"Black Jack, as a man out of time, is an excellent
character, and this series is the best military
SF I've read in some time."
—*GeekDad*

Praise for The Lost Fleet
THE LOST FLEET: BEYOND THE FRONTIER: DREADNAUGHT

"Campbell combines the best parts of military SF and grand
space opera to launch a new adventure series . . . Geary's
Star Trek–like mission of exploration sets the fleet up for
plenty of exciting discoveries and escapades."

—*Publishers Weekly*

"The story line is, as always, faster than the speed of
light . . . Jack Campbell creates a terrific unexpected spin
to his great outer-space saga."   —*Alternative Worlds*

"Campbell is to be commended for another excellent addition to one of the best military science fiction series on the
market . . . [*Dreadnaught*] delivers everything fans expect
from Black Jack Geary and more."   —*Monsters and Critics*

"Another exciting installment . . . Those who enjoy space
opera will be intrigued."   —*Night Owl Reviews*

"An invigorating return to the universe of Black Jack
Geary . . . a fun ride."   —*Geek Speak Magazine*

"An exciting adventure . . . But *Dreadnaught* isn't just an
action book—characters are well developed, realistic, and
people you'd care for."   —*TCM Reviews*

"Fans of the previous novels will no doubt enjoy this
installment . . . [*Dreadnaught*] is full of tense battles,
political maneuvering, and close calls."

—*. . . th Librarians*

THE LOST FLEET: FEARLESS

"Straightforward, solidly written military space opera."
—*Critical Mass*

"Another satisfying [Campbell] cocktail to slake the thirst of fans who like their space operas with a refreshing moral and intellectual chaser . . . *The Lost Fleet* deserves to find a home on your bookshelf."   —SF Reviews.net

"A great and gripping read. It's a fast-paced roller coaster of action and intrigue, with realistic characters and situations."   —*TCM Reviews*

THE LOST FLEET: DAUNTLESS

"A rousing adventure with a page-turning plot, lots of space action, and the kind of hero Hornblower fans will love."
—William C. Dietz, author of *A Fighting Chance*

"Jack Campbell's dazzling new series is military science fiction at its best. Not only does he tell a yarn of great adventure and action, but he also develops the characters with satisfying depth. I thoroughly enjoyed this rip-roaring read, and I can hardly wait for the next book."
—Catherine Asaro, Nebula Award–winning author
of *Carnelians*

"Black Jack Geary is very real, very human, and so compelling he'll leave you wanting more. Jack Campbell knows fleet actions, and it shows . . . [*The Lost Fleet: Dauntless* is] the best novel of its type that I've read."
—David Sherman, coauthor of the Starfist series

"A slam-bang good read that kept me up at night . . . a solid, thoughtful, and exciting novel loaded with edge-of-your-seat combat."   —Elizabeth Moon, Nebula Award–winning author
of *Echoes of Betrayal*

"Rousing military-SF action . . . [*Dauntless*] should please many fans of old-fashioned hard SF."   —*Sci Fi Weekly*

THE LOST FLEET

BEYOND THE FRONTIER

DREADNAUGHT

JACK CAMPBELL

ACE BOOKS, NEW YORK

THE BERKLEY PUBLISHING GROUP
Published by the Penguin Group
Penguin Group (USA) Inc.
375 Hudson Street, New York, New York 10014, USA
Penguin Group (Canada), 90 Eglinton Avenue East, Suite 700, Toronto, Ontario M4P 2Y3, Canada
(a division of Pearson Penguin Canada Inc.) • Penguin Books Ltd., 80 Strand, London WC2R 0RL,
England • Penguin Group Ireland, 25 St. Stephen's Green, Dublin 2, Ireland (a division of Penguin
Books Ltd.) • Penguin Group (Australia), 250 Camberwell Road, Camberwell, Victoria 3124, Australia
(a division of Pearson Australia Group Pty. Ltd.) • Penguin Books India Pvt. Ltd., 11 Community
Centre, Panchsheel Park, New Delhi—110 017, India • Penguin Group (NZ), 67 Apollo Drive,
Rosedale, Auckland 0632, New Zealand (a division of Pearson New Zealand Ltd.) • Penguin Books
(South Africa) (Pty.) Ltd., 24 Sturdee Avenue, Rosebank, Johannesburg 2196, South Africa

Penguin Books Ltd., Registered Offices: 80 Strand, London WC2R 0RL, England

This is a work of fiction. Names, characters, places, and incidents either are the product of the author's imagination or are used fictitiously, and any resemblance to actual persons, living or dead, business establishments, events, or locales is entirely coincidental. The publisher does not have any control over and does not assume any responsibility for author or third-party websites or their content.

THE LOST FLEET: BEYOND THE FRONTIER: DREADNAUGHT

An Ace Book / published by arrangement with the author

PUBLISHING HISTORY
Ace hardcover edition / May 2011
Ace mass-market edition / May 2012

Copyright © 2011 by John G. Hemry.
Excerpt from *The Lost Stars: Tarnished Knight* by Jack Campbell copyright © 2012
by John G. Hemry.
Cover art by Peter Bollinger / Shannon Associates.
Cover design by Annette Fiore DeFex.

ISBN: 978-1-937007-49-2

ACE
Ace Books are published by The Berkley Publishing Group,
a division of Penguin Group (USA) Inc.,
375 Hudson Street, New York, New York 10014.
ACE and the "A" design are trademarks of Penguin Group (USA) Inc.

PRINTED IN THE UNITED STATES OF AMERICA

10 9 8 7 6 5 4 3

ALWAYS LEARNING   PEARSON

To my uncle Oliver Holmes "Rick" Ulrickson, who sailed for his last home port in May 2010. The youngest in my mother's family, with six older sisters, he somehow survived childhood to serve in the Navy, work in aerospace (including NASA's Johnson Space Center Mission Control tracking system), and mentor many students at Texas Christian University. He was an amateur historian, he read a lot, he sang, and he was active in the civil rights movement in the sixties and seventies, but his proudest achievement in life was undoubtedly his family. You'll be missed, Uncle Oliver.

For S., as always.

ACKNOWLEDGMENTS

I remain indebted to my agent, Joshua Bilmes, for his ever-inspired suggestions and assistance, and to my editor, Anne Sowards, for her support and editing. Thanks also to Catherine Asaro, Robert Chase, J. G. (Huck) Huckenpohler, Simcha Kuritzky, Michael LaViolette, Aly Parsons, Bud Sparhawk, and Constance A. Warner for their suggestions, comments, and recommendations. Thanks also to Charles Petit for his suggestions about space engagements.

THE FIRST FLEET OF THE ALLIANCE

ADMIRAL JOHN GEARY, COMMANDING

SECOND BATTLESHIP DIVISION
Gallant
Indomitable
Glorious
Magnificent

THIRD BATTLESHIP DIVISION
Dreadnaught
Orion
Dependable
Conqueror

FOURTH BATTLESHIP DIVISION
Warspite
Vengeance
Revenge
Guardian

FIFTH BATTLESHIP DIVISION
Fearless
Resolution
Redoubtable

SEVENTH BATTLESHIP DIVISION
Colossus
Encroach
Amazon
Spartan

EIGHTH BATTLESHIP DIVISION
Relentless
Reprisal
Superb
Splendid

FIRST BATTLE CRUISER DIVISION
Inspire
Formidable
Brilliant
Implacable

SECOND BATTLE CRUISER DIVISION
Leviathan
Dragon
Steadfast
Valiant

FOURTH BATTLE CRUISER DIVISION
Dauntless (flagship)
Daring
Victorious
Intemperate

FIFTH BATTLE CRUISER DIVISION
Adroit

SIXTH BATTLE CRUISER DIVISION
Illustrious
Incredible
Invincible

FIFTH ASSAULT TRANSPORT DIVISION
Tsunami
Typhoon
Mistral
Haboob

FIRST AUXILIARIES DIVISION	**SECOND AUXILIARIES DIVISION**
Titan	*Witch*
Tanuki	*Jinn*
Kupua	*Alchemist*
Domovoi	*Cyclops*

THIRTY-ONE HEAVY CRUISERS IN SIX DIVISIONS

First Heavy Cruiser Division	Third Heavy Cruiser Division
Fourth Heavy Cruiser Division	Fifth Heavy Cruiser Division
Eighth Heavy Cruiser Division	Tenth Heavy Cruiser Division

FIFTY-FIVE LIGHT CRUISERS IN TEN SQUADRONS

First Light Cruiser Squadron	Second Light Cruiser Squadron
Third Light Cruiser Squadron	Fifth Light Cruiser Squadron
Sixth Light Cruiser Squadron	Eighth Light Cruiser Squadron
Ninth Light Cruiser Squadron	Tenth Light Cruiser Squadron
Eleventh Light Cruiser Squadron	Fourteenth Light Cruiser Squadron

ONE HUNDRED SIXTY DESTROYERS IN EIGHTEEN SQUADRONS

First Destroyer Squadron	Second Destroyer Squadron
Third Destroyer Squadron	Fourth Destroyer Squadron
Sixth Destroyer Squadron	Seventh Destroyer Squadron
Ninth Destroyer Squadron	Tenth Destroyer Squadron
Twelfth Destroyer Squadron	Fourteenth Destroyer Squadron
Sixteenth Destroyer Squadron	Seventeenth Destroyer Squadron
Twentieth Destroyer Squadron	Twenty-first Destroyer Squadron
Twenty-third Destroyer Squadron	Twenty-seventh Destroyer Squadron
Twenty-eighth Destroyer Squadron	Thirty-second Destroyer Squadron

FIRST FLEET MARINE FORCE
Major General Carabali, commanding

3,000 Marines on assault transports and divided into detachments on
battle cruisers and battleships

ONE

INNUMERABLE stars like brilliant diamonds carelessly flung across endless space shone upon the hull of the civilian passenger ship. Bright, but cold, their light far too distant to give any warmth, the stars formed constellations in which humans tried to find meaning. Admiral John "Black Jack" Geary, watching those stars, thought about the fact that the constellations changed depending on where you were, but the meaning of it all somehow didn't change.

He just wished he knew what that meaning of it all was. He had lost one battle, long ago, and discovered much later that the loss had meant something much different than he had imagined. Lately, he had won much bigger battles; but what those meant, what his future would be from this day forward, remained as uncertain as whatever messages the stars wrote across the sky.

The passenger ship had exited the hypernet gate at the particular star known to humans as Varandal. Over the dozen decades since it had been built, the ship had traveled between many stars, and while the stars themselves had burned on unchanging to the naked eye, the ship had felt those years. Men and women had worked to keep its systems functioning and its hull strong, but where the life of stars was measured in billions of years, the life spans of human creations were often less than a century.

This ship was old, moving almost as deftly as ever, but feeling the accumulated stress of years in the materials from which it had been built. It should have been replaced long ago. However, a civilization caught in a seemingly endless war couldn't afford such luxuries; instead, it diverted those resources to warships to replace countless other warships lost in countless battles.

But on this voyage, now that peace had come a month ago, the crew had spoken of rumors of new ships. No one knew for sure. So far, peace hadn't brought any major improvements, hadn't brought money or lives to replace what had been lost in the long war with the Syndicate Worlds. No one even knew exactly what "peace" was. No one living had been alive the last time humanity knew peace, before the Syndics attacked the Alliance a century ago.

No, that wasn't right. One man still living had been alive then, miraculously surviving a century in survival sleep to lead the fleet to victory, to bring this peace, which somehow felt not all that different from the once-endless war that had finally come to an end. And now he looked at the stars and wondered what new turns awaited his life.

Alliance government warns of threat to all humanity from alien race.

Geary lowered his gaze back to the news headlines scrolling under the star display. "When we left Varandal a few weeks ago, the existence of intelligent aliens was still supposed to be secret."

Sitting on the bed nearby, Captain Tanya Desjani glanced over at the headline before resuming her scrutiny of a ration bar. "We fought a battle with them. The whole fleet knows they're out there." She waved at another display set on one bulkhead, the new ring on one of her fingers flashing a moment as the star sapphire set within it caught the light.

A virtual window, the display showed another view outside their passenger ship; but on this one, the countless stars and the planets illuminated by the radiance of Varandal were dimmed by symbols revealing things invisible to human eyes from that distance. Hundreds of glowing images, representing the warships in the main Alliance fleet, hung apparently unmoving against the backdrop of space even though those warships were in fixed orbits about the star. The scene conveyed two very different sensations, one of them awe at the scale of humanity's achievements. But against that awe was the reality that, as massive as the fleet's battleships, battle cruisers, and lesser warships were in human terms, they were tiny when measured against the expanse of the star system and completely insignificant compared to even a small region of the galaxy.

Geary let his eyes linger on the view, realizing how much he had missed those still-unseen, utilitarian, and battle-scarred ships. His own home world had become foreign to him, but for all the changes a harsh century had wrought, the fleet had remained a place in which he felt he belonged. The men and women who had grown up with war and seen all of its terrors, who had been shaped in part by those bloody experiences, still remained sailors like him. Also, the formal end of hostilities with the Syndics should have brought rest from their labors, but this version of peace seemed unlikely to offer that. "I thought we were trying to figure out how to keep from fighting any more battles with the aliens. Why is the government now broadcasting all over the place their existence and the danger they pose?"

"Read some of the other headlines," Desjani suggested before biting off a piece of the bar. "These Yanika Babiya ration bars aren't bad. For ration bars, that is."

Geary focused back on the news, trying to catch up after resolutely ignoring events for much of the past month. *Ruling parties swept from power in special elections called in ninety-two star systems.*

The Rift Federation has voted to renegotiate its ties to the Alliance.

Fingal becomes the thirty-sixth star system to demand

reduction of its defense commitments and taxes to the Alliance central government.

Black Jack Geary, in comments made on Kosatka, offers only qualified support for the current government. "What? *Qualified* support? What the hell are they talking about? When that guy asked if I'd follow orders from the government, I said yes, I would."

Desjani swallowed her bite of ration bar and raised an eyebrow at him. "You said that you'd follow all lawful orders."

"So?" Geary demanded.

" 'Lawful' is a qualifier. Even a dumb sailor like me knows that."

"When did saying something that should be a given turn into something subversive?" Geary grumbled.

"When a majority of the population considers the elected government to be corrupt and full of crooks," Desjani replied. "To many citizens of the Alliance, 'lawful' implies sweeping out the criminals."

"I shouldn't have answered that guy."

She shook her head. "And leave the question unanswered? 'Black Jack Geary refuses to say he supports the government.' That wouldn't have produced a better outcome, darling."

Her use of the endearment calmed him. "Was it only four weeks ago that we got married?"

"Twenty-six days. Even though we won't be able to act as a married couple aboard my ship, you're still expected to remember all anniversaries and significant dates, you know." Desjani coolly took another bite.

"Yes, ma'am." He liked seeing the annoyed look she usually gave him when he responded like her subordinate, but this time all Tanya did was shake her head at him. Geary eyed her, wondering at how composed she had been since their arrival in Varandal Star System, then finally realizing that Desjani always got calmer when she sensed combat approaching. "Do you expect something to happen when we dock at Ambaru station?"

"I've been expecting something since this ship arrived back in this star system, but everything seems quiet so far. No government ships intercepting us to arrest you, no mutinous fleet ships intercepting us to declare you dictator, and no fighting going on between any factions and the government." She glanced around their compartment, a high-end passenger cabin whose dated but still-luxurious touches had disconcerted both Desjani and Geary, since they were used to the fairly Spartan accommodations on warships. But the government in Kosatka had insisted on providing "appropriate" transportation when the orders demanding that Geary immediately return to Varandal were received. At least the charter had prevented having to deal with other passengers on the way back.

Desjani shook her head again, her eyes this time on the outside display. "Maybe it's my ancestors talking to me. I can sense the tension here, like a star about to go nova, and I don't like going into action aboard an unarmed ship."

"It's not a battle cruiser," Geary agreed.

"It's not *my* battle cruiser," she corrected him. "I shouldn't have left *Dauntless* for so long."

"I'm sure she's fine. *Dauntless* has a good crew."

"Excuse me?"

"What I meant to say," Geary quickly added, "is that *Dauntless* has the best crew in the fleet. As well as an exceptionally good commanding officer."

"You're a bit biased when it comes to the commanding officer, but her crew is the best." Desjani took a long, slow breath. "My point is that the government may not want you near any battle cruiser or any crew, and we don't know if any of those warships are planning to act independently. Be prepared for anything when we dock."

"The message from Duellos we got after arrival implied everything is quiet."

She considered that, then shook her head. "We can't be sure he really sent it, or that the content wasn't modified en route to us."

Geary closed his eyes to block out their comfortable surroundings, trying to get back into a combat mind-set. "Surely they aren't still considering arresting me as a threat to the government."

She grinned, her canines showing to give the expression a fierce cast. "They wouldn't dare try that openly now. But you could just disappear, and supposedly be on a special assignment. They'll try something."

" 'They'? Which 'they' do you mean?"

"Someone. There are a lot of possibilities. You're too dangerous."

He thought about the crowds they had encountered on Kosatka, Desjani's home world. Often huge and always enthusiastic to the point of worshipful, they had been inescapable and unnerving in equal measure. Entire cities had seemed to pack into the streets for the chance of a glimpse of the great Black Jack Geary, legendary champion of the Alliance, the man who had stayed with his ship to the end, fighting off a surprise attack by the Syndics to allow other ships to escape. Everyone had thought that Geary had died during that fight at Grendel a hundred years ago; but he had been barely alive, frozen in survival sleep in a damaged escape pod. Geary had finally been found not long ago, awakening to find himself among people who had been taught to believe that he was an incomparable hero. *Who do they think Black Jack actually is? I certainly don't know. He's someone the government dreamed up to inspire everyone when the initial Syndic surprise attacks knocked the Alliance back on its heels.* "The next time the government tries to create a hero to motivate and inspire the population, they'll probably try harder to make sure that hero is really, absolutely, positively dead."

Desjani gave him one of those looks that could be as unnerving as the crowds. "The government thought it was creating an illusion. The politicians didn't realize that the living stars had their own plans and that you could not only reappear, but also be in reality more than the official illusion claimed."

"I thought that was over," he mumbled, looking away.

She had looked at him in exactly the same way when he had first awakened from a century of survival sleep. Belief in him and in what he could do, believing that he was someone sent by the living stars themselves at the behest of everyone's ancestors to save the Alliance. Usually, now she seemed to see him as a man, and treated him as a husband and an officer; but occasionally her faith that he could be more than that shone through.

She leaned close, reaching to grasp his chin gently and turn his head to face her again. "I see you. I see who you are. Don't forget that."

The statement had two possible meanings, but he preferred to believe that it meant she knew he was human and very imperfect. His own ancestors knew that he had given her enough demonstrations of his fallibility since being awakened. "Who does the government see?"

"Good question." Desjani leaned back, sighing. "In answer to your first question, though, about the aliens, as you can see from the rest of the news, the government is under so much pressure that it's telling everyone about the aliens to distract them. The war held the Alliance together. The war excused all kinds of things. Now, thanks to you more than anyone else—and don't try to deny that—we're at peace, and if war is hell, then peace seems to be like herding cats. I didn't figure that out myself, by the way. One of the politicians at that last reception on Kosatka told me that. He said that star systems all over the Alliance are rethinking their need for common defense now that the big, bad Syndic wolf at the door has been drop-kicked into the nearest black hole."

"You talked to a politician?" Like most fleet officers, Desjani had a well-developed dislike of the political leadership, born of a century of inconclusive and bloody warfare and a need to attach blame for the failure to win.

She shrugged. "He's an old friend of my mother. She vouched for him not being as bad as the others, and since my mother hauled me up to meet him, I couldn't very well about-face and walk away. The point is, Admiral Geary, that he told me no one really knows how to handle peace. It's been a hundred years since the war with the Syndicate Worlds started, so the politicians have never experienced an environment without an active threat. The government is falling back on what it knows. It thinks it needs a new threat to keep the Alliance unified. And it's not like the aliens aren't a threat. We know they're willing to attack us. We know that they carried out hostile actions before the Alliance even knew they existed."

"I wish those weren't just about the only things we do know about them," Geary grumbled, turning back to the headlines. *Prisoners of war coming home soon, say authorities.* Finally, some good news. Many men and women captured in the course of the apparently endless war, people who had never expected to see their homes again, would now be reunited with their loved ones. Bringing home the living would be a welcome job, even if it was tarnished by sad reality. Too many prisoners of war had already died far from their homes, during decades in captivity, their fates unknown. Tallying up the numbers and names of those who had died in Syndic prison camps would take long and cheerless years of investigation. "We're cruel enough to our own kind. Why do we need hostile aliens to add to our problems?"

"Ask the living stars, darling. I'm just a battle cruiser captain. The answer to your question is way above my pay grade."

The next headline bore no silver lining.

Reports of internal fighting in many star systems within Syndicate Worlds' territory as Syndic authority continues to collapse.

"Damn. Whatever is left of the Syndicate Worlds is going to be a small fraction of the region it used to rule."

"You say that like it's a bad thing," Desjani commented.

"Chaos will breed a lot more deaths and trouble for us," Geary countered, indicating the next headline. *Refugees fleeing fighting in former Syndic territory arriving in Alliance star systems.*

She shrugged, but he could hear in her voice the tension that Desjani was trying to mask. "They're Syndics. They started the war, they kept it going, and now they're paying the price. You don't actually expect me to feel sorry for them, do you?"

He thought about how many friends and companions Tanya had seen die in the war, including her younger brother. "No. I realize that very few people in the Alliance will shed any tears for the suffering of any Syndics."

"With good cause," Desjani muttered.

"I've never argued otherwise."

One corner of her mouth curled upward in a sardonic smile. "You just reminded us that our ancestors and the living stars don't look kindly on the slaughter of civilians or prisoners. Fine. We stopped killing everyone but combatants. But that doesn't mean we want to help any Syndics who survived the war."

"I know." He still had trouble grasping that: how the long war had poisoned the natural human tendency to offer aid to those in distress, even if those others were former enemies. But then, he had slept through the vast majority of that war, not felt it through every day of his life. "What I'm saying is, purely in terms of self-interest, the Alliance may have to help clean up the mess in what was Syndic territory. Something is going to replace Syndic authority in areas that slip from the grasp of the central government. Trying to ensure that those successor governments are representative and peaceful rather than dictatorial and aggressive just seems like smart policy."

Instead of replying directly, Desjani glanced at his display. "Speaking of messes, how's our own government doing these days?"

"Not too well, apparently. The next headline says, 'Newly elected Alliance senators demand investigations into wartime corruption.'"

"Investigating wartime corruption in the government would keep a lot of people busy for at least a few decades," she observed.

"As long as I'm not one of them." Geary read the next headline with growing disbelief. *Authoritative accounts reveal that Black Jack demanded and received a free hand from the Alliance grand council for the campaign that ended the war.* "That's not true! I didn't demand anything. Who the hell leaked that?"

Desjani took a look at the headline. "Somebody who's unhappy at the way the politicians are all trying to claim credit for the end of the war. Some other politicians angling for advantage. Fleet officers who guessed at the truth and assumed you had to threaten the council. There are plenty of possibilities."

"No wonder the government still sees me as a threat."

"You are a threat," she reminded him. "If you hadn't convinced Captain Badaya and those like him that you're actually running the government covertly, making the big decisions behind the scenes, then they would have already staged a coup in your name. Things could be worse."

He studied the headlines again, trying to read between the lines. "Someone in the government must realize as well as we do what's holding the fleet back. Overt action against me could still trigger a coup I couldn't forestall, then civil war as some star systems simply pulled out of the Alliance in response." It had taken a long time to accept that, the idea that the Alliance could be so frail, but a century of all-out warfare with its immense costs in lives and money had badly frayed the seams of the Alliance.

"That doesn't mean they won't still try something," Desjani observed.

"Could the government be that stupid?"

She smiled scornfully. "Yes."

Citizens' coalitions demand that Black Jack be brought to Prime to clean up government, the next headline screamed. Next to a coup by his misguided supporters, Geary thought, that would be his worst nightmare. Why did anyone believe that the ability to command a fleet meant that he could also run a government? He looked at the display showing the distance remaining to Ambaru station and the time remaining until the ship docked, wondering what awaited him and Tanya there.

"What's the matter?" she asked, her tone softer.

"I was just thinking."

"You've been promoted to admiral again. I'm not sure that much thinking on your part is permitted."

"Very funny." His gaze went to the stars again. "Before . . . before the war started, I never worried that much about the future. Most of it was out of my hands. I had serious responsibilities as an officer in the fleet, and at the last as commanding officer of a heavy cruiser, but what we did and where we went was never up to me. Then the war happened, and I ended up in command of the fleet a century later. For months after that, the future was a very narrowly focused thing. We needed to get the fleet from one star to the next, and eventually home. Then we needed to deal with the Syndics and do something to hold off the aliens. The future aimed itself. Do this. Then do that. Figure out how, right now, or there's no more future."

Geary paused and looked toward her. Desjani met his eyes, her expression somber but calm. "Now, the future is a huge, vague thing. I have no idea what tomorrow is supposed to hold, what I should do, what I'll be called upon to do. I know because of everything that's happened that the future depends a lot upon my own actions and decisions. And I no longer have any idea where those should take us."

She gave him one of those unnervingly confident looks. "Yes, you do, Black Jack. You have the same ideas you had when you assumed command of the fleet back then. Do the honorable thing, do the right thing, do the smart thing. Even if you're tempted to do otherwise, you stick to what you believe in, and what you believe in is what our ancestors believed in. That, and you believe that we're all worth saving. Which is why I know that if anyone can lead us through whatever the future brings, it's you. And that is why not only

I, but a lot of other people, will follow you and give you everything we've got."

"As long as I've got you."

"*That* future didn't aim itself," Desjani said. "You had a lot of options. You chose the hardest one, and the most honorable one, and the right one. That's why we're together now."

"You wouldn't have—"

"Yes, I would have, and you know that. I would have done it because I thought you needed it, and what you needed to do was far more important than me or my honor. I was wrong. You were right." She smiled. "Which isn't to say that you aren't wrong at times. But I'll be here to let you know when that happens."

THEY came out of the access from the passenger ship onto the dock at Ambaru station, side by side, both Geary and Desjani alert for trouble but trying to look relaxed despite their tension.

Two lines of armed ground forces soldiers awaited them, their weapons held in salute position, forming a corridor down which Geary and Desjani walked. Were the soldiers just an honor guard? Or thinly disguised muscle to back up another arrest attempt? This time he didn't have Marines escorting him to prevent such an overreaction by the government.

At least the soldiers weren't armored, instead resplendent in dress uniforms. If he was to be arrested, at least his captors would look their best.

On either side of the honor guard, more soldiers held back crowds packed into the walkways between docks, crowds who erupted into cheers at the sight of Geary. That was also a good sign, since it seemed unlikely the government would be crazy enough to arrest him publicly. What would happen if the soldiers tried to restrain or arrest him, and he instead walked to the crowds? Would that one action be the loose thread whose unraveling would tear apart the Alliance?

Despite his nerves and discomfort with the adulation, Geary forced himself to smile and wave one hand to the crowds, then saw Admiral Timbale waiting at the end of the ramp and felt some of his tension draining off. Even though he was as political as most senior officers these days, Timbale had seemed both honorable and firmly in Geary's camp before they left Varandal. Now Timbale saluted Geary and returned Desjani's salute, giving the gestures the crispness of someone who had recently learned saluting and wanted to show off. "Welcome back, Admiral Geary. It's nice to meet you in person, Captain Desjani."

"Thank you, sir," she replied, her return salute casually correct. Geary had no doubt that Desjani saluted in that fashion to subtly emphasize that, for her, the gesture had been common practice for months. "I'm surprised to see civilians here, sir," she added, indicating the crowds.

Timbale's smile hardened. "There weren't supposed to be any. Your arrival was supposed to be quiet and low-key, to avoid 'disruptions.' Or so I was told. But somehow word got out, and once the civilians started crowding through the barriers to see Black Jack, what could we do?" He glanced around. "Standing orders from fleet headquarters came in two weeks ago. We're to avoid any actions which 'improperly highlight any individual officer' and instead direct attention to 'the achievements of all personnel.'"

"I can't honestly object to that," Geary commented. "In fact, I think it's a good idea."

"It is," Timbale agreed, his tone becoming sardonic, "but since the brass at fleet headquarters got there by playing up their own roles in every success in every possible way, I find their newfound interest in individual humility by others a bit hard to swallow." Nodding to the commander of the honor guard, Timbale turned to go. "If you and Captain Desjani will please accompany me?"

Geary followed, wondering if the honor guard would also

come along. But the soldiers remained in place, their eyes straying to the sides to catch glimpses of him as he left.

Timbale nodded again as if reading his mind. "Nothing quite so obvious this time," he muttered to Geary. "Especially with all of those spectators."

"What is going on?" Geary asked.

"I don't know exactly." Timbale frowned as they entered passageways from which other military and civilians had apparently been barred, the path stretching empty before them. Metal and composite bulkheads, which in Geary's time a hundred years earlier would have been covered by skins showing images of natural materials or outdoor scenes, were instead bare, revealing rough repairs and exposed surfaces, just another sign of the strains so many decades of war had put upon the Alliance and everything built to further the war. "Varandal is not technically in a state of martial law, but in practice it's very close to that. The government seems to believe that if things are going to explode, Varandal will be the first charge to go off, and I don't think I have to explain who they think the detonator will be."

"Yet they've kept the fleet concentrated here," Desjani observed.

"Yes, Captain," Timbale agreed. "They're afraid to keep it in one place, and they're afraid to disperse it and not have it in one place where they can watch it all at once. So they've done nothing with it." He quirked a smile at her. "Forgive my manners. Congratulations to you both. You must have had to move fast to get married in the brief interval when you were both captains and neither of you was in the other's chain of command. You ticked off fleet headquarters no end, you know."

"Thank you," Geary replied, while Desjani just smiled. "It's nice to know that we accomplished that much. Where are we going?"

"Conference room 1A963D5. I only know for certain who one of the occupants is." Timbale gave Geary a glance. "Senator Navarro, chair of the grand council."

"He's not alone?"

"There are people with him, but I don't know how many or who they are. The security perimeter is seven layers thick, and every layer is as tight as a sailor coming back from liberty." Timbale hesitated, then spoke softly. "A lot of people assume that Navarro is here, so you can give him orders. I don't believe that's the case because I've met you and spoken with you before, but I've heard plenty of assertions that you're really pulling the strings."

Geary was trying to figure out the right response when Desjani answered. "Strategic success may demand tactical deception, Admiral Timbale. Many officers are pleased to believe that the government is doing as Admiral Geary says."

Admiral Timbale nodded. "Whereas they'd be unhappy if he wasn't. I understand. But we're balancing on a knife-edge here. Fleet headquarters keeps issuing draconian commands apparently designed purely to show that they're in charge. The fleet is obeying, but they're increasingly unhappy with the arbitrary and sometimes pointless demands."

"I've heard from some of the warship commanders already," Geary commented. "No one knows what's going on. They just keep orbiting here."

"I don't know any more than anyone else, but the fact that the chair of the grand council is here makes it seem to me like they've been waiting for you to get back so they can tell you to do something." Timbale frowned, uncertainty plain to read in him. "And they do intend to task the fleet with some mission. Even though funding is being cut all over the place, I've been directed to ensure that repairs continue here for all damaged warships. Given how much those repairs are costing, those orders must have come through the government as well as fleet headquarters. Keep them here, get them fixed. Those have been my orders."

"Have you had the chance to talk to any fleet officers about what's going on?" Geary asked.

"Yes, but most of them assume that *you* ordered the repairs to continue for reasons of your own. No one else seems to have any clues, which is very unusual. You know how hard it is to keep things secret."

Desjani shook her head. "How can you properly prepare the fleet for a mission without knowing what the mission is?"

"Damned if I know." Timbale let his unhappiness show.
"The government stopped totally trusting the military decades ago, but it's still annoying to be treated as though they
don't trust us. I've been told nothing of substance, just things
like the orders for today, under the seal of the grand council
regarding security arrangements. I also haven't been invited
to this meeting, Admiral Geary. I was told it was for you
alone."

Desjani kept her expression professionally unrevealing,
but Geary could tell she wasn't happy with that. Nor was
he, until he considered having both of them firmly within
seven layers of very tight security. "To tell you the truth,"
Geary said to Timbale, "I think it might be good to know
that you and Captain Desjani are outside the meeting, in
communication with everyone else, and able to act or react
as appropriate."

This time, Timbale smiled tightly. "There are some parties who wouldn't listen to me but will accept anything
they're told by the captain. It's a given that she speaks for
you."

Geary caught the flash of melancholy in her eyes at that
praise, but Tanya simply nodded. "I will keep an eye on
things while you're in the meeting, Admiral," she said.

"You don't have to be formal with your husband among
just us," Timbale advised her.

"Yes, sir, I do," Desjani told him. "When in any professional context, he is Admiral Geary, and I am Captain Desjani. We're both agreed on that."

They turned a corner and at the other end of that corridor
saw what must be the first layer of security, a checkpoint
occupied by an entire squad of soldiers. "How many of these
are there?" Geary asked Timbale.

"Enough soldiers and checkpoints spread through this
sector of the station to occupy an entire ground forces bri-
gade," Timbale said. "No money for a lot of other things but

plenty of money for obsessive security. Every way in and out, and I mean *every* way, has more than one checkpoint securing it. No communications in or out, either. Totally secure and totally isolated. Once you get past a couple of those checkpoints, you won't be able to send or receive messages."

Geary's comm link beeped urgently. "I guess we're lucky that whatever this is got here now." He gave it a look, saw whom the message was from, and called it up while still walking. As he read, he came to an abrupt halt, causing Timbale and Desjani to stumble to a stop as well and stare at him with mingled curiosity and worry.

"What's happened?" Desjani asked.

"Nothing yet. But—" Geary choked off his words, fury building inside him as he tried to stay calm. "Captain Duellos informs me that the fleet has just received notification of courts-martial charges being filed against a large number of commanding officers. He's forwarded the message to me."

If Timbale was feigning surprise and disbelief, he was doing a good job of it. "What? I haven't seen— May I, Admiral?"

Geary offered his unit, and Timbale read rapidly. "Unbelievable. Over a hundred of the current commanding officers. The charges are technically justified, but what kind of idiot . . ." His jaw tightened. "Actually, I can think of several idiots who might be responsible. A few of them are assigned to fleet headquarters at the moment. I told you that headquarters was trying to assert their control, but I didn't think they'd do something this stupid."

"I see that I am also under charges," Desjani said, her voice again deadly calm. "They want to gut the fleet's command structure, Admiral."

Timbale waved his free hand at the comm unit. "Every one of those commanding officers would have to be at least temporarily relieved of command! While we're still trying to get the fleet repaired, refitted, and resupplied! It'll cause total chaos!" He made a motion as if to throw the comm unit in frustration, then remembered that it was Geary's and handed it back. "It's a good thing you got here just before this broke. If it had been received earlier, all hell would have broken loose. You're the only one who can stop a very serious overreaction by the fleet."

But Desjani had adopted her combat-cool attitude again, her eyes fixed on Geary's own. "It might be that you're wrong, Admiral Timbale. Not about the fleet's reaction, but about when this message was supposed to be received. Is it possible that somebody jumped the gun? Perhaps it was intended for this to be received by the fleet while Admiral Geary was already inside with representatives of the government and thus unable to learn of it in time to do anything about it while facing the government representatives, or to keep the fleet from immediately overreacting when the fleet heard of it."

"Is that the intention?" Geary asked from between clenched teeth. "Making the fleet overreact? My first thought was that this is directly aimed at me, because most of these officers could be seen as loyal to me, but . . ."

Admiral Timbale took a moment to calm himself, then shook his head. "Maybe. Maybe. But with you out of communications, we also wouldn't have been able to tell the fleet what you were doing, what your status was. If anyone wanted to assume that you'd been seized by the government—"

"That's too big," Desjani said. "You're right, Admiral Timbale. It could far too easily happen, but I can't believe anyone would be stupid enough to *want* it to happen."

"As opposed," Geary said, "to being stupid enough to cause it unintentionally?"

Timbale nodded quickly. "Yes. That would fit with the other things that fleet headquarters has been doing. 'We're in charge!' They probably got some reports back of the fleet's attitudes toward their earlier dictates and are escalating with this."

"Probably not the government, then?" Navarro had not struck Geary as the type, or as foolish enough to push such an action, but then, Geary wasn't a politician.

"No." Timbale looked down the passageway toward the checkpoint, where the soldiers were all pretending to be paying no attention to the obviously agitated cluster of high-ranking officers. "Where's the advantage to the government? They're worried about revolt, and this is just the sort of thing to trigger it. I don't have a very high opinion of the intelligence of politicians, but even I know how good they are at self-interest and survival. I don't see any self-interest or survival upside for the government in pushing this now in this manner. And he's also inside the conference room waiting for you and out of communications, so he, too, wouldn't know about this matter until your meeting was over."

Desjani's eyes narrowed. "That would give him deniability."

"When he's in charge of the government? Claiming he didn't know what was going on wouldn't help him at all. It would make him look worse. Assuming that the fleet didn't blow the station open and kill him."

"Being a martyr might help his reelection prospects," Desjani suggested dryly. "Even I might be inclined to vote for a dead politician."

"Dead heroes don't always stay dead," Timbale said, inclining his head toward Geary.

"So what do we do?" Desjani looked at Geary, as did Timbale.

That hadn't changed, either. He didn't even have any command assigned at the moment, but everyone was still looking to him for what to do. "We're agreed that the bottom line is that the fleet will go ballistic. The order is from fleet headquarters. The only way to get it canceled is to go over fleet headquarters, to the government. I need to go on to this meeting. That's the best way, and probably the only way, to get this matter resolved fast."

"Sir," Desjani said, "the blowup in the fleet has probably already started."

"I know." He brought up his comm unit, scowling as he saw the no-link icon. "Why can't I send a message? I got that one a minute ago."

Timbale grimaced. "It's the station. We've got so many passageways, conduits, and compartments that act as reflectors, channels, and traps that it makes the perimeter of the security zone fluctuate. There's no telling how far back you'll have to go to get a link again."

"We don't have time for that." He pushed record and spoke with care. "All warships in Varandal Star System, this is Admiral Geary. I have just been apprised of the communication regarding charges against many fleet officers. I am in the process of dealing with it. All units are to hold in assigned orbits and to refrain from any unauthorized actions. To the honor of our ancestors, Geary, out."

He handed the comm unit to Desjani. "I need you to start putting out this fire now. Get outside the security block and transmit that, then keep anyone from doing anything stupid."

"I'm not one of the living stars," Desjani complained as she took the comm unit. "And even they can't stop stupid."

"If you tell everyone that I just found out and am dealing with it, they'll believe you. They'll listen to you."

Her eyes locked on his. "In what capacity am I acting? According to this message, I should immediately surrender command of *Dauntless*."

"You are commanding officer of *Dauntless* until you hear otherwise from *me*." It wasn't proper. It wasn't by the book. He had no authority to tell her that except for his superior rank. But Black Jack Geary could get away with doing it. If he didn't disregard the book at that moment, then the mess facing them would spiral into a destructive reentry very quickly. "Admiral Timbale, I would appreciate your assistance to Captain Desjani in this matter. I don't know how much influence she'll have over nonfleet military in this star system."

"Probably more than you think," Timbale suggested. "Everyone knows your . . . relationship. But it will take both of us to try to keep a lid on this. If I read attitudes in the fleet correctly, they'll be certain these charges are just the first salvo, and your arrest will be right behind it. Too many warships will want to start peeling this station open like an onion until they get you out. And if that happens, somebody else will surely shoot back."

"Maybe I should go back with you," Geary said. "Postpone the meeting and—"

"Then the government might well assume that you're behind the fleet's sudden aggressive movements! There's no guarantee that the fleet will immediately accept messages from you as being legitimate, unforced, and unaltered."

All he could do was look to the one person who had never failed him. "Tanya."

Desjani held up both hands. "All right. I'm on it, Admiral. I'm not Black Jack Geary, but I'll do my best." Another one of those sayings common in the fleet that made Geary wince when he heard them, but in this case all too literally true. She stepped back and saluted.

He returned the salute, thinking of all the things that could go wrong, of all the Alliance military units and warships in that star system suddenly erupting into a burst of fratricidal warfare, and of the number of people who would surely die if that happened. Possibly including Tanya. The Alliance itself might well die as a result, spinning apart with less bedlam than the Syndicate Worlds but with the same apparently unstoppable momentum. "Good luck, Tanya."

"Don't worry about me. I'm a bad-ass battle cruiser captain. You're the one who has to keep the politicians and fleet headquarters from screwing up the universe. If anyone can stop them, it's you."

"Thanks. I appreciate the lack of pressure."

"Don't mention it. And don't take too long in that meeting, or there won't be much left of this star system."

TWO

IT was easy to forget how much you depended on being able to get information quickly. Easy until you were inside a security perimeter that jammed all signals to ensure that no information leaked out and cut off connections to interior databases and displays. Now, with the fleet certainly in turmoil, he had no idea what was happening and how successful Tanya was being at keeping the situation under control. Not that he doubted her abilities, but anyone with common sense knew that there were always some factors beyond the ability of any human to direct.

He wanted to get to the meeting *now* and get things under control *now*, but the damned station was too big, every passageway too long, every checkpoint too slow to pass him through. With every step, Geary feared feeling the shudder of explosions being transmitted through the structure of the station as open combat erupted. He had felt the impacts of weaponry on ships. The hammerblows of missiles striking home, the trembling as hell-lance particle beams tore through metal and everything else in their path, the brutal hail of grapeshot pounding a hull in staccato rhythms.

Would those things feel different on something as massive as this space station? How deeply would a hell lance penetrate into the structure if fired from close in?

Oddly enough, wondering about those things and trying to figure out answers from his experience served as a calming distraction. Trying to anticipate the effects of combat damage was comfortingly familiar, whereas confronting politicians with unknown agendas remained something Geary found uncomfortable and foreign. *I'd rather be shot at than deal with politicians. And the strange thing is that every sailor in the fleet would understand that and agree.*

The soldiers he encountered at different checkpoints were drawn from a variety of units and organizations. He had experienced very little interaction with ground forces since being awakened from survival sleep, and all of that limited contact had been in the last couple of weeks. Now he studied these men and women, trying to evaluate their capabilities, their feelings, and their effectiveness. The fleet and even the notoriously tradition-bound Marines had been changed by the very long and very bloody war. How deeply had the ground forces fallen into the fleet's regression to charging straight at the enemy without regard for odds, tactics, or maneuvering? Had the ground forces also fallen back on rigid definitions of honor and an emphasis on blind courage to replace the skills of leaders who rarely survived long enough to become veterans?

All of the soldiers were stiffly professional with him, doubtless fearing that they were somehow being monitored by more than one superior officer; but most still looked at Geary in a way that revealed their feelings, no different from those of the civilian crowds even if much more disciplined and concealed.

Geary passed through checkpoint after checkpoint, everything remaining quiet as far as he could tell, though buried inside the station he could discern very little. The absence of anyone else at some points in the passageways between checkpoints felt eerie, like being in a derelict facility in a meager star system bypassed by the hypernet and now abandoned by its few human inhabitants. After weeks of trying to avoid crowds, he found himself wishing for at least a few other people within line of sight.

Finally, six more checkpoints beyond the first, Geary found himself being led toward a conference room remarkable only for the symbols by its open door that revealed it to be a high-security, sealed compartment guaranteed to be as impervious to outside surveillance as any room could be. "How tight is this conference room?" he asked the Alliance special forces commandos forming the last layer of security, wondering how much security technology might have advanced but also recalling the many times that Victoria Rione had demonstrated the ability to get through security barriers with the right equipment and software.

The major in command looked momentarily stunned at being personally addressed by Geary, then recovered. "Completely tight, Admiral Geary. According to specifications on these systems, even the environmental systems are self-contained. Once the hatch is sealed, you are as totally isolated from the outside universe as human engineering can manage. Nothing comes in or out. There are even quantum-level jammers that were very recently installed, though no one can actually conduct surveillance at that level yet."

No one human could, anyway. The politicians had, so far at least, kept secret the aliens' ability to use quantum worms in human operating systems. "Impressive," Geary said. "How does the room handle trapped heat from people and equipment if it's that tightly sealed off?"

The major looked to a lieutenant, who looked to a sergeant, who replied in the brisk tones of a senior enlisted telling officers things they should already know. "There is no way to bleed off trapped heat, sir. It builds up and creates a serious problem within half an hour given three or more occupants using personal electronics."

"Will that be a problem, Admiral?" the major asked.

"Not at all," Geary said. "I need to get things done fast right now, and in general, I like the idea of a conference room that becomes uninhabitable after half an hour."

The major hesitated as if not certain what he was allowed to say, then grinned. "I've wished for that more than once myself, Admiral."

The commandos assumed sentry positions as Geary rapped on the hatch, opened it, and walked into the room.

His eyes went first to the familiar face of Senator Navarro, who was rising from his chair to greet Geary. Beside him stood another male politician from the grand council, the enigmatic Senator Sakai, who had accompanied the fleet on the campaign that had ended the war. But he had done so as a representative of those members of the grand council who trusted Geary the least. How much had the experience convinced Sakai that Geary was no threat to the Alliance? On the other side of the room sat Senator Suva, a thin woman whom Geary also remembered being on the council, and who had demonstrated as little trust in the military as the military itself had in politicians.

Three senators. No military besides him. The room was even smaller than the conference room on *Dauntless*, but with its security requirements must lack any virtual conference capability that would allow many more people to attend. To one side, a display showed the star system and all of the military units within it; but the display was static, clearly not receiving any inputs to keep it constantly updating. Geary saluted, trying to keep from exploding with impatience. "Senator Navarro, I—"

Navarro smiled politely as he broke in smoothly. "Welcome back, Admiral. There are—"

"Senator," Geary interrupted, "something critical has come up." He saw the wariness that immediately sprang into Navarro's eyes, the way he tensed at Geary's words. He could almost hear Navarro's thoughts. *He's doing it. He's taking over.* "I don't wish to be abrupt, sir, but it is *extremely* critical, so I request that we discuss it before anything else."

Sakai answered him, his voice and face revealing little of his feelings. "What is so critical, Admiral?"

"A message was received by the fleet as I was on my way to this meeting. The message states that more than a hundred commanding officers of fleet warships are being court-martialed. They're supposed to be immediately relieved of command pending resolution of the charges."

Like Timbale, all three senators appeared stunned, though there was no way of knowing how much of that was feigned in the case of each politician. Navarro shook his head in bafflement, but his voice stayed guarded. "What are the charges? What are these officers accused of?"

Suva spoke up, her own suspicions clear. "Are these officers being court-martialed for actions or plans against lawful authority?"

"No, Madam Senator," Geary said. "They are not accused of any actions against the government. The charges are that they allowed their ships to get far too low on fuel reserves," Geary continued with what he considered remarkable control.

"Low fuel reserves?" Navarro asked after a long moment, as if wondering whether Geary was telling a strange joke. "You're serious? I remember being told that the fleet was very low on fuel when it reached Varandal. Some of the ships actually ran out during the battle here, didn't they?"

"Yes, sir. We were extremely low on fuel as a result of the long journey from the Syndic home star system and the battles we had to fight along the way."

"Of course." But Navarro didn't convey understanding. "But you won the battle. You got all of those ships back here. What was the crime?"

"Letting fuel cell reserves get too low is a violation of operating regulations," Geary said. "A ship that is too low on fuel might be caught unable to fight well, or be unable to respond to orders to proceed to battle. Commanding officers are required to ensure that their reserves don't get too low. The lower the fuel state, the more serious the violation."

"But . . . if you had come all that way and fought all those battles . . . successfully fought them . . . and arrived here in time to defeat the Syndicate Worlds' attack at Varandal . . ."

"Sir, the charges pertain to a purely technical violation of regulations, disregarding actual operational circumstances."

Senator Sakai nodded, his eyes hooded. "But it was a violation of regulations, you say."

"Yes, sir."

Navarro frowned down at the table's surface. "It seems ridiculous, but that means the military will reach the same conclusion after the court-martial proceedings have run their course. It's unfortunate, but not something we should intervene in."

Somehow he had expected the civilians to understand, to realize both how brainless were the charges and how serious the consequences of bringing them would be. Geary paused to reorder his thoughts, then spoke with great care. "Senator, every one of these officers has performed valiantly and loyally in the defense of the Alliance. They are now being relieved of command and ordered to submit to courts-martial on technical violations of regulations that were beyond their ability to prevent. It is an extreme and unwarranted insult to the honor of every one of them."

Senator Suva spoke, her voice as carefully modulated as Geary's. "Who brought these charges, Admiral?"

"Fleet headquarters, Madam Senator."

"Then it was the fleet's own superiors who initiated these charges. If what you tell us is true, then those superiors doubtless felt obligated to bring charges because of their own responsibilities. They understand the importance of abiding by regulations, rules, and laws."

The underlying implication was clear enough, a jab at Geary as if questioning his own understanding of that issue. "A good leader also understands when the letter of law, regulation, or rule will lead to unjust and improper outcomes. An automated system could govern us if all it took was abiding strictly by written rules."

Sakai watched Geary intently. "You are criticizing the judgment of your superiors?"

Geary stared back at the senator for a moment. It was the

sort of loaded question that usually only left the options of a sunk career or a hasty retreat. *But what the hell can they do to me if I answer honestly? The worst they can do is to send me to duty on a ship far from home, feed me lousy food, and make me work twenty hours a day when I'm not getting shot at by people who want to kill me.* "Yes, sir, I am saying that whoever approved bringing these charges suffered from a serious lapse in judgment."

The three senators exchanged looks, then Navarro sighed. "Admiral, I realize that this may offend your sense of justice, but we cannot interfere with the process, especially since you are so certain that the military justice outcome will exonerate your officers."

"Perhaps I haven't been clear as to what will happen as a result of this." Geary was surprised by how calm his voice sounded. "The least consequence would be serious disruption of the fleet as so many commanding officers are relieved all at once. But that will not happen, because the fleet will regard this as a move by the government against the fleet, against officers who have thus far sacrificed and fought loyally and well for the Alliance. I, and other officers, believe that they will not simply accept such an action but will regard it as a breaking of faith and an attack on the fleet by its own government."

Suva stared at him. "You are predicting that the fleet will mutiny."

"I regard it as highly probable," Geary said, the words feeling heavy as they left him.

"By your orders? You're not trying to stop this?"

It was Geary's turn to stare in disbelief. "I have never ordered anyone to act against the elected government of the Alliance, and I never will. As for trying to stop it, what do you think I'm doing now? Before I entered this meeting, I sent two other officers with orders to communicate to the fleet that it should do nothing."

"Then there shouldn't be a problem," Navarro said.

"I have no confidence that the fleet will accept those orders, Senator!" Why couldn't they understand? "I know that you're aware of sentiments in the fleet. You must be able to see that something like this crosses the line, will make too many officers believe that now they must do something. Yes, every man and woman court-martialed on those charges should be exonerated, but very few of them will trust that the right and proper outcome will occur. They will regard these charges as attempts to smear their honor beyond redemption before they are handed over to kangaroo courts!"

"But you're asking us to circumvent both military authority and the military justice system? How is that supposed to build respect for authority and the law?"

Suva chimed in again, her voice cold. "How is having the government give in to demands from military officers a means to prevent the military from controlling the government? Are you proposing that we win by surrendering?"

Sakai shook his head. "It is a legitimate question, but Admiral Geary's honor should not be questioned."

"I agree," Navarro said. "In light of what Admiral Geary has done, and what he has *not* done, it would be improper to doubt his word. *But* . . . this matter is not one in which we can take action. Your military superiors have made their decisions, our intervention in the military justice process at this point would be improper, and you will obey orders as honor demands." Despite his calm tone, Geary thought he could sense an undercurrent of tension, of fear, in the senator. "You, Admiral, will tell the fleet's officers to also obey orders and to trust in the integrity of the system. That course of action is the only salvation for the Alliance in the long run."

Navarro's words were true, but . . . they ignored the short-term danger. Geary knew this decision was wrong. He knew that if the senators did not act, disaster was a certainty. But they would not act on their own.

For months, he had feared reaching this point, ever since Rione had convinced him that he had the power to defy the civilian leadership of the Alliance. Why would he ever consider such a thing? Such defiance had been unthinkable to him a century ago, but now he could see every alternative flaming out, see that precipice of defiance approaching, had no idea what lay at the bottom, and could no more alter his course than could a ship trapped too deeply within the gravity well of a dead star.

Where did honor lie? What would be best for the people who trusted him and for the Alliance? "Sir, I must once again emphasize in the strongest possible terms that the fleet will not simply accept this kind of action."

"They will if Admiral Geary tells them to."

"I do not have confidence that is the case, sir, nor do I feel comfortable endorsing such actions."

"Nonetheless," Navarro insisted, "you have your orders and will obey them." Outwardly, he seemed irritated by Geary's persistence. Yet the subliminal signs of nervousness were more obvious as the senator spoke with apparent resolve. "We cannot violate your fleet regulations or the rule of law in the name of justice."

It sounded right and reasonable, but it also ignored reality. In this case, the rule of law was being used for injustice. But, technically, that didn't excuse him from his own obligation to do as ordered.

Geary took a slow count inside to steady himself. "Can we get an update of events outside this room, sir? Are any inputs allowed?" He knew what the answer was supposed to be but had already learned how many things that weren't supposed to be had a way of being so.

Navarro frowned, looking toward Sakai, then Suva. "We don't have . . . Can we manage a brief one-way feed?"

"A microburst of incoming information will still be entirely too hazardous," Suva replied. She had been looking at Geary with an increasingly unyielding expression. "I don't know what the purpose of that would be, in any case."

"I think it's important for us to know what the fleet is doing as we speak," Geary replied. "Despite my orders to them to remain in position."

Sakai spoke. "I believe this would be wise. My experience with Admiral Geary is that if he says we should know this, we should listen."

"Black Jack—" Suva began.

"Is not a god and knows he is not a god," Sakai broke in. "He knows there are limitations on his abilities. We should not assume that what he wants is inevitable."

Navarro stared at Geary, then at Sakai, some unspoken message passing between the two senators in that gaze. "All right. Get us an update and a download of recent transmissions," Senator Navarro said to Suva, who glowered at her data unit as she rapidly tapped in some commands.

The display flickered as the data on it updated and a string of high-priority message headers appeared to one side, then everything froze again as the security barriers locked back down. Everyone's eyes went to the display, where the neat arrays of warships locked into fixed orbits had been disordered, scores of vessels frozen in the act of maneuvering off station, their course vectors aimed at Ambaru station. Not just cruisers and destroyers, but the fast menace of battle cruisers and the ponderous threat of battleships moving toward Ambaru.

Geary could see the identifiers for the ships accelerating toward the station. *Illustrious*. Naturally, Captain Badaya would be the loosest of cannons in this situation. But Geary hadn't expected Captain Parr on *Incredible* to be moving in Badaya's wake, and *Implacable* was vectoring to join them, along with *Intemperate*. The new *Invincible* had also left position, as if choosing to unite with *Illustrious* and *Incredible*, the other two battle cruisers in her division, but *Invincible* had barely accelerated, as if trying to satisfy orders to remain on station and also go with the other ships at the same time, which meant that *Invincible* actually seemed to be doing neither.

The real shock was seeing the battleship *Dreadnaught* on the move. Why had his own grandniece disobeyed orders to stay on station? Jane Geary had impressed him as both solid and imaginative enough to be a reliable commander, but not only her battleship but also *Dependable* and *Conqueror* were in motion. That in turn seemed to have convinced *Gallant*, *Indomitable*, *Glorious*, and *Magnificent* to get under way. Seven massive battleships, any one of which could reduce Ambaru station to junk in a very short time.

Everywhere, heavy cruisers, light cruisers, and destroyers were also surging into action singly and by divisions and squadrons.

Against those were the ships standing fast. First and foremost *Dauntless* herself, with *Daring* and *Victorious*. Captain Tulev's battle cruiser division, of course, with *Leviathan*, *Dragon*, *Steadfast*, and *Valiant*. Captain Duellos holding firm with *Inspire*, *Brilliant*, and *Formidable*. There was little surprise that Captain Armus on *Colossus* had stayed on station. Armus was too slow-moving to leap into any new situation, which could be a problem at times but was a blessing in this instance as the example of *Colossus* and the rest of Armus's division seemed to be helping restrain a lot of other battleships and escorts.

Perhaps most surprisingly, the seemingly jinxed *Orion*, which in the past could always be counted upon to do the opposite of what was demanded, had held station just as Geary had ordered.

Elsewhere, on planets, moons, and orbital installations, including Ambaru itself, system defense forces were springing to higher alert levels and activating shields and weaponry. None had yet targeted any of the fleet's warships, though.

Not as bad as it could be, but pretty damned horrible. If one shot was fired, by anyone, it could set off civil war.

Navarro had frozen momentarily as he stared at the display but finally jerked back into motion, touching one of the messages.

An image of Tanya appeared. "All units are to hold position by order of Admiral Geary. All ships are to immediately return to their assigned orbital locations. You have all received Admiral Geary's order. Cease unauthorized actions and return to station now." Desjani was radiating all of the command authority she possessed. Which in Tanya's case was considerable. But it clearly wasn't enough.

His expression grim, Navarro touched a later message. Admiral Timbale, speaking quickly. "Stand down. All military forces within Varandal Star System are to stand down immediately. Halt all unauthorized movement. No one is to fire under any circumstances. I repeat, stand down now. Weapons are code red status null. No firing is authorized."

"Why aren't we seeing any messages from the warships?" Suva demanded.

Sakai answered. "Because they are most certainly using back doors within the command and control system to communicate. Those messages will not appear in official records. Is this not so, Admiral?" He had been with the fleet on its last voyage and had doubtless learned that firsthand.

Geary nodded, not bothering to try to hide his worries. "You can see that we're trying to keep things under control—"

"Under control?" Suva glared at him. "That other admiral told the defense forces here not to fire!"

"That's because a lot of people are still on the fence," Geary insisted. "Once someone starts shooting, it will force people to take sides. Under that kind of pressure, too many people will reflexively take the side of the comrades they've fought beside. We saw that in the Syndic home star system when rebellion broke out there. Don't you understand? This situation is degenerating fast. Not acting is *not* an option." He pointed to the display. "I can't control this!"

"We can't surrender to a coup before it even begins!" Suva almost shouted back at him.

"Follow orders, Admiral," Navarro urged, open desperation tingeing his voice. "Senator Suva is right. Giving in to this kind of pressure would amount to a coup in and of itself. No one in the fleet is going to act against the commands of Black Jack Geary. Tell them to stop and obey all orders."

Despite all of his efforts, the precipice was there, right at his feet. Like whoever had brought the charges against his officers, the politicians were technically in the right. He didn't have legal grounds for doing anything other than saluting, saying, "Yes, sir," and doing his damnedest despite his certainty of disaster. Doing otherwise would betray his oath, and he was the only person who had the tiniest chance of succeeding. But simply following orders would betray those who had followed him in battle, and too many officers would assume he had either been forced to say they should obey or that he had sold them out. Given the likely consequences in the fleet, obeying orders could well be the final nail in the coffin of the Alliance.

He had only one weapon left to use, one last means of trying to rein in a situation already almost too far gone. Geary hesitated, fear and uncertainty blossoming inside, then felt a strange calm descend upon him. It was as if something spoke to him with an authority far beyond that of any living thing. *This is the only path that offers a chance.* He took a deep breath. "No, sir." It came out firmly but not too loudly.

The three senators stopped moving, not even an eye blinking. "What is it you don't understand, Admiral?" Navarro asked.

"I do understand, sir. But I will not obey those orders, sir. I hereby tender my resignation from the fleet."

THREE

THE silence in the room was so absolute that Geary realized everyone must have even stopped breathing for a moment. Absurd as it was under the circumstances, he couldn't help wondering how that would affect the comfort level in the sealed conference room over time.

He hadn't known what to expect but was still surprised when Senator Navarro just looked over to Sakai, then back over to Suva, as if once again wordlessly conveying something that had already been understood.

Finally, looking at Geary again, Navarro clasped his hands before him on the table as he spoke. "Just to be clear, are you formally declaring an intent to no longer follow orders from the government?"

Geary wondered whether or not recording devices on the senators were working right now, ready to catch his confession to treason. "No, sir. That is not an option for me. But I can and will declare my resignation from the fleet, effective immediately, which means I will not be subject to orders."

"But," Sakai said, shaking his head, "as an officer, you serve at the pleasure of the government. The government need not accept your resignation. If what you say about the fleet's reaction to that message is true, then the Alliance *needs* you to help deal with this problem."

"If the Alliance government wants to deal with this problem, then the Alliance government can take the necessary action," Geary said. "I've told you what that action is, in my best judgment. I will not be a party to an unjust and dishonorable process."

"Even if your resignation is refused?"

"Even if my resignation is refused. The fleet may then court-martial *me*."

Navarro once again surprised him, sitting back and giving Geary a stern look. "You know as well as we do what would happen if the government brought charges against you. The fleet be damned, the government would collapse under popular pressure. Don't pretend that you don't realize how much power you can wield here."

"If you know that I have that much power, and surely you have some idea how little I wish to use it, why won't you listen to me?" Geary said.

"Because we can't ignore the law! We're already under immense pressure, and more investigations are being launched every day! *Any* violation, *any* favoritism, would be used against us, and to be perfectly honest with you, Admiral, I do believe that having the government fall apart would destroy the Alliance just as surely as would a revolt by the fleet! What would you have us do?"

"Find a way, sir. That's the job of a leader, isn't it?"

Senator Navarro sighed and closed his eyes for a moment, raising one hand to cover them. "We need . . ."

Whatever he had meant to add, if anything, was forestalled as Senator Suva, her eyes betraying calculation and assessment, spoke in an unemotional tone, surprising Geary with her words. "Admiral, you said that these charges should not have been brought, and even if they were brought properly, the implications for the impact on the fleet were not taken into account?"

"Yes, Madam Senator."

"Do we regard Admiral Geary as authoritative in these matters?" Suva asked the other two senators in a way that sounded rhetorical rather than like an actual question. "Yes? Then we must conclude that we have strong evidence that the process for bringing these charges was not properly followed. Certainly, any measures with such extreme consequences for the defense of the Alliance should have been coordinated with the Alliance Senate in its role as supreme authority on military issues before action was taken."

Navarro dropped his hand and gave Suva a sharp look. "The charges were brought using a flawed process."

"We have grounds for believing so." She didn't actually sound like she believed it, but Geary said nothing, wondering what the politicians were up to.

"Then we have an obligation to revisit and reexamine the process," Navarro concluded. "We must ensure that no mistakes were made and all necessary factors were considered. Charges this serious should not be brought in error." He turned a hard look on Geary. "We can, we *should*, cancel these charges while the decisions and process involved in bringing them are thoroughly reviewed."

Geary hesitated. "If they reappear at a later date—"

"That's not going to happen, though you won't get that in writing."

Sakai spoke in a musing tone. "But, if these officers received commendations from the government for their actions, specifically citing their success in bringing their ships home despite seriously low levels of fuel brought on by circumstances beyond their control, it would eliminate any grounds for prosecuting them for the same actions."

"Yes." Navarro smiled. "That will be done, Admiral Geary. I swear it on the honor of my ancestors."

Suva, her expression still oddly neutral, gestured to Geary. "Record a message, Admiral. Tell the fleet the charges are being dropped right now. We can burst transmit it out of here and calm things down."

He quickly composed something, hoping it would be what Desjani and Timbale needed to keep things under control. "This is Admiral Geary. The government has agreed that the charges against fleet officers were brought in error. They will be withdrawn. I am still in consultations with the government and unable to conduct routine communications but expect everyone to follow standing orders and my directions as relayed through Captain Desjani. Any ship that has left its assigned orbital station is directed to return to station immediately. All ships are to refrain from any actions contrary to standing orders, rules, and regulations. To the honor of our ancestors, Geary, out."

Suva tapped her controls to drop the security barriers for the tiny fraction of a second needed for a burst form of the message to be sent out.

That should be enough to calm things, but he wouldn't know for certain until he left the meeting. He also couldn't help wondering what might lie beneath the apparently solid assurances that he had just received. The grand council had made assurances to him before and lived up to them to the letter, all the while planning to circumvent their intent. Why had the senators caved so quickly after resisting so long? And why had Suva suddenly come up with a rationale that allowed the government to intervene in the matter after seeming so resistant to that?

"Now," Navarro said briskly, "if we can get to the reason for this meeting—"

"Senator," Sakai interrupted, "we have one more matter that must be resolved. Earlier, Admiral Geary formally tendered his resignation from the fleet."

"Oh. Yes. Is that withdrawn, Admiral?"

Geary let out a long, slow breath. "Yes, sir. I hereby withdraw my resignation."

"Good." Navarro spent a moment looking silently across the small room. "Unfortunately, a barrier has been breached. Your ability to pressure the government is out in the open now, at least between us. I hope in the future we can count on your loyalty to the Alliance and your sense of honor to ensure that nothing like this happens again."

"I didn't choose to have it happen this time, sir," Geary

said, hearing the stiffness in his own voice. He felt guilty, knew he should feel guilty, yet also resented it.

"Of course not." Navarro tapped some controls, and the display changed to show an area of space newly familiar to Geary. "We have a very important mission for you, Admiral. We have a problem on the far side of Syndic space, a problem you discovered. Senator Sakai has taken pains to assure us that your actions in dealing with the alien race were appropriate, but we have no means of knowing how decisive they may have been in the deliberations of these aliens. We know almost nothing about them, and that has to change."

All Geary could do was nod in agreement.

"You're going to find out more about these aliens, Admiral." Navarro gestured to the display. "Your orders are to go back there, only this time you're not to halt at the border the Syndics have maintained with the aliens. You are to enter the regions claimed by the aliens. And since we know what has happened to many Syndic ships at the hands of the aliens, you're going to have a strong force with you.

"You are to assume command of the newly organized Alliance First Fleet," Navarro continued, now clearly reading from words projected before him. "Following your assumption of command, you are to plan and execute with all due speed a full-force expedition to explore and investigate the alien race that was recently proven to occupy star systems on the far side of Syndicate Worlds' space. You are to take every needed measure to discover the strength, capabilities, and characteristics of the alien race, while also taking every reasonable precaution to avoid hostilities to the maximum extent possible. It is critically important to determine the extent of the region occupied by the aliens, so you are to identify the parameters of that region. You are to establish meaningful communications with the aliens while respecting whatever customs or characteristics have led them to be so secretive, and, if at all feasible, negotiate agreements to prevent further hostilities while also taking care not to compromise our ability to take any future actions in defense of the Alliance."

He paused to see how Geary was taking it. "You'll receive copies of all this before you leave this station, Admiral. Are there any questions?"

It was a major assignment to grasp all at once. Geary's mind focused on one key issue. "This First Fleet, sir. How many ships will be in it?"

Suva answered, smiling with tight lips as she waved broadly toward some vague area outside the station. "Everything out there, Admiral Geary."

"Everything at Varandal?" he asked, not believing the answer.

"Yes," Navarro confirmed. "And some more. Assault transports. You'll have more Marines. And more of the . . . uh . . . repair ships."

"Auxiliaries."

"Yes."

"You're calling this the First Fleet," Geary said. "But if you're giving it so many of the warships the Alliance currently has . . ."

"There will be two other fleets," Sakai said, his expression once more closed down. "The Second Fleet will be responsible for defense of the Alliance. That is, it will not leave Alliance space but remain within our borders. The Third Fleet will exist for training and repair."

Another alarm rang in Geary's head. "If the Second Fleet is supposed to stay within the borders of the Alliance, that implies First Fleet will have missions outside the borders."

"Yes," Navarro said. "You, yourself, in your reports stated that there would be many situations in Syndicate Worlds' space, or where the Syndicate Worlds used to rule and now independent star systems or anarchy reign, that the Alliance must address. That will be the task of the First Fleet."

The mission description felt reasonable. And giving him command of a fleet wasn't unexpected. He had done a decent job of commanding the fleet before. But, especially after the confrontation he had just had with the senators, it seemed strange to be handed formal control of that much firepower. "The government still trusts me with command of a fleet?"

"Of course," Navarro said without hesitation. "I'm sure you're aware that you're the only logical choice for such an assignment. You're Black Jack Geary. You've already proven to be far better at combat command than any other senior officer in the fleet. And even if you weren't, there'd be tremendous popular pressure to place you in such an important job."

"There are other factors of which you should be aware," Senator Sakai said, still impassive. "Much military funding is being cut. You will not be receiving more ships."

Navarro nodded. "No. The government is canceling most of the warships under construction. They're not needed anymore, and we can't afford them. Partially completed warships are being scrapped or placed into preservation status pending any future need to finish work on them. There are a few new warships that were far enough along in construction that canceling them would have cost more than completing them. They'll go into the Third Fleet until they're ready to join the Second Fleet."

"I understand," Geary said. It made sense, and it was consistent with the news reports that he had seen. Even the reduced fleet the government was talking about would be a few times the size of the peacetime Alliance fleet a century ago. "But that will mean Second Fleet will be spread out a great deal, with few ships covering a very large region of space."

"Well, yes. But that fleet will only have to deal with anything leaking over into Alliance space from the mess in what used to be the Syndicate Worlds."

"Then you intend to have the First Fleet often operating outside Alliance space?" It seemed important to get that said up front.

"Yes," Suva replied.

Geary eyed both Navarro and Sakai, but neither elaborated.

"There are some things you may not have heard," Senator Suva added. "You should understand the situation that we are facing. There's a growing faction within the Senate that believes our existing military forces should be cut far more than has been proposed so far. Some of them don't trust the military, and others want to divert that money to other purposes or use it to cut taxes, and some are motivated by both reasons."

"Yet," Sakai said, "the external threats remain."

"So, our problem," Suva said, "is how do we justify the continued size of the Alliance fleet? We have to be seen *using* those warships, and using *most* of them, not just small portions of the existing fleet. Otherwise, there will be unbearable pressure to either decommission or scrap those warships."

That, too, made perfect sense, except for the part about Senator Suva expressing concern for the fate of the military during peacetime. During Geary's one earlier and admittedly fairly brief encounter with Senator Suva, she hadn't impressed him as being deeply invested in the military. What had changed her mind, that now Suva wanted to provide reasons to keep the fleet at its present size? "Senator," Geary said, "I do think the Alliance is going to need those warships."

"Of course." Outward agreement but little feeling of real concurrence. "There is another issue, bearing on events that have just occurred. We have numerous agents within the fleet, reporting on morale and other matters vital for the government to know. Loyalty to the government is not a powerful component of the fleet." Suva turned a look upon Navarro, as if emphasizing some point they had argued before. "Those warships can be characterized as a threat to the government. If knowledge of that grows in the Senate, the pressure to eliminate those warships will become very strong."

" 'Eliminate'?" Geary asked, surprised by the use of that term.

"Pardon me," Suva said. " 'Decommission' is the right term? That is one factor. The other thing our agents report is that the longer the fleet sits in orbit, the more restless its crews might become. If we keep those warships idle, their crews will become harder and harder to control. I assume you see the truth in this."

Geary nodded back, the movement sharp. "I won't argue that, Madam Senator. But the crews of those ships have had very little chance to visit homes or families during the war. They deserve that opportunity now. If they don't get it, we'll have big morale problems from that, likely even more quickly than from giving the crews too little to do."

"What do you suggest, Admiral?" Navarro asked.

"More time at home for them. You say we need to carry out this mission into alien space quickly, but if we could delay that for a couple of more months—"

"No, no. That's impossible. We have an active threat that needs to be investigated. I've been convinced of that by the other members of the council," Navarro said, giving Geary the first hint that there had been debate within the council on his orders, "and I understand the need to act quickly. It cannot be months."

Instead of arguing for a more specific time frame, Geary just nodded, suspecting that they would keep pushing for less than whatever he asked for. Ruling out "months" did not make a single month an unreasonable period for his own planning on when the fleet should leave. But if he asked for a month, the grand council and fleet headquarters might insist on a period of only a few weeks instead. *Don't ask questions you don't want to know the answer to.* "Yes, sir."

Senator Suva was watching him closely. "Admiral, if those warships are sitting inside the Alliance, they pose a great threat to the Alliance. Today's events prove that." She leaned forward. "You have surely heard that there are those who wish you to become ruler of the Alliance. With you and those warships outside the Alliance, the threat posed by you is much reduced. We have been told that matters to you, that you don't wish to destabilize the government or cause a coup. Now is the time to prove that you truly believe that."

It was all true enough, but he once again felt that he was being forced into something by arguments he dared not openly disagree with. "I do believe it," Geary said, "and I believe that my actions have already proven the truth of my commitment to the government."

Navarro smiled slightly. "You have every right to say that. Please understand that we're trying to thread the needle on this, keeping the fleet strong enough for what needs to be done but avoiding situations where the fleet can threaten what it's supposed to defend. That's very hard for me to say, but you know the truth of it. Plenty of people in the government fear the military, and plenty of politicians want to use the military for their own ends. A lot of people also fear *you*, or they want to use you for their own ends."

"I have been made aware of that, sir."

Navarro took a deep breath. "Then you also understand that we need to keep that fleet out of the grasp of people who want to use it in ways that will harm the Alliance, and we need to keep you out of their reach as well. I admit it. You've done nothing wrong, and your example is an important factor in helping to keep the Alliance together. You're a hero of the Alliance, Admiral, not of any particular planet or political party, even though I understand that Glenlyon and Kosatka have already started arguing over which planet owns the rights to claim you now. But your continued existence is also a threat to everything you and we want to preserve."

That sounded very wrong. "My continued existence?"

"I'm sorry, that wasn't what I meant."

But Sakai's face revealed nothing, and Suva kept her gaze off to one side so that Geary couldn't read any feelings in her eyes.

Navarro sighed. "I won't be chair of the council much longer, Admiral. You'll be dealing with someone else in that position. But we've all discussed this and agreed that the mission is very important and that you are the person to undertake it. No one else could be trusted with it, and I'm not trying to flatter you when I say that I think no one else would have nearly the same chance of success. But let me tell you, if you get offers to make you ruler of the Alliance, you'd be well advised to turn them down. It can get ugly, and the strain is unremitting. I was even accused by my political foes of having been bought by the Syndics, and that's the sort of charge that might have led some misguided zealot to try to assassinate me."

"I thought the government had seen my report, Senator. The Syndic CEO we had captive said those impressions that you had sold out were deliberately created by the Syndics to harm the Alliance government."

Navarro smiled again, though in a pained way. "Facts, Admiral, do not play a major role in the perceptions of some individuals. Though I did appreciate the exoneration. Now, Admiral Geary, are you prepared to carry out your orders?"

"He should either accept the authority of the government or not," Suva argued. "We can't constantly be asking him if his orders are acceptable to him."

"I will carry out my orders to the best of my ability," Geary said, before any further debate could erupt over his earlier actions. "But entering alien space and attempting to communicate with them may prove very difficult. Not that I want to fight them again, but as Senator Sakai surely told you, the aliens showed no interest in negotiating or peaceful relations during the encounter our fleet had with them."

"Perhaps after the losses you inflicted on them," Navarro said, "they'll be more willing to talk. We need a better grasp not only of their strength and technology but also who they are and how they think."

"We know they can be ruthless," Geary pointed out. "They destroyed their own damaged ships to keep us from capturing any of them and learning anything about them."

"Yes." Navarro visibly hesitated, looking to both Suva and Sakai again, both of whom nodded back firmly. "But that makes it all the more critical that we know more about them. What do they look like? What are their cities like? What kind of culture do they have? If we can learn those

things, perhaps we'll learn how to avoid further bellig-
erence."

"Senator Navarro, I feel obligated to point out just how
dangerous this mission could be. We have no idea what kind
of defenses the aliens might have within the region of space
they occupy, nor how many warships they might have."

"I worried about those same issues, Admiral, but that's
why you must go! It's simply unacceptable, scientifically,
morally, and in terms of risk, for us to know so little of the
first intelligent nonhuman species we've encountered." Navarro glanced at the display and pointed to the representation
of Varandal's hypernet gate there. "Humanity's ignorance
was almost our undoing. We might have wiped ourselves
out, or crippled our species beyond hope of recovery, thanks
to attractive but potentially deadly gifts we didn't know we
had received from aliens we didn't know existed."

"You will have a secondary mission," Senator Sakai
added. "The Alliance also needs firsthand reports, as timely
as possible, about what is happening within Syndic territory.
Our ability to collect information within Syndic space is fragmentary and mostly confined to star systems close to the
border with the Alliance. Which star systems does the Syndicate Worlds' central government still control, which have
declared independence, which are fighting the central government or each other, which are a developing threat to not
just their neighbors but in time to the Alliance itself? You
must travel through Syndic space in order to reach the border
with the aliens, which will give you the opportunity for
firsthand collection of information deep within Syndic
territory."

Geary added it all up. "That's quite an opportunity to
excel, Senator."

"Excuse me?"

"I mean that it is a demanding set of orders. But I'll do
my best," he repeated, "as I know every man and woman in
the fleet will as well."

"Then this meeting is completed," Suva said.

"In that case, it's probably best that I get out of here and back where I can communicate with the outside, so I can ensure that the situation is back under control."

Navarro looked toward the unmoving ships on the frozen display, but Suva had her eyes on Geary. "You will receive confirmation of these orders from your fleet headquarters, Admiral," she said.

"I may need some extra authority when dealing with fleet headquarters to ensure that I get the ships and supplies I need for this assignment."

Senator Suva smiled reassuringly. "Certainly."

The promise had been given too easily. Victoria Rione's voice whispered in Geary's head. *Don't trust anyone any more than you have to.* But he couldn't see what could be gained by pushing the point at this time. The politicians would just provide more verbal assurances and wouldn't provide any written guarantees. Better to get the current situation stabilized, then push for whatever he needed in the future.

Navarro alone walked Geary to the hatch and followed him out. "Give Admiral Geary an escort to help him get back out through the checkpoints as quickly as possible," Navarro told the commandos standing guard outside.

"Yes, sir." Beckoning to four other commandos, the major in charge saluted Geary. "Sir, if you'll permit us to escort you?"

"I'd be honored. But we do have to hurry."

"Yes, sir!"

They rushed through the next three checkpoints, at each one the commandos making gestures to the soldiers on guard that all was well, producing not-entirely-suppressed smiles. Tension seemed to be draining out of the air as he went, the soldiers' attitudes relaxing even though they maintained rigidly correct postures, presenting arms instead of just passing Geary through. He saluted them in return, trying not to let his own worries show.

As Geary cleared the third checkpoint, he must have also passed out of the jamming zone. The major's comm unit chimed. The soldier gave Geary a questioning look, got a quick nod of approval in reply, and answered the call. "There's a general call out for you, Admiral. Urgent request for you to contact a Captain Desjani."

"May I borrow your comm unit?" Fortunately, the government-issue units were standardized, so he didn't have to figure out how to work a piece of ground forces equipment as he punched in the familiar contact data. "Tanya?"

"Where are you, Admiral?" Desjani asked, her voice clipped but also very calm.

The security jamming still had enough effect to block any video, but her tone of voice told him that the situation hadn't resolved itself yet. "I'm halfway back out through the security cordons and heading for you. What's going on?"

"Your second message helped a lot, but I've still had limited success with controlling the situation. Rumors are proliferating faster than we can shut them down. We still have warships out of their assigned orbital positions and vectoring toward Ambaru station."

"I saw a bit of that. Why didn't they respond to my second order?"

Desjani's voice stayed calm but got colder. "Questions have been raised as to whether it was authentic or some disinformation cobbled together by the government to keep the fleet quiet."

He had trouble controlling his own anger when he heard that. "Where's Admiral Timbale?"

"In the central command compartment. He's trying to keep the other military forces in Varandal from reacting to the ship movements. I strongly recommend another personal statement from Admiral Geary to the fleet, and I recommend it be sent out five minutes ago."

Geary stared down the empty corridor he was now rushing through, his commando escorts keeping up on both sides. "You don't even know what other news I have."

"Whatever your news is, it can't be worse than what I've had to work with," Desjani replied.

He tapped his unit irritably. "I still can't get a broadcast link from where I am with this comm unit. Can I relay through your comm unit?"

"I believe so, Admiral. Wait one. Got it. Voice only. You will have a broadcast link in three . . . two . . . one . . . now."

The broadcast icon popped up on Geary's comm unit display. He slowed down to keep from breathing hard from exertion as he held the device closer to his mouth and began speaking clearly. "All units in the Alliance fleet, this is Admiral Geary. All ships are to return to assigned orbital stations immediately. I do *not* want to have to repeat this order again." He let a full measure of anger and disappointment sound as he said that. Should he threaten the errant warships with relief of their commanding officers if they didn't obey this time? No. Let his expectations be clear and give the officers responsible for overreacting some way of covering their retreat without seeming to surrender. In this fleet, with its concepts of honor, threats might well backfire.

"The fleet headquarters message," Geary continued, "which notified the fleet of pending charges against numerous commanding officers in the fleet, has been canceled effective immediately." The senators hadn't actually told him that in so many words, but this was no time to leave any ambiguities hanging. "I say again, the fleet headquarters message is canceled. No actions ordered by that message remain in effect, and it will not be retransmitted. I will be proceeding directly from Ambaru station to my flagship, and once aboard *Dauntless*, I will immediately hold a conference to brief all commanding officers on the situation. To the honor of our ancestors, Geary, out."

He took another deep breath, keying off the broadcast link before speaking to Desjani again. "How was that?"

"Acceptable."

"Thanks. Assuming things calm down, you and I will need a shuttle to *Dauntless*."

"I already ordered one dispatched. It's about fifteen minutes out from docking. Where do you want it brought in?"

Good question. Already worn-out, Geary considered a

nice, secure, and more isolated military dock. But he realized the tension within Varandal hadn't dissipated by a long shot. Plenty of people must have felt something was wrong even if they hadn't noticed warships on the move. *I need to show everyone that everything is fine. Civilians as well as military.* "Make it a civilian dock. Ask Admiral Timbale to deploy the same soldiers who were working crowd control when we got here to set up things at whatever dock gets assigned. Don't try to seal it off. Let people see us and see that everything is okay."

"I understand, Admiral," Desjani said, her tones getting a little sharp again. "I will be happy to assist you."

Ouch. "If you please, Captain."

"Certainly, Admiral. I am happy to report that all ships off station seem to be turning around. I don't think any of them wanted to find out what would happen if you had to give that order a fourth time."

"Thanks, Tanya."

He closed the call, handing the comm unit back to the major with his thanks. The major took the unit with an awed expression. Would he keep it, Geary wondered, or put it up for auction as a device actually used by Black Jack himself?

Geary took it slower after that, walking at a good but not hurried pace, now wanting to convey a lack of anxiety to anyone watching. Calm continued to spread through the station. The last few checkpoints were passed with the soldiers not even bothering to check him through this time but just making shows of saluting him.

Geary dutifully returned every salute, surprised to see that the old gesture of respect was spreading so quickly through the rest of the military. When he had been awakened from survival sleep, only the Marines had still retained saluting. The rest of the military, scarred and bled white repeatedly by the never-ending war, had let the custom lapse. "Did your chain of command order everyone to start using salutes?" he asked the major.

"No, Admiral Geary," the commando said, his shy smile at strange odds with the number of battle awards he wore on his left breast and the scars mottling one side of his face. "The fleet's sailors came in doing it, and they said you thought it was a good idea, so everyone else is picking up on it. Our ancestors did it. We should. No one had to order anyone, sir. Although . . . well, it was a little hard to start copying Marines."

Geary grinned although feeling awkward again that a veteran of so much combat should be overwhelmed by him. "There are worse fates, Major . . . ?"

"Sirandi, sir," the major said, coming to attention for a moment.

"Sirandi?" *Where have I heard that name? On the old* Kutar. "I served with a Lieutenant Sirandi on a destroyer. He was from . . . Drina."

The major's eyes widened in astonishment. "My family has relatives on Drina."

"Perhaps he's one of them." Geary paused as time rushed over him again. He hadn't looked up the fate of Lieutenant Sirandi, as he had avoided learning about the deaths of most of those he had once known, but the man had surely died long ago, either in battle or from old age. "Perhaps he was one of them, I mean."

Major Sirandi's eyes were shining. "It is a great honor to know one of my ancestors served with you, Admiral Geary."

Trying to shake off the melancholy that still threatened to hit him when reminded in a personal way of the century lost to survival sleep, Geary shook his head. "The honor is mine, to have served with him, and now to be in the service while you are as well. Your ancestors, the ancestors of all of you," he said to the other soldiers, "are surely proud of you for the way you honor them with your lives of duty and sacrifice."

The phrase sounded old-fashioned, and it was for these soldiers even if it had been in common use in Geary's time; but for some reason that seemed to please the soldiers even more. Tradition meant a lot, especially when other certainties had been rocked on their foundations. As they walked onward, Geary took careful looks at the commandos, seeing that the major and most of the others had not just the combat awards but also the brooding eyes of veterans who had seen too many things and lost too many friends. They might be demobilized someday, sent off to rejoin the civilian world, but they would never truly be civilians again. "How are the ground forces doing?" Geary asked. "Is there much demobilization going on?"

Major Sirandi hesitated, his lips pressing together tightly for a moment. "Do I have permission to speak freely, Admiral?"

"Yes."

"It is very disorganized right now. Some units are told they will disband immediately, others told there will be no major downsizing. Then the next day everybody is told the opposite of what they were told before. Our own unit has been informed that we will remain active, but I don't know." The major paused again. "I have tried to imagine what I would do. I don't know. All my life I've trained to fight, and I have fought. It's what I know."

The other commandos nodded in agreement, even the younger ones. "My family served for three generations in the war," one of them said. "I always knew I would serve when I grew up. Now I don't know what the future is."

"You're not alone in that," Geary said, surprised to hear these soldiers expressing the same sentiments he had spoken of to Tanya. "None of us know what the future holds."

The soldiers exchanged quick glances, none of them saying what they doubtless all believed, that Black Jack, rumored to have spent his century of survival sleep among the living stars, might indeed know more than other men and women.

"You have your Marines in the fleet, Admiral Geary," Major Sirandi said in a sudden rush. "But if you need good commandos, men and women who can fight better than anyone, please remember us."

Geary met his eyes. "Major, rest assured that I will remember you, and everyone else here."

A minute later, the major's comm unit chimed again.

"Dock 71 Beta," he reported to Geary. "Your shuttle is docking there."

"Thank you," Geary said. "That's Captain Desjani?"

"Just a text, Admiral. It also says . . ." The major frowned in puzzlement. " 'Mother was right.' "

Geary couldn't help grinning. "It's . . . a code, Major." Of sorts. He remembered the shock on the face of Desjani's mother when they'd met her on Kosatka, and the first words her mother had spoken to Tanya. *You are going to have a very interesting life, Tanya. Just remember, if it gets too interesting, that you chose it.*

They had cleared all but the last security checkpoint when Admiral Timbale came toward them. The commandos stayed walking with Geary but fell back a few steps so he could talk to Timbale privately. "Is everything all right on your end?"

"For the moment," Timbale said. "I'll be happy once the extra troops and assorted senators leave, and my station starts getting back to normal. I take it you have orders now?"

"You're talking to the new commander of the First Fleet." Geary waved to encompass the whole star system. "I hope congratulations are in order."

"Me, too."

"Is *Dauntless* part of your fleet?"

"Yes." Geary hadn't had a chance to let that soak in before now, to realize that his orders would not force a separation from Tanya.

Timbale grimaced. "We don't have much time before we get to the dock, but there's one other thing I should tell you while I have a chance to speak privately, something I heard rumblings about. Maybe just scuttlebutt, but it sounded legitimate to me. Have you wondered why your orders didn't send *Dauntless* and her commanding officer off to one end of the Alliance and you off to the other end?"

"To be perfectly honest, I hadn't gotten around to wondering about that yet," Geary said. "Though I had worried about the possibility."

"It's not out of concern for your happiness. You and

Desjani maintained a professional relationship while you were single." Timbale gave him an apologetic look. "Some people are questioning how well you can do that when you're married. If you're separated, there's no chance for failure. But if you're together . . ."

"We might slip up?" He felt beyond anger, wondering at the minds who spent their time creating trouble for others instead of trying to solve problems.

"Just a warning. There are people watching for that, *hoping* for that, for some chink in the armor of Black Jack."

He felt a short laugh escape. "Hell, if they want to know that I'm human, I'll be happy to announce that to the universe."

"Not too human," Timbale warned. "You and Desjani getting married raised some eyebrows despite what was known or suspected about your feelings for each other. But you'd done nothing wrong that anyone could turn up, and the marriage was perfectly proper by rule and regulation. But if you two acted inappropriately now, it would give some individuals what they consider legitimate grounds to call into question whether there were improper actions before."

Geary realized he truly didn't care what others might suspect about him, but Tanya was another matter. He couldn't allow her honor to be questioned, especially not because of something he might do. "Thanks for the warning. We weren't planning on doing anything while aboard *Dauntless*, but it doesn't hurt to be reminded that we'll still be watched." *By those who are hoping that we fail.*

Once past the last checkpoint, Geary and Timbale started to encounter other people in the corridors again, his commando escort now moving to march proudly ahead to keep the path clear. The civilians smiled and called out greetings, while the military personnel smiled and saluted. Geary kept returning salutes, hoping they would reach the shuttle before his arm gave out.

Desjani waited near the boarding ramp, standing at parade rest and looking as if no crisis had threatened them just a short time ago. The two ranks of soldiers were once again drawn up as an honor guard. Nearby, other dense lines of soldiers once more restrained crowds whose cheers and cries of "Black Jack" echoed off the walls.

Major Sirandi and his commandos escorted Geary up to the ramp, then the major saluted Desjani. "Captain, the 574th Commando Regiment is honored to return Admiral Geary to the warships of the Alliance fleet."

"Thank you," Desjani replied, herself coming to attention and returning the salute. "The fleet appreciates your returning the admiral. We'd hate to lose him. Admiral, I suggest departing as quickly as possible so you can address necessary issues in the fleet."

He nodded, wondering what Desjani hadn't been able to tell him over the borrowed comm unit, thanked the commandos again as they beamed under the envious gazes of other nearby soldiers, forced himself to wave to the crowds, smile, and look calm and confident, then walked between the lines of the honor guard, saluting once again with an arm grown sore from exertion, before entering the welcome sanctuary of the fleet shuttle.

No, not sanctuary. Just a means of getting quickly from this crisis to the next one.

FOUR

DESJANI sat silently for a few moments after the hatch sealed. "Did your message to the fleet constitute formal notification that *Dauntless* will once again be your flagship?" she finally asked, looking straight ahead rather than at Geary.

Oops. "I guess it did. Until I went into that meeting, I didn't even know what kind of command I'd have or if *Dauntless* would be a part of it."

"So after you left the meeting, you told the fleet. Before you told me."

Geary didn't quite avoid wincing. "You told me I had to broadcast something to the fleet as soon as possible."

She gave him a sidelong look. "What exactly will *Dauntless* be the flagship of?"

"The First Fleet."

"That *sounds* impressive."

"It is," Geary assured her. "Most of the ships we've worked with so far will be part of it."

"And yet something is really bothering you," Desjani observed, facing him. "What's the catch?"

Geary activated the privacy fields around their seats. The

pilots weren't supposed to be listening in, and the privacy fields wouldn't defeat sophisticated surveillance systems, but he wasn't telling her anything that he wouldn't soon be telling the rest of the fleet's commanding officers. He explained his assignment and the mission while Desjani listened with occasional grunts of exasperation.

When he finished, she shook her head. "I never knew that even Alliance politicians could pack that many contradictory commands into one single order. How are you supposed to penetrate space belonging to a species with proven hostile intent while also avoiding hostilities? How are you supposed to establish communications with them while respecting their concepts of privacy, whatever those are? And how are you to reach any agreements with the aliens without somehow restricting our own options in the future?"

"Beats the hell out of me," Geary admitted. "How big a problem do you think we'll have with the crews? Being sent out on a mission like this when they had every right to expect a long time at home?"

"Problems?" Desjani exhaled with obvious annoyance. "The government knows that the only leader the fleet would follow is you because they trust *you* to bring them home again. If anyone else were in command, there'd be major trouble."

That made him feel worse. "Because they trust me, they'll follow me into what could be a major mess."

"Admiral." Her tone made him look directly into Tanya's eyes. "You have a very difficult course to steer. Without you, the fleet would currently be blowing apart Varandal."

"If I weren't here, that problem wouldn't have even come up."

"Oh, *excuse me*, Admiral. If you weren't here, then the fleet would have been destroyed several months ago back in the Syndic home star system, and the *Syndics* would be blowing apart Varandal and everything else they could reach in the Alliance."

"Why isn't that enough?" Geary demanded. "Why does the fate of the Alliance still depend upon me?"

"I told you that the living stars might not be done with you," Desjani said. "As to why, we'll have to ask our ancestors that question, but one thing I do know is that, in this case, those responsibilities have been given to someone who can handle them."

"Tanya." He pressed one palm hard against his eyes. "How am I supposed to support the government, and support the fleet, when each of them thinks the other is out to destroy it?"

Desjani's hand came to rest on his, and he heard her speak in a somber voice. "Try to keep either one from doing anything stupid."

"Is that all?" He felt a disbelieving laugh coming and let it out, the sound filling the compartment for a moment. "How can anyone keep other people from doing stupid things? Humans are good at doing stupid things. It's one of our talents, and one we like to exercise frequently."

She didn't answer immediately. "If you don't exercise a talent, you get rusty," Desjani finally said. "We stay in practice by doing stupid things often. Can you imagine if humans were bad at being stupid? It might take centuries to do the amount of damage to ourselves that we can now achieve within months."

He opened his eyes, staring at her serious expression, then noticed one corner of her mouth quivering as Desjani tried to keep a smile suppressed. "When did you acquire this wicked sense of humor, Tanya?"

"It's a small part of my attempts to remain sane. And, speaking of insane people, shall we talk about events during the almost revolution a short time ago? You should have a rundown on that before you meet with everyone."

Geary grasped her hand for a moment before releasing it. "I may have to steer the course, but you're keeping me on it. You're right. I couldn't hear any of the messages that must have been flying in the back channels. I saw one update, so I know some of the ships involved. *Illustrious*, of course."

She bared her teeth. "Badaya kept raising hell. He was the hardest to deal with, insisting that the government was trying to get rid of you and all of your supporters in the fleet while all but calling me a widow. If we'd been in the same compartment, I would have been extremely tempted to empty a sidearm into him."

"That would have shut him up," Geary said.

"Well, yeah, that would have been an extra benefit."

Deciding not to pursue the problem of Badaya for the moment, Geary mentally ran through the long list of warships present in Varandal. "*Dreadnaught*."

"Yes." Desjani seemed uncomfortable, then shrugged. "She insisted that you needed help."

"Even though you passed on my order."

"Right. Jane Geary was very aggressive about confronting the government, and she hauled more than one other warship in her wake, as you probably saw."

It didn't make sense. "She wasn't one of the officers being charged or relieved of command by that message. *Dreadnaught* wasn't even part of the fleet until after the battle here. And Jane ended up in command of a battleship instead of a battle cruiser because she was judged not to be forceful enough. What made her fly off the handle?"

"I really don't know. But people noticed that she was urging everyone to do what I was telling them not to do. On the private channels, there was a lot of chatter about how she wasn't backing me up. Not that I took that personally," Desjani took pains to add. "Professionally, I was seriously ticked off, though. I would suggest talking to her."

"I will." Geary went through his memories again. "Did anything or anyone else stand out on your end?"

"Hmmm." She thought, then gave Geary an enigmatic look. "*Dragon*."

"*Dragon*?" Commander Bradamont, one of Tulev's officers. "What was surprising? All of Tulev's battle cruisers, including *Dragon*, stayed on station."

"That's right," Desjani agreed. "But in the private channels, Bradamont was out in front when it came to backing me up."

"Why is that a problem?" Geary paused to think. "It's unusual, isn't it?" His memories of Bradamont were of a commander who fought her ship well and aggressively, but at conferences always remained silent and in the shadow of Tulev. He couldn't recall her ever speaking up or even doing anything that would have drawn attention at conferences.

"Right again. Bradamont's been keeping her head down since assuming command of *Dragon*, and for good reason."

"Wait a minute." Something about Bradamont teased at his memory. Her service record. Something unusual. "She was a Syndic prisoner of war."

"Very good, Admiral. Who got liberated while she was being transferred to another POW camp." Desjani gave him another hard-to-interpret look. "Her transport was intercepted by an Alliance raiding force. That didn't happen very often. Neither did transfers of POWs from one Syndic labor camp to another."

Geary sat back and watched Desjani. "There was a security flag on her record, but nothing high priority, so I hadn't gotten around to checking it."

"I'm not surprised. About the security flag, that is. It's funny how hard it still is to say it."

"To say *what*?"

"Bradamont fell in love with a Syndic officer while she was a prisoner of war."

That had been the last thing he expected to hear. That she had been a difficult prisoner, prone to organizing resistance among other prisoners. Or that she had been in possession of special intelligence that the Syndics were trying to pry out of her. Or that Bradamont had some family connections in the Alliance that the Syndics wanted to try to exploit. "She fell in love. With a Syndic. In a POW camp?"

"He was some kind of officer or liaison at the camp." She saw Geary's expression. "Now you know why she's stayed quiet. No sense attracting attention with that in your past."

Hatred toward the Syndics had grown poisonous during the extended war, its corrosive effects on honor and professionalism shocking to Geary when he had learned of those things. But even without that, such a relationship between officers on opposite sides was hard to understand. "How did she get command of a battle cruiser?"

Desjani shrugged. "Excellent question, Admiral. But no one knows why. It's absolutely certain that security must have given her a clean bill of health after debriefing her. Naturally, everyone has their own theories about connections she might have had or if she was on some secret mission while a prisoner. All I know for certain is that after being cleared by security, Bradamont was assigned to be executive officer on *Dragon*, and after Captain Ming transferred off *Dragon*, Bradamont was promoted to command. Bloch was in charge of the fleet then, and at the time I heard him grumbling about the command being given to Bradamont by higher authority rather than his being able to use it as a reward for some officer politically loyal to Bloch."

"She seems like a good officer and good fighter, but . . ."

"Yes," Desjani said. "But. For a while, I couldn't even stand to look at her."

He watched Desjani curiously, remembering that soon after they had first met, Desjani had expressed regret at not being able to wipe out entire Syndic planets. "How do you feel now?"

"She's . . . done her duty. Fought bravely." Desjani gave him a cross look. "I respect her actions in battle. Just before you assumed command, in the chaos of the Syndic ambush, Bradamont made a risky firing run with *Dragon* that drew fire from two Syndic battleships that had *Dauntless* in their sights. She probably saved my ship."

Geary nodded slowly. "Then she probably saved both of our lives, too."

"That had also occurred to me, but that was less important than the fact that she fought her ship as well as Black Jack." Desjani paused. "That's an old saying in the fleet."

"I've heard it," Geary replied.

"Sorry." She knew how little he liked most of the sayings about and attributed to the legendary Black Jack, especially since he couldn't recall ever actually having said most of them. "Anyway, that's why I've been all right with Bradamont since then. That and, uh, gaining some personal understanding of the tricks a heart can play on people whether they want it to happen or not. Obviously, Bradamont never compromised herself in that prison camp, or security wouldn't have cleared her even if she was a Geary. Sorry. That's another saying. But that's why Bradamont tried not to draw attention to herself. Which makes her highly visible attempts to help control things a short time ago unusual. Things have changed a bit, of course. Not too long ago, if she'd spoken up, someone like Kila or Faressa would have gone after her, but the war is officially over, and they're both dead, may my ancestors and the living stars forgive me for not being the least bit sorry in either of their cases."

Another pause, then Desjani smiled for a moment. "I missed Jaylen Cresida, but Bradamont . . . she felt like Jaylen was there backing me up."

"That's pretty high praise."

"I mean it." Desjani eyed him. "But not everyone took her high profile in this matter well. How do you intend explaining to Badaya and his faction why you're leaving the Alliance when they think you're actually running everything?"

The change in topic threw him off for a moment, as did the realization that he had no answer to the question. "I'm open to suggestions."

She checked the display in front of her. "Twenty minutes until we reach *Dauntless*. I'd rather spend it necking with my new husband since the living stars alone know when next we'll have an opportunity for that, but it looks like we'll have to devote that time to using our brains."

"I share your sentiments." Geary activated his own display. "Let's see if there are any ideas here. Search . . . leader . . . no, ruler . . . fighting . . . outside . . . borders." An extremely long string of results stared insolently back at him. "Great. How do I sort through all this?"

Leaning close to him, Desjani pointed to one. "Marcus Aurelius? That's a strange name. Look how old that citation is. Roman Emperor, What is a Roman Emperor?"

"What *was* a Roman Emperor," Geary corrected, staring at the dates. "A long time ago, on Old Earth. What does that have to do with . . . Ruler of his Empire, but he spent his time fighting on the borders."

"Sounds like we found our precedent."

"Let's hope so." Geary kept reading. "He was also some kind of philosopher. 'If it is not right do not do it; if it is not true do not say it,'" he quoted.

"Easy for him to say," Desjani complained. "In order for you to do the right thing, you have to be pretty careful what you say. Maybe things were simpler back in the times of this Roman Empire. It all happened on one planet. On part of one planet. How complicated could things have been?"

"I guess that would depend on how much people have changed since then, or if they've changed at all. This Aurelius had to fight on the borders of the Empire, to maintain security," Geary mused. "While trusted subordinates ran things back home. That's our answer. Everybody says I'm the only one who could handle these aliens, so we tell everyone that I have to go do that while my trusted agents follow orders back inside the Alliance."

"Smooth," Desjani approved. "And the identities of the agents have to remain secret?"

"Naturally." But he said that in a sour way that drew another sharp look from her.

"Admiral Geary, you're only misleading those who would otherwise do things that would cause a lot of trouble for everyone, including themselves. Now, straighten up your uniform."

"It looks fine—"

"You're an admiral, and you have to look your best. Besides, I don't want us walking off this shuttle looking like I've been groping you."

"Yes, ma'am."

That earned him another look, some annoyed eye rolling, and a heavy sigh of exasperation.

ABOARD *Dauntless*, the shuttle resting securely in the shuttle dock, he walked down the ramp and onto one of *Dauntless*'s decks, memories flooding in of events here. Geary's last words with the flawed and doomed Admiral Bloch, his later first encounters with Alliance men and women liberated from Syndicate Worlds' labor camps, and his frantic departure about four weeks ago, trying to stay ahead of a new promotion and new orders as he sought to catch up with Desjani.

The short notice before their arrival didn't seem to have fazed *Dauntless*'s crew. A perfectly turned-out set of sideboys rendered honors as Geary reached the deck. An announcement echoed through the ship. "Admiral Geary, arriving." He raised an arm, which had just begun to recover, and returned their salutes with his own.

As Desjani came down the ramp behind him, honors were rendered again, followed by the declaration, "*Dauntless*, arriving." By ancient traditions regarding commanding officers of warships, Desjani went by the name of her ship in such matters.

Geary stopped and waited for her, his eyes running over the entire complement of officers on the ship drawn up in ranks, behind them more ranks of sailors and Marines representing the rest of the enlisted crew. They looked fine. They looked more than fine. He realized he was smiling at the sight, and left the smile in place, knowing they could see his reaction.

Desjani paused beside him, her face professionally dispassionate, then nodded to her executive officer. "The crew appears to be in acceptable shape."

"Thank you, Captain."

"The admiral and I will be attending an emergency fleet

conference. I'll conduct an inspection of the ship once that is completed."

"Yes, ma'am." The executive officer took a rectangular object about a half meter wide and perhaps a quarter of a meter high from one of the other officers, then offered it to Desjani. "From the officers and crew of *Dauntless*, with our compliments and congratulations to you and Admiral Geary, Captain."

Desjani frowned slightly as she took the object, then one corner of her mouth bent upward, and she turned the article so that Geary could see. A plaque made from real wood, inlaid with a shining metallic star map of the course the fleet had followed under Geary's command through Syndicate Worlds' space, passing through star system after star system, each labeled with its name, until ending at Varandal within Alliance space. Under the inlay, actual twine sealed to the wood had been formed into the names Geary and Desjani, the strings tied together between the names in a beautifully formed knot. He had seen sailors practice such knot tying since he was a junior officer, and had been told the knots were incredibly ancient, and still valuable when tying something down could be as important as it had been on the earliest trading ships on Earth's seas. "Very nice," he commented. "Thank you."

"Yes," Desjani agreed. "Thank you all," she added at a volume that effortlessly carried through the hangar deck. "Please deliver this to my stateroom," she asked the executive officer in a much lower voice, handing it carefully back to him. "The admiral and I will proceed to the conference now."

"Yes, Captain. Welcome back."

She finally smiled. "It's nice to be back. You have doubtless already heard this, but I am happy to provide formal notice that *Dauntless* will once again be Admiral Geary's flagship. Please inform the crew."

Geary walked with Desjani out of the hangar as the officers and crew broke ranks behind them, a buzz of conversation erupting over Desjani's news. He let out a long, slow breath, happy to be walking familiar passageways. You couldn't get lost anywhere there was a comm connection to walk you through any location, but there was still comfort at being in a place where you needed no directions. "You want the plaque in your stateroom?" Geary asked.

"Yes, sir. It goes on a bulkhead in *my* stateroom. It's much less public that way."

"If it's in your stateroom, I might never get to see it. I thought that we'd agreed I shouldn't visit you there for the sake of appearances."

She frowned in thought. "Maybe I'll let you borrow it every once in a while."

"Thanks."

THE conference room was familiar, too, but not so comforting. There had been too much drama in that compartment for it to carry any sense of relaxation. Geary sighed and sat down, checking the conferencing software and thinking through what he would say. The fleet was currently spread out in orbits around Varandal, with the farthest ships from *Dauntless* almost ten light minutes distant. "That's going to cut down on real-time questions and answers," he said.

"You wish," Desjani commented as she checked things on her own display.

As usual, she had understood how he really felt. "I can dream, can't I?"

Further conversation was cut off as virtual images of commanding officers began popping into existence along the table. The table, and the compartment, seemed to grow in length to accommodate their rapidly increasing numbers. They were familiar faces now. Most of them, anyway, though with hundreds of commanding officers to deal with, Geary knew only a few well and some hardly at all. He took a moment to focus on *Orion*'s latest commanding officer as Commander Shen's image appeared. Shen was thin, small in stature, and wore an annoyed look that seemed perpetual rather than the result of any particular event. Geary resolved to check on the man's service record as soon as possible.

But Desjani glanced up when she realized that Shen had arrived, then smiled and gave him a friendly wave. Commander Shen's eyes went to her, then the lower half of his face seemed to crack like rock being ravaged by an earthquake as he briefly returned the smile before nodding in reply and resuming his irritated expression.

"You know him?" Geary asked Desjani.

"We served together on a heavy cruiser," she replied. "He's a very good officer." As if knowing what Geary was thinking, Desjani added one more thing. "Looks can be deceiving."

"I'll take your word for it when it comes to him, anyway."

"*Orion* followed orders," Desjani pointed out.

"Very good point." If Shen could turn around *Orion*, he would earn the right to bear any expression he favored.

A moment later, Geary blinked as another commanding officer appeared. This captain seemed to be nearly a twin of Commander Shen, right down to the aggravated appearance, which looked like it rarely varied. Sensing Geary's focus, the meeting software brought the captain's image closer and identifying information appeared next to him. *Captain Shand Vente*. Invincible.

"What happened to Commander Stiles?" Geary asked in amazement.

Desjani glanced up again, then at Vente with clear distaste. "Somebody more senior in rank and with better political connections must have pulled some strings and gotten orders to assume command. Remember, command of a battle cruiser is regarded as an essential ticket punch on the way to making admiral, and if it was hard to make admiral during the war, it's going to be damn near impossible now that admirals won't be dying by the handfuls in battles." Her glance strayed to Geary. "Except for you, of course, who can't stop getting promoted to admiral over and over again."

"Lucky me," Geary muttered. Every once in a while,

something like this still happened, something that drove home just how much the century-long war with the Syndics had warped the fleet. It wasn't that politics had been foreign to senior officers a hundred years before, but political jockeying had been carefully hidden, never blatantly displayed by acts such as relieving another officer of command after only a few months so someone else could get their promotion ticket punched. "Is Vente related to Shen?"

"Why—?" She looked at Vente and did a double take. "Not that I know of."

Vente, alerted by the conference software that Geary was looking his way, turned his face toward the head of the table. Unlike Shen's, his annoyed expression didn't waver as he hesitated, then nodded abruptly before resuming his stare at the table before him as if something irritating rested there.

Feeling sorry for the crew of *Invincible* but not sure that he would be able to do anything about Vente in the time available, Geary felt comforted by the arrival of Captain Tulev. Almost immediately after Tulev, the commanding officers in his division showed up in their seats, including Commander Bradamont. She sat quietly, looking at no one in particular, just as Geary recalled seeing her at past conferences when he had noticed her at all. If he hadn't had so many other things to worry about, he probably would have wondered why someone so forceful in combat was so retiring in conferences. But then, considering his problems during that period with officers like Captain Numos, who were more forceful in conferences than in combat, if he had really taken much notice of it, he would probably have just been grateful.

That thought diverted him enough that Geary entered a fast query on Numos's status. *Still awaiting court-martial. The wheels of justice grind slowly sometimes. But they still had time to generate those idiotic charges against over a hundred fleet commanding officers when they should have been dealing with Numos.*

Images were flooding in by then, the room seeming to expand at a rapid pace to accommodate their numbers. Captains, commanders, and lieutenant commanders in charge of battle cruisers, battleships, heavy and light cruisers, fleet auxiliaries, and destroyers. Captain Duellos leaned back casually, as if the fleet hadn't been on the verge of mutiny a short time before. Captain Tulev sat stolidly, little emotion apparent, but he nodded a welcome-back to Geary. Captain Badaya peered around suspiciously, plainly still expecting government agents to pop out of the bulkheads and start arresting officers. Captain Jane Geary just sat calmly, giving no outward sign that she had been agitating for trouble not long ago. Captain Armus also revealed no uneasiness, not that he had cause for it, as usual appearing as ponderous as the battleship he commanded. Geary hadn't fully appreciated until now just how solid and reassuring that kind of ponderousness could be when others were dashing around in alarm.

The final officer flashed into existence, and Geary stood up, the images before him reacting in staggered motion, those on ships closest to *Dauntless*, within a few light seconds or less, responding almost in real time, while those on the most distant ships, light minutes away, might still be reacting to his standing up when he had finished talking. "Let me start by laying out the situation. I have been assigned command of the new First Fleet. Every ship here is also assigned to that fleet, so as of half an hour ago, I am officially your commander once more."

Badaya's suspicious look vanished, replaced with smug assurance. Others reacted with obvious relief or cheerful smiles, though the delayed reactions allowed Geary to easily see that some others took the news either stoically or with some worry.

"As you have no doubt guessed, the First Fleet was created for a purpose. We are to deal with threats to the Alliance before they reach the Alliance. We have been assigned our first mission in keeping with that responsibility. It's a demanding task, but I'm certain that this fleet will be able to carry it out." Tapping controls, Geary brought up a display of far-distant but recently familiar space. "You all know this area. Part of the Syndic border facing the alien race we fought. The Alliance needs to know more about these aliens. A lot more. Especially how big a threat they might pose to us. So we're going back there, and this time we're entering alien space and getting some answers."

The smiles were faltering, shading into surprise and some concern. "How big a threat can they be?" Captain Armus asked, his broad face set into its usual slightly stubborn and slightly challenging expression. "We beat them."

Desjani answered. "We surprised them. But they demonstrated some impressive maneuvering capabilities. We want to be sure that we keep surprising them and that they don't spring any more surprises on us."

Geary nodded. "Don't forget about the hypernet gates. The aliens tricked us there so successfully that they might have eliminated most of the human race."

Commander Neeson had brightened at Desjani's words. "If we can find out how their maneuvering technology works, it would give us a huge advantage if the Syndics try anything else."

Commander Shen looked around the table. "I know that this fleet destroyed many alien warships in the engagement at Midway. How rapidly could they recover from such a blow?"

"We have no idea," Geary replied. "We don't know how powerful the aliens are, how many star systems they occupy, what sort of population they can call on, or any other information vital to evaluating the threat they pose."

"But we are going to fight them?"

"Our objective is to establish contact and to learn. We'll fight only if necessary." He saw the variously time-delayed reactions to that statement appear, oddly mixed in with reactions to his previous announcements. "It's true that the aliens showed no interest in negotiating last time we met them, but we kicked them back into their own territory when we fought. They may react a little differently this time, if only out of respect for our own ability to inflict damage on them."

Captain Parr of the battle cruiser *Incredible*, who had

been having the good grace to look a bit chastened because of his earlier involvement in the movements toward Ambaru station, now grinned. "They know now that we're not as easy to fool or fight as the Syndics were."

A comment from Captain Casia of *Conqueror* regarding some earlier statement finally arrived. "It appears the Alliance has no fear of attack now, Admiral Geary, if it is sending us all out so far from its own territory. Will there be nothing left in Alliance space to guard it but system defense forces?"

He answered that immediately, knowing others must be curious about the same thing. "You've probably heard that most warship construction has been canceled. But a few new hulls will be completed. Those will form a much smaller fleet dedicated to defense of Alliance space."

"When do we leave?" Captain Vitali of the battle cruiser *Daring* asked.

"I need to evaluate the state of our ships, how much work still needs to be done, how many personnel have had chances to go home on leave, and how many still need that opportunity," Geary said. "But I intend taking at least another month to prepare. The crews of our ships deserve that much."

"They deserve more time at home," *Warspite*'s captain grumbled.

They did, but as Geary tried to come up with an adequate reply, Captain Parr spoke again as he gestured to the star display. "What about the humans the Syndics said were lost inside alien space? On planets and ships? Are we going to try to learn their fates? Finding out what they did to human prisoners would tell us something about these aliens."

"Some of those humans are still alive," Badaya said, startling everyone with the confident assertion. "I just came to that conclusion," he added, as all eyes rested upon him. "During the . . . confusion earlier today, I was thinking about how easily we could be fooled. Easily not just because we're all human but because those fooling us are also human. We understand our weak spots, the ways our minds work, the things we overlook, the best and most effective ways to trick other humans."

Duellos gave Badaya a look of grudging respect. "But these aliens also fooled us in more ways than one, and tricked the Syndics for a century. Which means they have some highly effective knowledge of how humans think."

"Yes! We could read all we wanted to about some other species, cats or dogs or cattle or fish, but we couldn't have any hope of understanding them without studying them in person."

Geary had to suppress a shudder at the thought of humans kept for study, and saw from others' reactions that he wasn't alone. "When we saw the ultimatum the aliens sent the Syndics, we thought it felt like something drafted by humans. Human lawyers, wasn't it?" he asked Duellos.

"Yes," Duellos agreed. "That was our suspicion from the wording of the ultimatum. Now, if the aliens have human lawyers imprisoned, I would personally recommend we leave them there. We have too many lawyers here as it is."

"They'd do plenty of damage to the aliens," Desjani agreed. "Better there than here."

"There are fates too horrible even for lawyers," Commander Landis of *Valiant* suggested apologetically. "My brother's a lawyer," he explained.

"You have our sympathies for your misfortune," Duellos commented.

"But I believe his sentiment raises an important point," Tulev said somberly. "We are dealing with Syndics here. Questions may be raised as to how much risk we should run to aid them. Will it depend upon their being slaves?" Tulev wondered. "Or lab rats?"

Jane Geary roused herself and shook her head. "It's possible they're being treated better than that. Imprisoned, yes, but in, uh, a natural environment. A town or something. Because if the aliens want to study how we react to things, they'd want to see humans who weren't in cells or labs but interacting more normally."

"Possibly they have treated *some* human captives that way," Tulev partially conceded. "But the number of Syndic citizens unaccounted for within territory occupied by the aliens is much more than they would need for such a purpose unless they have set aside a planet for such research."

"Then we can find that planet," she said.

"Yes. The argument remains the same. I would suggest that we must find these humans, if any live, and Captain Badaya's suggestion on that issue may be true, so they may be freed, even if they are Syndics, or are descended from Syndics."

Coming from Tulev, those words meant a great deal. His home world had been rendered unlivable by Syndic bombardment during the war, and all of his relatives were dead.

"Even Syndics don't deserve that fate," Armus agreed. "And it's not impossible that they have some Alliance citizens, too. Their ships could have penetrated as far as Alliance space without being spotted, thanks to those worms."

"A real possibility," Badaya said. "Who would believe their naked eyes when sensors reported seeing nothing? And if they did believe it, who would believe them? There'd be no record in any system to back up their statements."

"What will we have," the commanding officer of *Revenge* asked, "to handle landing operations? The fleet's normal contingent of Marines is easily overtaxed on such missions."

"General Carabali will be with us," Geary replied. "Along with a reinforced Marine contingent. There will be some assault transports added to the fleet to help carry them, as well as help transport any prisoners we liberate from alien territory or Syndic territory."

Armus made a face. "Lots of Marines. The living stars help us if they go on liberty. They always raise hell planetside."

"Carabali's not too bad to work with," Duellos suggested. "For a Marine, that is."

"Yes. She's not too difficult for a Marine." Armus looked

back at Geary. "What exactly are we being called upon to do when penetrating alien space?" Like the battleship he commanded, Armus wasn't particularly quick, but he had a tendency to bull through to the heart of a matter.

"We have four basic tasks," Geary explained. The written orders the grand council had downloaded to him had helpfully spelled those out, along with the contradictory cautions. "We need to establish communications with the aliens." He couldn't help glancing at Desjani. "Communications by some means not involving weaponry, that is."

"Our hell lances got their attention," Desjani observed.

"Damn right," Badaya agreed.

"Granted," Geary said. "But we have to try to find other ways to talk to them. If possible. The second task is to try to establish how powerful these aliens actually are. If we can negotiate with them, it may be possible to figure that out without learning the answer the hard way."

Duellos leaned back, sighing. "It would be nice to know how many more warships they have left. I assume we're also tasked with finding out what other kinds of armaments they might have?"

Geary nodded. "Preferably without having those armaments fired at us."

Tulev made a face. "At least for once the government is not trying to do something too cheaply and with too little. They are giving us most of the Alliance's remaining offensive warships for this mission."

Badaya frowned importantly. "What else are we going to accomplish, Admiral?"

Geary waved toward the star display. "We want to gain some idea of how large a region the aliens occupy. It's likely that will require penetrating quite a ways into their space, which is why we'll have extra auxiliaries along. I fully intend moving fast while scouting out the limits of alien space."

Neeson had his eyes on the star display. "What lies beyond the borders of the space controlled by those aliens, I wonder? Other sentient nonhuman species?"

"That's one of the things we need to learn."

"Potential allies," Badaya murmured.

"Possibly," Geary agreed.

"Or," Armus observed with a sour expression, "more hornets' nests to poke with sticks. You spoke of four missions, Admiral. I've counted three so far."

"We've already discussed the fourth." Geary paused to ensure that his next point stood out. "We know that human-crewed ships have vanished in space occupied by the aliens. We know that the Syndics weren't able to fully evacuate some of the star systems they abandoned under alien pressure. There are humans unaccounted for." Eyes were on him, faces stiffening with resolve even before Geary said more. "We're going to look for any signs of human presence, any signs of human prisoners, any signs of any human who needs to be rescued."

A long silence followed, then Shen grimaced. "Even though they're Syndics?"

"In this case," Tulev said, "the fact that they are human takes precedence over any political allegiance they may have."

Shen nodded. "If you are willing to say so, then I will not object."

"Pragmatism demands it of us even if our duties to the living stars and the honor of our ancestors does not," Duellos said. "These creatures, whatever they are truly like, cannot be allowed to think that humans can be treated in such a way."

"Except by other humans," Armus grumbled.

"Well . . . yes. Only we have the right to mistreat others of our species. It's an odd moral stance, but I can't think of a better one."

Commander Landis of *Valiant* spoke up. "Admiral, I was as happy as anyone when you told us that headquarters' message regarding the courts-martial had been canceled. But I was surprised that it ever got sent in the first place." He glanced toward where Badaya sat, who nodded back to him. Geary had never been certain that Landis was one of those in Badaya's faction, but now it seemed pretty clear. Still, *Valiant* had followed orders earlier.

He decided that the best way to form his response was by continuing to defuse the tension and phrase his response in vague terms. "Believe me," Geary said with exaggerated sarcasm, "you weren't the only one who was surprised." Delayed reactions showed around the table. "Orders get given, but sometimes it takes a while for people to respond." The double edge to that statement should keep those who had overreacted on the defensive. "And sometimes we have to deal with aberrant actions by those who should know better. I assure you and everyone else here that everyone knows better now." He had to keep promises to a minimum because there was no telling what else headquarters, in a moment of imbecility, might decide was a good idea.

"The issue is settled," Tulev said. "Admiral Geary has told us so."

"Lessons learned," Badaya agreed with a glance at Landis, who nodded back.

Geary waited for a couple of minutes to see if more comments came in, finally seeing the commanding officer of the heavy cruiser *Tetsusen* stand up. "Admiral, it sounds as if we'll be spending a long time away from home in the future. I'll be the first to admit that I don't know what to expect from peace, and that it's nice to have a firm idea of what the future holds after all of the uncertainties about whether we'd be demobilized quickly or left to orbit here indefinitely or whatever. But, sir, we have homes and families. Will we see them as rarely in peacetime as we did in time of war?"

He answered quickly, wanting to allay those real concerns as best he could. "Commander, it is my intention to have this fleet inside Alliance space as much as possible given the exterior threats we may face. This fleet will remain here for another month before leaving on its first assignment because you all deserve that time. To my mind, this fleet needs to be in a position to respond to external threats, not be tied down fighting those threats, and that means this fleet needs to be home as much as possible."

It felt like the right thing to say, and it must have been the right thing because all of the other officers nodded back, though Badaya had another questioning expression.

Geary looked slowly along the vast virtual length of the table, trying to personally make eye contact with every officer. "I am honored to be given the opportunity to command you again. Welcome to the First Fleet. For now, continue with previously assigned actions. I'll be reviewing the status of ships and making any changes necessary to ensure we're all ready in a month's time."

They all stood, the motion staggered a great deal by the time lags created by the distance of some ships. Some of the commanding officers would still be standing up ten minutes from now. But as each rose, he or she saluted, then disappeared.

Most of the images disappeared as quickly as they had arrived, but one cluster of officers remained in place. Studying them, Geary saw that all were commanding officers of warships from the Callas Republic and the Rift Federation.

Captain Hlyen of the battleship *Reprisal* saluted in an almost ceremonial fashion. "Admiral, though we currently remain assigned to the Alliance forces, and therefore accept our placement within the First Fleet without reservation, we anticipate being ordered to return home in the near future. As the most senior officer among the contingents from the Callas Republic and the Rift Federation, I wish to extend our formal appreciation for the honor and the opportunity to have served under your command. We know that victory, and our own survival through many battles, is owed in great part to your leadership."

The other officers saluted with the same flourish that Hiyen had used, and Geary, with a small smile he couldn't suppress, returned the gesture. "The honor has been mine to be offered the chance to fight alongside ships and crews such as yours. I'll always be grateful for the contributions that your republic and federation provided for the victory we all fought to achieve." It saddened him to think of losing those ships, but given the politics roiling their homes, he could scarcely have expected the bulk of the warships making up the fleets of the republic and federation to remain under Alliance control.

The allied officers vanished as well, leaving Geary alone with the images of Badaya and Duellos, and the real presence of Desjani.

Badaya sat back, frowning. "While you spoke during this meeting, over the back channels I heard quite a few concerns being raised. Now that you've given the official story for public consumption, Admiral, many of this fleet's officers have some serious questions that *must* be answered."

FIVE

HAVING prepared himself for just this line of questioning, Geary simply nodded in reply. "What's bothering them?"

Badaya gave Geary a curious look. "I trust you, of course, but I admit to also being confused about this. Why are you leaving Alliance territory? It's obvious that the politicians are barely under control. This mess with the attempts to court-martial half the fleet on ridiculous charges is a clear sign of that. Who knows what else they might do in your absence?"

"The problem with the court-martial charges originated at fleet headquarters," Geary said. "I dealt with it. Everyone should have trusted that I would do so."

Seemingly unfazed by the once-again barely veiled rebuke, Badaya spread his hands. "You're right that confidence means we have to assume you're on top of things. But you've been gone for a little while, and although everyone knows you were actually putting the government in its place under cover of a honeymoon, we also understand that straightening out the Alliance is a difficult job for anyone."

"Yes," Desjani commented in innocent tones. "We have

been doing a *lot* of political maneuvering for the last few weeks."

"Naturally," Badaya replied, seemingly oblivious to alternate meanings to Desjani's statement, though Duellos seemed on the verge of choking for a moment as he coughed several times. "The point now is, you're heading out. A long ways out. What happens here while you're far from home?"

Desjani answered him again, this time speaking with flat, professional tones. "There's a major threat outside of Alliance space that must be evaluated and confronted, and if necessary defeated once more. Who would you select for that task?"

Badaya stayed silent for a few moments. "I don't know. I couldn't do it. If I'd been in command at Midway, I wouldn't have figured out what was happening in time, and those damned aliens would have hurt us very badly and won the star system. As good as you are, Tanya, and you, Roberto, I don't think you would have done so, either. Not on your own." He sat back, rubbing his chin, his eyes going from Geary to Desjani. "Some tasks can be delegated, but when it comes to fleet operations . . ."

"Admiral Geary has no equal," Desjani finished, acting as if she were oblivious to Geary's discomfort at the statement. "There are messes inside the Alliance, political messes, which others can contain and control. But the threats outside the Alliance require his personal attention. Do you agree?"

"Absolutely! These others . . . do you trust them?"

Geary thought about the grand council, the worn-out but apparently sincere Navarro, the hard-to-read Sakai, and the worrisome Suva. Not to mention the other senators he had met previously. What option did he have but to trust them? And whom did he know better qualified or more trustworthy, even if he could pick and choose? "They're what we have to work with," he finally said.

"The old dilemma of any commander," Duellos commented. "You have to carry out actions with what you have, not what you'd like to have. More than one disaster has taken place when people operate as if what they wish for was what they actually had."

"I'd say countless disasters," Badaya agreed. "But, speaking of what we have, the ships from the Callas Republic and the Rift Federation seem very confident that they'll be leaving us soon."

"It's understandable," Duellos said. "They were attached to us for the war, and the war is now officially over."

"But official endings leave a lot of messes behind, don't they?" Badaya frowned again. "There are rumors that the Callas Republic and the Rift Federation are actually going to leave the Alliance, sever all ties now that they think they don't need us anymore."

"There's talk of that," Geary said. "They were always independent powers who chose to join with the Alliance during the war."

"But to let them walk away from the Alliance now—"

"The Alliance never controlled them," Duellos pointed out. "We don't control them now. They have independent ground forces and space forces, and independent governments."

Badaya made a disgusted face. "We'd have to defeat them to keep them in the fold. Civil war."

"Or a straight-out war of conquest," Duellos agreed, "depending on how people chose to define the current relationships of those powers with the Alliance. But either way, it would be the sort of action for which the Syndicate Worlds have long been notorious."

"They're not worth that kind of stain on our honor," Badaya grumbled. "You made a good decision to let them go if they want, Admiral."

Duellos coughed slightly, probably covering up another laugh, as Geary nodded to Badaya as if he had indeed decided what would happen. "The departure of those ships will leave a hole in the fleet," Geary said, "but nothing we can't handle. It's not as if we could keep them by force in any event. I'll miss having them, but I don't want to go into battle alongside people who are only on our side because we have guns at their backs."

He paused, watching Badaya. As difficult a problem as Badaya could pose, he was also a decent commanding officer with a quick mind. He was also, as far as Geary could tell, honorable enough except for his willingness to act against the government of the Alliance. But even that willingness Badaya justified by believing the Alliance government had become too corrupt and no longer representative of the people of the Alliance. *And I hate even misleading people like Badaya about my role now. I hate lying to them even worse. If I can walk them toward accepting the government now . . .* "In the long run, the government has to be trusted again."

"You have no disagreement from me on that," Badaya said.

"That's another reason why it's important for me to not be home too much," Geary continued, wondering what was inspiring these words. Maybe his ancestors had given him the arguments he needed to make. "We can't have people believing that I'm the only who can do things, that I have to be in charge. I can't be indispensable because I do make mistakes, because I can't be everywhere, and because the day always comes when all of us leave our lives and join our ancestors. The Alliance can't be dependent on me."

"This fleet," Duellos suggested, totally serious now, "recalled much of its past honor with your example. Perhaps there's hope for the government, too."

"Politicians don't change their stripes that easily," Badaya said. "But you're right, Admiral. Absolutely right. The citizens have to vote in a government worthy of the name. It's their responsibility. It's like being in command of a ship. You're important. Your decisions are important. But if you die, and the remaining officers can't keep that ship going because you've never prepared them for that, then you've failed in one of your most important duties."

"Exactly," Geary said. "Does that mean the questions you had are now answered?"

"You answered some that I hadn't thought to ask." Badaya stood up and saluted. "Oh, and congratulations to you two, if I can step outside of formal bounds for the moment." He beamed at Desjani. "And you did it by the book! Not a rule broken! I hope that you had plenty of time for more than politics on your honeymoon!" Winking broadly, Badaya vanished.

"I am going to kill that oaf someday," Desjani announced.

"Make sure you do it by the book," Duellos suggested, then looked to Geary. "You made a good point about not wanting to be indispensable as far as the Alliance is concerned. Now that you have a long-term command, you might want to consider what happens if we lose you as fleet commander."

Geary sat down, resting his head in one hand, feeling immensely tired after recent mental and emotional strains and wanting nothing but to relax for a little while. "I do need to designate a formal second-in-command."

"You can't pick just anybody," Desjani said.

Duellos nodded in agreement with her. "Seniority and honor, Admiral. That's how we've been doing command for a while."

"When Bloch designated you as acting fleet commander," Desjani added, "you weren't just Black Jack. You were also by a wide margin the most senior captain in the fleet based on your date of rank a century ago. And even then you had some who were willing to contest the validity of your date of rank. Remember?"

"There's a lot about that period that I'd be happy to forget," Geary replied. "Who is next most senior in this new fleet?"

"It might be Armus," Duellos said, his brow furrowing in thought. "But even if he were, battleship commanders often stood aside or were cast aside when such issues arose."

"Tulev might be the most senior battle cruiser captain," Desjani said, her own expression brightening. She tapped her personal unit several times, then her smile faded. "No. He'd be third in line. You're eighth in line, Roberto."

"And you would be seventh in line," Duellos acknowledged with a slight bow in her direction. "I always respect my elders."

"Go to hell," Desjani replied without any heat.

"Who's senior to Tulev?" Geary asked.

"Badaya is number two, and number one is . . . Vente on *Invincible*."

"Ancestors preserve us." A familiar headache was threatening to make another appearance.

Duellos rubbed his chin. "Badaya wouldn't simply accept Vente. He would try to get the rest of the fleet's captains to back him as commander. Which would create quite a problem if he succeeded. And Badaya probably would succeed since Vente is new and needs to build up support."

"But how can I get Badaya to not object to my designating Tulev as second-in-command, and commander if I'm killed?" The silence that answered Geary's question confirmed his worries. "I haven't even started organizing this fleet, and I've already got a major organizational problem."

"Just wait until you get the organization order from fleet headquarters," Desjani said cheerfully. "They'll tell you exactly where everyone and every ship and everything is supposed to go."

The headache was definitely here now. "And exactly why do you find that funny, Captain Desjani?"

"Because fleet headquarters always sends out detailed organizational orders," Duellos explained, "and operational commanders always completely ignore them. It's not practical to have someone scores of light years away trying to decide which ships go together and how many should be in each division or squadron, and how crews should be distributed, and exactly which ship and which department and which stateroom should be occupied by Lieutenant Generic Average Officer after his original ship got shot out from under him, but that's never stopped headquarters from trying."

"They send out their extremely detailed message," Desjani added, "and periodic updates and corrections and additions and addenda—"

"Not to mention appendices and annexes," Duellos said.

"—and headquarters thinks that every particle in the

universe is aligned just as they've mandated. That makes
headquarters happy. We ignore their message, so we can
actually do our jobs, and that makes us happy."

"No wonder the war lasted a century," Geary said.

"Headquarters no doubt deserves considerable credit for
that," Duellos agreed. "How to get Tulev accepted as your
successor, in the unfortunate event that becomes necessary,
is a real matter to deal with. Alternately, we try to figure out
how to make sure Badaya will act responsibly. Frankly, that
may be the better option since bypassing Badaya will be
very difficult. Those are real matters of concern; but when
the organizational message arrives, you may read a little of
it, then hit the delete button, happy to know that you need
not do anything it says."

"Great. Thanks for helping to keep a lid on things when
that stupid court-martial message came in."

Duellos nodded again but lost his amused look. "That
was a very serious piece of stupidity. Someone with much
seniority and little brains almost did a lot of irreversible
damage." He stood up and shrugged. "Why should that surprise me? My congratulations as well to you both. May the
living stars shine on your union."

After Duellos had left, Desjani stood up, sighing. "I suppose we shouldn't stay alone in here for any longer than
necessary. I thought you handled everything pretty well.
Will you be using this compartment for any follow-up meetings with individual officers?"

He hesitated. "I'd been planning on using my stateroom . . ."

"Using this compartment instead of your stateroom will
convey a message in itself," she suggested. "Assuming you
wish to convey disapproval of recent actions by anyone in
particular. Especially if they're related to you."

"Why do I even pretend that you don't always know
exactly what I'm doing?" Geary asked.

She just smiled and left.

Bracing himself, Geary called *Dreadnaught*'s commanding officer. "I need a private conference with you."

It only took a couple of minutes for Jane Geary's image to reappear. "Yes, Admiral?" she asked, betraying no sign of discomfort.

He didn't ask her to sit down. That, like the choice of this room over his stateroom, would also send a message. "Captain, after reviewing the communications records, I'm concerned about your recent actions." He had chosen to say it that way to keep Desjani out of it, to prevent implying that he was acting because of what she had reported. "To be specific, I don't understand why you acted as you did."

Jane Geary's voice and expression both reflected composure. "I acted as I thought best, Admiral."

"You had orders from me that all ships were to remain on station. Not only did *Dreadnaught* leave her assigned orbit, but you encouraged other ships to do so as well."

"Under the circumstances, I thought it wise to ensure that pressure was maintained on those who had created the crisis."

"Even though you had orders from me to the contrary?" He heard the disbelief edging into his voice, knew he was beginning to sound angry and didn't bother trying to hide it.

"Comms can be faked, Admiral."

"You were speaking with Captain Desjani, who was conveying orders I had given to her in person."

"Her comms could have been altered en route to us as well," Jane Geary explained. "You were both under control of outside forces."

Something had happened to her. But what? Geary sat down, leaving her standing. "Captain Geary," he said, using the formal title to emphasize his words, "I was speaking to members of the Alliance government. They are not outside forces. I want to be clear about my reasons for unhappiness. I am concerned not just because my orders were disobeyed but because of how you acted. From the first time I saw you in action, defending Varandal, I was impressed by your judgment and restraint. You did not act recklessly or impulsively."

Those words got some response, something flickering in her eyes as her mouth tightened slightly. "I took what actions seemed required by the situation," Jane Geary said. "Just as you always have, sir. I was selected to command a battleship, not a battle cruiser, but that does not mean I lack the spirit of a Geary."

He couldn't help a small frown of puzzlement. "No one's ever questioned that."

Her eyes met his. "Yes, Admiral, they have."

The past slammed down between them again, like an invisible wall that forever divided Geary from his surviving relatives. *Tell her I don't hate you anymore.* Michael Geary's last words to him. To those who came after him, Black Jack Geary had been the impossible-to-equal, and impossible-to-escape, symbol of his family. His relatives had grown up fated to serve in the fleet because of their supposedly dead and supposedly heroic ancestor. "Jane, I have told you before this that I consider you one of the better commanding officers in this fleet. That includes all of my battle cruiser commanders. You're one of the best."

"Thank you, sir."

She didn't believe him. What had changed for her while he had been gone? "I want the officer I saw defending Varandal. Forget Black Jack. I want you to be Jane Geary."

"Yes, sir."

Damned military formality. When all else failed, it offered the perfect hiding place for real feelings and thoughts. Geary leaned back, tapping the table. "Sit down, please, Jane. I have to confess that I thought you'd leave the fleet and get on with your life now that the war's over."

She sat but still seemed rigid. "Not every mission is over," Jane said quietly.

"If Michael still lives, I'll find him."

"You have plenty of other jobs, Admiral. I can do that one."

"Is that why you're staying in the fleet? To search for Michael?"

Jane hesitated. "There are a number of reasons."

"You've done your part," Geary urged her. "I'm stuck here. You can do something else."

"I'm a Geary." She said it in a low voice, but the force behind the words carried clearly. "More so than ever."

He stared at her, unable to find words for a long moment. "Let's just be clear that I believe that you have a right to your own life. Don't stay in this fleet because of me. I've done enough damage to the family. But if you do stay, I need to know that I can count on you."

"You can count on me." She watched him steadily, no wavering in her eyes.

"I have always known that." This wasn't going anywhere. "Jane, as your commanding officer, I hope you will keep me informed of any matters that might impact your ability to continue serving as well as you have in the past. As your uncle, I hope you will feel free to speak with me on any matter."

Jane didn't reply for a long moment, then shook her head. "I'm older than you are, Uncle. You spent a century not aging."

"I've been making up for it since being recovered from survival sleep. With everything that's been happening, I think I've been aging a few years every month." The attempt at humor didn't change her expression, so Geary gestured to her. "That's all I had to say."

"Thank you." She stood once again, saluted even though the meeting had become informal, then her image vanished, leaving Geary glowering at the space where she had been. *What the hell? "I'm a Geary." That's what she ran away from all her life. Why is she embracing it now? And how would that—*

Damn. Is she embracing the legend? *Does she now think she has to live up to that?* I *can't live up to that.*

She can't be thinking she has to be like Black Jack.

But what Jane Geary had Dreadnaught *do during that mess over the courts-martial. Isn't that what the myths say Black Jack would have done?*

Please let me be wrong. The last thing this fleet needs is that mythical Black Jack.

* * *

FINALLY free to hide in his stateroom for a few minutes, Geary found himself too restless to sit there. He decided to take a walk around the ship. As he went through the familiar passageways, he felt a lightening of his spirit. *Dauntless* had been built to as austere a scheme as Ambaru station's new sections, but the battle cruiser had something the station did not. *Dauntless* felt like home.

He wasn't surprised to encounter Tanya, walking steadily along, checking out everything on her ship. *Dauntless* had probably been a beehive of activity before she arrived, with everyone striving to ensure that not a single speck of dust marred any surface and not a single item was out of place or functioning at less-than-optimum levels. "Good afternoon, Captain Desjani."

"Good afternoon, Admiral Geary," she returned in the same tones, as if they had spent the last few weeks just working side by side as usual.

He fell in beside her as they walked, being careful to maintain a distance between them. This was her ship, and the crew would surely note any unprofessional familiarity. "It's odd. Being back in my stateroom, I started to feel like everything in the previous weeks was some kind of dream."

She raised one eyebrow at him, then brought up her left hand, holding it straight up with the back facing him so that the new ring on it glinted clearly. "I don't usually acquire jewelry in my dreams."

"Me, neither."

"Something has you on edge. How did your individual meeting go?"

"Well enough, but odd." He got another questioning look as he described his meeting with Jane Geary. "I don't know what's gotten into her. Jane made it clear when I first talked to her that she only joined the fleet because she had to, because she was a Geary. The war's over now. She's done her duty, and then some. There's nothing holding her to the fleet."

"*Something* is holding her to the fleet."

"I told her she was free to leave, to get on with her life."

Desjani smiled wryly. "Life isn't usually what we plan. Whatever Jane Geary once thought she'd be, she's spent her adult life as a fleet officer. Maybe she's finally realizing that *this* has become her life. Maybe she no longer knows what else she wants to do. And maybe . . ."

"Maybe what?" Geary asked.

"You've told me about your family issues, how they felt about Black Jack." Desjani bit her lower lip before saying more. "Maybe part of her was *not* being Black Jack, because she could hate him and think he was nothing actually worth emulating. But now she knows the real Black Jack."

"Black Jack was never real."

"Are you always going to be in denial about that? The point is, Jane Geary may be trying to figure who she wants to be now. Not just 'not Black Jack.' Something else."

He grimaced. "That's what I'm worried about, that she might want to be more like the imaginary Black Jack. Not like the real me. I wish she'd talk to me about it. I'm going to go talk to my ancestors. Maybe they'll offer some understanding."

"Have fun and say hi to them for me," Desjani said. "I need to finish looking over the ship. I'll go down to the worship spaces after that. To give thanks," she added with a meaningful look at him, "for all that has gone well and all that could have gone much worse."

"Message noted, Captain Desjani." They were together, even if that togetherness would be severely limited, and only a fool wouldn't give thanks for worst cases that had been averted today.

THE organization message from fleet headquarters had arrived just as Desjani and Duellos had predicted, one week after Geary had assumed command of the fleet and four days after he had organized the fleet himself. He hadn't been sure how much the other two might have been joking about the nature of headquarters' micromanagement, but couldn't resist a grunt of disbelief at the size and detail of the message. *Put* Inspire *and* Leviathan *in the same battle cruiser division? Why the hell would I do that since it would mean Duellos and Tulev would both be in the same division instead of leading their separate divisions as they've done so well? Why scramble the battleship divisions instead of keeping the ships with the comrades they've been working with for a while?*

No further promotions had been approved. Not the ones Geary had proposed, and none based on length of service or heroic actions or new assignments. With the end of the war and the freezing of the fleet's size, officer promotions had skidded to an abrupt halt, a standstill all the more jarring for the officers nowadays, who had been accustomed by constant and serious battle casualties to expect promotions as fast as other officers were killed in action and needed to be replaced. Aside from the Alliance's apparent need to keep promoting him to admiral, and Carabali's promotion from colonel to general, no one else had been approved for higher rank, not even Lieutenant Iger. "Unfair" was the mildest way of describing it, but the system had been carefully designed so that promotions were never guaranteed, so there were no legal grounds for fighting the lack of promotions. Geary wondered how long it would be before his officers began chafing at the sudden halt to upward mobility and the apparent failure of the fleet to any longer recognize superior performance with higher rank.

And they would be looking to him, wondering why he didn't fix things and get promotions going again. *Field promotions. Maybe headquarters forgot to restrict my ability as fleet commander to promote officers in the field for exceptional performance. But I'll have to make a bunch of those all at once because once I do it the first time, headquarters and the government will realize that loophole still exists.*

He paged down deep in the message and saw the crew lists. Sure enough, every man and woman, officer and enlisted, was assigned by ship, duty, and berthing compartment or stateroom. *Can I really just ignore this?* He wondered for the first time about the fleet status reports that went out when the fleet was in home space. He knew the reports he received from each ship were accurate, but what got forwarded to headquarters?

Desjani blinked at the question after he called her. "It's a simulation," she explained. "You don't have to do a thing. The fleet database is set to automatically generate a simulation based on headquarters messages like that one. It gets updated by real data when necessary, like combat losses and damage, but administratively it's an alternate universe that gets fed back to headquarters to keep them quiet. Didn't you do that a century ago?"

"No." Should he be horrified? Or thankful that a cure for bureaucratic meddling had been discovered by the operational forces? "Why hasn't headquarters figured out what's happening?"

"They know it's happening. Of course, operational units are so far away, it takes headquarters a while to figure it out. Then they tell us to do what we're told and stop running the simulation, and the simulated fleet agrees and tells them everything is fine. After a while, headquarters figures out they're still hearing from the simulation and tell us again, and the simulated fleet agrees again. And so on and so on. Officers at headquarters vow to change the system, but if any of them ever get out with the operational forces, their perspective changes."

It made sense, but it could also be an enormous practical joke on him. Geary studied her intently, looking for any sign that Desjani was pulling his leg. "Nobody ever talks about it?"

"We don't have to talk about it much. It's all automatic on our end, though I guess headquarters devotes a lot of effort to telling our simulated fleet how to behave. Haven't you heard anyone talk about the Potemkin fleet? I don't know where the name came from; maybe it was the name of whoever first designed the system, or maybe it was a name someone found in a database that seemed to fit. The point is, it means the fleet that headquarters wants to see, so that's what we show them. We follow operational orders, of course, but the micromanagement of everything else is just ignored."

After he had ended the conversation, Geary still spent a few minutes staring at the message. Despite Desjani's ease with the situation, part of him still revolted against the idea of feeding headquarters a lot of simulated data. But then he took another look at the detailed instructions, focusing on one line pertaining to one officer on one ship. *Ensign Door should make reports twice each week to his department head Lieutenant Orp on his progress in qualifying as an emergency damage repair party leader per fleet instruction 554499A. Should Ensign Door fail to make adequate progress, reports documenting his shortfalls should be prepared weekly using form B334.900 . . .*

Geary deleted the message from his queue.

Naturally, it was only the first of many from fleet headquarters.

The next arrived the following day in the form of a high-priority alert flashing an angry demand for attention. That alone gave Geary a bad feeling since he was busy reviewing the readiness state of the ships assigned to the First Fleet. With a sigh of resignation, he tapped receive, seeing the image of the new chief of fleet headquarters for the Alliance, Admiral Celu, appear standing before him. Celu had a strong chin, which she jutted out as if challenging Geary.

"Admiral Geary, we are in receipt of reports that indicate that you do not intend proceeding on your assigned mission for thirty standard days after assuming command. This mission is of the highest priority to the security of the Alliance. You are directed to move up your intended date of departure by a minimum of two weeks. You are to acknowledge receipt of this message and respond with your intended date of departure as soon as possible. Celu, out."

Not even a polite and proper "to the honor of our ancestors" at the end of the message. And not a simple text message or even a video headshot to convey the short message, but a full-body image plainly intended to impress or intimidate. At one time it would have driven home to him the need to comply with an order whether he thought it wise or not. But in the last several months, he had done a lot of operating without the benefit of senior guidance, faced down plenty of opponents doubting his authority, and sent far too many men and women to their deaths on his orders during battle. His own perspective had shifted quite a bit, and actions aimed at pleasing his superiors even at risk to his subordinates had even less appeal than they had once had. Having confronted more than one collapsing hypernet gate, the image of an admiral standing before him held far less impact by comparison.

Geary paused the message to look Celu over. A very nicely cut uniform. Many decorations. Something about the image reminded him of the Syndic CEOs he had seen in their perfectly tailored suits. A certain cast to her expression, which, together with the tone she had used, made Geary willing to guess that Celu was the type of officer known as a "screamer" to subordinates, the sort of commander who thought that volume of voice and anger were the only two essential components of leadership.

Celu clearly intended to establish her relationship with Geary as commander and subordinate. He had no problem with that. It was only her due, and the chain of command had to be respected, but he didn't like the way she was doing it. He never had liked headquarters, which even in his time too often had seemed to consider itself a self-licking ice-cream cone whose existence justified itself by existing and making demands on the warships it was supposed to be supporting. Apparently, that had worsened significantly during the long war as a gap had grown between headquarters staff and the operational officers.

So now Geary paused, thinking. A way existed to avoid moving up the date of the fleet's departure despite that explicit order from Celu. Or a way had once existed, anyway. He called up fleet regulations, searching for the right phrase, and smiled when it popped up. *Ultimate responsibility for the safety of ships and personnel, and for successful com-*

pletion of assigned tasks and missions, rests with the com-
manding officer. It is the duty of the commander to take into
account all potential factors when implementing orders.

Over a century ago, Geary and his fellow officers had
called that the "you're screwed" regulation. Obey an order
when some of "all potential factors" might have made obedience unwise, and it was the fault of the commander in the
field. Disobey an order when some of "all potential factors"
made such disobedience wrong, and that was also the fault
of the commander in the field. He shouldn't have even wondered that a regulation designed to shield higher authority
from fault would have been removed at any point.

But he could use it against higher authority. He could
respond to these orders with a very detailed report laying
out all of the potential factors that justified what he believed
to be a necessary delay in beginning the mission. More
repairs, more supplies to be brought in, crew members on
leave who wouldn't be reporting back early unless emergency recalls were sent out. Drafting such a justification
would require his full attention for at least a day, and there
would be no guarantee that anyone at headquarters would
read beyond the executive summary at the beginning and
no guarantee that headquarters would pay attention to any
arguments contradicting its own chosen version of reality.

But he couldn't lie, either. A Potemkin fleet might be all
well and good when dealing with purely administrative matters, but lying about the fleet's readiness status and when it
was leaving on a mission would be criminally deceptive.

All potential factors. New officers used to complain that
there was no way to describe all potential factors, and we'd
laugh and tell them that was the whole idea of the regula-
tion. All . . . Potential . . . Factors.

I've never really taken advantage of being Black Jack,
the popular hero. But I've never liked people like Celu. And
I have a lot of other things I should be doing besides justify-
ing my decisions to a bunch of bureaucrats at headquarters.
I will not screw the crew members who are taking leave now

and earned that leave in plenty of battles. Nor will I rush a mission that requires substantial preparation.

There wasn't much I could do about this kind of thing before. But they need me in command of this fleet. And, by regulations, I have ultimate responsibility for deciding what to do here. I just have to justify my decision.

He carefully composed a text reply. *In response to your message (reference a), per fleet regulation 0215 paragraph six alpha, I am required to take into account all potential factors in carrying out orders. The current projected departure date on my assigned mission reflects my assessment of all potential factors, including but not limited to the time necessary to meet essential logistics, readiness, repair, personnel, and planning requirements. Justification for this assessment and delineation of all potential factors is contained herein (attachment b).*

He had offered no give on his chosen departure date, though that was slightly hidden in a nicely vague, politely worded, and deceptively brief message containing no real information. The information would be taken care of by the attachment. *They want all possible factors? I'll let them read through everything to see if they can find any grounds for saying my decision isn't justified.*

Geary instructed the fleet database to copy every official file it held on any subject (though he did exempt anything related to the Potemkin fleet simulation) and drop the entire collection into a single folder to attach to his message. The fleet's massed computing power, every warship linked into a single networked system, chugged away at that one task for several minutes. He hadn't imagined it was possible for any task to take that long for the fleet's systems to handle and was wondering if he had somehow managed to crash the network when the result finally flashed onto his screen.

Geary paused then, awed by the sheer magnitude of the resulting attachment to his message. The mass of information was so huge that it would probably give even a black hole indigestion.

That made him wonder what would happen when all of

that information got dumped into headquarters databases already renowned for their musty size and scale. Could a large enough mass of information result in a collapse into a virtual black hole of degenerate information from which nothing could escape? If the result meant that headquarters would have trouble sending out more messages, it was certainly worth a try.

He took another look at Celu's image, thinking of her order to respond quickly, then gave his reply the highest nonemergency priority. *You asked for a reply as soon as possible. You're going to get it.*

Could a single courier ship even carry that much data? It would be interesting to find out and interesting to see how long it would tie up headquarters just downloading the attachment. Smiling, Geary tapped the command to send the message, then went back to work.

HE usually only quickly scanned headquarters messages after that, seeing whether they needed a vague reply or could just be ignored or perhaps actually required action. But two weeks into his command, a very odd message came in, one that made him pause and read through it. *Identify for transfer on a high-priority basis all fleet personnel, officer and enlisted, with formal or informal expertise on workings of hypernet systems. Personnel so identified are to remain at Varandal until reassigned.* Transfer? Yanking experienced crew members off ships about to head out for a perilous mission— *Wait a minute. Wait a damned flipping minute.*

He didn't know how many personnel in the fleet qualified as having "formal or informal expertise" when it came to the hypernet, but he knew that one of them was Commander Neeson, commanding officer of the battle cruiser *Implacable*. He was supposed to identify for transfer a veteran commanding officer two weeks before leaving, then leave that officer behind when the fleet departed? How many other critical personnel would be covered by this latest demand from fleet headquarters?

A quick search of the fleet database popped up a long list of names, almost one hundred men and women, officers and senior enlisted, who had been assigned secondary codes for hypernet-related skills. Aside from Neeson, four others were commanding officers, including Captain Hiyakawa of the battle cruiser *Steadfast* and the captains of two heavy cruisers. But as far as he could tell from reviewing the skill code criteria, hypernet expertise was an ill-defined area. Checking the primary skill codes of the senior enlisted, which by contrast were well-defined, Geary shook his head in disbelief. *I can't afford to let these people go. Not many of them. Not any of them if I have any say in it. Why the hell does headquarters need them?*

He called Commander Neeson, whom he had worked with before on hypernet issues. "Commander, how big an impact would you have on any Alliance research or development or building project concerning the hypernet?"

Three light seconds distant on his ship, Neeson seemed startled by the question. "You mean, me, personally, Admiral? Not much. None, really. I know some things about the hypernet, theory and practice, but nothing compared to real experts. I know of at least a half dozen officers at headquarters who could run rings around me when it comes to hypernet matters. We haven't talked, but I've seen their names on research papers."

"What about anyone else in the fleet? I understand Captain Hiyakawa has that skill code."

"I don't know Captain Hiyakawa well, Admiral," Neeson replied after the six-second delay caused by outgoing and incoming transmission times. "But we've talked a little. He's about at my level. Sir, the only fleet officer who could have contributed significantly to such an effort was Captain Cresida. Not because of her education on hypernet matters but because she was intuitive and brilliant. I'm just a plodder, and I'm as good as anyone now in this fleet as far as I know."

"Can you think of *any* hypernet project in which your experience would make a significant difference?" Geary asked.

"Outside the fleet? No, sir. I could get coffee during meetings, but that's about it as far as usefulness."

"Thank you, Commander. I appreciate your assessment." After the link had ended, Geary sat watching the empty space where the comm window had been. *No difference. Not when it came to hypernet skills. But a very big difference if the skills of those fleet personnel in other areas were lost to me now. And fleet headquarters already has people who are far more qualified.* And *the message from fleet headquarters didn't even promise me any replacements.*

Cresida was the only fleet officer who could have contributed . . . Damn, I miss Jaylen. A fine officer. Brilliant, like Neeson said. But if she was the only one who could be said to have real expertise, according to Commander Neeson, who is perhaps the most capable hypernet knowledgeable person I still have in the fleet, then I believe I am justified in responding appropriately to this message.

Geary tapped the respond command. "In reply to your request, a review and evaluation of fleet personnel turned up none who in my judgment satisfy your needs."

The worst they could do was question his judgment, and he was getting used to having people do that. Since being awakened from survival sleep, he had seen his judgment questioned more often than since he was an ensign. But all that mattered in the short term was avoiding losing a lot of personnel his ships needed. Maybe whoever at headquarters had generated this odd request would manage to shoot another demand to him before the fleet left in two weeks, but he could stall that one easily with the little time that would be left at that point. In any case, it was better to receive a complaint that he hadn't offered a good enough reply this time than to transfer all of those men and women before the fleet left Varandal.

At least most of my problems seem to be at headquarters these days instead of being here in the fleet.

Another chime sounded, alerting him to a call. *Timbale. This shouldn't be too bad.*

Admiral Timbale's image appeared, smiling encouragingly. "Good news."

"I could use some."

"Your experts are arriving tomorrow."

Geary waited, then asked, "Experts? On what?"

"Intelligent nonhuman species."

"We have experts on that? Until we found the enigmas, we didn't even know any existed, and we just confirmed the existence of the enigmas a few months ago."

"That's true," Timbale admitted. "But science and academia have nonetheless been producing experts on the subject for centuries now. Not too many in recent centuries, I gather. Apparently, the dearth of intelligent nonhuman species actually discovered managed to slow down the production of experts on that topic. But there are some. You're apparently getting most of the experts on the subject who exist within the Alliance. They are, I am told, thrilled to be coming along."

Geary felt the old headache making another appearance. "How many?"

"Twenty-one. All civilians. Fourteen of them are full-scale doctors."

"I'm still waiting to hear the good news. Where am I supposed to put twenty-one civilian experts on nonhuman intelligent species who have never actually heard about or read about or encountered an actual nonhuman intelligent species?"

Timbale made an apologetic gesture. "They are the best humanity has on that topic. If I may make a suggestion, one of the assault transports would be a good place to keep them. You should have plenty of extra staterooms on one of them, and if the professors and doctors get bored, they can study the Marines."

"That should generate some interesting conclusions," Geary said. "Thanks for the heads-up. I'll have General Carabali take our experts in hand and decide which transport to put them on."

* * *

A week later, he looked up in alarm. The knocks on his stateroom hatch were so forceful that they evoked images of grapeshot slamming into a warship's armor at a velocity of several thousand kilometers a second. Before the tremors from the last of the knocks had subsided, the hatch slammed open, and Tanya Desjani stormed into the stateroom, looking inflamed enough to spit plasma. *"What is that woman doing on my ship again?"*

SIX

GEARY knew how stunned he looked because that matched how he felt. There was only one woman who could produce a reaction like that in Desjani. "Rione? Victoria Rione?"

Her eyes fixed on him, blazing with anger. "You didn't know?"

"She's aboard *Dauntless*? When? How?"

Still plainly enraged, but mollified by Geary's surprise at the news, Desjani nodded stiffly. "She came aboard with the routine daily shuttle flight. I didn't learn that until she came off the shuttle a couple of minutes ago." Pacing back and forth, Desjani turned a sour look on him. "You're lucky that you're such a lousy liar. That made it obvious you hadn't known she was coming. If you had known and hadn't told me—"

"Tanya, I'm not that stupid. What the hell is she doing on *Dauntless*?"

"Since you can't tell me, I suppose you'll have to ask her."

Wondering what he had done to cause the living stars to call this particular fate down upon him, Geary nodded in what he hoped was a calming gesture. "Where is she?"

"Right now? Knowing that woman, she's probably on her way to this stateroom."

On the heels of Desjani's words, Geary's hatch alert chimed. Desjani crossed her arms and stood there, plainly not intending to go anywhere. He braced himself, then keyed the hatch open again.

Any lingering hopes that it might be some other Victoria Rione vanished as he saw her standing there, her expression reflecting polite interest. "I'm not interrupting anything, am I?"

Desjani's face, already reddened, darkened toward an ominous purple, her jaw clenching as well as her left fist so that the ring on one finger stood out clearly. Yet somehow she managed to speak in an almost emotionless voice. "I was not informed that you were coming to visit my ship."

"It was a last-minute assignment by the government," Rione said, answering Desjani's question while somehow making it seem as if she were replying to something Geary had asked.

"Won't the Callas Republic miss you?" he asked.

"Sadly, no." The first flickers of real emotion flashed across Rione's face, there and gone too fast to read. "Special election. You may have heard of them. The voters have judged me too focused on the Alliance and not engaged enough in issues purely of interest to the Callas Republic."

That took a moment to sink in. "You're no longer Co-President of the Callas Republic?"

"Not Co-President, and not Senator of the Alliance." Rione's voice stayed light, but more emotions flared within her eyes. "Someone judged to be more loyal to the Alliance than to the Callas Republic would be a poor representative on the issue of whether or not the Republic should withdraw from the Alliance now that the war is over, don't you agree? After all, the Republic only became part of the Alliance in the face of the Syndic threat. Taking advantage of my lack of other responsibilities at the moment, the Alliance government has appointed me to be an emissary of the grand council."

"Emissary of the grand council?" Geary asked. "What the hell does that mean?"

"Whatever the grand council, and I, wish it to mean."

She's enjoying this, Geary realized.

Desjani had clearly come to same conclusion and was struggling to keep her temper in check. "I'm certain that you'll need to complete your business with the admiral before the shuttle departs, so—"

"I will be staying," Rione interrupted, speaking again to Geary. "The grand council wishes that I stay on the same ship with the admiral for the duration of its next mission."

Worrying that Desjani would actually explode on the spot, Geary frowned at Rione. "You'll leave when we return to Alliance space?"

Did something else show in her then? Something too strong to completely hide but so well concealed that he couldn't even be certain that he had seen it? "That depends upon my orders from the grand council," Rione said.

Ancestors preserve us. Stuck on the same ship with Desjani and Rione again. Stuck on the same ship *between* those two women. "I will send a message—"

"Don't bother. Really. It would be a waste of time. The grand council wants me here. The other emissary appointed by the grand council will be arriving soon." Rione finally acknowledged Desjani, turning a frosty smile upon her. "But I have been remiss. Congratulations to you both. How fortunate that everything worked out when the fleet last returned to Varandal."

Desjani stiffened again, her eyes going to Geary for a moment while he now tried to avoid showing any reaction. If she ever guessed that Rione had played a role in helping him catch up with Desjani that day, there would be hell to pay. *And Rione knows that, so why did she hint at it in front of Desjani? What's going on inside her head this time?* "What exactly is your role supposed to be?" Geary demanded.

"Representing the government," she said, glancing toward Desjani.

Tanya got the message, glowering as she turned to face Geary. "By your leave, sir, I will return to my duties."

"Thank you, Tanya." He tried to put extra meaning into the words and perhaps succeeded, because her rage seemed to subside a little.

The hatch had no sooner sealed behind Desjani than Rione flopped down in a chair, her expression suddenly haggard. "I'm truly sorry for the lack of warning about my arrival."

"You didn't need to provoke Tanya that way."

"No, but I'm a bitch, and I have to stay in practice. As for why you got no warning, that wasn't my doing. The grand council is doing a lot of shooting from the hip these days. My co-emissary should be arriving within the next couple of days."

"He'd better, because we're leaving in about a week. Is it anyone I know?" Geary asked, sitting down opposite her.

"I doubt that you know him. Retired General Hyser Charban." Rione smiled sardonically. "He's not trying to achieve power by the coup route, but in the old-fashioned way: accumulating favors from powerful politicians before he runs for office on his own."

"General? A Marine?"

She laughed. "No. Ground forces. I don't know Charban personally, either. The reports I've seen characterize him as a 'pragmatic dove, sadder and wiser for his experience with the limitations of firepower when it comes to achieving end-goals.' " Rione recited the words with an ironic lilt.

"There's nothing wrong with being aware of the limitations of firepower," Geary observed.

"Not if that's what you truly believe."

"What exactly *are* you emissaries coming along with the fleet to do?"

She paused, as if deciding what to say. "Our job is to represent the government."

"That's what you said before," Geary pointed out. "It tells me nothing."

"You're getting better at this. Let's put it this way. Since neither Charban nor I holds elective office, we can't be voted out of power while in the middle of a voyage, something that would cast our legitimacy as representatives in doubt if it did happen."

"Victoria, tell me why you're coming with the fleet."

She looked into a corner, her expression guarded. "Perhaps you should ask me instead what it is the government really wants accomplished on this mission."

He took his own time answering, making sure he framed the words right. "My understanding is that I'm to learn more about the alien race, especially about their technology and strength, and attempt to establish peaceful relations with them."

"More or less." Rione closed her eyes, looking tired again. "What the government really wants is the cheapest, easiest solution to a big, complicated, and possibly very expensive problem. That should mean talking to the aliens and stopping any conflict. But maybe not. The aliens will surely want something in return. They may need to be pressured. It is the task of myself and Charban to make sure you take the path with the least costs and least risks up front."

Geary blew out a derisive breath. "What about the long-term costs and risks?"

"Long-term problems can be confronted when they get here," she said, her voice once again betraying no hint of her own feelings, "with more cheap and easy short-term solutions that push the problems further down the road for someone else to handle someday. That's how politicians think. I thought you knew that by now."

"*You're* a politician."

"One who got voted out of office." She smiled without humor. "The government, *all* of the governments in the Alliance, are in survival mode right now. They're afraid of you, but they also need you. So you're being sent off to be heroic, far, far from any opportunities to cause problems."

"I already knew that. Sort of like when I was dead. The government got the benefit of who they claimed I was but didn't have to worry about what I'd actually do."

"Yes, it is sort of the same thing, isn't it? But you are alive, and capable of doing all sorts of things. General Charban and I are to judiciously guide your choices into directions most beneficial to the government."

Maybe he had spent too much time around Rione because he immediately caught the significance of her words. "Beneficial to the government. As opposed to beneficial to the Alliance."

"But aren't those the same thing?" she replied in a bland voice that confirmed his statement without actually saying so. "Now you know where you stand and where I stand."

"I know what you say your orders are," Geary countered.

Another smile, but one that could mean anything. "Yes."

"Why the hell did you come here, Victoria? You must have known how Tanya would feel."

"I had my reasons, and I had my orders from the grand council." Rione made a casting-away gesture with one hand. "Since I was between jobs, I wasn't in any position to turn down the grand council's offer."

"I still can't believe they really voted you out of office," he said.

"The gratitude of the people tends not to extend very far." Bitterness crept into her voice. "I was willing to state unpleasant truths. Unfortunately, I'd been influenced in that regard by a certain relic from an earlier age, a man commonly known by the name 'Black Jack.'" She fixed the cool look on him that he remembered all too well. "My opponent was willing to promise the voters anything they wanted, and promise that they wouldn't have to sacrifice in any way for it. A majority of the voters thought that was a wonderful idea."

Geary looked back at her steadily. "So you lost the election because you insisted on being honest."

"That *is* ironic, isn't it?"

"As you once took pains to point out to me, some of the ships in this fleet are from the Callas Republic. Their crews, and the crews of the ships from the Rift Federation, are expecting orders to go home. They haven't received them yet, and I've been trying to decide whether I should leave those ships at Varandal."

Rione looked away again and shook her head. "They'll be waiting a long time for such orders. The government of the republic won't be calling back those ships. Don't expect me to say that publicly, and don't expect any official acknowledgment of that policy from either the republic or the federation."

He thought about the hopeful looks on the faces of those commanding officers, who thought they would soon be returning to their home space. "That makes no sense at all. If they want to loosen ties with the Alliance, why should they leave the bulk of their warships under Alliance control?"

"Because they fear those warships." Rione turned her head and regarded him with a somber gaze. "The new government strongly suspects that the crews are more loyal to Black Jack Geary than they are to the government of the Callas Republic. They're probably right."

His temper flared, all of the anger he had felt during his confrontation with the grand council surging to life again. "Suspicions don't excuse treating those crews that way after all of their courage and sacrifice! How can they treat their own people like that? If they distrust me, fine! I'm getting used to it. But I will not allow those ships to be exiled from home because of vague concerns about what I might do someday!"

She confronted his anger without flinching, simply gazing back at him, then shook her head slowly. "You're letting the Alliance do it to their own warships, aren't you, Admiral?"

"My Alliance ships will be coming home between missions!"

"Of course." Her tone conveyed no hint of agreement or emotion.

"I'll send those ships home," Geary said. "On my own authority. I'll tell those ships to return to the Callas Republic and—"

"I did bring orders with me, but the orders from the republic are for those ships to remain with the fleet. The orders imply the continued duty here is temporary but don't actually say so." Rione's eyes were fixed on some point in one corner, avoiding his own gaze. "Understand this. You can't change those orders without overriding political authority, and the new government in the republic has a lot of excellent-sounding reasons for keeping those ships with you."

"I don't get it." The flat anger in Geary's voice drew her gaze back to him. "Nobody in the government trusts me, but they want all of these warships to remain under my command. The Callas Republic wants to loosen ties with the Alliance, but it also wants the bulk of its warships kept under my control. Are they all insane, or am I?"

She closed her eyes once more for a moment. "You'll keep the ships. Other admirals would consider that a gift."

"What's the catch?"

The silence dragged on for so long that he had decided she wouldn't answer, but abruptly Rione did. "Don't expect to see much support from the Callas Republic for those ships. The crews will be paid, but repairs and operating costs will be dealt with piecemeal, grudgingly and slowly, and there will be no replacements to keep the crews up to strength."

It took a moment for that to sink in. "They'll just be allowed to wither away, then? Until they're destroyed in action or not worth keeping going and what remains of their crews are sent home, now safely diminished and without warships to threaten anyone."

Rione didn't answer at all that time.

"What about the Rift Federation ships and crews?" Geary asked.

"I'm from the Callas Republic—"

"I didn't ask where you were from. Do you know anything about their government's intentions for them?"

Anger flared in her own eyes. "I have reasonably reliable reports that the Rift Federation will follow the same policies as the Callas Republic regarding the few ships it has left in this fleet."

"Damn." There didn't seem to be anything else to say. Geary felt pain in one hand and looked down to see that he had clenched one fist so hard it seemed locked into a single ball of muscle and bone. "How can the governments of the republic and the federation explain to their own people why their ships aren't coming home?"

"First of all, Admiral," she said, "there aren't that many ships left. Before you assumed command, many of the republic and federation contingents had already been lost. Some more were lost in subsequent battles. It's not a matter of bringing home huge numbers of men and women, but rather the survivors. And measured against the populations of their homes, those survivors are *very* small in number."

His anger seemed to have burned out, replaced by a dull heat that brought no warmth. "Like the Alliance fleet, before the war. Most people didn't have anyone closely related to them in the military back then."

"Yes. So you see the logic. Those two governments will keep the threat of the warships and their crews far from home, and few will complain because few still have a personal stake in their absence. But the presence of those warships with you will serve as a basis for proud declarations of their government's continued support for the great hero, Black Jack."

"I'm still being used," Geary said.

"Yes, you are. What are you going to do about it?"

"I could resign—"

Emotion blazed in her again. "Who else could better keep them alive, Admiral? Resign, and they'll be in the hands of some fool like Admiral Otropa. Do you want them dead?"

"That's completely unfair!"

"You still believe in 'fair'?" Rione asked.

"Oddly enough, yes." But she had spoken a truth. *Their own people are casting them aside. Someone has to look out for them. Until I can think of somebody else, that someone has to be me.* "I'll do my job to the best of my ability."

"You'll still follow your orders?" Rione asked, her voice growing softer but more intense.

"Yes." Geary bared his teeth at her. "As I see them. That means doing everything I legally can for the people under my command."

"And the aliens?"

"You have your instructions, and I have mine. *My* orders require me to not only deal with short-term threats and problems, but also to handle them in ways that work in the long term. If the government or its emissaries have any problems with that, they can find someone else to use as their toy soldier."

Rione slowly smiled, though she still looked tired and somehow older. "Everyone underestimates you. Everyone but me."

"And Tanya."

"Oh, but she also worships you. That I won't do." Rione hauled herself to her feet. "I need some rest. Charban shouldn't show up before tomorrow at the earliest. You may consider yourself once more politician-free for a while."

"I'm sure your stateroom is ready." He eyed her, wondering why he kept getting the impression that Rione was slightly different from when he had last seen her. "Are you all right?"

"I'm fine." She smiled again, the gesture this time as empty of real feeling as the smile of a Syndic CEO, her eyes betraying nothing.

After she left, he stayed seated for a while, thinking through their conversation. Some of the things she had said, like alluding in front of Tanya to her role in getting him and Desjani together, had been uncharacteristically reckless. But Rione had also given the impression at times of playing a more subtle game than in the past, even when she seemed to be speaking candidly. *Why did you really come back to this fleet, Victoria? How much are you an ally of mine, how much are you following the government's line, and how much are you working to further your own goals, whatever those are?*

Under the cover of what you did tell me, how did much did you not *tell me?*

*   *   *

MUCH later that day, he met Tanya walking through the passageways again. "Did you get a chance to look at those special orders from the grand council?" The orders Rione had brought for him. The orders marked for his eyes only. *To hell with that. I want other inputs on this.*

Desjani grimaced. "Yes. Painful."

"Yeah. A lot of 'do this unless you shouldn't and don't do that unless you should' directives."

She didn't answer again for a moment, her eyes fixed straight ahead. "Please understand that my personal feelings aren't factoring into this. That woman brought special orders for us. What are her orders?"

"I've wondered the same thing."

"They didn't need her just to be a courier. She's here for another reason or reasons. Until we find out what those are, please treat her as a potential threat."

"I will," Geary said. "I'm already unhappy enough with the orders she let us know about, or at least the part telling us to go to the Dunai Star System. I was planning on jumping to Indras in Syndic space and taking the Syndic hypernet from there all the way to Midway before jumping into alien space. Simple and as fast a journey as we can make it. But instead, the grand council wants the fleet to go via Dunai to pick up the Alliance prisoners at a Syndic POW camp there." He felt angry and trapped. These orders he couldn't ignore. "The extra stops and jumps will add three weeks to our journey before we reach Midway."

"Why Dunai?" Desjani pressed. "What makes the POW camp there more important than all of the other camps still full of Alliance prisoners in Syndic territory?"

"The orders don't say, and Rione insists that she doesn't know."

"Let me put her in an interrogation cell for half an hour—"

Geary made a helpless gesture. "I wish I could, but there are no grounds for treating a civilian and a governmental representative that way. We have to go to Dunai, Tanya."

"Then why aren't we going by Dunai on our way home?" she asked. "The supplies we use during that extra travel time may be needed once we're inside alien space, and it would make a lot more sense to pick up those POWs on our way home than it would to have them aboard our ships when we're entering alien space."

"You're right. But there's no time to appeal the order, not without delaying our departure for weeks, and how can I do that when the side trip to Dunai is an annoyance but not a critical issue? I can't refuse that order. It's operational, it's fully within the rights of headquarters to mandate that, it's not unduly dangerous or risky to our knowledge, and it doesn't significantly compromise our assigned mission. It's not like the court-martial issue."

"Yes, sir."

"Tanya, there may be good reasons for us to go to Dunai. You don't have to like it . . . I don't like it . . . but please respect that I have to accept the authority of those over me when it is legitimately employed."

"I do." She smiled apologetically. "You're already under plenty of pressure. I know how unhappy the warships from the federation and republic are. Believe me, if anybody but you was commanding this fleet, they'd probably mutiny and sail for home on their own accord. At least you can blame that witch for it since the orders came with her." Rione's stock with the fleet, never high, had sunk to lows approaching absolute zero. "Our own crews aren't thrilled, but they trust you to bring them home."

"I know." That pressure never abated, the confidence of these men and women that he would treat their lives as the valuable-beyond-measure things they were. But he knew that he would be ordering those same men and women into situations where they might well die, that some of them would very likely not come home.

"I'm sorry. But there's something else you need to know about. I'm actually on edge because of another thing. It has nothing to do with politicians. I think. But it's odd. *Dauntless* lost another power distribution junction today."

"You mean it's too far gone to repair?" he asked, wondering why she was bringing that up. Junctions failed sometimes. The failures were pretty rare, but nothing worked forever.

"It's completely burned-out. There's not even anything left worth salvaging." She stopped walking and turned to face him, her eyes fixed on Geary. "I don't normally bother you with materiel problems. Keeping *Dauntless* going is my job, not yours. But *Dauntless* had three power distribution junctions fail while I was gone. That is, two failed inspection, and a third was so shaky that my executive officer wisely chose to have it powered down as well. Fortunately, Varandal could manufacture replacements, but now we've lost another."

Geary looked away, trying to think. "Four junctions? In a few months? That's a very high failure rate for a ship that hasn't suffered battle damage during that period. I can't recall hearing about anything like that a century ago."

"Ships were probably built differently a century ago," Desjani observed, "and didn't have to deal with the combat these ships have seen. But *Dauntless* hasn't had a problem like this in the past. I told my people to find out what was causing these failures, but all the engineers aboard *Dauntless* and on the auxiliaries can tell me is that the junctions suffered 'serious component malfunction significantly impacting operating parameters.' Which is how engineers say, 'It broke.' "

"That many equipment failures and no indication why?" He frowned down at the deck, then gestured to her. "Come on. Let's look into this." He led the way back to his stateroom, waving Desjani to one chair, then seating himself. Geary called up the fleet database, then narrowed the information display to junction distribution failures within the last several months. A tremendous number of tags related to battle damage popped up, so he narrowed the search to the last two months. "*Dauntless* isn't the only ship that has had that problem. *Warspite* has lost five, *Amazon* three, *Leviathan* four . . ." Frowning, he told the system to identify common aspects for the warships with the failures, then stared at the answer. "The oldest ships in the fleet. Including *Dauntless*."

"*Dauntless* was launched nearly three years ago," Desjani said. "There aren't a lot of ships that survived that long during the war," she added proudly.

"*Warspite* is actually older than three years by a couple of months." Geary called up his comm screen. "I need to talk to Captain Smythe about this."

The fleet had gathered its units closer together as the time for departure from Varandal approached, so *Tanuki* and the other auxiliaries were only a few light seconds distant. Captain Smythe's image appeared in Geary's stateroom with only a small delay. Smythe saluted in his usual slightly sloppy fashion, his customary cheerfulness not evident. "Yes, Admiral?"

"We seem to have a problem with power distribution junctions on the older ships," Geary began.

Smythe sighed heavily. "By older, you mean anything over two years since launch, is that right, Admiral?"

"You don't sound surprised."

"I've been looking into it and reached some unpleasant conclusions this morning after the most recent reports of equipment failures on *Dauntless* and *Warspite* came in. I wasn't quite ready to report to you, but my results are far enough along to brief you now since you've asked." Smythe looked down, his mouth working, then up at Geary again. "Your last ship, sir. *Merlon*. How long was she designed to remain in commission?"

He had to stop and think about that. It seemed an eternity ago that he had strode the decks of *Merlon*, even though he had slept frozen in survival sleep through the intervening century between then and now, and his memories were still vivid. "She was about thirty years old when I assumed command. Her planned hull life was one hundred years. That was the working figure for ships of her class. The hull life could be extended if necessary, but it would have required exhaustive overhaul and replacement to keep one of those heavy cruisers going for another several decades beyond the century mark."

Desjani had a look of total disbelief. "A hundred years? They actually built ships assuming they'd last that long?"

"They *did* last that long," Geary said, "until the war started. We'd upgrade systems along the way to keep it all state-of-the-art, of course."

"Astounding," Smythe murmured. "I wish I could have seen that ship. The engineering must have been exceptionally high quality." He shook his head, smiling sadly. "Do you know how long these ships of ours were built to last, sir?"

The memories of Geary's first impressions had not faded. "Rough edges, sloppy welds. They were built fast. I've heard they weren't expected to last long."

Smythe nodded. "Expected combat life spans were measured in months. Maybe a couple of years at the outside. Hardly any hulls made it to three years before being destroyed. Five years? Nothing survived that long. Absolutely nothing." He waved around. "With apologies to her commanding officer and crew, *Dauntless* is quite an old girl now by the standards she was designed and built to meet."

Perhaps it was because the idea was still foreign to Geary, but Desjani understood first. "*Dauntless* wasn't designed for this long a career. Her systems are wearing out."

"Exactly," Smythe agreed. "Dying of old age, to use a living organism's equivalent. The power distribution junctions failing on *Dauntless* and the other older ships are sort of canaries in the mine shaft, the first components to begin breaking down because they were never designed to work this long. See here." A window popped up next to Smythe, and he pointed to some of the information displayed. "The junctions that failed on *Dauntless* in the last few months were ones that had somehow failed to be damaged or destroyed in battle up until now. They're original equipment, and they've exceeded their planned life spans. It's the same on the other ships of age in this fleet."

Geary winced, thinking about the scale of repair work that represented. "We're going to have replace most of the power distribution systems on the older ships?"

"No, Admiral." Smythe spread his hands apologetically. "*Everything* on these ships was built with the expectation that it would only have to last a few years at the most."

"Ancestors preserve us."

"I've been talking to mine," Smythe said. "Unfortunately, I doubt that our ancestors will show up to shower us with new equipment and help install it."

Desjani was watching Smythe with a horrified expression. "If all of the older ships are developing these problems . . ."

"Then every ship in the fleet will develop them within the next few years, yes." Smythe sighed again. "That's the bad news."

"There's good news?" Geary asked, wondering what this information might do to his plans for departure.

"Relatively good." Smythe called up another window, pointing to the graphs and curves on it. "First off, the failures won't all cascade at once. There'll be a curve, starting out slowly as older ships like *Dauntless* hit their limits. For some time, if the auxiliaries we have work at it and aren't diverted by the need to repair battle damage and manufacture weaponry and such, we can not only make new components faster than they fail and replace the old systems with equipment that should last longer, but we can get a little ahead of the game. We'll still face a serious crunch about a year and a half down the line, of course, when the bulk of the existing fleet starts hitting the two-and-a-half- and three-year points in their lives."

Geary studied the data, nodding. "Is that all the good news?"

"Well, the main problems are in systems and sensors. The hulls and structures are fine. They had to be built to certain tolerances and durability in order to withstand combat maneuvering, which also means the hulls and structures are durable enough to last. The government couldn't cut too many corners there, or the ships would have come apart in action. That means we don't have to worry about them cracking into pieces purely because of age, though I recommend we do step up inspections for weaknesses in the hulls and structures developing as a result of accumulated strain."

"That seems like a good idea." Geary used one finger to trace a curve on a graph. "If this holds, in a year and a half, about a third of the ships in the fleet will be as seriously degraded as if they had suffered major battle damage."

"It could hit one-half," Smythe cautioned. "I used best estimates, but if contractors and shipyards cut corners, the equipment might not even hold up as long as that. And, of course, if you insist upon fighting battles, that will complicate matters as well because of the need to repair battle damage and manufacture replacements for battle-damaged parts and expended weaponry."

"I'll keep that in mind. What about regular overhauls back here in Alliance space? Are those factored in?"

Smythe made a face. " 'Overhaul' these days probably doesn't mean what you think it does. What it means is making sure all damage is repaired and everything works."

Geary realized that he was staring at Smythe again. "What about replacing old systems? Upgrades?"

"If it's not broken going in, it doesn't get repaired or replaced." Smythe shrugged. "This way of doing things developed in the course of a very long war in which ship survival times were very short. Why go to the expense of upgrading a ship that would very likely be destroyed within a year and be replaced with a new ship?"

Slumping back, Geary tried to take in the implications. "Things have to change. The system has to start assuming that ships will remain in commission for extended periods, and the overhaul, construction, and repair requirements have to be changed so that they're based on that."

"What construction?" Desjani asked. "A few hulls are being finished and everything else shut down."

Smythe smiled wryly. "Just so. What you say makes sense, Admiral. But it will not only require a change in mind-sets among senior officers and the entire fleet bureau-cracy as well as substantial parts of the government; it will also require significant sums of money."

"They did this on purpose," Desjani growled. "They knew what was happening, and they still handed this whole mess to Admiral Geary."

"I don't think so," Smythe suggested. "Or perhaps not the full implications. Even we hadn't realized what was go-ing to happen. In Admiral Geary's case, it's because his experience with such things is prewar, and for you, me, and all of the other fleet officers, it's because we've never en-countered this problem. If somehow a ship survived past the life of its systems, it would undoubtedly have been so battered by combat as to be good only for scrapping to re-cover materials."

Geary looked at the graphs again, trying to sort out what he was feeling at this moment. "But just because we tell the government and fleet headquarters about this doesn't mean that they'll fix it. They might just let the fleet shrink rapidly through end-of-hull-life attrition." Which didn't mean they would also shrink missions to match fewer ships, naturally. He wondered how long ago it had been that people were first told to do more with less. Probably it had been when some protohumans were without enough stone tools. "Money, you said. How much can we afford to have your auxiliaries do? I know they can manufacture and install what we need, but how much will it cost?"

Smythe smiled like a pirate eyeing a fat prize. "There we have some intriguing possibilities, Admiral. It would depend upon how we charged the work. I have training accounts. This would certainly fall under that. Battle damage must be repaired per fleet regulations and charged back to various headquarters accounts, but evaluating the extent of battle damage that must be repaired is an uncertain art. Some-times, such damage can't even be identified until quite a while after a battle, and then it's a judgment call as to whether the failure was battle-related or not. I'm certainly not going to second-guess assessments that any failures are related to earlier combat engagements. And, of course, if we encounter failures of equipment during operations, then that would fall under operational accounts."

For the first time during the conversation, Geary felt like smiling back at the engineer. "How much could you soak fleet and government accounts before someone caught on and tried to rein us in?"

"I'd never do anything *improper*, Admiral," Smythe said piously, "but my responsibility is to keep this fleet's ships running well. That will take work. The funding runs through many channels, many departments and organizations, depending on exactly what is done and why. Deciding how and what to charge and where to charge it and how to justify it, well, in the normal run of events that keeps a lot of people busy who should probably be doing other things. Under these particular circumstances, those decisions will require very judicious decision-making. Some of it may be a trifle difficult to sort out on headquarters' end and inside government departments, especially since rumors are that financial tracking positions are being cut with the war over, but I'm certain that if anyone sees any irregularities in the process or finds a way to total up the sums involved across the board, they will get back to us regarding those matters *eventually*."

"Absolutely," Geary agreed. "You're already working up a plan?"

"It's close to completion, but some details still need work, and, as I said, funding considerations will need to be flexible." Smythe grinned at Desjani. "Have no fear, Captain. *Dauntless* will have her youthful vigor restored so that you operational types can charge around trying to break her again. *Titan* has the most experienced crew, so I'll assign her to get to work on *Dauntless* right away if that is acceptable, Admiral."

"Perfectly acceptable." Geary gestured widely. "What about the fleet's plans? How does this impact our intended operations?"

"Ideally, we'd stay here and replace everything," Smythe

said, "but somehow I doubt the government would want us doing nothing but boring holes in space around Varandal for the next couple of years. If you're asking whether this means we can't head for strange and unknown areas beyond human frontiers, well, I don't think it will prevent that. Better we go sooner than later, really, while fewer ships are actually suffering failures."

"Thank you, Captain Smythe." After the engineer's image had vanished, Geary looked to Desjani. "It's bad, but it could be a lot worse."

"Thank the living stars we've got eight auxiliaries now," she replied. "Did you see the look on Smythe's face when he talked about gaming the system? This isn't the first time he's done that sort of thing."

"He's doing it for a really good purpose," Geary pointed out.

"He's doing this part of it for a really good purpose," she countered. "What else is he up to? What's he already done without being caught? Smythe might have casinos operating on all eight auxiliaries."

"Who do we know who could watch for that sort of thing?"

Desjani paused to think. "I don't know. Roberto Duellos likes to posture as a rogue, but he's actually as upright as they come. What we need is someone who knows how things in Smythe's world work so well that he or she could spot a quark out of place or hide a battleship in plain sight if they wanted to. At least a senior enlisted, maybe an officer who's a former enlisted. I'll talk to some people and see if they know any candidates."

After she left, Geary called up data on his eight auxiliaries so he could comfort himself by reviewing their capabilities. *Titan*, *Tanuki*, *Witch*, *Jinn*, *Alchemist*, *Cyclops*, *Kupua*, and *Domovoi*. He was extremely lucky to have *Kupua* and *Domovoi*, both of them part of the larger *Titan* class and both of which had been completed just before news of the end of the war triggered an immediate halt to most new construction. Having eight auxiliaries along during the long retreat from the Syndic home star system would have made that voyage a lot easier. Instead, he had been forced to make do with half that number, and lost *Goblin* along the way. This time out, having eight auxiliaries and fewer warships depending on them for resupply and repair should grant a decent logistics safety margin for getting well into alien territory and out again without anything running short.

Naturally, there was a price to be paid for that logistics safety margin. The massive auxiliaries *Titan*, *Tanuki*, *Kupua*, and *Domovoi* could charitably be described as sluggish when their raw materials bunkers were fully loaded. *Witch*, *Jinn*, *Alchemist*, and *Cyclops* were smaller and a bit more maneuverable, but still far from justifying the official designation of Fast Fleet Auxiliaries. When in star systems, the fleet would have to limit its speed to accommodate the slow-moving auxiliaries, and if the fleet did end up fighting again, then protecting the lightly armed auxiliaries would be a major concern.

Barely an hour later, Desjani called him. "We have a shuttle from *Tanuki* on approach. There's a visitor for you aboard it."

Given the ease of virtual visits among ships, an actual physical journey between ships for consultations was a rare thing. However, even the most secure software didn't ensure no one was eavesdropping on virtual visits, and apparently Captain Smythe thought there were some more things to say that shouldn't run any risk of being overheard.

But the officer who arrived at Geary's stateroom twenty minutes later wasn't Smythe but a lieutenant. A lieutenant with green hair. Not just shades of green within another color but brilliantly green. "Lieutenant Elysia Jamenson, sir. Captain Smythe believed I should meet with you in person to discuss my role in assisting fleet readiness and repair, Admiral."

He invited the lieutenant to take a seat opposite his own, taking a moment to try to size her up before asking the obvious question. "Just why does Captain Smythe think I need to meet with you in person, Lieutenant Jamenson?"

Sitting with her back straight instead of relaxing, Jamenson replied in a matter-of-fact voice. "Captain Smythe has ordered me to work in direct support of you regarding the fleet's maintenance requirements, Admiral Geary. I will be responsible for formatting reports, requisitions, and all other supply and logistics issues related to keeping the fleet's warships at the best possible state of readiness, as well as providing you with status reports on those matters."

He leaned back, resting his chin on one fist. Jamenson seemed to be in her midtwenties, consistent with her rank but an oddly young age for such a responsibility. "What is it about you that makes Captain Smythe certain that you're the right person for that job?"

"I confuse things, sir."

"What?"

"I confuse things." Jamenson gestured around to encompass the universe with a wave of her hand. "I can take information, data, reports, and requisitions and render them in a form almost impossible to understand."

Geary barely managed not to laugh. "I'm sorry, but I've met any number of people, and any number of lieutenants, who could do the same thing."

"Yes, Admiral, but you see, I can do it on purpose, and I don't actually *change* the information, or do anything wrong with it, or put it into a form that doesn't meet the requirements of the regulations and other rules. The information is still complete, accurate, and properly rendered. It's just very, very hard to understand."

This time Geary did laugh. "So you'll do that in regard to the work by the auxiliaries to keep our ships going, and, therefore, keep headquarters and the civilian bureaucracy so confused they won't be aware of how much we're spending?"

"Those are my marching orders, yes, Admiral."

No wonder Smythe hadn't wanted any record of this conversation within the fleet comm systems. "And how am I or anyone else in the fleet supposed to keep track of what's actually going on?"

Jamenson smiled confidently. "I can also work in reverse, Admiral. As long as the information starts out valid, I can unconfuse it and render it in a form easy to grasp."

Geary realized that both of his eyebrows had risen as he looked at Jamenson. "That is an extremely impressive set of talents, Lieutenant. Where did you learn how to do that?"

"I came by it naturally, sir. My father says I got it from my mother."

"I see."

Jamenson's voice took on a trace of apology. "I was also ordered by Captain Smythe to inform you that he would take it very badly if you poached me for your staff, Admiral."

Another laugh. "Captain Smythe, and you, can rest easy on that count. I prefer my staff to have other jobs, so they do what I need them to do without trying to fill spare time finding extra things for themselves or others to do."

"I'll inform Captain Smythe of that, sir."

"Thank you." Geary paused to look her over again, wondering just what uses Smythe had found for Jamenson's talents in the past. The ability to confuse the bureaucracy as to your actions could be invaluable. "I'd like to ensure we're on the same page when it comes to our goals. What do you see as your responsibility?"

"To do all I can to assist in maintaining the fleet at its current state of readiness and in upgrading of existing systems to ensure long-term readiness," Jamenson recited.

"Perfect. Do you have any questions about what I want?"

She hesitated for the first time, something that reassured Geary. Officers who were too confident could too easily overreach or make mistakes. "My understanding is that you prefer to work within regulations, sir."

"That's correct."

"Are there circumstances," Jamenson said carefully, "under which you would approve actions contrary to—"

"No." He smiled encouragingly to take any sting from the blunt reply. "If we need something that bad, I expect people like you and Captain Smythe to figure out how we can get it within regulations. Somehow. Some way. Find a loophole or an interpretation that could be defended as justified." Memory of the near disaster involving the mass courts-martial for low fuel cell levels crowded in then, making Geary's smile vanish. "I don't want anyone making the mistake of thinking that I want them to break regulations. If that's the only alternative, then I take that responsibility openly. We don't do something like that under the table even if we can make it hard for anyone to figure out that we did it."

Lieutenant Jamenson had been listening intently, and nodded. "I understand, Admiral."

"Good. Anything else?"

"Captain Smythe asked me to invite you to visit *Tanuki* in person whenever it is convenient, Admiral," Jamenson said. "I should mention that *Tanuki*'s wardroom has one of the finest selections of wines, liquors, and other distilled and fermented beverages in human space."

That helped explain some of what Smythe had been up to. Geary wondered how many VIPs had found their shipments of luxury goods mysteriously shorted as a result of something like "damaged in transit" and how many requisitions from *Tanuki* for unusual items had gone unremarked because of creative formatting. "Thank you, Lieutenant Jamenson. I don't know when I can manage a visit to *Tanuki* in person, but I'll keep the offer in mind. I look forward to working with you."

"Most of my visits will be through the fleet virtual-meeting system," she added, "but Captain Smythe thought it wise that I explain my role in person."

Desjani had been right. Smythe was clearly an old hand at playing games in which he didn't want to leave any unnecessary traces inside official records. "Good idea. Lieutenant; there's one other thing that I have to ask you, given that both you and Captain Smythe understand the need for keeping a low profile."

"My hair, sir?" Jamenson asked.

"Yes. I've seen a few other sailors with green hair but

never talked to any of them about it since it was within regulations. But it's still a bit flamboyant."

Jamenson smiled ruefully. "It's my natural color, sir. I'm from Éire."

"Éire?" The name didn't ring a bell, so Geary called up a star map. "That's pretty far distant, one of the star systems colonized directly from Old Earth."

"Yes, Admiral. The first colonists on Éire had a fondness for such shades of green and may have been a wee bit too free with genetic engineering." She touched her temple lightly. "It can be reversed, but many of us think that it would be improper to change something that meant much to our ancestors, is mostly harmless to us, and causes no harm to others."

"Mostly harmless?" he asked, thinking that he had wondered why a fleet officer would choose such a shade.

"I can't change how others see it, Admiral. But it's also given me a nickname. I've been called Shamrock since before I left Éire."

"Shamrock? That's a plant, isn't it?"

"A green plant. It's everywhere on Éire." Another rueful smile. "Something else dear to our ancestors, apparently."

After Lieutenant Jamenson left, Geary walked up to the bridge. With the fleet's departure looming near, he had grown increasingly restless to be on the move, to be about the purpose for the fleet's existence, and to get away from further messages from headquarters and the possibility of more order changes from the government.

Desjani was already on the bridge, of course, just finishing running her bridge crew through a training simulation. "Have a nice meeting?" she asked.

"Instructive."

"Since you're apparently going to insist upon my asking directly, why did Captain Smythe send a green-haired lieutenant to speak with you in person?"

"Her job is to confuse things."

Desjani waited a moment to see if Geary would betray signs of joking. "If you wanted a lieutenant who would confuse things, I have at least one on *Dauntless* who would fill the bill."

"Noted. I'll explain her particular skills in that area later on." The privacy fields about his and Desjani's seats on the bridge were good, but Geary knew from his own experience as a junior officer that amazing amounts of information could still be gleaned by close-though-covert observation of senior officers as they talked. He settled into his seat, looking about the bridge of *Dauntless*, having to suppress a sigh of contentment. "You know, after dealing with the grand council and Alliance politics and headquarters, it's actually going to be something of a relief to be dealing with lying Syndics and homicidal aliens again."

"Dangers make you yearn for distant home," Desjani mused, "but when you get home, it can have a way of quickly making you yearn for distant dangers."

"You really do have a way with words, Captain Desjani. When we were on Kosatka—"

"All four days?"

"—did you get a chance to talk to your uncle the literary agent?"

"Only once." Her eyes took on a distant look. "He wanted me to write an account of the journey back to Alliance space from the Syndic home star system. I told him it was mostly boring."

"Except when it was terrifying?"

She grinned. "And I told him I wouldn't say a *word* about personal matters. You could see the man's dreams crumble into dust."

Geary had to muffle his own laughter. "You crushed the dreams of a literary agent?"

"That almost makes me a writer already, doesn't it?" Desjani asked.

THE rest of the week passed far too slowly in the sense of wondering what might happen next, and far too quickly in terms of the work remaining to be done. A flood of personnel returning to their ships from leave kept the fleet's shuttles busy, while Geary's walks through the passageways of *Dauntless* involved more and more detours as engineers off *Titan* blocked movement in a constantly changing dance of barriers while they enthusiastically ripped out components and installed newly constructed replacements that were built to have much longer lives.

Dr. Setin, who announced himself to be in charge of the group of experts ("though not their leader in a strictly hierarchal fashion"), managed to escape from *Tsunami*, where Carabali had stashed the experts, long enough for a shuttle flight to *Dauntless*. "An amazing opportunity, Admiral," he told Geary. "Can you imagine the thrill of actually encountering an intelligence different from our own?"

Thinking back to the battle at Midway, Geary just smiled politely. "Yes."

"But then, you have encountered them! What was it like?"

"Thrilling."

Dr. Setin had come with authorizations allowing him to see what records existed of the fleet's contacts with the enigma race, so Geary provided him with the information and sent him back to *Tsunami*.

The day before they were to leave, Geary took a virtual tour through *Orion*, wanting to personally size up the state of repairs to the battleship and assess the morale of the crew. He had grown depressingly used to having *Orion* fail him whenever the ship's contributions were most needed and, despite Desjani's faith in Commander Shen, couldn't help thinking that turning the ship around might be beyond the ability of anything short of divine intervention.

Shen looked as aggravated as usual as he led Geary's virtual presence through *Orion*, occasionally pointing out items but mostly letting his crew do the talking. A remarkable number of repairs had been accomplished, but that impressed Geary less than how keen the crew members were to show him what they had done. "All battery members fully certified, all hell-lance projectors at one hundred percent," one chief announced proudly, as Geary paused to look over his battery.

Peering around with an expression as if he had a blister on one foot, Shen focused on the chief. "Lironi got his qualifications completed?"

The chief indicated one of the sailors standing in ranks nearby. "Yes, sir."

"About time." Shen addressed the sailor directly. "You could have done it six months ago and be commanding this battery yourself by now. Next time, don't let down *Orion* or yourself."

"They're looking good," Geary told Shen before he departed. "The crew and the ship."

Shen, frowning as if the statement simply pointed out the obvious, saluted stiffly before Geary broke the connection. Geary stood there in his stateroom for a moment, rubbing his neck and wondering what *Orion* would do the next time he called upon that ship.

The next day, he and Desjani sat on the bridge of *Dauntless* as Geary prepared to give the orders for the fleet to leave orbit about Varandal and head for the jump point for Atalia inside Syndicate Worlds' space. Or rather, inside what had been Syndic space before Syndicate authority began collapsing. Atalia's current status was ambiguous, which was better than hostile.

As he had been half-fearing, and half-expecting in a resigned way, an urgent transmission came in. "Admiral Timbale?" Geary asked. Timbale had remained supportive and dependable, but at present he had a rigid set to his expression. "I'm hoping you're just calling to wish us on our way." That was something Timbale had already done some hours ago, but Geary could always hope.

Timbale's response was delayed almost half a minute by the current distance to Ambaru station. "Admiral Geary, have you received any orders concerning any of your auxiliaries?"

"My auxiliaries?" Had Smythe's plan already been

compromised? The fleet was literally leaving within the hour. "No."

"I am in receipt of high-priority orders instructing that I take immediate control of *Titan*, *Tanuki*, *Kupua*, and *Domovoi*. They're to be detached from your fleet pending other assignments."

SEVEN

"WHAT?" He couldn't believe what he had just heard. Not just half his auxiliary force, but the four big auxiliaries. In terms of capability, taking those four would amount to losing two-thirds of his auxiliary support. "Why?" Could someone have already discovered Captain Smythe's scheme? But the first requisitions based on those had only been forwarded two days ago, far too short a time for them to have reached headquarters, let alone be analyzed. These orders must have originated roughly a week ago.

"No reason given." Timbale kept his voice level, but he was clearly upset.

"The other fleets are intended to operate inside Alliance territory. They'd have no conceivable requirement for auxiliary support."

"I know. I thought at first it might be a cost-cutting measure, a very ill-advised cost-cutting measure, but the orders clearly state the auxiliaries will be sent on new assignments, not decommissioned."

"I'll—" What? What could he do? The orders were to Timbale, not Geary. "Those ships aren't even under your command, Admiral. Why would those orders have been sent to you and not me?" *Unless headquarters has figured out that I actually am taking into account all potential factors when I decide how to carry out my orders, and so is trying to end-run me this way because they know I'd find reasons to keep those auxiliaries with me.*

Timbale paused, thinking, then nodded. "You're right. Admiral Geary. It is my professional assessment that these orders were sent in error and cannot be accurate. The ships in question are assigned to you, under your command, so these orders should have gone to you. At the very least, notifying you as part of their current chain of command would be required. Surely, headquarters would not intentionally have failed to inform you on this matter since that would be a violation of operational procedures." Admiral Timbale was speaking slowly and clearly, ensuring that the record of their conversation would lay out justification for his actions. "Since I also cannot think of any possible reason for detaching these ships from your command at this time, it follows that this message must have been sent in error, perhaps a training or contingency message that was accidentally released for transmission."

"Surely," Geary agreed, knowing that both he and Timbale were aware that headquarters had very likely excluded him on purpose. But they had to speak as if innocent of any intent to disregard a valid order. "Higher-priority tasking should have been specifically identified in the orders."

"Therefore, I cannot execute these orders," Timbale continued. "Administratively, I'm not sure I have the authority to remove ships from your control, and, operationally, the orders don't make sense. I will reply to headquarters, expressing my assessment that the orders are erroneous, and requesting clarification. Given the uncertain nature of their validity, I strongly advise that you do not halt ongoing tasking in order to carry out orders not even transmitted to you. I will await confirmation of the validity of the orders before carrying them out."

Even if Timbale sent that query out immediately, and Geary suspected that Timbale would take a while to actually do that, by the time a courier ship had reached headquarters and a reply had come back, weeks would have passed, and Geary's fleet would already be well outside Alliance space. But headquarters would still have Timbale within their reach. "Admiral Timbale, I appreciate your willingness to do what seems proper, but I am concerned about possible misinterpretations of your intent to properly carry out your orders."

"Thank you, Admiral Geary, but I have no alternative. My duty to the Alliance demands that I ensure orders are valid before I carry them out." Timbale actually seemed very tranquil as he said that. "You know, Admiral, we talked once about the cat in the box, about not knowing whether you'd do the right thing, no matter what, when the time came. I'm happy to inform you that the cat is alive."

"I'm pleased to hear that. Rest assured that I will take my own steps regarding this matter when I can."

"Are they trying to outright sabotage you?" Desjani asked in disbelief as Timbale's image vanished.

"I can't believe anyone would do that," Geary said slowly. "There are other explanations."

"I'd love to hear them."

"Maybe someone got hints of what Smythe is up to—"

"Not enough time has gone by, Admiral. Try again."

She would keep him honest no matter how much he wanted to avoid considering some possibilities. "Maybe someone finally ran the numbers," Geary said, "and realized how much it's going to cost to keep those four big auxiliaries in commission and figured getting rid of them would save a lot of money. The orders didn't say that was the intent, but that might have been a deliberate move to avoid letting us know that we'd lose the support of those ships not just temporarily, but permanently."

"Humph," Desjani snorted skeptically. "It might save money in one or two places but add a lot of expenses else-

where. Who would they have to pay to do the jobs that the
auxiliaries are doing? Private contractors? Didn't we hear
that the Syndics use that kind of system?"

"Yeah. And their mobile forces hated it." Geary checked
his display. "All ships are reporting readiness for departure.
What do you say we get the hell out of here now instead of
waiting another half hour?"

"I say that's an excellent idea, Admiral."

He sent the orders, watching as nearly three hundred
warships, auxiliaries, and assault transports lit off their main
drives and began moving into formation for the transit to
Atalia. Even though the war with the Syndics had ended,
and even though Atalia had declared its independence from
the rapidly imploding empire of the Syndicate Worlds,
Geary had decided to make jumps in formations suitable
for immediate combat just in case unexpected threats
materialized.

The growing experience and skill of his crews had led
him to choose a formation that involved six subformations.
Five of those were built around cores of battleships or battle
cruisers, with heavy cruisers, light cruisers, and destroyers
arrayed around them. The sixth was made up of the eight
auxiliaries, divided into two divisions, and a single division
of four assault transports. He had a lot more Marines along
than before since no one knew what he might need when
dealing with the aliens, but the Marine force commanded
by General Carabali only required two transports to carry
those Marines not dispersed among the major warships. As
a result, *Tsunami*, *Typhoon*, *Mistral*, and *Haboob* were only
half–loaded out with Marines and their equipment, as well
as the small contingent of civilian experts on nonhuman
intelligent species. The extra capacity to carry people in
those four transports would be useful when they picked up
the POWs at Dunai, and in case they found any humans
alive and captive inside alien space.

The subformations were arranged with the largest combatant subformation in the lead, the auxiliaries and transports behind that, and the other four combatant subformations

spaced evenly around the support ships, as if the warships formed a huge cup, bottom facing forward, holding the auxiliaries and transports inside. Front and center in the largest subformation was *Dauntless*, the flagship, literally the moving point around which the rest of the fleet aligned itself.

He felt a sensation of being watched and looked over to see Desjani gazing at him and smiling. "Now what did I do?"

"It's just so obvious how proud you are of them," she replied. "When I watched Admiral Bloch, and some other admirals, at times like that I always got the feeling they felt that having lots of ships respond to their orders showed how powerful and special they were. From you, as you watch those ships, I get the feeling that you feel privileged to command them."

"I am privileged," he muttered. "Do you know what tomorrow is, Tanya? It will be the one hundred and first anniversary of the day I assumed command of the heavy cruiser *Merlon*. I found the responsibility of being *Merlon*'s commanding officer to be very humbling. Now all of these ships are under my command."

"They all will be if we can get out of this star system before any more messages come from headquarters."

At point one light speed, it took almost three days to reach the jump point for Atalia, but the only surprise occurred on the second day, when two civilian ships jumped in from another Alliance star system and began broadcasting messages, which finally reached the fleet's ships hours later.

"Do not export human aggression!"

"Exploration not conquest!"

"Keep our taxes and our soldiers at home!"

"I don't disagree with the sentiments," Geary commented. "Except for the fact that they seem to think we're the ones picking a fight with the aliens."

Desjani, uncharacteristically, didn't reply for a moment, but finally shrugged. "It was a long war. You know how we all felt. Most of us kept fighting because we didn't see any good alternatives. I lost a lot of friends, so I understand why some people wanted other decent choices. But wanting it didn't make it so. It still doesn't."

He nodded slowly to her. "True. Right now I'd love some good alternatives to going across half of human space, then jumping into alien territory armed to the teeth. But from what we know, none of those alternatives would be better than what we're doing."

She smiled wryly. "I wonder what they'd do if they actually encountered the aliens they're worried about us attacking."

"Our job is to make sure they don't, or if they do, that the aliens are willing to talk and coexist."

This time Desjani laughed briefly. "Which means if we succeed at what we want to do, then those protestors will probably never realize what we did."

"Somebody asked me why I still believed in 'fair,'" Geary commented. "When I think of things like you just pointed out, I have to admit that's a good question. As a matter of fact, I'm not sure I've ever actually seen 'fair.'"

"Just because you've never seen something doesn't mean it's not real."

He was still contemplating that statement when the communications watch made a report. "They're broadcasting their junk on every channel, Captain, official and unofficial. Apparently that's become standard protest tactics."

Desjani shook her head. "Idiots. They're blocking emergency coordination frequencies. The people in this star system won't be sympathetic to their messages anyway, but that move will ensure any possible agreement is swamped by irritation. I hope Varandal's defense forces can catch those fools."

One of the watch-standers grinned. "Those ships couldn't outrun specters, Captain."

Instead of smiling in return, Desjani gave him a flat look. "We don't fire on peaceful protestors, Lieutenant. If those people transmitted on authorized frequencies only, then they'd be allowed to as long as they wanted. We're the Alliance, not the Syndics."

"Yes, ma'am," the lieutenant said, reddening slightly in embarrassment. "I wasn't serious."

"Understood. But people controlling the amount of firepower that we do have to be careful of the jokes we tell."

Geary nodded to Desjani, then checked his own comms. "Most of my channels are still clear."

"Admiral, that's because our transmitters are powerful enough to punch through the interference from distant ships," the comm watch explained.

"Good. I guess we just ignore those guys, then. They're not our problem, and they're not telling us anything we haven't already thought about."

A couple of destroyers assigned to Varandal's defenses were still chasing the protestors the next day, when the fleet reached the jump point for Atalia. Geary took a deep breath, wondering if jumps would ever feel routine again or if he would always be haunted with worry about what might await at the exit for another star. "All ships, jump at time one zero."

On the outside views, the endless stars and the black night between them vanished, replaced by the gray nothingness of jump space. As if greeting the fleet's arrival, one of the strange lights that came and went in jump space grew in brilliance somewhere directly before them, near or far impossible to tell since there was no means of determining the distance to it, though it somehow felt close. The light glowed briefly, then faded out to be lost amid the drab gray.

It took Geary a moment to realize that while he had been watching the light, everyone else on the bridge had been watching him. The moment they realized he might be aware of that, they all busied themselves at their jobs. All except Desjani, who glowered around the bridge menacingly before giving him a rueful look. "They still wonder if you were in those lights for the century you were gone."

"If I had been, wouldn't I know something about them?" he snapped in reply, irritated. "I told *you* that I wasn't there."

"You told *me* that you couldn't *remember* being there."

He could stay angry to no purpose, because there wasn't any proof either way, and there couldn't ever be, or he could accept that the question was going to dog him for probably the rest of his life. "I guess there are some things I'll never be able to get away from."

She nodded. "Not totally. But once we get into Syndic territory, everybody will have other things to occupy their minds."

ATALIA hadn't changed much in the few months since they had last passed through the star system. Even though new buildings were no longer being turned into craters by Alliance bombardment almost as soon as something important could be built, and even though the Alliance and the Syndicate Worlds would no longer be using the star system as an occasional battleground, there was a tremendous amount of damage to clean up, and Atalia wasn't a wealthy star system. Even if it once had been prosperous, the frequent fighting within it would have reduced it to poverty over the century of war.

One difference was that an Alliance courier ship hung near the jump point, ready to tell the Alliance if anyone attacked Atalia. Thus far, that was the sum total of the Alliance's commitment to the defense of Atalia.

Desjani sat with her chin resting in one hand as she looked at her display. "It doesn't seem right to be here and not be blowing up things."

"There's not much worth blowing up." Geary shook his head as he looked at his own display. "The war did a number on this star system."

"Actually, it got off fairly easy." Her voice had suddenly become tense. "Compared to others."

"I know." Sore subject. Too many star systems had been battered into far worse condition. Too many of those star systems had belonged to the Alliance. He had avoided any information on how many billions had died during the war on both sides, not being willing to face that. But Tanya, like the others in the fleet, had grown up with such awful statistics, had seen them continue to rise year by year. Time to talk about something else. "They've got a HuK now."

"I noticed." One Syndic Hunter-Killer, a warship slightly smaller than an Alliance destroyer, orbited in the inner system. Even if it hadn't been almost six light hours distant, the single small warship posed no conceivable threat to the Alliance fleet. "I wonder if it's here by orders of the Syndic government or if it's declared allegiance to Atalia?"

"I'll let our emissaries worry about that," Geary said.

"Good idea! Maybe we could leave one of them here." Desjani glanced back to the empty observer's seat. "I suppose I should be grateful that they're not hovering on the bridge constantly. That general likes to walk around trying to ingratiate himself with the crew—"

"He's practicing to be a politician."

"—but I haven't seen the other one at all."

Geary nodded, thinking that was one more thing about Rione that had changed. "She was always very careful and calculating before, trying to keep on top of everything. Now she sits in her stateroom."

"I'm not complaining," Desjani said. "I hope that you're not worried about her."

"Tanya, she brought new orders for us. As you already pointed out, we don't know what orders she might have been given." He hunched forward, clasping his hands tightly together as he remembered his conversation with Rione. "When I talked to her right after she came aboard, I got the feeling that she wanted to see how far she could lean over the edge of a cliff without falling off. There was a heedless quality, a sense that she'll jump off that cliff just to see how it feels on the way down."

"Normally," Desjani murmured, "I'd just wish that she'd jump. But if she has other orders from the government that we don't know about . . ."

"Orders that may account for the changes I've noticed in her."

"Something she knows?" Desjani asked. "You never

could trust her. I hope you understand that now. Maybe it's something she did. There have to be a thousand skeletons in *her* closet. Or maybe it's something she has to do. Though I find it hard to believe that her conscience is bothering her."

Geary made an exasperated gesture. "If it's something purely personal, then that's unfortunate for her but unlikely to impact us. But she is an emissary for the government."

"Wouldn't that general . . . what's his name?"

"Charban."

"Yeah. Him. Wouldn't he also know if it involved some orders for the emissaries?" Desjani paused, her expression hardening. "Unless he's a throwaway. A dupe to give cover for her. He's a retired general. What if he's being used?"

Too many questions and, as usual, not nearly enough answers.

EVEN though Atalia was an easy destination from Varandal, there weren't many good options from Atalia, one of the things that had kept the star system from being battered even worse during the war. One option was Padronis, a white dwarf star that had never had much human presence, even the small orbital station once maintained by the Syndics having been abandoned decades ago. The other choice, Kalixa, had once been a good option itself, a fine star system with a large population and a gate in the Syndicate Worlds' hypernet system. But that gate had collapsed and annihilated the human presence in Kalixa, apparently on orders from the same alien species Geary's fleet was en route to investigate. Now the only signs that humans had ever been there were shattered ruins on the wreck of what had once been a habitable world.

But from Kalixa, the fleet could jump to Indras, where a Syndic hypernet gate should still be intact. The Alliance had already used that gate once, in the final campaign against the Syndics.

Geary stood before the conference table, once more viewing the images of the fleet's captains sitting around it. This time, the fleet being in a much more compact formation, only the most distant ships would have any noticeable time lag. He gestured to the star display. "We'll have to go through Kalixa again."

Most of the officers listening displayed distaste or unhappiness at the idea of revisiting that star, where the dead emptiness somehow emphasized the millions of lives that had been destroyed there. But they knew as well as he did that the only efficient path for the fleet led through Kalixa.

"Then back to Indras," Geary continued. "My initial plans had been to take the Syndic hypernet from Indras directly to Midway, keeping travel time to a minimum. However, we'll be going via Dunai, which means taking the Syndic hypernet to Hasadan, making a short jump to Dunai, then jumping back to Hasadan to reenter the hypernet for the transit to Midway." Laying it out that way only emphasized what a pain in the neck this diversion was. "Dunai has a Syndic labor camp still holding an estimated six hundred Alliance prisoners of war. We're going to lift them out of there."

"On the way out?" Captain Vitali asked. "But if we waited until the way back, they'd be in Syndic custody for months longer, wouldn't they?"

"Exactly," Geary agreed. If Vitali's suggestion hadn't been so convenient, Geary would have been seriously irritated. It had taken him hours to come up with that same explanation for the diversion since parts of the fleet didn't believe he could be ordered to Dunai by the government; but Vitali had thought of the same rationale in two seconds. "If we still have extra passenger capacity on the way back, we'll pick up more prisoners in another star system." That wasn't in his orders, but it wasn't forbidden by his orders, either. "We don't anticipate any trouble at Dunai."

Tulev tightened his lips slightly before speaking. "If the Syndics intend to drag their feet on any aspect of the peace treaty, Dunai will tell us."

"Does the treaty allow us to go anywhere we want in Syndic space without their approval?" one of the heavy cruiser commanders asked. Noticing the expressions on the other captains at his question, he hastily added, "Not that I care whether they approve or not."

"Yes, it does allow us to enter and leave Syndic territory," Geary said. "When the treaty was being hastily negotiated with the new Syndic government, the newly in charge CEOs desperately wanted the Alliance fleet to go to Midway to defend it against the aliens, so our ability to go through Syndic territory was part of that agreement. I'm sure the Syndics intended that as a onetime deal, but our negotiators worded that part of the treaty so it's actually open-ended."

"Sometimes even our politicians come in handy," Duellos remarked.

"I suppose they have to get something right every once in a while," Badaya replied.

"The key," Geary said, "is that the treaty allows our movement through Syndic space as long as we're going to and from Midway Star System. Which we are, despite the detour to Dunai. I'm mentioning this because future missions may also require visits to Midway, not because we want to go there but because it will meet the legal requirements of the peace treaty."

Commander Neeson chuckled. "That'll probably come as a surprise to the Syndics at Midway."

"I imagine that it will."

When the others had left, Duellos remained seated, his eyes on Geary. "How are you bearing up?"

"I've been worse," Geary replied, sitting down. "How about you?"

Duellos grinned. "Only one thing has been bothering me lately. Curiosity. I'd like to know how your brief visit to Kosatka went."

"My honeymoon, you mean?"

"Yes. When I've asked Tanya, all she does is mumble a lot."

Geary paused, bringing up the memories. "We both figured that as soon as the passenger ship we were on exited the hypernet gate at Kosatka, the crew and passengers would be fighting to see who could alert the media first that we were aboard. Or, to be accurate, that I was aboard. Just in case they weren't doing that, a couple of hours after our ship arrived, a fast fleet courier popped out the gate and started broadcasting orders for me to return to Varandal, which even the dullest mind could take as a hint that I was at Kosatka."

"I assume it also broadcast your promotion back to admiral?"

"Yeah, that, too. Too late to stop us from marrying. Tanya had admiral's insignia with her, naturally, and immediately pinned it on me, all the while grumbling about how only a total idiot would have given up the rank of fleet admiral. Anyway, the local government and defense forces and media were all reacting about as calmly as you can imagine, which meant not calmly at all. Tanya was determined that she would tell her parents about our marriage before anyone else could. She knew plenty of people in Kosatka, and one of them had access to a shuttle, so the shuttle came winging in and plucked us off the passenger ship while it was still a half hour out from the main orbital spaceport, where everybody was waiting for us. Then the shuttle dove for the planet in a hot, steep reentry while various government, military, and media shuttles chased after."

Duellos grinned. "You were probably missing the relative peace and quiet of a battle by then."

"It got worse. We made a secondary landing field without getting overtaken, one the media hadn't yet staked out, and another of Tanya's old friends was there with a private vehicle, so we got bundled into that and tore off into the city while Tanya's friend demonstrated combat driving skills to get around traffic. We made it to the high-rise where Tanya's parents lived, and it was one of those secured-access places, so we jumped out of the car, ran up to the access panel, and Tanya pounded on it, yelling, 'They changed the access code! Mom, Dad, let us in!' "

"I've seen movies like this," Duellos said.

"And we can hear sirens all over the place, getting closer,

and Tanya's wondering if her mother and father were working extra shifts and not home yet, but finally her mother answers, and says, 'What are you doing back on Kosatka? Who's "us"? Who's that with you?' and Tanya says, 'My husband.'" Geary returned Duellos's grin. "For what seemed forever, her mother didn't say anything, then she looks at Tanya, and says, 'I thought you were married to that ship of yours,' and Tanya gets all upset, and says, 'Her name is *Dauntless*, Mother, not "that ship." Now let us in!'

"We got inside and up to the floor where her parents lived, and her mother opens the door, looks at me, sort of freezes when she recognizes me, then finally looks back at Tanya and says in this real quiet voice, 'You're trying to kill me, aren't you?' Tanya says, 'No,' and her mother says, 'Were you hoping for a stroke or a heart attack?'"

Duellos nodded thoughtfully. "I see where Tanya gets some of it from."

"Naturally, her mother was horrified that we'd gotten married on the ship, saying that the whole planet would have wanted to see the ceremony, and it would have been the biggest thing on Kosatka since the royal wedding one hundred and ten years ago, and Tanya demands to know if her mother wants Tanya to have a stroke, and to try to calm everyone down, I mention that I was at that royal wedding over a century ago, and that didn't exactly work as far as making me seem like just some average sailor who married her daughter.

"By that time, everybody has tracked us down to that building thanks to the city security-camera system, and we're pretty much besieged in there. Tanya's father got escorted through, wondering what the hell is going on, and we try to talk and get to know each other while every dignitary on Kosatka tries to crowd into the place. The local military had to establish a fortified perimeter with portable, high blast barriers, because by then the word was spreading and the crowds were . . ." Geary's smiled faded. "Ancestors help me, Roberto, the crowds. Everywhere I went, and on all the media channels, the crowds."

"Chanting, 'Black Jack,' no doubt."

"Yeah. I don't think before then it had really hit home to me just how dangerous I really was to the government. To the Alliance. Nobody should be that popular, have that much adulation, and especially not me."

Duellos nodded, his own grin much smaller. "You're lucky you didn't see what was happening on my home world. I had people wanting to see me, to touch me, because I'd worked with you. The living stars alone know what sort of thing Jane Geary encountered when she went back to your home world, Glenlyon, for a short visit."

"She did?" Was that what had caused the changes in Jane Geary? "Has she talked to you about that?"

"No." Duellos gave him a quizzical look. "She hasn't spoken to you of it, either? But her behavior in command does seem to have altered a bit since then."

"Yes." Maybe knowing that, he could finally get Jane to admit to whatever had caused her to act differently. "So . . . the crowds. Everywhere. Tanya could tell how those crowds are bothering me, and she wasn't exactly thrilled that the times she got mentioned it was usually as 'Black Jack's new wife' rather than Captain Tanya Desjani. We had to attend a number of official functions so the local authorities wouldn't feel snubbed, but after a few days, I was happy to have the excuse of my orders to have to leave the planet."

"You would think," Duellos said, "that your obvious discomfort with the adulation would have reassured the government."

Geary shrugged in reply. "Maybe the government is afraid I'll get used to it."

THE distance between the jump point from Varandal to the jump point for Kalixa was four light hours, which meant a forty-hour transit at the fleet's velocity. With the primary inhabited world at Atalia orbiting on the far side of its star, the authorities there didn't even know the Alliance fleet had arrived until more than five hours later. As a courtesy, Geary had sent a brief message to them saying that the fleet was simply passing through en route to business elsewhere. Their reply to his message took another five hours to reach Geary.

He listened, feeling growing discomfort, as the new rulers of Atalia fell over themselves offering greetings to the fleet in general and to Admiral Geary in particular. It was glaringly obvious that they feared him, they needed him, they wanted the protection of the fleet he commanded against their former Syndicate masters, and the barely concealed pleas from them left Geary unhappy. *I'm not the master of this fleet. Ultimate authority rests with my government. Don't they understand that? I can't do what they want, what they need. The Alliance has a courier ship here, and, while that in itself offers no defense capability, it is a symbol of the Alliance's interest here. Or at least the Alliance's interest in knowing what happens here. That might not be much of a deterrent, but it's something.*

After several hours of postponing a reply, he sent another message, telling the rulers of Atalia that his fleet was proceeding on a mission elsewhere, and that their requests for further assistance would be passed to the Alliance government. *Next time I guess I should let the emissaries talk to the Syndics, or used-to-be Syndics.*

Aside from some wishes for a safe journey and swift return sent in answer to Geary's last message, nothing else of note happened for the rest of the transit. The jump for Kalixa brought a different kind of dread, a reluctance to view that ruined star system again. He wondered if it would be easier to see it the second time.

It wasn't.

The exit from jump at Kalixa still felt curiously abrupt, as if the impact of the hypernet gate's collapse there had strained even the structure of space itself. A few moments' observation confirmed that the star's intensity continued to fluctuate rapidly. The storms had subsided a bit in the thin atmosphere, which was all the formerly inhabited world had left, but that just made it easier to see the lifeless and almost waterless landscape. Men and women on the bridge of *Dauntless* muttered prayers to themselves as they gazed on the destruction, and Geary believed crews were doing the same on every ship in the fleet.

He ramped the fleet up to point two light speed through Kalixa, cutting the amount of time spent there in half. It cost in fuel cell usage, but the benefit to morale was worth it.

Indras hadn't offered any problems the last time the fleet had been through there, and as long as its hypernet gate was still in existence, the fleet wouldn't linger at that star. "Do you think we should try out one of the copies of the Syndic hypernet key?" The original key aboard *Dauntless* had been painstakingly reproduced, but only a few copies were still available when the fleet had left. One had been installed on *Warspite* and the second on *Leviathan*.

Desjani shrugged. "If you want. The copies should work fine. But I'd advise against it."

"Because?"

"The Syndics should be able to tell which ship used a key at the gate. They already know about the key on *Dauntless*. Keeping them in the dark about which other ships now have keys might be a good idea."

He nodded in agreement. There might formally be peace at present, but trust would be a very long time in coming.

INDRAS and Hasadan had once been military objectives, enemy star systems to be attacked. Now they were simply waypoints, occupied by former enemies who could only watch the Alliance warships passing through their star systems. The hypernet transit from Indras to Hasadan was . . . boring, Geary decided. Jump space felt like a place even though it was a place with nothing there but the mysterious lights, which gave it a sense of being occupied by something unknown and perhaps unknowable to humans. A place humans didn't belong, and felt increasingly uncomfortable being in the longer they were in jump space.

But for a ship conducting a hypernet transit, there was

only an absence of everything, the feeling that the ship was nowhere, something Captain Cresida had once painstakingly tried to explain to him might be literally true. *Our best theory is that as far as the outside universe is concerned, ships inside a hypernet have been transformed into probability waves that don't really occupy any point.* They really were nowhere.

And nowhere didn't have a lot to recommend it, aside from the fact that it got you somewhere else very, very quickly compared even to jump space. "I wonder how jump space feels to the aliens?" Geary wondered out loud. "Does hypernet travel feel like being nowhere to them?"

Desjani, walking beside him down one of the passageways of *Dauntless*, frowned. "That's an interesting question. How does nothing feel? Maybe you should pass that on to our experts, so they'll have something to do."

Fortunately, once the fleet popped out of the hypernet gate at Hasadan, it was only a short jump to Dunai.

Dunai was a decent star system from a human perspective but had little to distinguish it, which was probably why it hadn't earned a hypernet gate of its own. Three inner planets, the second one orbiting about nine light minutes from its star in the sweet spot where worlds habitable for humans could usually be found. Much farther out, three gas giants orbited, and on the fringes of the star system, a pair of frozen minor planets orbited around each other as they also whirled about their star more than four and a half light hours distant.

The habitable world looked to be comfortable, resources in the solar system more than adequate, a decent amount of civilian space traffic could be seen moving between planets and orbital installations with raw materials, manufactured goods, foodstuffs, and passengers, and the total population was well into the hundreds of millions. A good star system from a human perspective, but not a remarkable one.

"It doesn't look bad at all from here," Desjani commented, as the fleet's sensors analyzed the second planet from the star Dunai. "Usually, the Syndics seem to place their labor camps on less desirable worlds."

"That's been our experience," Geary agreed, studying his own display. A variety of climates, some nicely temperate, plenty of water, an atmosphere close to the habitable standard, and lots of well-maintained towns and cities balanced by some areas left wild. "It's nice."

"Too nice," she muttered.

"Sir?" A virtual window had popped open near Geary, from which his intelligence officer, Lieutenant Iger, gazed out. "We've confirmed the existence of the prison camp and fixed its location." A glowing dot appeared on the map floating to the other side of Geary.

Geary knew he was frowning from the way Iger's expression grew uncertain. "That's good work, but isn't the location here a bit surprising? This seems to be a pleasant world, and that's a decent spot on that planet instead of the camp's being set somewhere with harsh conditions."

"Yes, sir, but I think these images we got of the camp help explain that." Another window, this one revealing a collection of buildings seen from overhead. Very high overhead, of course, since the fleet's optical sensors had spotted them from many millions of kilometers distant.

He frowned more deeply, staring at what seemed to be well-maintained structures that, from their arrangement, were probably barracks-type buildings. The three fences enclosing the entire place inside multiple layers of security had only a few guard towers, and only about ten meters of dead ground inside them. Most of the area inside the camp appeared to be covered with grass instead of pavement or crushed rock, but there were a number of shade trees as well. Good roads led into the camp to large parking areas. "It looks like the prisoners get moved from the camp fairly frequently."

"Daily is our guess," Iger explained. "You notice the camp is not far from a large city. We're estimating from the arrangement of the camp and some of the Syndic messages and transmissions we're picking up that the Alliance prisoners have been used as laborers. That's not unusual for the Syndics, but we're more used to seeing our prisoners of war having been forcibly employed in mining or agriculture, well away from cities."

Geary sat back, drumming his fingers on the armrest of his seat. "You don't think they've been employed in hard labor?"

"They could be, sir. Roadwork, for example. But it could also have been easier labor, such as cleaning buildings. Once we get the former prisoners aboard and can debrief them, we'll know exactly how they've been mistreated."

The use of the term "mistreated" came automatically to Iger, and Geary knew from the labor camps they had already encountered that it was very likely accurate. Still, this labor camp looked much nicer than the bleak prison complexes the fleet had seen in the past. Definitely a prison camp, but not a hellish one. "Let me know if you find anything else."

As the window containing Iger closed, Desjani leaned back with a sigh. "Nothing much to worry about here. No warships except a couple of Nickel corvettes in that dockyard orbiting the second planet."

Geary tapped on the symbols for the corvettes, reading details of what the fleet's sensors had seen. "Our systems estimate the corvettes have been gutted but not for scrapping. There are indications they're being refitted with new systems."

"Maybe they've got a Captain Smythe here."

"Partially completed warships' hulls," Geary mused, pointing to a couple of other orbital shipyards. "Three Hunter-Killer-size warships there and one light cruiser–size hull at that other one. They're not close to completion."

"Somebody seems to be building themselves a little fleet," Desjani commented. "Those HuK hulls vary from Syndic standards. Maybe they're not being built under contract for the central government."

That was interesting. "Is the local CEO getting ready to defend this star system or preparing to lean on other star systems? Maybe just extortion backed by firepower, maybe outright expansion of control."

"Is whatever Syndics do to each other our problem?" Desjani asked.

"No. Not this kind of thing, anyway. If we came across an attack under way, we could intervene, though I have no idea if we'd want to, and our orders are extremely vague on what to do in those circumstances."

"Those ships under construction are easy targets," she commented. "It would probably be an act of great charity for surrounding star systems if we blew those hulls into tiny fragments."

He gave her a lopsided smile. "As impressed as I am by your newfound humanitarian impulses, we are at peace with the Syndics now. That means we need a really good reason to blow up something."

"Well, if you want to get technical about it." Desjani shook her head. "But, seriously, won't this be a problem at some point? As long as we're transiting Syndic space, that is, which as far as I know may happen a lot, and as long as Syndic government control continues to collapse, which as far as I know is going to keep on getting worse, then sooner or later we're going to come across some shooting going on when we reach a star system. What if it's one Syndic star system attacking another? The defenders will ask for our help. What do we say? And what if the attackers belong to the Syndic government, and they're bombarding their own people to reestablish control over that star system? Are we just supposed to sail on through and pretend nothing's happening?"

He sat back, drumming his fingers on one armrest as he thought. "Our orders dance around that question. They can be interpreted to allow us to act, or to require us to act, or to restrain us from acting, or to outright prohibit us from acting."

"Meaning that neither the government nor headquarters knew what to do so they left you to deal with the hard choices. I am shocked. Shocked."

Geary nodded. "With all the focus on the aliens, and my plans to transit Syndic space as quickly as possible, which would hopefully avoid those situations, I haven't tried to really analyze that problem. Our actions are going to be heavily dependent on the exact circumstances. Maybe our emissaries have some instructions about that particular question that they haven't shared with us yet."

"Were they going to tell us before or after we open fire?" Desjani wondered.

"I'll ask. After we take care of business here." Geary tapped an internal comm control, bringing up windows showing Rione and Charban. "Madam Emissary, General Charban, please contact the senior Syndic CEO in this star system and make whatever arrangements are necessary for our pickup of the Alliance POWs here. We'll use our own shuttles to lift them off the planet. We won't need any Syndic assets or assistance beyond making the former prisoners available and providing any relevant records on them."

"We're on it, Admiral," Charban announced as if he were still on active duty and working with Geary on a military operation. "The peace treaty obligates them to turn over the prisoners without hindrance, so there shouldn't be any trouble."

Rione simply inclined her head toward him in wordless acceptance of the task, her eyes hooded.

"Thank you," Geary said. "Let me know if any problems do develop."

"Admiral," the maneuvering watch called, "if you intend maintaining point one light speed, systems recommend the fleet come starboard one five degrees and down zero four degrees for an intercept with the second planet."

Geary checked the system recommendation himself, seeing the long, smooth curve of the fleet's projected path arcing through the star system. They were intercepting a moving object, the inhabited planet, so the actual path they would have to take was much longer than a simple straight-line distance. "A bit less than six light hours to where we'll intercept the planet in its orbit."

"Yes, sir. Two days, eleven hours' travel time at point one light speed."

"All right." He called the fleet. "All units, come starboard one five degrees and down zero degrees at time two one. Maintain current formation and current velocity."

Two and a half days' travel time to the planet, maybe half a day around the planet while the fleet picked up the prisoners, then another two and a half days back out to the jump point. Allow some time for unexpected delays. *Call it six days. The government and headquarters didn't want me to delay another two weeks, but their little rescue mission here has delayed our transit to alien space by about a week. Add in the transit times through Hasadan and the jump times to get to Dunai and back, and it totals a lot more than two weeks. At least we're doing some good by picking up those prisoners.*

The images of the two emissaries were wearing poker faces when they called Geary back. It had been ten hours since the fleet arrived in Dunai, with forty hours' travel time left to get to the primary planet. "You asked us to call you if any problems developed," Rione said, displaying some of her old fire.

"What problems do we have?"

"Perhaps," Charban suggested, "you should view the reply we received from the Syndic CEO in charge of this star system. Dunai is still nominally loyal to the Syndicate Worlds, by the way."

Another window popped open in front of Geary, and a moment later, the image of the Syndic CEO appeared, looking disturbingly like almost every other Syndic CEO he had ever seen. The CEOs weren't actually cloned, and they had the usual physical variations between different men and women, but every one of them wore suits that seemed cut identically from the same material, all wore similar perfectly cut hair, and all of them had the same range of practiced and meaningless expressions. It was as if a wide variety of persons had been forced into molds that eliminated most of their individuality.

The Syndic CEO flashed the standard and obviously insincere CEO smile that must require considerable practice to master. "We are happy to deal with Alliance forces operating under the treaty approved by the Syndicate Worlds. Since the prisoners have constituted a significant burden to our world, one we have gladly shouldered to ensure the prisoners had access to adequate housing, food, and medical care, we trust that the Alliance is prepared to compensate us for those expenses incurred by Dunai. We're certain that the Alliance will not shirk its own obligations. Once we've agreed on the sum for compensation, we'll discuss arrangements for the turnover. I've attached our accounting and a preliminary figure for payment as a starting point in our negotiations."

The window faded away, and Geary looked back at Rione. "How much?"

She named a figure that made him stare in disbelief. "It's a common Syndic negotiating tactic to open with something too one-sided to be acceptable, then bargain for a lesser deal," Rione explained, as Charban listened silently. "He doesn't expect us to agree to that, but he does think we'll settle on some lower figure."

"He's thinking wrong. Even if this fleet had access to funds like that, I wouldn't agree to such a thing."

"Then we will inform the CEO of that," Rione said, "and tell him there will be no negotiations for payment. However, he is very likely to continue to insist upon it since he holds the prisoners on his world."

"Despite what the treaty says."

"Yes."

"In that case," Geary said, "you might remind him that I hold an entire fleet of warships in this star system."

Charban frowned slightly. "We need to be careful about implying a willingness to use force."

"I'm sure that two emissaries of the grand council of the Alliance are able to imply not only carefully but also ably."

That made Charban's frown take on a puzzled aspect, as if he wasn't certain whether to be upset at Geary's statement, but Rione smiled sardonically. "We'll see what we can do, Admiral," she said.

Desjani waited to comment until the images of Charban and Rione disappeared, then a grunt of disbelief escaped her. "That CEO is shaking us down. The arrogant little bastard actually expects us to pay him for letting us have our people." She turned a pleading look on Geary. "Now can we blow up something? Just to show him we mean business?"

"Sorry," he told her. "Not yet."

"Peace sucks," Desjani grumbled.

But her suggestion had gotten him thinking. "Which doesn't mean we can't demonstrate how we might blow up something, or a lot of somethings, if he keeps trying to impede our pickup of those personnel."

She raised an eyebrow at him. "Maybe a warning shot?"

Geary paused. "More like a demonstration shot, hitting some worthless real estate."

"We need to hit something they care about."

"We can't," he insisted. "Not without a lot more provocation. I'll have our emissaries inform that Syndic CEO that we're conducting a weapons test and see if that helps get our point across."

"A weapons test. Aimed at nothing. But at least those two emissaries will be doing something to earn their keep," Desjani said in a voice just loud enough for him to hear, looking seriously irritated as she kept a fixed stare on her display.

She needed to be mollified, and there was one thing almost guaranteed to make Tanya Desjani happy. "Why don't you pick out a target? I'll let you know when to launch the rock."

"Just *one* rock?"

He sighed. "All right. Two rocks."

"Three."

"Okay, three. But make sure your targets are nowhere near any Syndics."

"Yes, sir."

"Tanya . . ."

"All right! But I'll pick spots where plenty of Syndics can watch the fireworks and worry about our next volley coming down on them!"

EIGHT

ANOTHER twelve hours had passed. One of the moons orbiting a gas giant planet had three more craters, and Rione had a glint of anger in her eyes. "We have another reply from the Syndic CEO."

"And?"

"I can let you watch if you have the stomach for it. But to sum up a long message, the CEO says he has regrets but is unable to comply with our requests until we have made mutually acceptable arrangements for compensation." Rione's lips moved in a humorless smile. "It appears that our weapons test wasn't persuasive enough."

Geary closed his eyes, slowly counting to ten inside, then opened them again. "Doesn't that make him in violation of the treaty?"

She glowered, though not at him. "Probably."

"Probably? What the hell does it take to violate the treaty?"

"I don't know! But whether this level of dispute is the sort of a matter that qualifies as a treaty violation is something that lawyers could dispute indefinitely."

Geary wondered just how stubborn and angry he looked because he knew that was how he felt. "We don't have an indefinite period of time, and I'm damned if I'm going to leave the fates of those prisoners up to the arguments of lawyers."

He had forgotten that Desjani was still linked in until she spoke in a deceptively mild voice. "We may not have lots of time or lots of lawyers, but we've got a lot more rocks."

Instead of rejecting or ignoring Desjani's words with disdain, Rione paused, her own expression still irate but also thoughtful. "Another demonstration might be a good idea, not because I think it will directly budge this CEO but because we need to find another way to put pressure on him. We need a demonstration that emphasizes to the population just how much their leader's behavior is endangering them, so that the people of Dunai will insist upon an end to actions that are provoking us."

Desjani, looking inspired, held up one finger, looking at Geary rather than Rione. "Hold that." She turned to address the combat systems watch-stander. "Lieutenant, you've heard of skip-shots with rocks?"

"Yes, Captain. When some error or unexpected factor causes a kinetic projectile to skip through the upper atmosphere of a planet instead of diving down at its target."

"Right. Find out if we can do that on purpose, ensuring that the rock either burns up without hitting the surface or bounces back into space after a few skips. We want a deliberate miss that burns through atmosphere."

"A light show?" Geary asked Desjani, smiling.

"A *big* light show," she replied. "Let me use more than three rocks this time, and we can light up the sky on that CEO's planet."

As usual, Rione didn't address Desjani directly, instead speaking just to Geary. "An excellent idea. Accompany that show with a message broadcast to the system populace, a message from you, Admiral. I think the pressure those things generate on the CEO may produce the results we want."

"If it doesn't," Geary said, "I'll drop a rock on his head and let the lawyers argue about whether that's a violation of the treaty."

That earned him a wry smile from Rione. "I was hoping you'd be a moderating influence on your captain, but it appears that, instead, she is influencing you."

As Rione's image vanished, Geary looked over to see Desjani beaming. "You know," Desjani confided, "that's the first thing that woman has ever said that I can honestly say I was happy to hear."

He didn't answer, wondering why something about what Rione had just said felt important. His thoughts wandered for a moment, recalling his first meetings with Desjani, his impressions of her, his shock at the things she once accepted as a natural part of Alliance military operations . . . "That's it."

Desjani gave him a questioning look, and he recognized that she had fallen silent when she realized he was lost in thought. She did that automatically these days, giving him time to work out things inside, and he rarely noticed it. "I assume you're talking about something more important than my opinion of a politician," Desjani said.

"Thanks for giving me time to think. You always do that, and it helps a lot. No. I'm talking about a politician's opinion of me." Geary pointed at his display, where the primary inhabited world glowed. "That Syndic CEO. He knows he's dealing with *me*. Not any other fleet officer. Me."

Her eyes lit with understanding. "The man who doesn't bombard planets indiscriminately. Who follows the old concepts of honor. We know that word of your policies got around Syndic space pretty quickly."

"Yes. Mostly to our benefit during the war. But now this CEO thinks he can play games with us because I'll be restrained and civilized." Geary turned a grim look on her. "I wonder if his attitude would change if he had to deal with another Alliance fleet officer?"

"One who's a bit less civilized?" she asked.

"Tanya, I don't mean—"

"I know exactly what you mean, and it's all right, because I think you nailed what's going on here." Desjani frowned at him. "I can be very intimidating, but—"

"I think the next message to that CEO needs to go out from the officer who has been delegated to deal with the POW issue, and you—"

"*But* are you sure it should be me?" she asked, her voice sharpening. "I can't always be your first choice for assignments."

"Good point." Even though Tanya was very well qualified for the job, they couldn't afford to have others think that she was receiving special treatment. He paused to think. "Tulev."

"Excellent," Desjani approved. "If the Syndic files on Alliance personnel are any good at all, they'll have Tulev listed as a survivor of Elyzia. That Syndic CEO will know he's dealing with a man whose home world was bombarded into an uninhabitable ruin by the Syndics."

"I'll call Tulev. You set up the light show. Between his message and your rocks, I think that CEO will rethink his attitude."

THE Alliance fleet was only thirty light minutes from the second planet when the light show began.

"What do you think?" Desjani asked a bit smugly.

"I don't know what effect it's having on the Syndics, but it's certainly impressing me," Geary replied. On a part of his display that had been set to show only visual light, the globe of the second planet hung like a marble mottled with white and blue on about a third of the face showing, the rest nightside dark spangled with lights from Syndic cities and towns. But those lights had been eclipsed by fiery streaks of brilliance slashing through the dark and on into the dayside, still so bright that they shone clearly against even the sunlit part of the planet.

Tulev's message would have reached that planet about half an hour before the aimed-to-miss barrage of kinetic projectiles. Tulev, his customary impassiveness even more evident, so that he seemed as emotionless as stone, had spoken in flat tones that somehow carried more menace than any anger or threatening voice would have. "Your leader is playing with your lives in an attempt to extort money from this fleet. I have been assigned the task of ensuring that all Alliance prisoners in this star system are liberated and taken aboard this fleet. I will carry out my orders by any means necessary and will not tolerate any delays or attempts to impose barriers. You have three hours to inform us of your readiness to peacefully transfer all Alliance prisoners to our custody without any preconditions or hindrances. If this deadline is not met, I will take necessary action. To the honor of our ancestors. Captain Tulev, out."

The fleet was already a lot closer to the planet, so the answer only took an hour. Geary was still on the bridge of *Dauntless* when both emissaries called.

"He's still holding out."

Geary took a moment before replying to Rione, making sure he had heard right "The Syndic CEO for this star system is still trying to extort ransom from us?" For some reason, he felt a need to spell it out, so there would be no possible misinterpretation.

"Yes. He's actually quite defiant about it." Next to Rione's image, another window opened.

In the recording of the transmission, the Syndic CEO now displayed an expression Geary had begun thinking of as Intimidating Frown, since he had seen exactly the same look on numerous CEOs. "We expected better of Admiral Geary than transparent attempts to strike fear in the innocent populace of our world. These are not the negotiating tactics of civilized people, and surely the living stars look upon these actions with disfavor."

The CEO's expression changed a bit, settling into what Geary thought of as Angry Frown. "We are not afraid of asserting our rights under the treaty by which the long and terrible war was finally brought to an end by the efforts of all our peoples. If necessary, we are prepared to defend ourselves by all available means. It is my responsibility to prevent any attacks or hostile landings upon our peaceful world."

Desjani made a gagging sound.

Now the CEO adopted the Sad But Reasonable expression. "It would be unfortunate for anyone to be harmed because of a refusal to discuss realistic compensation. Money is not more important than lives. I await word of your willingness to turn aside from force and embrace negotiation to find a mutually agreeable solution to our disagreements."

As the CEO's image blanked, Geary stared at where it had been, not trusting himself to speak for a moment.

"Okay," Desjani said in a calm voice, "now I only need one rock. And the coordinates of that scum's location."

"He's not showing any signs of bending." General Charban stated the obvious. "We need more leverage. Something to convince him that we do mean business. Another, bigger demonstration, perhaps."

Desjani, unseen by Charban, rolled her eyes, but her voice was loud enough for the emissaries to easily hear. "They're *still* gaming us because those Syndics think the humanitarian and honorable Black Jack won't blow them to hell. They'll keep stalling, keep demanding, because no matter what we do they'll convince themselves that it's a bluff."

Geary nodded, finally able to speak coolly. "I think you're absolutely right. And if the CEO here thinks that, then there must be CEOs all over Syndic space who believe the same thing, that my desire to avoid civilian casualties and indiscriminate bombardments means I'm soft."

"And," Desjani continued, "that means if this one gets away with it, we'll face similar ransom demands in every star system that holds Alliance prisoners."

He took another glance at the emissaries. Charban was scowling and shaking his head, but Rione simply sat looking back at Geary, not giving any sign of agreement or disapproval. "We only have five hours left before we reach orbit about that planet," Geary said. "We have already made our position clear, a position fully in keeping with the peace treaty. In my opinion, we now have no alternative except to show these Syndics, and everyone else who will hear about this, what happens in response to such tactics. They need to know that my being an honorable man does not mean that I am an easy mark or that extortion is a viable tactic against the Alliance."

"What do you intend?" Rione asked. "We are at peace with these people."

"A peace that obligates them to do certain things they refuse to do. That CEO stated that military force will be used to prevent us from pulling out our people."

"Yes, he did," Rione agreed, causing Charban's scowl to shift from Geary to her.

"Therefore, I intend to go in there with the amount of force necessary to conduct a safe extraction of our Alliance personnel. That means knocking down any defenses that might imperil the landing force or the ships in orbit, isolating the camp from ground force reinforcements, and dealing with any attempts to attack or otherwise interfere with our operation."

To one side, Desjani mouthed a silent and gleeful, *Yes!*

Charban, though, shook his head. "It's too early to embark on such a drastic course of action. The legal ramifications—"

Thoroughly fed up at the moment with politicians of all types, Geary interrupted. "That may be your opinion, General, but I am in command of this fleet, and you are not."

The general reddened slightly, looking to Rione. "We cannot approve of this action."

Rione, though, stayed silent again and gave Charban no more sign of support or agreement than she had Geary.

Geary moved his hand toward the control that would end the conversation. "Unless either of you has the authority to relieve me of command," he told the emissaries, "I intend taking this action whether you approve or not. Thank you for your input." He tapped the control, and the images of both emissaries disappeared.

Desjani, her eyes shining, actually grabbed his arm and turned him to face her. She leaned in close to speak in barely a murmur despite the privacy fields, which should have kept anyone nearby from overhearing normal conversation. "The perfect decision *and* perfect treatment of those politicians. By the living stars, I love you, Admiral."

"That's not a very professional thing to say, Tanya," he reminded her in the same low tones.

"To hell with that. Let's kick some Syndic butt, darling."

THE hastily convened fleet conference had no doubt raised some eyebrows, but as Geary laid out his decision, any signs of concern faded into smiles of approval. No one in the fleet would object to hammering Syndics, peace treaty or no. Which was why Geary took pains to pound home his restrictions. "We have to limit our actions to those justified by the treaty. The Syndics in this star system are in violation of that treaty and have threatened military action to prevent us from exercising our rights under that treaty, giving us the authority to free our personnel by whatever force is necessary. We will *not* exceed the requirements of necessary force. General Carabali."

She nodded to Geary, all professional composure.

"The fleet's targeting systems will draw up a list of bombardment targets in order to establish a safe transit corridor for your landing force. I want you and your shuttle commanders to review that list and ensure that it provides the required margin of safety."

Another nod. "What will be the rules of engagement for my Marines?" Carabali asked.

"Your landing will be preceded by broadcasts telling the Syndics that no one who avoids engaging our forces will be targeted, but that anyone or anything who fires on or locks targeting on or points weapons toward or advances toward our forces will be neutralized using all necessary means."

Carabali actually smiled thinly. "That should provide adequate guidance for my Marines."

General Charban spoke up, his attitude now that of a comrade among his peers. "It is critically important that our Marines follow those rules of engagement and exercise a high degree of restraint in their actions."

"That is understood," Carabali replied politely.

"And in any event," Duellos commented, "Marines are renowned for their restraint."

A low wave of laughter rolled around the table. Carabali nodded to Duellos, her smile still in place, but Charban's own belated smile seemed a bit strained.

"We are going to tear up a decent-size area going in," Tulev commented. "That is not only required for the safety of our forces but should also serve as an object lesson to CEOs in other Syndic star systems that they cannot demand ransom for our personnel without paying a large price."

"Exactly," Geary said. "An important secondary objective of this operation is to drive home to anyone holding Alliance prisoners of war that those prisoners cannot be employed as bargaining chips. If someone does try that, they're going to end up losing a lot more than they can hope to gain. We don't want to face this nonsense in any other star systems. Now, there's no threat from warships, so all we have to worry about are defenses on the planetary surface and in fixed orbits. Don't underestimate the threat from those weapons. A particle beam powered by planetary-based sources can be powerful enough to blow right through the shields and armor on even a battleship. All ships are to conduct random evasive movements within their assigned positions. Any questions?"

"We can't take out the warships under construction in this star system?" Commander Neeson asked.

"No. They pose no possible threat to us or to the operation. Destroying them would unquestionably fall outside the bounds of what we're allowed to do to enforce our rights under the peace treaty." Geary looked around the table. "We're doing this right. Not because of what the Syndics might say about our actions but because this fleet does things right. Let it be clearly understood that there will be *no* 'accidental' firing of any weapons at anything other than approved targets. No 'unexplained events' in fire-control systems, and no 'glitches' in launch mechanisms."

Some of his officers tried to look innocent, some feigned shock at the suggestion, and a few openly grinned. But he thought they would all abide by his clear instructions. "Are there any more questions? We don't have much time to get this operation under way, so if you see any roadblocks, let me know as soon as possible so we can keep things moving."

There weren't, though after he ended the conference, Jane Geary gave him a long look before her image vanished. He hadn't expected many questions, not from this fleet. The hard questions would have come if he had chosen not to employ force under these circumstances.

The vast majority of the captains departed in a flurry of disappearing images, both political emissaries going as well, until only Captains Badaya and Duellos remained with Geary and Desjani.

Badaya beamed approval at Geary. "I could tell how little those politicians liked your decision. This operation will help keep the Syndics in line, but it's also worthwhile as a reminder to them of who's in charge."

"Hopefully," Geary agreed, projecting general agreement with Badaya but keeping his own words as vague as possible. Such political behavior irked him, but given Badaya's potential as a loose cannon, he had no alternative.

With another broad smile and a wink at Desjani, Badaya saluted and also vanished.

Looking annoyed, Desjani glared at Duellos. "I hope you're not also going to imply anything."

"Me? Imply anything?" Duellos raised one eyebrow at Desjani. "I just want to know how you did it."

She gave him a guiltless look in return. "I had nothing to do with it. The admiral reached the appropriate conclusions on his own."

"*Completely* on his own?"

"Yes," Desjani replied. "Mostly."

"Mostly?" Duellos nodded and spread his hands. "I'm not thirsty for blood, Admiral, but I do think you reached the right conclusions, mostly completely on your own, about the required course of action."

"I take advice from all quarters," Geary replied. "But since I value your experience and judgment, I particularly appreciate your agreement."

Duellos stood and made a mock bow toward him. "We are wasting time here," Duellos said. "A distraction and a diversion. Why did the government insist upon it when learning more about the aliens seems a far more urgent priority?"

"If you figure that one out, be sure to let me know."

Duellos made a move as if to leave, then paused. "How ironic. We spent long months getting home, trying to guess the motivations and thinking of the alien race we suspected existed. Now we're devoting our time to trying to guess the motivations and thinking of our government. That reminds me, you are going to keep a close eye on the Marines, aren't you? Those rules of engagement could too easily be interpreted as a license to kill anything that strikes them as hostile."

"Carabali can be trusted to keep them in line, but I'll make doubly sure she knows that we need to be able to justify every use of firepower."

"That's probably wise, as was your admonition to my fellow commanders." Duellos seemed to be looking at something distant for a moment. "A lifetime of shooting at anything Syndic is not easily overcome," he added, his voice shading into sadness.

After Duellos had left, Geary spent a while just looking at the space vacated by Duellos's image. *A distraction. Yes. And Duellos just pointed out how big a distraction it could be even once we're done with liberating those prisoners.* "Tanya, make sure I stay focused on the aliens once we're out of this star system."

She gave him a puzzled look. "You're worried about that?"

"I don't know what's in that prison, or rather *who's* in that prison camp, but we can't afford for me to be dealing with issues from that when I need to be thinking about what's ahead. If something we find there is a major distraction, help me keep my focus."

"I wish you'd mentioned that before Roberto Duellos left. Your head is so hard sometimes that I might have to borrow a brick from him."

A number of Syndic satellites once orbiting the planet, satellites that had been part of the command and control for Syndic defenses or held sensors employed by the defense forces, were now dead objects tumbling into catastrophic reentries of the atmosphere. Four orbiting platforms that had held missiles were also gone.

As the fleet itself swung into orbit about Dunai's primary world, Geary took one more look at Rione, who continued to reveal no sign of what she thought about his course of action. "Still nothing from the Syndic CEO?"

"No. Just a litany of complaints about your 'unprovoked' destruction of some of their satellites."

He called up a comm window to his left. "General Carabali, how's it look?"

Carabali, her eyes on another part of her own display so that she was looking to one side of Geary, gave him a respectful nod. "It's a fine day for a nonpermissive personnel extraction operation, Admiral."

"They're still prepared to resist?" Geary asked her.

"Ground forces are dispersed in combat formations around the prison camp," Carabali replied. A window popped up for Geary, zooming down to the area around the main prison camp. "But we haven't seen any attempt to bring the prisoners out of their barracks and make them human shields. The Syndics have grounded all of their aircraft, but there are numerous artillery and missile assets within range of the prison camp."

"Do you think they'll fight?"

"I think, Admiral, that they're still expecting you to hold back at the last moment. That would explain why they're not using the prisoners as outright hostages, which could really piss us off. If that's the case, they may fold when we come in. But they could also have orders to resist to the best of their ability if we actually start sending Marines down."

Geary pressed one hand against his forehead, thinking. "Madam Emissary, I would appreciate your assessment of what that CEO is thinking right now."

He wondered for a moment if she would reply, but finally Rione began speaking. "He has staked his authority and judgment on the idea that you would give in. Your refusal to give in and his continued insistence on his chosen course of action have increasingly backed him into a corner. If he now offers no resistance when you strike, it will make him look very weak and very foolish. If he fights, it will make him look foolish in his judgments, but not weak. A leader thought to be foolish might survive, especially if he is seen as willing to fight to the end, but a leader believed to be weak and foolish has the chance of a snowball in hell. That is what I would assume he is thinking."

Desjani frowned, glanced back toward Rione, then shrugged in an annoyed manner. "I agree," she whispered to Geary.

"Then I've only got one option." He activated the bombardment command, the clock on the time-to-launch running steadily down toward zero, then tapped approve and confirmed the order. A few minutes later the countdown spiraled to zero, and warships began spitting out kinetic bombardment rounds.

The barrage came down through the planet's atmosphere like a fall of deadly hail, each solid piece of metal dropping at tremendous speed, gaining energy as it plummeted to the surface, until at impact, that energy was released in a burst of destruction. The people on Dunai could see the rounds coming, could determine their targets pretty closely, but had no means of stopping the projectiles and, with the fleet's warships in high orbit, had only minutes in which to react.

Personnel could be seen fleeing targeted facilities and for-
tifications in vehicles and on foot. Other vehicles with the
military units near the prison camp frantically tried to scoot
out of danger.

The bombardment had been timed for every round to hit
home as close to simultaneously as possible in order to enhance the psychological impact of the blows. There wasn't
any need to enhance the physical impact as the kinetic projectiles struck their targets. Weapon sites became craters,
buildings holding sensors or command and control facilities
were blown apart, and roads and bridges disappeared where
the rounds hit. In a wide area along the path down which
the shuttles would bring the Alliance Marines, and in an
extended perimeter outside the prison camp itself, organized
planetary defenses ceased to exist within less than a
minute.

"Launch the recovery force," Geary ordered.

Shuttles dropped from all four assault transports and
from several battleships and battle cruisers as well. Carabali
had decided on overwhelming force within the prison camp,
and Geary hadn't hesitated to approve that choice, memories
of the fight on Heradao still far too vivid.

As the Alliance shuttles penetrated the atmosphere and
dove for the prison camp, Geary noticed that Desjani was
watching them with a bleak expression. "Are you all right?"

"Just remembering." She said nothing else, and he left it
at that, knowing that Desjani was not yet ready, perhaps
never would be ready, to share some of the memories that
haunted her.

The Syndic defenses seemed to be in total confusion as
a result of the bombardment. Aside from disrupted ground
forces milling about outside the prison camp, nothing else
had gone active. "Twenty-five minutes to first shuttle landings," Carabali reported to Geary. She was on one of those
shuttles but would be among the last to land. "No resistance
noted."

"We have missile launches from the surface," the combat
systems watch announced at the same time alerts blared on

Geary's display. "Medium-range ballistic missiles from an installation to the northwest of the camp, and low-level cruise missiles from someplace to the east."

It took three taps of commands to get recommendations from the combat systems. "*Fearless*, *Resolution*, and *Redoubtable*, make sure those ballistic missiles are stopped. *Leviathan* and *Dragon*, eliminate the launch site with kinetic bombardment."

But the cruise missiles were another matter. Their flight path was taking them at low altitude over a sprawling metropolis with extended suburbs. Hitting them from high up without also striking the civilians below would not be easy. "*Colossus* and *Encroach*, destroy the cruise missile launch sites now but wait to engage the cruise missiles until they clear those suburbs, then take them out."

"Those suburbs come close to the prison camp," Desjani pointed out. "You didn't give them much of a window for engaging those cruise missiles."

"We can't just punch hell lances through civilian dwellings."

"They're forcing you to make that choice!" Desjani insisted, as hell lances from *Fearless*, *Resolution*, and *Redoubtable* tore apart the ballistic missiles at the peak of their trajectories, and the rocks from *Leviathan* and *Dragon* headed downward for the place that had launched the missiles. It might be a case of slamming the barn door after the horses escaped, but that particular barn wouldn't be letting any more horses go after it was turned into a field of craters.

"I know, but—" Geary broke off speaking as something caught his eye on the display. "What's *Dreadnaught* doing?" The battleship was veering downward, leaving high orbit to skim the upper reaches of atmosphere. He hit the comm control viciously. "*Dreadnaught*. What are you doing?"

Jane Geary seemed preoccupied as she answered, her attention focused to one side. "*Dreadnaught* is engaging threats against the landing force and the prisoners, Admiral."

The only threats *Dreadnaught* was moving to engage were the cruise missiles. "*Colossus* and *Encroach* are assigned those targets, *Dreadnaught*. Return to station now."

"If we missed hitting any planet-based particle beams, *Dreadnaught* could get speared by one in that low an orbit," Desjani said.

"I know!" *Dreadnaught* hadn't altered her vector. "Captain Geary, get back into higher orbit and return your ship to her assigned station *now*."

Jane Geary's expression didn't alter, intense concentration visible there, and she didn't answer immediately.

"*Dreadnaught* is firing hell lances," the combat systems watch reported.

There were ten cruise missiles. *Dreadnaught* fired ten hell-lance shots. Geary, his display cranked to high magnification, watched as each particle beam ripped through a cruise missile as the missile crossed open areas like streets or narrow strips of woodland.

"Targets destroyed," Jane Geary reported. "No collateral damage. *Dreadnaught* is returning to station."

"Very well." That was all he trusted himself to say as Jane Geary's image vanished.

Desjani cleared her throat. "You'll have to decide whether to give her a medal or relieve her of command."

"Tanya, damn it to hell, I don't need—"

"And in this fleet," she continued, "you know which action will be regarded as justified."

"She went against my explicit orders—"

"She got the job done." Desjani gestured toward the planet. "And she did it aggressively and with style. Think before you act on this one. Sir."

He took a deep breath, then nodded. "All right." *What the hell is Jane thinking? She's thinking that she's Black Jack, that she has to be him. And, dammit, she did a good job just like Tanya said. But what will happen next time she disregards orders to demonstrate her status as a "real" Geary? Maybe disaster, like the sort of brainless courage that cost us* Paladin *at Lakota. But I have to deal with that later. Focus. I've got Marines about to land. Is anyone else acting up?*

Invincible stood out on the display, not for what it was doing, but for what the battle cruiser *wasn't* doing. Every other warship was making small changes in its orbit at random intervals to throw off targeting by surface-based weapons. But *Invincible* sailed along without any variations in her orbit, locked into the exact center spot of her assigned position in the formation. "*Invincible*, begin evasive maneuvers as previously instructed."

Captain Vente, who had never spoken up at fleet conferences, sounded peevish now. "No specific maneuvering orders were issued."

"*Random*, Captain Vente. Make random changes in your ship's movement," Geary ordered.

"What *kind* of random changes?"

Desjani gestured to attract Geary's attention. "Combat maneuvering subroutine 47A."

"Execute combat maneuvering subroutine 47A," Geary repeated to Vente.

"Oh. Very well."

Orion. What was *Orion* up to? If any ship was going to have problems doing what it was told . . .

But *Orion* was in position, jinking randomly in her orbit, all systems reporting combat readiness.

The first shuttles were dropping fast to the surface inside the prison camp, their ramps out so that the moment the shuttle touched, Marines in full combat armor were rolling out and dashing for cover. Close-in weapons on the shuttles still coming down lashed at guard towers and other defensive positions, ensuring that any prison guards still at their posts stayed under cover. Within moments, the first wave was down, the shuttles lifting again for safety while the Marines headed for their objectives, and the second wave came in behind them.

The buildings there were more like multistory dormitories than the low, warehouse-type structures Geary had seen at previous Syndic labor camps. Rows of small windows looked down on the courtyards where the shuttles were dropping Marines, but no fire came from any of the windows.

Geary took a long look at his display. *Dreadnaught* was almost back on station, and everyone else seemed to be behaving themselves. The annihilation of the launch sites appeared to have discouraged any more attacks on the prison camp area, with even Syndic ground forces lying low. *Their leader may be stupid, but they aren't. None of them want to face this fleet's firepower just to salvage their leader's pride.*

He called up windows for the Marine unit leaders, momentarily surprised by the number that appeared. He had more than twice as many Marines as had previously been with the fleet, meaning twice as many unit leaders. He touched one face, the subdisplay showing activity in the prison camp immediately highlighting that officer's position near the shuttles. Trying again, Geary got a lieutenant who was leading a platoon inside one of the buildings, and called up another window offering a view from that Marine's combat armor.

A moment's disorientation vanished as Geary's mind made sense of the images, seeing a darkened hallway lined with doors. The Marines moved quickly, weapons ready, all the way to the end of the hallway; then, at the lieutenant's command, one of them reached for a locked door and twisted the lock with the enhanced strength of the combat armor. With a squeal of protesting metal, the lock snapped, and the door swung open.

Two men in faded Alliance ground forces uniforms stood within, not moving, their hands out. They had enough sense not to do anything while nervous Marines had weapons trained on them. "Where are the guards?" the lieutenant asked them.

"Even floors, guard stations at the end," one of the prisoners immediately replied. "Normally three guards."

"Got it. Stay put until the follow-on forces come through." The lieutenant sent her men up the stairs at the end of the hall, the combat armor allowing them to leap several stairs at a time until they crashed through the doors onto the next floor.

The guard station was deserted, its alarm panel blinking frantic and futile warnings. "Guard stations in this building are abandoned," the lieutenant reported. "Roger," Geary heard her captain reply, his voice sharp. "Make sure you check every one. Combat engineers are coming through to disable alarm panels and ensure they aren't linked to any dead-man traps. Make sure your Marines don't touch them."

"Understood." A moment later, the lieutenant roared at some of her own Marines. "Orvis! Rendillon! Don't touch those damned buttons!"

Geary closed the window, feeling guilty at concentrating on a single, small piece of the picture when the entire fleet was his responsibility. "Why is it that whenever sailors or Marines see a button, they want to push it?"

"Did you ever wonder what they did before humans invented buttons to push?" Desjani asked. "There must have been something they weren't supposed to do."

"No resistance," Carabali reported. "The guards are hunkered down in their barracks and surrendered to the first Marines to breach the doors."

That was going well, anyway. "Any problems?"

"Not yet. Seventy-five percent of the prison camp is now secured. Estimated time to completely secured is five minutes."

"Thank you." Things were going far too well, but he couldn't spot any problems hiding, ready to pounce. He tried to relax while staying alert and shifting his attention between different displays, watching his ships jink and dodge slightly at random intervals to confuse any attempt to target them from the planet's surface, watching the green "cleared" areas on the prison camp display grow to cover the entire area, waiting as the Marines ensured that no booby traps were active before they began breaking open doors wholesale and herding newly liberated prisoners into courtyards where shuttles waited.

Another window popped open next to Geary. "We're getting identifications on the prisoners, Admiral," Lieutenant Iger said. "It looks like this was a VIP labor camp."

"A what?"

"VIPs, sir. Every other prisoner ID we're getting is for an admiral or general. The lower-ranking officers among them, and by 'lower-ranking' I mean usually fleet captains and colonels, all seem to be men and women who were highly decorated and influential before being captured. Now we know where the general officers have been, why the prison camps we've liberated prior to this had captains and colonels as the senior officers. There are a few civilians so far, but even those are high-ranking officials or political leaders who were nabbed in raids or assaults on Alliance worlds. No enlisted personnel at all."

"Highly decorated and influential," Geary repeated, something telling him that those words were critically important.

"Yes, sir. Like, um, Captain Falco."

Captain Falco. A single individual who had triggered mutiny against Geary and caused the loss of several ships. And this Syndic labor camp was full of individuals with similar backgrounds. "Thank you, Lieutenant."

"Is there anything else, sir?"

"No. Thank you." He had to think about this. Were these individuals still valuable to the Alliance? To the government? But if they followed the molds that Geary had seen thus far, they would be thorns in the government's side. "Wait. Lieutenant, I'd like you to go through their records. From before they were captured. What I'd like to know is whether any of these VIPs had some special knowledge, skills, or political relationships that would still be important for their rapid return to the Alliance." Phrase it that way, so it didn't sound like he was trying to discover the government's reason for sending him here.

"Yes, sir."

"What did he say?" Desjani asked, as Geary ended the

call. The concern in her voice told him that his expression was giving away too much.

"Let's talk later." Right now he had to do something else. Was it better to have the VIPs underfoot on *Dauntless*, or stashed somewhere where he wouldn't have to fend them off? *I can more easily transfer them to other ships, if I want to, if they're first warehoused somewhere.* He quickly called Carabali. "General, change of plans. I'd like all of the liberated prisoners delivered to *Typhoon* and *Mistral*. The assault transports are better suited to rapid screening and medical exams."

The Marine commander paused, then nodded. "Yes, sir. I'll direct the shuttles to head for *Typhoon* and *Mistral*. Are both of those ships aware of the change in plans?"

Carabali could be very diplomatic for a Marine. "I'm notifying them once I finish speaking with you."

"Very well, Admiral. I should inform you that the first shuttle has already launched with orders to proceed to *Dauntless*. Should I divert it as well?"

Damn. An obvious change in destination for that shuttle at this point would raise too many questions. "No. We'll take them aboard here."

Back to Desjani. "*Dauntless* will only get one shuttle. The others are going to *Typhoon* and *Mistral*."

She eyed him curiously. "All right. We were planning on processing more than that, but it's your fleet. Do *Typhoon* and *Mistral* know—"

"I'm calling them now!"

"Excuse me," Desjani muttered just loud enough for him to hear, then raised her voice. "Lieutenant Mori, we're only getting one shuttle. Inform everyone on the intake teams."

Finishing informing the commanding officers of *Typhoon* and *Mistral* of the change, and wincing inside as he knew how much of a last-minute scramble those orders would cause on those ships, Geary turned to a stony-faced Desjani. "Sorry. It's because they're VIPs."

"*Who* are VIPs?"

"The prisoners."

"All of them?"

"Damn near."

After a moment, Desjani asked another question. "Military VIPs?"

"Yeah. Like Falco."

"What the hell?"

"My feelings exactly."

With no opposition, the Marines on the ground were moving very quickly. "There were fewer than three hundred prisoners in this camp," Carabali reported. "Most of the cells were unoccupied. We have all of the POWs in hand and are loading the last ones into shuttles now. I've already started lifting Marines out, too. Estimate fifteen minutes until the last Alliance personnel are off the surface."

"Excellent." It all went like clockwork, even as he waited for something to go wrong, some unexpected factor to suddenly throw a wrench into the smoothly working operation. But the last Marines dodged into the last shuttles, the last ramps rose, and the last shuttles leaped into the air, leaving ranks of disarmed Syndic prison guards standing around apparently uncertain of what to do next.

"Shuttle on final," the maneuvering watch reported. "Estimated time to dock five minutes."

"How long until the last shuttles are recovered?" Geary asked.

"Forty minutes, sir."

Every Syndic on the planet seemed to have gone to cover. Nothing was moving in the sky or on the roads or in open country. "Looks like the Syndics here finally figured out what a bad idea it was to mess with this fleet," Desjani commented, drawing grins from her watch-standers.

Geary stood up. "I'm going down to greet that shuttle, Captain Desjani. I'll be back here within half an hour. I need to see some of these VIPs and talk to them." *Maybe then I can get some clue as to the reason we were sent here.*

Desjani just nodded, her eyes on her display, her brow furrowed in thought.

He walked briskly, trying not to reveal any disquiet to the crew members he passed, who all seemed cheerful as a result of the one-sided fight and victory, word of which was already flashing through the fleet. Inside the shuttle dock, Geary paused to take in the sailors forming up to serve as a combined honor guard and intake force to get the newly liberated prisoners evaluated, assigned quarters, and given necessary treatment.

"We meet again," Rione murmured as she came up beside him.

"What brings an emissary down here?" Geary asked.

"I may not be a senator anymore, but I still have an obligation to pay respects on behalf of the government to those who have been imprisoned."

And you're probably hoping to find someone who knows something about your husband. But he didn't say that out loud, knowing that in her place, he would have done the same.

The shuttle swung in, easily visible behind the shield keeping atmosphere in this part of the dock, then came to a gentle landing as the outer doors sealed and the shield dropped. Geary waited as the ramp extended and the shuttle's hatch opened, watching the men and women who came down the ramp. Despite their VIP status, they resembled the other prisoners of war liberated by the fleet in the last several months. A mix of ages, some of them captured so long ago they were now elderly. Threadbare uniforms mixed with articles of cast-off Syndic clothing. Thin from hard work and just enough food. And looks of mingled disbelief and joy as if they feared this was a dream from which they would soon awake.

The only difference was the amount of rank present. As far as Geary could tell, there were only a few commanders or majors among them, everyone else being at least colonels or captains, and almost half wearing the tarnished insignia of admirals and generals. Iger hadn't been exaggerating in the least.

He was gazing at the prisoners, searching for Captain

Michael Geary even though he knew the odds of his great-nephew being alive and being here were very small, when a noise from Rione caught his attention. A wordless gasp, it somehow carried across the dock. Several of the former prisoners heard and turned to look, one man among them stumbling to a halt, then running toward her. "Vic! By the living stars, is it really you?"

Geary took a step away as they embraced, feeling embarrassed to be witnessing such raw emotion, actual tears flowing from Rione as she held him.

He started to look aside, then focused back on Rione's face. Amid the wonder and happiness, did he also see horror? How could that be?

But then she noticed him and averted her own face for a moment. When he saw it again, Rione had only the natural emotions from such a reunion visible.

She broke the embrace, turning toward Geary, reestablishing the iron control Rione usually displayed. "Admiral, may I present Commander Paol Benan, my husband."

Geary waited for a salute, which didn't come, and he belatedly realized that, of course, these officers had been imprisoned when he had reintroduced saluting to the fleet.

Benan grinned broadly. "It's really you. Well, damn, of course it is. The Marines told us Black Jack was in command. Who else could have brought the fleet this deep into Syndic space? You must have them on the run. We can beat them now, crush them so they never again pose a threat to the Alliance! Now that we're off that planet, you can hit it with everything you've got!"

It took both Rione and Geary a moment to realize what he meant, that the Syndic authorities here had cruelly withheld news of the end of the war. "Paol," she said, "the war is over. We already won."

"What?" Benan looked completely lost for a moment. "When? How?"

"Admiral Geary. He wiped out the Syndic fleet and forced them to agree to peace."

"Peace." Benan said the word as if he had heard it for the

very first time in his life and had no idea of its meaning. "That's . . . But you attacked the planet. The Marines assaulted the camp."

"The Syndic CEO here balked at his obligations under the peace agreement," Geary explained. "We took necessary actions to liberate you and your fellow prisoners."

"Yes." Benan still seemed uncertain. "We can help with some targeting for your follow-up bombardments. There are some buried installations, well concealed, that we know the locations of."

"There will be no more bombardment of that planet, Commander."

"But . . . the manufacturing centers . . . population centers—"

Geary heard his voice hardening. "This fleet no longer wars on civilians, Commander. We attack military targets only, and those attacks now will come only as necessary to ensure that the Syndics abide by the peace treaty."

Benan simply looked at Geary as if he had heard words in an unknown language.

Taking his arm in a gentle grasp, Rione spoke for them both. "My husband needs to be checked in and receive his medical evaluation, Admiral. I will have an opportunity to bring him up-to-date while that is under way. I hope you will forgive us now."

"Of course." He felt ashamed for his anger of a moment earlier. Benan and the others liberated with him were still stressed by the long captivity and bewildered by recent events. They needed to know how things had changed, that the fleet had returned to the honorable practices of their ancestors.

Gazing back at the other liberated prisoners, Geary saw an admiral and a general looking his way. *Time to reposition before I get pinned down.* "I need to return to the bridge," he said to no one in particular in a voice loud enough to carry. He offered the prisoners a quick wave and smile, then dashed off before they could leave the line.

He made it there only twenty minutes after leaving, finding everything still going well. Of course, he could have directed the operation from anywhere within *Dauntless*, but humans had long since learned that leaders needed to be seen and needed to issue orders from professionally appropriate locations. Geary had discovered that the old (and apparently true) story of the admiral who had issued orders during a battle from the comfort of his stateroom while drinking beer was still well-known.

Carabali's shuttle was the last to dock on *Tsunami*. "All shuttles recovered, all Marines accounted for, all prisoners located and liberated," she reported to Geary. "No damage to shuttles, personnel casualties limited to several sprains incurred during the landings."

"Outstanding job, General." Geary let out a long breath that felt like he had been holding it for hours. "All units, execute Formation November at time four zero."

Forming into five rectangles, broad sides facing forward, the largest rectangle in the middle itself centered on *Dauntless*, the Alliance fleet accelerated away from the Syndic planet, heading for the jump point that would take it back to Hasadan. But this time, from Hasadan the fleet would take the Syndic hypernet to Midway. He stood again, stretching out the accumulated tension. "I think I'll take a break in my stateroom, Captain Desjani."

"Get something to eat, too," she said.

Resisting the urge to say, "Yes, ma'am," and salute her in front of the bridge crew, Geary headed for his stateroom by way of a mess compartment to pick up a battle ration. It wasn't the best food, and arguments within the fleet debated whether battle rations qualified as food at all using most definitions of that word, but the rations filled you up and met minimum daily nutrition requirements.

He was almost to his stateroom when Desjani came quickly toward him down the passageway, her expression stiff. She gestured wordlessly toward Geary's stateroom, letting him enter and following closely behind. Once inside she closed the door with great care, then turned to him, her face a mask of barely contained fury, all the more fearsome for the coldness of the fire in her eyes. "Request permission to speak freely, sir."

"You never require permission to do that," he replied, keeping his own voice low and steady.

"I have been informed of the identity of one of the liberated prisoners. *Her* husband."

"That's right." He wondered if her anger was directed at him for not telling her, but it seemed aimed elsewhere.

"What an amazing coincidence. She came aboard with new orders, diverting this fleet from its planned course and its planned mission in order to come to the prisoner-of-war camp in this star system, a camp that just happened to have her husband among its number." Desjani's words came out clipped, hard as a barrage of grapeshot. "We came here on *her personal errand.*"

"That's possible, but—"

"*Possible?* She *jerked* around this *fleet* for her own *personal* purposes—"

"Tanya, hear me out!" He waited as she took a deep breath, the heat in her eyes subsiding to a controlled blaze. "I've had time to think about this. First, my impression was that she was shocked to see her husband. But she's very good at concealing her real feelings, so that's far from definitive."

"She's—"

"I'm *more* worried about dealing with all of the *other* VIPs."

Desjani took a long, slow breath, still furious but keeping the feelings on a shorter leash. "Like Falco."

"Multiplied a hundred times."

Her eyes narrowed as the fires in them became a white-hot, focused torch. "Why? She didn't like Falco. Neither did the government. Why unleash dozens more like him?"

"I don't know." He sat down, one hand to his forehead, trying to blank out anger and frustration. The battle ration sat untouched, his appetite fled for the moment. "All I know for certain is that they're here, and we're taking them into alien space with us."

"Hundreds of loose cannons." Now Desjani seemed baffled. "What possible advantage does that give anyone?"

"I think Rione knows why we were sent here to get them."

"Her secret orders. But why wouldn't the government want those Falco-wannabes left in Syndic hands as long as possible? Why make them a priority for release?"

"I don't know." Geary let his eyes rest on the star display floating above the table, which he had left centered on Dunai Star System. "Even if Rione knew that her husband was at Dunai, why would the government have agreed to let her divert this fleet for a personal matter? She's not that powerful. She's been voted out of office. And what possible reason would the government have for agreeing if it had any idea that all of those other senior officers were there?"

"It must have been a price," Desjani insisted. "Something she demanded in exchange for agreeing to go on this mission and carry out whatever orders she has." Desjani seemed ready to order Rione's arrest.

"She's still a legal, authorized representative of the government, Tanya. Even if the government agreed to order us to this star system to satisfy Rione's personal agenda, it's within the rights of the government to do that."

Desjani sat down, too, glaring at him. "Are you sure you don't want to be dictator?"

"Yes." That brought up another thought, though. "We know the government fears this fleet. They fear what I might do with it. But now they've ensured that lots of other senior officers who might back a coup are also present with the fleet. It's either irrational or so brilliantly Byzantine it only seems to make no sense at all."

"What if those secret orders jeopardize the safety of this fleet?"

"We don't know that—"

"We don't *know* anything." Desjani jumped up, walked to the hatch, and yanked it open. "It's like dealing with the aliens."

* * *

"SOME amount of disorientation is normal in cases like this," the fleet's senior medical officer explained to Geary. "But the readjustment difficulties are higher than usual for these individuals. It was a good idea to place many of them on *Mistral*, where I could conduct personal examinations."

Geary smiled and nodded as if he had indeed thought about that on the spur of the moment.

"Call me old-fashioned," the doctor continued, "but I think even the best virtual-meeting software misses things. Tiny things, but important in evaluating an individual."

"Can you summarize your impressions?" Geary asked.

"I already did." The physician hesitated. "I could go into a little more detail, I suppose. As I said, some disorientation is normal. They've been in a Syndic labor camp for years at least and, in many cases, decades. They are accustomed to being confined to certain areas, to being subject to arbitrary rules, to having their actions controlled by authorities whose judgment can't be questioned."

That sounds a lot like just being in the military, Geary thought.

"But in addition to that, there's the fact that basic certainties are different. The war is over. That's a major alteration in what they considered a fixed reality, and unlike those of us who were free to see events unfold recently, it is hitting them all at once. They have been told an intelligent species of aliens exists beyond human space, something totally unexpected. Then there's you, yourself, that Black Jack, against all rational odds, did indeed return from the dead (figuratively speaking, naturally) and achieve the seemingly impossible. To these former prisoners, it's as if they have suddenly found themselves in a fantasy world rather than the universe they occupied before being captured."

The fleet physician looked down, sighing once, before focusing back on Geary. "There's one other factor unique to these prisoners. As you may have already been informed, many are fairly senior officers. Before being captured, they were used to either being in charge or being highly influential. Many of them believed that they would play an exceptional, personal role in the war because of their own abilities, that they were fated to do great things. There's a medical term for this set of beliefs."

Geary fought down his own sigh. "Geary Syndrome."

"Yes! You've heard of it?" the doctor said in surprised tones, as if amazed that a nonphysician would have such knowledge.

"It's been brought to my attention."

"Then I'm sure you understand that they find it hard to deal with a situation where they lack authority in this fleet despite their rank and seniority. Many of them believed that somehow, despite being imprisoned, they would still save the Alliance and defeat the Syndics. Such beliefs helped sustain them. But you already won the war, leaving them without any clear sense of their own destinies."

He didn't need any further explanations to see how much trouble all of those disorientations could add up to. "I'm going to speak with them as a group. It's already set up for ten minutes from now."

"They'll expect one-on-one meetings with you. I've already heard scores of slight variations on 'I'm certain that I'll be assuming an appropriate command position very quickly.' More than one expect to assume command of this fleet."

"I understand, but I don't have time for individual meetings before we jump for Hasadan." The inability to communicate between ships in jump space except in very brief forms was usually a hindrance, but in this situation, it was a blessing.

"Your meeting should be most interesting," the doctor remarked. "May I sit in?"

"Certainly." *You'll get to watch the original Geary talking to lots of Geary Syndrome sufferers. That ought to inspire a nice paper for your medical colleagues.* "Just do so using the blind participant setting so no one else knows you're watching and listening."

A few minutes later, the conference room grew rapidly in size as the virtual presence of more than two hundred former prisoners flooded in, even those on *Dauntless* using the software since the actual size of the conference room was too small to accommodate all of them. Geary had intended to speak with them alone; but as he waited, the virtual presences of General Carabali, Captain Tulev, Rione, and General Charban appeared. "Captain Desjani indicated you wished me to attend," Carabali explained, to which the other three nodded in agreement.

All right, Tanya. Maybe it'll be good to have that backup. On a sudden suspicion, he checked the software and saw that Desjani herself was also monitoring the meeting in blind mode.

Geary swept his eyes around the table, already knowing that none of the freed prisoners was Michael Geary but unable to keep from looking for him one more time.

He stood up to speak, only to have one of the admirals shoot to his own feet. "It is necessary to discuss command issues as soon as—"

Geary had been through variations on this before, during the long retreat from the Syndic home star system. He already had the right control ready and silenced audio from that officer. "I am Admiral Geary," he began, as if no one else had already spoken. "I am in command of this fleet."

Rione made a small gesture, as if unable to stop herself, and Geary paused in reaction, only then realizing the pause gave his statement more force. *Is she helping?*

Geary went on, welcoming the freed prisoners and explaining the mission. "Unfortunately, even though you all deserve to be returned to Alliance space as soon as possible, we are deep within Syndic space. I can't detach any of the assault transports to take you back, not unless I escort it with a strong force of warships, and given our lack of knowledge about the threats we will face inside alien space, I don't feel comfortable diminishing my force at this point.

"Also, unfortunately, it's impossible for me to speak individually with each of you. We'll be jumping back to Hasadan soon, then using the Syndic hypernet system to proceed to Midway, so there will be little opportunity to communicate between ships."

Finally, the question he didn't want to ask. "Are there any questions?"

More than two hundred men and women started talking at once. The software automatically blocked all of their audio, highlighting each individual so Geary could choose who would be heard. "One at a time, please," he said, more loudly than necessary since he didn't actually have to shout everyone down. Resigning himself to the inevitable, he indicated the admiral who had first tried to speak. "You have a question?"

Standing up again, his face set, the officer looked around the table as he spoke rather than aiming his words at Geary. "Fleet procedures need to be followed regardless of circumstances. We are combat commanders, highly skilled and respected. Our first order of business must be to establish an agreed-upon fleet commander—"

This time the admiral was interrupted by another former prisoner, also an admiral, who pointed toward Geary. "Chelak, use your head for something besides making noise. That's Black Jack. He's our equal in rank, he's in command, and every sailor and officer I've talked to in this fleet supports him."

"My date of rank is much earlier than his! I earned respect for that, as did you all!" Chelak insisted.

"He's earned some respect, too," a female general replied. "I'm still trying to catch up on things that have happened since I was captured, but it's obvious that none of us has enough of a grasp on the current situation to supplant someone who does."

"That doesn't mean we ignore honor and tradition," a female admiral shot back.

"We're supposed to give lessons in honor and tradition to Black Jack?"

"We don't know that he's really—"

"Read up on the last several months," the second male admiral suggested.

A hundred officers started talking this time.

General Carabali stood, drawing their attention. "The fleet's Marines will follow the orders of Admiral Geary." She sat down again, the flat statement seeming to echo amid the sudden silence.

"Some of you may know me," General Charban suggested. "I can assure you that the government and headquarters placed Admiral Geary firmly in command."

"As if we care for what either one does," someone called out.

Another outburst, hundreds of voices being shut off so that images of high-ranking officers yelled silently at one another.

Tulev looked at Geary, speaking on a private circuit. "This is unmanageable. You could spend weeks speaking with them and get nowhere."

Carabali nodded. "Too many alphas in one fleet. You'd be best off packing them all on *Haboob* and disabling all the comm systems."

"Seconded," Desjani's voice sounded in his ear.

Geary looked at Charban and Rione. "What are the government's wishes?"

She looked back at him. "I have no instructions for disposition of freed prisoners."

Charban spread his hands. "I have none, either."

Geary switched to a private circuit with just those two on it with him. "The government ordered us to liberate this bunch. I was ordered to bring the fleet here. Why? What do they want with them? Why did we need to pick them up before proceeding into alien space?"

"I have no instructions," Rione repeated, her expression unyielding.

That did it. "Then I consider this a matter that must be dealt with using my authority. Neither of you is an elected official. Under Alliance law, outside of Alliance territory, a fleet commander has authority over civilians who work for the government or anyone contracted to the government. You and General Charban are hereby assigned to act as primary liaisons with the freed prisoners. You two are their first points of contact, and you two will attempt to resolve any and all issues concerning them. I will be informed of any actions posing a threat to the fleet or violating regulations or Alliance law. Otherwise, the government wanted them, so the government can have them."

He looked down the table again as Charban stared at Geary, aghast, and Rione reddened slightly but otherwise remained impassive. Keying his override, Geary spoke to all of the prisoners. "Thank you for your sacrifices and service to the Alliance. Governmental emissaries Rione and Charban will now be your primary points of contact on all matters. I look forward to your safe return to Alliance space." *By the living stars, do I look forward to that.* "Thank you. To the honor of our ancestors."

Cutting himself, Carabali, and Tulev out of the conference, so their presences disappeared as far as everyone else was concerned, Geary left the compartment.

He spent a while roaming the passageways, not wanting to be alone with his thoughts in his stateroom and too restless to sit anywhere. Stopping to talk with some sailors as they worked was comfortingly familiar, as if the century he had lost had never been. The equipment might be different, but sailors were always sailors.

Tanya ran him down at one point, walking beside him silently for a while before speaking. "Giving them to the emissaries was brilliant, but it's not really a solution, you know."

"I know. Some of them could still make major trouble."

"Your grip on the fleet is much, much stronger than it was when Falco made his moves. Plus, you've been formally appointed to command instead of being an acting commander. And as far as we know, none of the current ship captains are working against you."

"As far as we know," Geary agreed.

He had no chance to say more as Rione appeared, coming down the same passageway with a clear intent to intercept them.

Rione came right up to them and stopped in their path. "Admiral, I need to speak with you."

"You and General Charban can sort out how to—"

"It's not about *that*." She took a deep breath, seeming to fumble for words for a moment, something unusual enough that Desjani's frown took on a different cast. "My—Commander Benan. He has been told . . . about events concerning you and me . . . in the past."

From somewhere in Geary's mind one question arose. "Are you in danger?"

"No! Not me."

"Not *you*." That left one other person.

But Rione shook her head. "I don't think he would—"

Hearing a sudden hiss of breath from Desjani, Geary looked up to see Commander Benan walking steadily toward him.

NINE

DESJANI took a step forward, putting herself between Benan and both Geary and Rione. "Is there a problem, Commander?"

"I must speak with . . . the admiral." Paol Benan's face was deathly pale, his voice rough. "There is a matter of honor between us. I must—"

Desjani broke in, her voice sharp, at command tone and volume. "Commander Benan, are you aware of fleet regulations?"

Those fevered eyes turned on her. "I do not need to be lectured on regulations by—"

"Then you know what will happen if you continue on your current course," Desjani said, her tone growing colder. "I will not have such a breach of discipline aboard my ship."

"Aboard *your* ship? After what you and he did? *You* disgraced your position and should have been relieved of command and called to account for—" Other members of the crew had halted to watch the scene, and now a low growl arose from them, menacing enough to draw Paol Benan's attention and choke off his words.

A chief petty officer stepped forward, speaking in a firm voice. "Sir, if there had been any grounds to question the honor of our captain, we would have been aware of it. She and the admiral never violated their duties or responsibilities."

"Their honor is not stained," an ensign added.

Whatever Benan might have replied was cut off by Victoria Rione, who pushed past Desjani to stare at him, then in a low, furious voice spoke to her husband. "We will talk. In private. Now."

A flush spread across Benan's pallor. "Anything you have to say—"

"If you still care about me at all, you will not proclaim in public anything regarding my honor or my actions," Rione said in a voice that seemed to physically force Benan back.

That got through to him. Benan swallowed, then nodded, suddenly subdued. "I'm . . . I'm sorry, Vic."

"Come with me. Please." Rione faced not Geary, but Desjani. "If you will excuse us, Captain. My . . . thanks," she got out in a strangled voice, then spun and led her husband away.

Desjani watched them go, then focused on her crew members, who were standing about, uncertain. "Thank you."

They nodded or saluted or smiled and moved on as Desjani beckoned to Geary. "Let's keep moving. That was close."

"What was close? What was Benan doing that you interrupted?"

She stopped in midstep to stare at him. "You really don't know what he was doing?" Desjani asked. "He was about to challenge you to an honor duel."

Geary wasn't sure that he had heard right. "A what?"

"An honor duel. To the death, usually." They reached her stateroom, and she gestured him inside. "Hopefully, you can spend five minutes in here without anyone assuming we're acting like rabbits in heat." Desjani flopped down on a chair in an attitude very different from her usual rigid posture, her face troubled. "Honor duels started, I don't know, thirty years ago maybe. Fleet officers calling each other out on matters of honor. We couldn't beat the enemy so we started eating ourselves alive." Her gaze locked on his eyes. "Matters of honor, like accusations of unfaithfulness."

"That happened in the fleet?" Geary demanded.

"You know what we're like even now! Honor is all that matters, displays of courage are all that matter." Desjani made a disgusted face. "Challenged officers couldn't back down without being accused of cowardice. We didn't have enough officers as it was, and those we did have were killing each other in a frenzy of misguided zeal. Finally, fleet stepped in with very harsh regulations mandating serious penalties for anyone making a challenge. It took a little while to stick, and more than a few firing squads; but by the time I entered the fleet, honor duels were just stories told by the few who were still alive from those days. But the regulations are still on the books. We had to memorize them in officer training. If that idiot had finished stating his challenge to you, I would have been forced to have him arrested and locked in the brig, pending court-martial upon our return." She gave him a speculative look. "Unless you decided on a summary execution in the field, which is permitted under the regulations."

Geary looked around. He couldn't remember ever being in her stateroom before. Choosing a seat, he sat down facing her. "That's not funny."

"I didn't think it was. He almost challenged me as well, or didn't you notice?"

He stared at her. "That bit when he began to say something about how you should have been relieved of command?"

"Yeah. That bit," Desjani spat out.

"Your crew defended your honor," Geary pointed out.

"That's because they don't know how dishonorable my feelings were," she said, bitterness growing in her words. "You could have had me for the asking. You knew it then, and if you're honest with yourself, you'll admit to that. Don't pretend I'm this model of honor when I would have done anything you asked of me even though you were my superior officer."

"You didn't— Tanya, you believed I had a vital mission to carry out. Even our harshest critics could never point to anything you did—"

"*I* am my harshest critic, Admiral Geary!" She glowered at him. "Haven't you figured that out yet?"

"I suppose I should have."

Desjani stared into one corner of the room for a while, then shook her head. "I could have been her. You know I had relationships before you. It's possible that one of them could have resulted in marriage, and at least one of the officers I could have married was captured by the Syndics. I could have spent years and years burnishing the memory of him and of our relationship, then found out when he was liberated just how much difference there was between those dreams and the reality of who he had been and who he now was. And be forced to explain and live with whatever I'd done while he was captive for what we all thought would be the rest of his life."

He lowered his head, seeing the emotions in her and not wanting to see them. "You wouldn't have—"

"I could have. You know that. Don't patronize me. Only chance kept me from living what she's stuck with right now."

He looked up, fixing a baffled gaze on her. "That's why you stepped between her and Benan? You wanted to protect her because you feel sorry for her?"

"I am the commanding officer of this ship! I will not tolerate breaches of discipline!" Desjani glared at him again. "*That* is why I intervened. Because it was my responsibility. Understand?"

He eyed her, knowing that this was a subject that Desjani would never discuss without holding a lot back. "Yes, ma'am."

"Dammit, Jack! Stop pushing me!"

He had never liked the Black Jack nickname, had been horrified to discover that the Alliance government had made it part of him while building him up as the greatest hero the Alliance had ever known, but Desjani had taken to on rare occasions calling him just Jack as a personal nickname, and

he had found he liked that. But for her to say it now spoke
to how upset she was. "All right. I really am sorry. How long
are you going to beat yourself up about your feelings that
developed when I was your superior officer?"

She flipped one hand toward him. "The rest of this life.
Part of the next one, probably. I'm sure by the life after that
I'll have plenty of other sins to occupy my sense of guilt."

"So what do I do if Commander Benan tries to challenge
me again?"

"I'd have the bastard shot, but that's just me." She
frowned down at the deck. "Sorry. I know you're asking for
advice. Assuming that the harpy he's married to hasn't already gelded him over this, you should just shut him up. Put
a fist in his gut if you have to. Keep him from finishing his
challenge. Otherwise, you'll face some ugly choices."

"All right." He stood up, knowing that eyes outside would
be on her closed door. "Thank you again for ensuring that
no incidents occurred on your ship."

She gave him a suspicious look. "You're welcome."

He started to go, then paused, looking at a plaque on the
bulkhead next to the entrance where Desjani would see it
whenever she left her stateroom. Names were listed there,
alongside dates and different stars. The long list had obviously been added to over the years. The earliest names were
those of junior officers, the ranks increasing in the later
years. "Who are these people?"

"Friends."

He spotted the last name on the list. "Captain Jaylen
Cresida."

"Absent friends," Desjani said.

He looked back at her. She had her eyes on the plaque,
avoiding meeting his. "May the living stars shine on their
memory," Geary said, then left, closing the hatch gently
behind him.

A very restless night, which finally found him walking the
passageways again. That required some good acting, to be

seen roaming the passageways in the middle of the night yet not appear nervous or worried to the crew members who worked that shift. *What the hell am I going to do about Jane Geary? Tanya's right. As much as I've managed to make this fleet more professional, the fact is they still place a priority on the attack, on being bold, getting to the enemy fast and fighting it out. And while Jane disobeyed orders, she did so for a daring attack that took out an enemy threat. In terms of getting the job done and protecting our troops on the ground while also minimizing the chances of Syndic civilian casualties, she did everything right.*

Which leaves me very little room to hammer her. I can't condemn initiative that effective, not without sending some wrong messages of my own. If I make obedience the only virtue that counts, I might be creating a culture that is at least as bad as the undisciplined mess I first found here. Do I want a fleet full of officers like Captain Vente, who apparently requires exactly what he's supposed to do spelled out for him? I have to find grounds for relieving him from command of Invincible, *but I don't have any yet.*

There were a lot fewer people out and about at that hour, and most of those were at duty stations, so when someone else turned a corner ahead of him, Geary instantly noticed her.

Rione.

She hesitated, then came on toward him until both stopped, facing each other.

"How are you?" Geary asked.

"I've been worse."

Guilt stabbed at him. "Is there anything I can say or do?"

"I doubt it. It's what you did, what *we* did, that led to this." She looked away. "The fault is not yours. It wouldn't have been even if you had dragged me into your bed because I was willing. In fact, I did the seducing, not you. And I have been candid with my husband about that. But it's not just about your and my shared past." Rione lowered her gaze, her expression somber. "Something's changed in him. He's darker, harder, more angry."

"A lot of the former prisoners have serious issues to deal with," Geary said.

"I know. His are worse. Your fleet medical personnel are worried." She shook her head. "All he talks about is vengeance. Getting even with the Syndics, getting even with people back in the Callas Republic who he imagines once slighted him, and of course now getting even with you. But I am told that thus far his expressions of anger are within acceptable parameters." She gave the last words an ironic and bitter twist.

"What about you?"

"Me." Rione shrugged. "I don't know. For the sake of the man he once was, I will continue trying to reach him. He is now under no illusions that I will tolerate behavior such as you saw today. But he has trouble accepting that I am not the woman that I once was, that I became a senator and Co-President of the Callas Republic, that I have done many things while we were apart. In his mind, I was always at home, waiting for him, unchanging. How can I be angry with him for clinging to that vision to sustain him in the darkness of that labor camp? But how could he not know that I would not sit alone in a silent home, endlessly waiting, but instead go out to do what I could?"

"It can be very hard," Geary said slowly, "to learn how much the world you once knew has changed."

"You would know." Her expression and her voice were both growing distant, taking on a strange remoteness even though Rione stood beside him. "And things are always changing, even as they always stay the same. Never trust a politician, Admiral Geary."

"Not even you?"

A long pause before she answered. "Especially not me."

"What about the senators on the grand council?" The question he had been wanting to ask for some time.

Rione took even longer to answer this time. "A living hero can be a very inconvenient thing."

"Is that how the government still thinks?" Geary asked, letting his tone be as blunt as his words.

"The government." Rione breathed a single, soft laugh

though her expression didn't change. "You speak of 'the government' as if it were a single, monolithic beast of huge proportions, with countless hands but only a single brain controlling them. Turn that vision around, Admiral. Perhaps you should consider how things would be if the government was in fact a mammoth creature with a single tremendous hand but many brains trying to direct that hand in its powerful but clumsy efforts to do something, anything. You've seen the grand council at work. Which image seems more appropriate to you?"

"What's going on now? Why are you really here?"

"I am an emissary of the government of the Alliance." Her voice held not a hint of emotion.

"Who made you an emissary? Navarro?"

"Navarro?" She looked right at him again. "Do you think he would betray you?"

"No."

"You're right. Not knowingly. But he was tired, worn-out from his duties on the grand council. Look elsewhere, Admiral. Nothing is simple."

"We didn't come to Dunai because your husband was here. You didn't know he was one of the prisoners here. Who did we come for?"

Another long pause. "Are you looking for one person?" With that, Rione began walking down the passageway away from him.

"Would you withhold anything I needed to know to get you and your husband home safe again?" Geary called after her.

Rione didn't answer, walking steadily away.

HE had managed to deflect some of the numerous requests and demands for personal meetings relayed through Charban until *Dauntless* and the rest of the fleet jumped into the nothingness of jump space. Out of respect for the rank and service of the liberated prisoners, Geary had found time to meet with a number of them, finding the meetings often difficult since he could offer those officers none of the things they expected, and more than one kept insisting on those things anyway.

He had never before appreciated just how pleasant the isolated nothingness of jump space could be.

The work on *Dauntless* continued to clog passageways, but the slow progression of work areas provided evidence of progress, interspersed by sudden leaps across areas in which earlier battle damage had already resulted in extensive replacement of original system components. "Rebuild work on *Dauntless* is fifty-one percent complete," Captain Smythe had proudly declared before jump. "Of course, that last forty-nine percent might be a real bitch. We've done the easiest-to-access work first."

Soon afterward, Desjani had shown up at Geary's stateroom. She indicated the sailor beside her, a master chief petty officer whose girth had to be right on the upper edge of fleet body-fat standards. However, the master chief's uniform was immaculate, and he wore the ribbons for some impressive combat awards. "Admiral, have you met Master Chief Gioninni?"

Geary nodded, having encountered the stout master chief a number of times. "We've talked."

"In those conversations, did Master Chief Gioninni ever mention that while he has never been convicted of violating a single law or regulation, he is nonetheless widely rumored to be constantly juggling so many schemes and scams that the tactical systems on the average battle cruiser would have trouble keeping track of them all?"

"Captain, there's no evidence any of those rumors are true," Gioninni protested.

"If we could find the evidence, you'd be in the brig for about five hundred years, Master Chief." Desjani made a gesture in the general direction of the auxiliaries. "Master Chief Gioninni is, I believe, the perfect individual to monitor activities on some of the other ships in the fleet for anything contrary to regulations."

"On account of my professionalism and keen observational skills, that is, of course," the master chief explained.

"Of course," Geary agreed. He wondered if Gioninni was the reincarnation of a senior chief that he had known a century ago. "Why would anyone running his own schemes and scams be interested in reporting on similar activities being carried out by others? I'm asking on a purely theoretical basis, of course."

"Well, sir, speaking purely theoretically, of course," Gioninni said, "someone who might be doing such improper and unauthorized things wouldn't want too much competition, and he . . . or she . . . wouldn't want the competition to maybe try to dig up evidence against him . . . or her. Not that there could be any such evidence, of course."

"Of course." Geary kept a straight face with some difficulty. "I do need to know what your first priority is, Master Chief."

"My first priority, sir?" Gioninni thought for a moment. "Even supposing certain rumors were true, Admiral, I swear by the honor of all my ancestors that I would never allow anything that endangered this ship. Or any other ship. Or anyone on any ship, for that matter."

Geary looked toward Desjani, who nodded her belief in what Gioninni had said. "All right, then," Geary agreed. "Keep an eye on things and let us know if there's anything we should be told about."

"And if we find out you've cut any deals to keep quiet in exchange for a piece of the action, you might find yourself among your ancestors a lot sooner than you expected to be," Desjani added in her sternest manner.

"Yes, ma'am!" Master Chief Gioninni saluted, then marched off with perfect military bearing.

"You haven't managed to catch him at anything yet, eh?" Geary asked Desjani.

"Not yet. Maybe it's just as well. There are times when necessary items for the ship can't be acquired quickly enough through official channels. At times like that, Master

Chief Gioninni can be extremely useful. Not that he's ever been told to bypass proper procedures, of course."

"Of course."

AT point one light speed, it was a day and a half travel time from the jump point they arrived at to Hasadan's hypernet gate. Geary had to fight down constant urges to ramp up the fleet's velocity, to get to the gate faster and get to Midway faster and finally take the dive into alien space.

Just before entering the hypernet gate, Captain Tulev asked for a personal conference, an unusual thing for Tulev, who customarily kept his thoughts and feelings to himself. But now he seemed lost for words for a moment. "Admiral, there is something I wish to be certain that you are aware of concerning the prisoners from Dunai. One of them, Colonel Tukonov, is my cousin."

Geary himself had trouble thinking of what to say. Tulev's entire extended family had been thought killed in the war and the vicious Syndic bombardment of his home world. "That's very good news."

"Yes. Colonel Tukonov was thought dead, lost along with the rest of his unit nineteen years ago. Now he lives." Tulev struggled for words once again. "The dead come back to life. You. My cousin. The war ends. Humanity finds that we are not alone. These are extraordinary times."

"You're starting to sound like Tanya Desjani."

A small smile appeared on Tulev's lips. "There are worse fates, Admiral. She is a formidable woman."

" 'Formidable' is as good a word as any for her. Thanks for letting me know about your cousin. It's nice to know one good thing came out of our liberation of that prison camp."

Tulev pondered Geary's statement for a moment. "They are very active, but most of it consists of arguing among themselves. Too many of them believe that they should be the leader now."

"It's a good thing their high rank and status is also their

greatest weakness," Geary remarked. "We have a few on *Dauntless* that I'm thinking of sending to join the others on *Haboob* and *Mistral*."

"Including the husband of Emissary Rione?" Tulev asked. "Do not do that, Admiral."

"Why not?" Commander Benan hadn't been any trouble since the confrontation in the passageway, but it had still seemed like a good idea to put him on another ship.

"You have told me that Emissary Rione has orders to stay on *Dauntless* with you," Tulev explained. "You would be sending her husband away, while you and she remain on the same ship."

"Oh." Damn. That sounded really, really bad. "Maybe that's the last thing I should do."

"I am not wise in such matters, but I think that is so." Tulev straightened to attention, plainly ready to depart. "You are watching the liberated ones? My cousin will tell me some things, but I cannot be sure that he would be aware of any . . . disruptive actions any of them planned."

"We're keeping an eye on them," Geary assured him, but after Tulev's image vanished, Geary sat down heavily. *Lieutenant Iger has limited assets for monitoring what those former prisoners are up to. I used to be able to count on Rione's agents in the fleet to learn about brewing trouble. Not that those agents discovered everything. Not by a long shot.* For the first time, he wondered if those agents were still active and still reporting to Rione. *She hasn't said one word about them since returning to* Dauntless. *She's still avoiding the bridge most of the time, which at least makes Tanya happy.*

He went up to the bridge, taking his seat and scanning the display that automatically popped into existence before him. The fleet had remained in Formation November, the five rectangular subformations closing steadily on the huge hypernet gate no longer far distant.

Geary tapped the control to speak to the entire fleet. "This is Admiral Geary. The latest news from Midway is months old. Hopefully, the bloody nose we gave the aliens the last time we were there has kept them away, but there's a chance the aliens returned and have occupied the system. All ships are to be prepared for combat the moment we exit the gate at Midway. If the aliens are at the gate, they are to be regarded as hostile and engaged immediately."

That hadn't been an easy decision to make. It wasn't impossible that the Syndics at Midway could have reached some agreement with the chastened aliens, allowing the aliens peaceful access to the star system. Coming in with all weapons blazing might destroy a newly arranged peaceful coexistence. But that possibility didn't seem very likely given what they had learned about the aliens, and requiring his ships to get permission to fire would cost precious seconds and minutes that could literally mean the difference between life and death.

A thought that fortunately reminded him of something else that needed to be said. "The Syndics in Midway Star System are not hostile and are not to be engaged without prior authorization. There may well be a Syndic warship or courier ship waiting by the hypernet gate. That ship is not to be fired upon.

"Assuming that the aliens are not present there, this fleet will transit through Midway to the jump point used by the aliens, then proceed into areas of space occupied by the alien race. The ancestors of everyone in this fleet will surely be proud of their participation in this historic exploration. To the honor of our ancestors, Geary, out."

Desjani glanced his way. "You gave the Syndics at Midway the secret of the alien quantum worms. With that, they might have been able to defend themselves using that small flotilla."

"It's possible. Make sure your fingers don't twitch on the firing controls if we see a HuK when we emerge from the gate at Midway."

She managed to look hurt. "I only fire weapons when I want to."

"I know."

* * *

THE disorientation on leaving the hypernet wasn't nearly as bad as that when exiting jump. Within a second after the fleet arrived at Midway, Geary was focusing on his display as the fleet's sensors rapidly updated information.

Sure enough, a single Syndic ship hovered several light minutes from the gate. At least it was distant enough to ensure that none of the Alliance ships would "accidentally" squeeze off a few shots. It wasn't a Syndic warship, though, but a civilian ship whose presence hanging around the gate was unusual. The only other ships within a light hour of the gate were a few civilian freighters, heading in-system or toward the gate at the lumbering but fuel-efficient pace that cargo haulers favored.

Midway hadn't altered much. The same planets and other objects swung in their orbits around the star as they had for years beyond counting, oblivious to the humans who for a very short span of time considered themselves rulers of this star system. The Syndic flotilla guarding the star hadn't changed a great deal, still comprising six heavy cruisers, but now with five light cruisers instead of four and only twelve HuKs. There were no signs any battles had been fought here since the Alliance fleet had confronted the aliens over three months ago.

Where space around the star had once been full of other ships trying to evacuate human inhabitants before the alien race's assault force arrived, now only routine cargo and passenger shipping could be sighted.

"Why do you suppose they have fewer HuKs?" Geary asked Desjani. "There aren't signs of any other battles being fought here since we left."

She twisted her mouth in thought, then pointed to the area around the hypernet gate. "There isn't a HuK nearby. Standard Syndic practice is to have a HuK lingering around a jump point or a system's hypernet gate so it can function as a courier. They're using a civilian ship, instead." Desjani looked over at him. "They probably used some of those missing HuKs as couriers to the central government back at the Syndic home system, and I'd bet you the central government didn't send any of them back."

"What's left of the Syndic government needs every warship it can get. But so do the people here. So you think the locals stopped using warships as couriers when they realized that they were running out of HuKs?"

"Even Syndics should have been smart enough to figure that out," she said. "Eventually, anyway. They've picked up another light cruiser from somewhere, maybe one passing through that they convinced to stay. But remember that these Syndics had the flotilla protecting them yanked away by the central government to fight us. They know that flotilla won't be coming home, and they know the Syndic central government left them with practically nothing to defend themselves against the aliens."

"They must know they have to depend on themselves," Geary agreed. "I'll let them know we're just passing through and see if they have any new information about the aliens."

"If they do, they'll want something for it."

"Maybe they'll still have some gratitude for when we saved them."

Desjani didn't even bother answering that suggestion.

The primary world here was almost on the other side of its star now, lengthening transmission times a few minutes. Since the total distance between the fleet and that planet was on the order of five light hours, that didn't make much difference.

The Syndics had waited to hear from the Alliance ships before sending any messages, so their reply didn't show up until the fleet had been in the Midway Star System for half a day and was well on its way to the jump point for the star humans had named Pele but which had been abandoned to the aliens decades earlier.

CEO Iceni herself was seated at a desk, her eyes wary as she spoke, which was understandable enough. She was communicating, after all, with a large fleet belonging to the

Alliance, which the Syndicate Worlds had been fighting bitterly for decade upon decade before the recent peace treaty. "I extend my personal greetings to Admiral Geary. In response to your question, we have not detected any activity by the enigma race since the departure of your fleet. It is the desire of the people here that this situation continue. We have no wish to provoke the enigma race into renewed offensive action.

"Please inform me of the reason for the return of your fleet to this star system after only a few months' absence.

"The people of Midway do of course remain grateful for your defense of this star system. However, you are a fleet belonging to a foreign power. Ambiguous wording in the peace treaty may allow this movement, but it is not the desire of the people of the Midway Star System that the Alliance consider such incursions into our star system to be routine. We will closely monitor your movements and insist that in the future, any visit to this star system by foreign warships be cleared in advance."

"You're welcome," Desjani muttered.

General Charban and Rione had come to the bridge, expecting to be there when the reply arrived from the Syndics. "She didn't threaten us," Charban pointed out, as if that were the height of courtesy.

"That's understandable," Geary said. "Unlike that idiot at Dunai, she wants to preserve what little defensive capability she has."

"I believe," Rione said, "that Iceni is much brighter than the CEO in the Dunai Star System. She knows a bluff against us would be stupid, so she's not trying. That's one thing that she didn't do." Rione gave Geary a searching look. "The other thing is that CEO Iceni did not say she would report our transit through this star system to the Syndicate Worlds' central government."

"What's left of the Syndicate Worlds' central government, you mean." Geary frowned, his eyes going to his display of their own accord. "We've been wondering why there wasn't a HuK posted near the hypernet gate to serve as a courier. We thought they'd simply decided to stop sending them back to the central government when none returned."

"That is probably one of the reasons, but I would urge you to consider the possibility that CEO Iceni is also deliberately distancing herself from the Syndicate Worlds' government with a goal of establishing an independent star system here."

"There have already been plenty of other star-system CEOs who have done the same. Assuming she succeeds, why does it matter to us?"

Charban looked pained. "Our treaty is with the Syndicate Worlds' government. Iceni might argue that her regime wasn't bound by that treaty and might demand that we renegotiate everything."

As if reading Geary's mind, Rione shook her head. "We can't treat this star system as we did Dunai. We want to come back here as often as necessary, and we want a stable star system with a stable government anchoring this part of human space facing the aliens. We could do worse than a government headed by Iceni."

"She's a Syndic CEO," Geary pointed out.

"One who chose to remain on her world with the bulk of its people when it was threatened by the aliens rather than flee on the fastest available ship crammed with all the treasure she could pack into it," Rione said. "She appears to have not only courage, but also some sense of duty to the people she leads."

"A Syndic CEO?" Desjani muttered.

"Syndic CEOs," Rione said to Geary, "like Alliance politicians, and fleet officers, are individuals. Each must be judged on their own merits, or lack thereof."

"Iceni doesn't want us to go into alien territory," Geary said, "but I don't want to lie to her about our plans, especially when it's obvious that we're heading for the jump point for Pele."

"Then don't lie," Rione said tonelessly. "Lying doesn't become Black Jack Geary under any circumstances."

Desjani gave her a sharp look, but she couldn't object to the words.

So Geary told the truth when he responded to Iceni. "We are en route to Pele, and from there intend to penetrate farther into alien space in order to learn more about the enigma race and hopefully establish peaceful relations."

It was well into the next day before he heard from CEO Iceni again, taking the message this time alone in his stateroom because the message was addressed to his eyes only. Transmission times had shrunk a bit, to only about four hours each way, which was at best a hard means of carrying on a conversation. Iceni had an expression that veiled her feelings, keeping them hidden without being obvious about it. She could teach the Alliance politicians, including Rione, a few tricks in that regard. "I will be blunt, Admiral Geary, because I know from your reputation and our previous conversations that you are not someone who likes to play extended word games. You intend taking your fleet into space controlled by the enigma race. I don't like that. We have enough problems here without worrying about an aroused and angry enemy in that area. But I am fully aware that I have no means of stopping you, or even hindering the movement of your fleet in any significant way."

Iceni leaned forward a bit, her eyes intent. "It is clear that you intend making use of the loophole in the peace treaty to use Midway Star System as a forward base for accessing alien space. Clearly, also, you would benefit from our active cooperation in that. I am willing to discuss such an agreement between this star system and you, on a mutually beneficial basis. I have more to offer than simply our agreement and support for your fleet's movements through Midway. There is something else I have that you need. In exchange, there is something I need from you. I will discuss a bargain, but only directly with you. Respond on this same channel, no other, if you wish to engage in negotiations with me. For the people, Iceni, out."

Now what? Ask Rione? She had stopped providing advice except in rare circumstances, and in any case, Iceni only wanted to deal directly with him. Charban might have political authority because of his emissary status, but Geary hadn't been impressed by Charban's well-meaning but unpracticed attempts at diplomacy.

What was it that Iceni had that she was certain Geary needed? Was that just bait to get him to respond to her, or something he, or this fleet, really needed?

Finally, he sent a response. "CEO Iceni, I am willing to speak with you on any matter. Be aware that I will not agree to anything contrary to the welfare of the Alliance. If you want to negotiate some kind of basing agreement, I will have to get the emissaries of the Alliance government involved. Please spell out your offer and what you want in return. To the honor of our ancestors, Geary, out."

WITH a turnaround time of eight hours, there wasn't any sense in waiting for a reply. He went back to work, trying to concentrate on administrative matters, until Desjani called. "A shuttle from *Tanuki* brought us some more parts, and a visitor for you. It's holding at the dock until you're done with your meeting."

"A visitor?" Captain Smythe himself, come to evaluate in person the work being done?

"Lieutenant Shamrock," Desjani replied dryly.

Lieutenant Jamenson's green hair seemed somehow subdued as she sat down opposite Geary. "Admiral, there's a matter on which Captain Smythe said I should brief you."

"A problem with the repairs to the fleet?"

"No, sir." Jamenson paused, as if uncertain how to proceed. "I told you that besides confusing things, I can unconfuse things. Captain Smythe . . . likes to keep abreast of everything going on, so he monitors a lot of traffic not specifically addressed to him or his command."

"I see." Meaning that while still at Varandal, Captain Smythe had been tapping into Alliance communications not intended for him. Somehow that wasn't too big a surprise. Technically, it was a violation of security rules and communications procedures, but in practice Smythe wasn't the only commanding officer who kept his or her eye out for things they might need to know even though they didn't have a formally established need to know. Besides, it never hurt to make sure that you knew something you needed to know about even if it hadn't been addressed to you specifically.

"We had a large amount of such messages backlogged from before we left Alliance space," Jamenson continued. "I've been getting to them slowly because there's a lot of minutiae in them, little details and unknown program codes and funding streams I don't recognize. But I think . . . I'm certain that I've identified a pattern in many of those messages."

Her attitude wasn't reassuring in the least. "Something concerning this fleet?"

"I don't know, Admiral. In a nutshell, there's still new construction of warships under way within the Alliance."

"We knew that," Geary said. "Completing full hulls that were almost finished."

"No, sir. Much more than that." Jamenson hesitated again. "I can't be absolutely sure of how much, but from the number of project codes, contract references, and funding streams, there seem to be at least a dozen battleships and a dozen battle cruisers being built, including some extensive new modification work on partially completed hulls, plus enough heavy cruisers, light cruisers, and destroyers to serve as escorts."

He just looked back at her for a long time, trying to fit Jamenson's information into what he had already known. What he had *thought* he already knew. "This is being kept hidden?"

"Yes, Admiral. We weren't supposed to see any of the messages concerning the construction, and it's all hidden in a mess of details. There aren't any single contract identifiers. It was hard to figure out what was really happening."

Another long pause as Geary tried to think. "Auxiliaries. Are any of those being built?"

"Um." Jamenson looked startled, then thought. "I haven't identified any indications of new construction for auxiliaries, Admiral."

Was that why headquarters had tried to yank the bulk of his auxiliary force? Or were these new ships intended only for defense of the Alliance and not for any offensive operations outside Alliance space, where auxiliaries would be needed?

Why had this construction been kept secret from him? Why had the grand council and everyone else told him that no new ships were being constructed? And what were these extensive modifications? Were the new ships being built for long hull lives? Which would mean that someone *had* realized what would be happening to the short-hull-life warships in Geary's fleet.

Jamenson was watching him worriedly, biting her lower lip.

Finally, Geary nodded to her. "Thank you, Lieutenant. This is important information, and your ability to pull it all together means we know about it. Is there anything else?"

"No, sir. That's all I can say at this point."

"But you do feel confident in saying that twenty-four major warships are under construction, along with sufficient escorts for those warships."

"Yes, sir. I can lay out all the details for you, Admiral."

"Just leave them with me." Geary paused again. "Please thank Captain Smythe for his foresight in telling me about this. Do we have any indications about how much the bureaucracy back home has figured out what *we're* doing to fix up this fleet?"

"No, sir, I'm sorry. Before we left, we saw no signs they had picked up on anything yet, though. I'm really working hard to confuse everything."

"I never thought that I'd be thanking a lieutenant for working so hard at that." Geary gave her his best look of approval. "Damn good job, Lieutenant Jamenson. Thank you," he repeated.

He would probably have to give her a medal when all

was said and done because her efforts would make such a huge difference in the readiness of the fleet. But how would he word the citation? *Under trying operational conditions and with limited resources, Lieutenant Jamenson success-fully and repeatedly confused higher authority, ensuring that superiors in the chain of command were totally unable to figure out what was actually happening.* Many junior officers (and more than a few senior officers) had inadver-tently done that in the past, but Jamenson might be the first to get a medal for deliberately doing it.

Twelve battleships and twelve battle cruisers. Something to keep quiet from the taxpayers, perhaps, and certainly something that the Syndics should be kept from knowing. But why the effort to keep him and presumably many others unaware of it?

CEO Iceni was smiling slightly, with the look of a partner, or of a co-conspirator. "I'll lay out what I want from you, Admiral Geary, then what I can offer in return, and you can decide if it's a fair bargain. I assure you, I'm not asking for anything you could not provide.

"What this star system is most in need of is your protec-tion from the enigma race. I believe I am safe in saying that the same provision of the peace treaty that your fleet is using to justify being able to travel freely through Syndicate Worlds' space to this star system could also be read to be an open-ended commitment by the Alliance to defend this star system from the enigmas."

That was a turnabout that Geary hadn't suspected. He had a feeling that this was another one of those "lawyers could argue indefinitely" issues, but if the Syndics could point to what the average person would interpret as an ongo-ing Alliance commitment to the defense of Midway, it would be hard to just disregard that interpretation. Especially when the Alliance was exploiting the same provision for its own ends.

"Beyond that," Iceni continued, as if the defense issue

were settled, "I would like your passive support and your active forbearance. My knowledge of the Alliance's remaining strength is far from complete, and the central government of the Syndicate Worlds has refused to provide specific information to us about their own strength right now, but I believe that I am safe in saying that you, and your fleet, are the dominant force in human space at this time. If it is implied or uncertain whether this star system is under your protection, it will give pause to anyone, human or not, who wishes to threaten us."

Human or not. Iceni shouldn't expect any threat from the Alliance. The only other dangers she would face aside from the aliens would be nearby star systems led by CEOs who had struck out on their own and started threatening their neighbors, and the remnants of Syndicate Worlds' central authority.

"Your active forbearance is critical as well." Iceni gestured to a star display next to her, which was centered on the Syndicate Worlds' home star system. "The central government has its hands full trying to maintain control of the star systems it still has. Every ship that arrives here brings reports of more star systems that are . . . seeking autonomy. The Syndicate Worlds' government cannot possibly force them all back under its control, not with the small forces remaining to it in the aftermath of your campaigns, Admiral Geary. But some star systems are more valuable than others. I know how badly the central government will want to retain control of *this* star system, both because of the hypernet gate here and because of its strategic location."

Iceni paused, clearly giving him time to think through her words. "Your help would be welcome in supporting the efforts of the people of this star system to find the freedom and independence the Alliance has always championed."

Is she actually going to ask my help in declaring independence from the Syndicate Worlds? Though I notice she mentioned freedom and independence as matters of importance to the Alliance but didn't say anything about democracy. I doubt that was an accidental oversight. And I doubt that she means freedom in terms of liberty for the average citizens of this star system.

"I understand," Iceni continued, "that active support of our endeavors may be impossible without clearly violating the peace treaty. All I ask is that you refuse to assist the central government of the Syndicate Worlds when they come to you saying that it is vital for the defense of human space that this star system remain firmly in their control."

Rione had been right. Iceni did plan on independence for this star system. Or rather independence for herself as ruler of this star system.

"Now," Iceni said, looking straight into the camera in what must be a remarkably good imitation of someone with nothing to hide, "there is the matter of what I offer in return." The display beside her changed, showing the Midway hypernet gate. "All of the gates in the hypernet system constructed by the Syndicate Worlds now have the safe-fail mechanisms on them, but as you are aware, all that does is limit the immediate damage if the gates collapse. Every time a gate collapses, we lose part of our hypernet, and our defense capability is harmed, as is our trade and other aspects of our economies. If the enigma race chose to collapse the entire hypernet constructed by the Syndicate Worlds, as we believe they could, the long-term impact would be horrendous. It is our assessment that the enigmas have refrained from this step only because they are trying to find a means of canceling out the effects of the safe-fail mechanisms so that the collapse of gates can once more cause the death of entire human star systems."

Geary stared at Iceni's image, grateful that she couldn't see his reaction. Collapse the entire hypernet? That wouldn't directly cause damage, but the tactic was so obvious now that Iceni had mentioned it. Once the aliens knew that humanity wasn't going to annihilate itself using the gates as weapons, there was no reason for them to continue allowing humanity all of the benefits from the hypernet systems.

Iceni made a dismissive gesture. "I realize that the Alliance must have reached the same conclusions and be working on its own defense against the loss of its hypernet system. However, we *already* have one, a mechanism that actually blocks the collapse command, so that each individual gate as well as the system as a whole is impervious to that form of alien attack. It has been tested. It does work."

Was the Alliance working on such a system? How could they not be? Was that why he had been ordered to detach those hypernet-knowledgeable personnel? But Commander Neeson had been certain that the fleet's personnel were not expert enough to make any difference to any Alliance efforts. Not with Captain Cresida dead.

But removing those personnel from the fleet would have gone a long way to ensuring that the fleet had no means of even realizing this particular threat might exist. As well as no means of constructing a device such as Iceni now offered.

Geary's eyes went to his own star display, imagining a journey back to Alliance space from Midway the hard way, jumping star to star, a distance well more than twice that which the fleet had covered in its withdrawal from the Syndic home star system. Even without the constant threat of attack, it would be a long and arduous trek, cut off from home the entire time. Fuel, food . . . how could he acquire what he needed for such a long journey without taking it under threat of violence?

And what if the fleet had returned to Midway from alien space, low on supplies and possibly battered by combat, to find that instead of a fast journey home, it would require close to a year?

Had the government realized that risk existed and thought the need to learn more about the aliens justified dealing with it? But why hadn't they told him about it? And why had fleet headquarters tried to yank the majority of his auxiliary support just before departure from Varandal, when that risk made having the maximum possible auxiliary support vital? Was that the reason the auxiliaries had been ordered away from him, and not the issue of supporting the new construction warships? Or was it a matter of both?

Why would the government and headquarters risk

stranding the vast majority of its fleet as far from Alliance territory as existed within human space? Stranding the fleet and . . . stranding him.

A living hero can be a very inconvenient thing.

He became aware that Iceni was speaking once again. "I'm sure that you appreciate the value of what I am offering to you. All you need do in exchange for the design of this extremely important system is to remain silent when it is implied that this star system is under your protection against *all* aggression, and to refuse any request by the Syndicate Worlds' central government for assistance if they seek to attack the peace-loving people of this star system."

Her smile took on the completely insincere cast of a standard Syndic CEO expression. "You see that this is a humanitarian issue as well as a matter of self-interest. I am willing to accept your . . . word of . . . honor on this matter. Simply say that is what you will do, and the design will be transmitted to you.

"I await your agreement, Admiral Geary. For the people, Iceni, out."

He covered his face with his hands, thoughts racing. *The government wouldn't be bound by any commitments of that nature that I made, but it seems Iceni believes, just like Badaya and his followers, that I'm actually running things in the Alliance now. Saying that I take my orders from the Alliance government is true, but she won't believe that's the real reason.*

The Alliance government that may have tried to strand me and the fleet out here. What would the aliens do when we penetrated their space? That could have triggered the wholesale collapse of the Syndicate Worlds' hypernet. Didn't anybody think about that? Is this a case of deliberate malice or just lack of foresight? The fiasco with that courts-martial message was proof enough that there are people in authority who aren't thinking through the implications of what they do, but when things keep happening, it forms a very disturbing pattern.

How much had Rione known?

Ironically, the Syndics had probably used the information that Geary had given them about the alien worms to develop their mechanism, along with the design of the safe-collapse system first developed by Cresida and leaked to the Syndics to ensure their gates wouldn't be used as weapons by the enigmas against the Alliance fleet. Or maybe it wasn't ironic at all. Those gestures had seemed the right thing to do. Humanitarian in the real sense of the word, and a means to ensure that the Syndics in Midway had a meaningful chance to defend themselves, as well as being aimed at aiding and protecting the Alliance. Thanks to those gestures, he had the opportunity to acquire what might be a critically important breakthrough. If the Alliance, absorbed in internal political squabbles, hadn't figured out that particular threat, or if it simply hadn't figured out how to build a device like that yet, wasn't it his responsibility to ensure that he brought back this Syndic countermeasure?

Iceni wasn't even asking for anything in writing. Well, of course not. She was clearly too smart to commit agreements to paper when her own government would consider those agreements to be treasonous. It had been saddening as well as instructive to see Iceni grope for the term "word of honor," an expression she plainly wasn't used to using. For a moment, he wondered what Syndic CEOs used among themselves as a guarantee that agreements would be honored.

I can't ask for advice on this one. If I reach an agreement with Iceni, it might be regarded as contrary to regulations, exceeding my authority, and unlawfully committing the Alliance to actions regarding the internal affairs of the Syndicate Worlds. Anyone I talk to before I make that decision would be implicated in it.

I have to decide alone, so no one else can take a hit for my decision.

He called up a report prepared by intelligence based on message intercepts in this star system and started reading it again. Iceni was still senior CEO here. No surprise there. The second-most-powerful CEO in the star system was the commander of the ground forces, a man named Drakon. Not much was known about him, but he had been involved in several battles along the border with the Alliance and been rated as highly effective by Alliance intelligence, before being mysteriously transferred to an assignment at the Syndic equivalent of the back end of nowhere.

Geary thought of Jason Boyens, the captured Syndic CEO they had brought back to Midway, who said that he had been assigned here, far from the front with the Alliance, as a form of exile. *I wonder who Drakon ticked off and what he did?*

Also listed was a CEO named Hardrad, who apparently commanded the internal security forces in the star system and whose status ranked parallel to Iceni and Drakon. From what he had seen, Syndic internal security forces wielded immense power. They always had, but that power had been enhanced during the long war, and in some Syndic star systems that had included nuclear weapons as an ultimate safeguard against mass rebellion by planetary populations. He wondered how Iceni planned to handle Hardrad, or if she had already turned him so he would support her.

In other star systems, he had seen firsthand the results of attempts to declare independence from the Syndicate Worlds, the open warfare between military factions, civilian groups, and internal security forces. He hated to think of Midway suffering the same fate, but that was a matter beyond his control.

The report listed more names of sub-CEOs who had been identified in Syndic message traffic, but offered little other information besides a fragmentary order of battle for ground forces and a complete listing of Syndic warships in the star system.

No answers there. Geary went for a walk, down to the spaces deep inside *Dauntless*, where worship rooms awaited those seeking privacy. He sat down in a vacant room, lighting the ceremonial candle. *Honored ancestors, you know the decision I must make. What is your guidance?*

He waited, felt nothing, rephrased the question, felt nothing, and finally snuffed out the candle and left.

Outside, he almost bumped into a sailor hastening into the rooms. With an almost comical expression of alarm, the sailor straightened to attention and saluted. "Excuse me, Admiral!"

"Not a problem," Geary replied, waving the sailor past. "You've obviously got some urgent questions to ask."

"Nothing that urgent, sir." The sailor smiled sheepishly. "Just me and . . . uh . . . a friend. Whether . . . you know. Personal things. I know the important stuff already, because you're in command, and you'll get us home. That's what my parents asked, will you get home? And I said Admiral Geary's in command, and they knew that meant the fleet would be all right."

"Thank you." He stood there a moment while the sailor rushed onward. Maybe his ancestors had provided an answer. *You'll get us home.* Regardless of what happened to him, what was most likely to get these ships and sailors home again?

Back in his stateroom, Geary tried to project matter-of-fact confidence as he sent an answer to Iceni. "I agree to your proposal. I will not provide any specific commitment to defense of this star system from attack by anyone but the enigma race, but you have my word of honor that I will also avoid outright denying such a commitment. I cannot guarantee that this fleet or other Alliance assets will not be ordered by our government to assist the Syndicate Worlds' central government in reestablishing control of this star system, but I will argue against allowing this fleet to be used in that way, and I will not command such a force.

"In exchange, in addition to the mechanism you have promised to provide, I want a commitment from you that you will not attempt to claim the support of this fleet for your own actions, or declare any backing by me for your plans. If you publicly claim such backing, I will repudiate it. And if you commit atrocities against your own people or attack other star systems, I will regard this agreement as void."

One other thing. "I would appreciate being apprised of

what happened to CEO Boyens after he was released. I await your agreement to my terms and the receipt of the plans for the collapse-prevention mechanism."

Less than ten minutes after the transmission, Geary's hatch alert chimed. He allowed entry, surprised to see Lieutenant Iger there. What could have required the intelligence officer to personally visit Geary's stateroom?

"Admiral," Iger said, visibly nervous, "there is a matter concerning a superior officer that I am required to take action on."

TEN

"**EXCUSE** me?" Geary asked. Had intelligence been monitoring his own transmissions? Was this the sort of loyalty policing he had heard about but had trouble believing would actually take place in the Alliance fleet?

Iger's nervousness increased. The man was more uncomfortable than Geary had ever seen him. "A . . . a matter concerning a superior officer, Admiral. I am required to report it to you, sir."

"Report it to *me*?" It wasn't about him, then. "Who are we talking about?"

"One of the captains, Admiral. One of the battle cruiser commanders."

Geary went rigid, staring at Iger. "What is this? Nothing like Captain Kila, is it?"

"No, sir!" Iger shook his head rapidly. "I'm sorry, sir. No. Nothing like that, but it is something I must report to you," he said for the third time.

It couldn't be easy making what must be a negative report about a superior officer. Forcing himself to calm down,

Geary nodded. "Let that be a lesson to you on how not to break news to me, Lieutenant. Which officer is this?"

"Commander Bradamont, sir. Commanding officer of *Dragon*."

Bradamont? Someone whom Desjani herself now trusted? "What has Commander Bradamont done?"

"Sir, Commander Bradamont has accessed the intelligence analysis we did regarding the Syndic military capabilities in this star system."

The same one that Geary had looked at a little while ago. "She . . . wanted to know about the military capabilities of a potential opponent? One of my battle cruiser commanders wanted to know about Syndic military forces in this star system?"

"Yes, sir."

"Exactly why is that a problem, Lieutenant Iger?"

Iger, who had been relaxing slightly in response to Geary's attitude, now grew more uncomfortable again. "Even though her position authorizes Commander Bradamont to access the report, and she has an obvious need to know the information, there's a security flag on Commander Bradamont's record, Admiral. I don't know if you're aware—"

"You mean when she was a prisoner of the Syndics?" He had accepted what Desjani had told him of the matter rather than dig into Bradamont's record personally, but it wasn't surprising to hear that security had kept a special watch on her. "I thought that was resolved."

"It was, sir, but we're still required to report under certain circumstances, and . . . sir, have you had the opportunity to review the analysis we did of Syndic military forces in this star system?"

He almost smiled at the extremely careful way in which Iger had asked if Geary had actually read the report yet. "Yes. I just reviewed it again a few minutes ago. What about it generates concern in the case of Commander Bradamont?"

"One of the Syndic military officers in this star system,

Admiral," Iger explained. "A sub-CEO fourth grade. His name is Donal Rogero. We believe that's the same Syndicate Worlds' officer with whom Commander Bradamont . . . uh . . . became . . . uh . . . involved while in captivity."

"Oh. I see."

"I'm required to report the matter to you," Lieutenant Iger continued apologetically. "Even though it involves a superior officer."

"I understand." He did as far as Iger's actions went. But what was Bradamont up to? "Is there any reason I can't ask Commander Bradamont about this directly?"

"No, sir. I'm not authorized to pursue the matter without approval, but there's no restriction on your actions aside from the normal rules and regulations. Nothing classified is involved of which Commander Bradamont isn't already aware."

"All right. Thank you. I appreciate your informing me of the matter, and doing so in an appropriate manner. I don't see any need for you to pursue it further." He had to say it that way to let Iger know that reporting adversely on a senior officer was indeed an unpleasant duty but that Iger had handled it properly.

The relieved lieutenant left for the sanctuary of the intelligence compartments, and as the hatch sealed again, Geary made another call, to *Dragon*. "I require a private meeting with Commander Bradamont. Have her call me as soon as she's ready."

Barely five minutes later, Bradamont's image appeared in Geary's stateroom. She saluted, giving no indication of anything but curiosity. "Yes, Admiral? A private meeting? Is it concerning *Dragon*?"

"No, Commander." Geary stayed standing, and so did she. Until he knew more, anything less formal didn't feel right. "It concerns a personal matter that also bears on your professional duties."

She didn't blink an eye, though the curiosity faded. "Rogero."

"That's right. Are you trying to determine whether the

Sub-CEO Rogero in this star system is the same man you had a relationship with while a prisoner of the Syndics?"

"I am fairly certain that he is that man, Admiral. The last I heard, he was under a CEO named Drakon, who was transferred to this side of Syndic space as punishment for getting on the wrong side of some very powerful Syndic CEOs."

Geary paused. Bradamont knew more about Drakon's status than the intelligence report that he had just read? What did that mean? "Commander, are you just curious? Or do you intend doing something about it if this is the same Rogero?"

Bradamont paused before replying. "I don't know, sir."

"Are you still in love with him?"

Another pause. "Yes, sir." She eyed him defiantly. "We're not at war with them anymore."

"No," Geary agreed. "But we're not exactly one big, happy family."

"Admiral, I'll swear by anything you want that I will not do anything contrary to my duties as an officer of the fleet, and that I will never fail in any aspect of my responsibilities as commanding officer of an Alliance warship. I will be happy to repeat that oath inside an interrogation compartment so there can be no doubt of my sincerity."

She certainly looked sincere, and if there had been any doubt on either of those counts, Bradamont never would have been passed by security to return to the fleet. "I don't think use of an interrogation compartment will be necessary, Commander. Can I ask you a personal question? Another one, I mean. We've fought the Syndics with you on *Dragon*. Did it ever worry you that Rogero might be on one of the Syndic warships we were engaging?"

"I could not afford to think about that, sir." Bradamont met his eyes. "I had my duty to do, and I knew he would understand that."

"Understand being killed by you in combat? Not every man would be that understanding, Commander Bradamont."

"He understands *duty*, Admiral. That's one of the reasons

why—" She gave him a straight look. "You want to ask another personal question, I know, how I came to fall in love with a Syndic officer."

"That's not my business," Geary said, though in truth he was curious.

"I'll tell you because I think you're more willing to accept what I say than others are." She looked to one side, not just as if gathering memories but also as if she was looking into the past. "A number of newly captured prisoners, myself among them, were being transported to the world holding the Syndic labor camp where we'd be held. The Syndic ship suffered a serious accident. We all very likely would have died. Rogero was in command of the Syndic ground forces also being transported on that ship. He ordered us freed from confinement to save us, then allowed us to work alongside the ship's crew to save the ship and ourselves." Bradamont gazed at Geary once more. "For this, he was punished with removal from command."

"He broke the rules."

"Yes. His superiors said he should have let us die. I know this because several of us were required to testify to events that day. Against our will, but in individual interrogation units we could hardly concoct consistent lies. For his punishment, Rogero not only lost his command of a ground forces unit but was also assigned to the labor camp as one of the Syndic officials there. That was a Syndic idea of a joke, Admiral. Since Rogero had cared enough about us to save us, he would be forced to be one of our jailers."

It made sense. "He was one of the senior Syndic officers at the camp, and you were one of the senior Alliance officers, so you had contact again on a regular basis."

"Yes, sir, and I knew something of his character from the actions that had resulted in his being there." Bradamont paused. "You and . . . Captain Desjani . . . are probably best suited to understand how I felt when I realized my feelings. It was not . . . something that I sought or welcomed. When I discovered he felt the same about me . . . impossible. He is a decent, honorable man, Admiral, even though he was trained to act differently. But . . . we both remained true to our duty. I never betrayed my oath to the Alliance, I never dishonored my ancestors, no matter what some—" She broke off.

"I see. The Syndics obviously took it poorly, too. You were sent to another prison camp, and he was exiled out here."

"Not initially. CEO Drakon had some pull back then and was eventually able to get Rogero back under his command, after I had left that labor camp. Admiral . . ." She hesitated longer this time. "There is a highly classified matter, involving Alliance intelligence and myself. I doubt that anyone in this fleet is aware of it, or was ever read into it. But I can't in good conscience leave you as my fleet commander unaware of it. The Syndics were allowed to believe that my feelings for Rogero had turned my loyalties. I have been feeding them occasional reports for years, through Alliance intelligence, which always provided me with the supposed secrets and misleading information that I was purportedly leaking to Rogero."

Another surprise. "What did the Alliance get from this? Just a channel to send bogus secrets to the Syndics?"

"And messages that occasionally came back from Rogero, supposedly providing intelligence on Syndic activities." She shook her head. "I have long suspected the messages from Rogero weren't really from him, and that if they were, they also contained no real secrets, just disinformation, both sides playing the same game so both could imagine success while neither actually benefited."

"Do you have any proof of what you're telling me?"

Bradamont shook her head again. "No, sir. Just the contact information for my Alliance intelligence handlers, back in Alliance space."

"That's a dangerous game to play." Geary finally sat down, eyeing her. "Is it possible that Lieutenant Iger has anything based on what Rogero reported? Do you know what Alliance intelligence reports called him?"

"Red Wizard, Admiral."

"Do you have a cover name that was used in those reports?"

"White Witch, sir."

Geary reached for his controls. "Lieutenant Iger. Do you have any intelligence reporting on file that was sourced to a Syndic source code-named Red Wizard?"

Iger couldn't prevent a baffled frown, but turned slightly to consult his database before turning a now-surprised look on Geary. "Yes, sir, but I have no record that you've ever been read into that program, sir. You would have been provided any information derived from it, but that source and code name is tightly restricted."

"Do you know the real name of that source?"

"No, sir. That wouldn't be in the files on any ship, to prevent it from being compromised in the unlikely event any of our files survived the ship being destroyed or captured."

"Has Commander Bradamont ever been read into that program?" Geary asked.

"No, sir! With her . . . background that would be . . . very unusual. With a security flag on her record, it wouldn't happen."

"Do you have anything on a source named White Witch?"

Iger checked, looking uncomfortable again. "Admiral, I have to ask where you're hearing these code names. These are highly restricted compartments."

"Is White Witch related in any way to Red Wizard?"

"Yes . . . sir, though the identity of that source is also not available to me. Admiral, I really have to insist that I can't talk about this any more unless you're formally read into these programs and sign the necessary security agreements."

"That's all right. Thank you." Geary ended the call and waved Bradamont to a seat. "What you told me checks out. Now what, Commander? If Rogero was sending you information, contacting him directly now might create problems for him."

"I agree, sir."

But I need to know what's happening in this star system.

"I'll be candid with you, Commander. If Rogero was willing to tell us about the situation in this star system, it would be worth a great deal. The senior CEO is up to something, and we have no idea what the positions of the other Syndic CEOs are."

Bradamont sat silent for a moment. "I don't wish to use him, sir, but I suspect both he and I understand how we've already been used by our governments. If I send him a personal message, he can choose how to respond. If we end up in contact, perhaps a means of passing information can be established, if he so chooses and does not believe that would conflict with his own honor."

"His honor?" Geary questioned without thinking, then gritted his teeth.

But Bradamont just smiled slightly. "I know the idea of a Syndic with a sense of honor is a difficult concept to grasp, sir. But he is just a sub-CEO, not a full-ranked CEO."

"My apologies, anyway. I feel obligated to point out that news of your message to Rogero might somehow get around the fleet."

Her smile grew wry. "What are they going to say about me that they haven't already said?"

He glanced to one side, where Bradamont's record hung in a window next to him. She had served well in the past. Tulev's evaluations of her were glowing, and when Geary had reviewed the battles in which *Dragon* had fought under Bradamont's command, he had found nothing to fault and much to admire. "Very well. Have your message sent to *Dauntless*. We'll forward it to the Syndics, so there's no question about your superiors being aware of it, with instructions to the Syndics to send the reply through us."

"I have no objections to that, Admiral. White Witch is a part of me that I would have happily seen retired long ago."

"Commander, if you hope to bring Rogero home with us when this fleet returns—"

"I don't think that's realistic, sir." Bradamont's voice grew wistful for a moment before taking on a professional lack of feeling again. "But if the messages I received from

Rogero are true, then this CEO Drakon is as good a commander as Rogero might find. He's supposedly loyal to those under his command. That somehow led to his disgrace and transfer here."

"Do you know anything about Drakon's relationship with Iceni?"

"No, sir. I'll see what I can find out."

DR. Setin had a querulous expression. "Admiral, how much longer until we encounter the enigma race?"

"We're heading for the jump point to a star controlled by them, Doctor," Geary assured him.

"Many of my colleagues are concerned about the violent nature of much of the human interaction with the enigma race to date."

"Believe me, Doctor, I'm concerned about it, too."

ICENI was smiling again. "I have no hesitation in promising to abide by your conditions, Admiral Geary."

No further bargaining, just an immediate promise. He was really starting to distrust politicians who quickly agreed to something. But he could always repudiate any claims beyond the terms of what he had agreed to, and Iceni's words would not bind him if they weren't true. Who would take the word of a Syndic CEO over his?

"The information you requested is being transmitted separately," Iceni continued. "That transmission identifies the gift of the design as a thanks for the services your forces have rendered to the defense of this star system. If your experts have any questions about the design or its operation, contact me using this same connection.

"As for CEO Boyens, he's not here. Not in this star system, I mean. He rode one of the courier ships back to the home star system, where he thought his information and experiences might prove to his advantage with the new government." Her smile twisted a little. "CEO Boyens is an ambitious man. I'm afraid that I can't tell you anything else. We have not heard from him since his departure. Our communications with the central government and the home star system have been sporadic over the last few months."

Her smile faded, replaced by what seemed to be real concern. "I will not attempt to minimize my worries about what might happen to your fleet inside enigma space, Admiral Geary. The Syndicate Worlds has lost many ships there, vanished without a trace. But that was before the discovery of the quantum worms. This time may be different. I cannot dictate your actions, but I ask you to keep in mind the welfare of my people when deciding on what to do, and if you have the opportunity to reach any agreements with the enigmas. I am providing you in another separate transmission with the latest information we have on file for the star systems now within enigma space, not because I must, but because we are allies in this matter, strange as that may seem, whether we will it or not. If you reference on any other communication channel our agreement, anything we have discussed here, or anything I have provided through this channel, I will deny any knowledge of it. For the people, Iceni, out."

THE Syndic flotilla, as hugely outnumbered as it was, had shadowed the Alliance fleet at a distance of two light hours all the way to the jump point. Before ordering the jump, Geary checked again to see if any reply had come from Rogero. But there had been nothing. The fleet's sensors hadn't picked up any unusual activity among the Syndics, so whatever Iceni was planning apparently wouldn't happen while the Alliance fleet was in this star system.

He called Commander Neeson on *Implacable*. "Have you finished analyzing that Syndic collapse-prevention system?"

"Yes, sir. It should work." Neeson pursed his lips. "I'm surprised that we didn't hear about anything similar being developed by the Alliance before we left, sir."

"Me, too, Commander. It could be they've already fielded a similar design back home."

"You're not sending a ship back immediately with this design, sir? Just in case the Alliance hasn't developed their own?"

Geary shook his head. "It's the same problem as the one with our high-ranking liberated prisoners. I'd need to send substantial forces back as escorts, and I don't want to weaken the fleet that much before we find out what kind of problems we're going to face inside alien space. Besides, that ship couldn't get home for weeks, and if the aliens intend collapsing the Alliance hypernet in retaliation, they would do it long before that when we enter their space."

"Perhaps we should delay entering enigma space until we know the Alliance has the devices installed, Admiral."

"No," Geary said. "I considered that, but the travel time alone for voyages back to Alliance space, then returning here would add up to a couple more months, even if the force we sent was not delayed or blocked. I don't know that the Syndic central government might not attempt to cut off and destroy a smaller, isolated force whose fate the Syndics could then claim to have no knowledge of. If the design made it home, it would take more time for the Alliance to actually test, manufacture, and install the equipment and receive verification of that from every star system on the hypernet. We can't afford to wait for how long all of that might require, not even knowing if a reply and confirmation will reach us out here."

One last transmission. "All units be prepared for combat the instant we leave jump at Pele. All ships jump at time three two."

THE fleet exited at Pele with every weapon ready, every man and woman in the fleet ready for a desperate fight. Instead, they found . . .

"Nothing."

Desjani glared at her combat systems watch-stander. "Are our systems being scrubbed for the alien worms?"

"Scrubs are under way and continuous, Captain. There's nothing here."

Geary kept checking his display, unable to believe that there was no sign of any alien presence at Pele. Tanya's suspicion about the alien worms had also been the first thing to occur to him. Those worms, using principles unknown to humanity, had been discovered only thanks to an intuition on the part of Jaylen Cresida before her death. Hidden inside the sensor and targeting systems on human ships, the worms had let the aliens control what humans saw of the outside universe. All too often, that had meant that the alien ships had been effectively invisible.

But there didn't appear to be any alien worms deceiving their sensors this time, and what the sensors could see wasn't impressive. Two inner worlds of modest size whirled about the star, but this star system lacked the usual array of gas giants farther out. Instead, a single massive planet orbited, so large it had become a brown dwarf, radiating heat but not strongly enough to classify it as a star in its own right. Between the star Pele and the brown dwarf, the two inner planets received an uncomfortable amount of heat, rendering all of them too warm for human habitation even though one of the worlds had some primitive extreme life-forms living on it.

On one of the inner worlds, a new massive crater could be seen, one that didn't exist on the Syndic records they had been provided. That same planet had once had a large Syndic facility in orbit. "The aliens deorbited it intact, and it made a big bang when it hit," Desjani commented. "Run the finest-grain analysis of this star system we can," she ordered her bridge team. "If there's an alien molecule here, I want to know where it is."

"Why wouldn't they at least have some kind of surveillance satellite?" Geary wondered. "Something to monitor the system and know if anyone else came here? Why don't

they have a picket ship watching to give warning that someone was heading into their territory?"

"Over-confidence?" Desjani suggested. "Maybe they
only wanted this star system as a springboard to attack Midway, not as part of their own security buffer."

"Maybe. As soon as the fleet's systems confirm the location of the jump point for Hina, we'll head for it."

"Hina? Not Hua?"

"Hua is a more direct line toward what we think is alien
territory," Geary agreed. "But the Syndics had placed a
colony at Hina. It looks like they intended to use Hina as a
source to seed other colonies and base their forces out here.
I want to see what's at Hina."

Another window popped up. "Admiral," Dr. Setin said,
"there are no aliens in this star system."

"We've noticed that, Doctor. We'll be proceeding directly
to another star system deeper in alien space."

"Will there be aliens there?"

"I hope so. How are you and the Marines getting along?"
Geary asked to change the subject.

"Very well! These Marines have a unique and fascinating
way of processing, evaluating, and understanding information. Their intellectual mechanisms are distinct from those
I have encountered in the past. In some ways it's almost as
if they were a separate variant of the human race."

"I've heard other people say much the same thing, Doctor. Please give my regards to General Carabali."

They had only been at Pele for an hour when Geary's
display flickered, then a few moments later flickered again.
Desjani's must have done the same, because the instant after
the second flicker, she was spinning in her seat to snap a
question at her watch team. "What happened?"

The communications watch answered. "Our systems carried out automatic resets in response to attempts to override
controls. Someone put a worm into our systems, but it's an
old design, so the security protocols were able to block it
immediately."

"How did the worm get into *Dauntless*?" Desjani demanded.

The lieutenant on communications watch shook his head. "It couldn't have come in remotely, Captain. Our systems would have blocked it there. Someone aboard *Dauntless* manually inserted it."

Desjani turned a narrow-eyed look on Geary. "Someone on *Dauntless*, using an old design. Who do you suppose could have been involved?"

He nodded back to her. "Some of our liberated prisoners. What was that worm trying to make the comm systems do?"

"Broadcast a message to the fleet, Admiral. The worm tried to self-destruct the message when it was blocked, but our systems recovered it." The lieutenant paused. "Sir, *Haboob* is reporting a similar attempt to commandeer her comm systems a few minutes ago."

"Oh, yeah," Desjani said sarcastically, "it's going to be very hard to figure out who was behind this."

"Can you route to me the message the worm tried to broadcast?" Geary asked the lieutenant.

"Yes, sir. The worm has been deactivated, and the message scrubbed for any other worms hidden inside it. It's clean."

"Let me see it, then." He noticed Desjani giving him another look. "And route it to Captain Desjani as well."

A window popped open before Geary. Several of the former prisoners, all now wearing new uniforms glistening with their rank insignia, decorations, and awards, stood as if addressing their own command. One of them, Admiral Chelak, launched into a speech about honor, fleet traditions, respect for seniority, and the opinions of other officers, the need to resolve command issues—

He cut it off.

"What took you so long?" Desjani asked.

"I wanted to see if they'd say anything that showed they'd been thinking." He glowered at his display. "But this appeal to the fleet's officers means the ones behind this still think they can work against my command even after talking to people in the fleet."

"Sabotage in a war zone—" Desjani began.

"I can't just start shooting them, Tanya. Especially since the worm wasn't designed to actually cause damage."

"It *was* designed to incite mutiny."

"That's true." He thumped a control. "Madam Emissary Rione, someone aboard *Dauntless* placed a worm in her systems. I will give you the opportunity to speak with Commander Benan about that before he is formally interviewed. If he was aware of or involved in the matter, an admission and cooperation at this point will be taken into account. While speaking with Commander Benan, you might also ensure that he is fully aware of recent history with worms in this fleet, both alien in origin and those created by internal enemies."

Rione gazed back at him, her expression as stiff as if molded of metal. "Thank you. I'll speak with him."

Desjani waited until Geary was done. "As commanding officer of *Dauntless*, I have an obligation to launch an investigation."

"Do so, Captain Desjani. Please take into account the status of those being questioned. We don't want to give anyone grounds for claiming they're being dishonored or disrespected."

"Yes, sir."

He gave her a sharp look. "I mean it."

"Yes, sir."

Before the day was out, Rione had asked for a private meeting with Geary, bringing along Commander Benan, who stood rigidly at attention as his wife spoke. "He says he placed the worm into *Dauntless*'s systems, Admiral."

"It was an exercise of our rights to be heard," Commander Benan said. "I was assured the worm would cause no damage to any ship or system."

"Nonetheless, Commander," Geary said, "placing unauthorized software into official systems is contrary to regulations, especially if such software is designed to override normal control functions. Are you aware of what happened to the heavy cruiser *Lorica*?"

Benan, already rigid, somehow stiffened even more. "I would never— *Nothing* would excuse such an action."

"An action that was justified by those who committed it on the grounds that they didn't believe I should be in command," Geary said.

"So I have been informed. I repeat, I would never commit such an act."

"I believe you, Commander. Would you inform me or someone else in authority if you are again approached to assist in actions contrary to regulations?"

Benan didn't answer at first, looking over at Rione, who looked steadily back at him. "Yes. My wife's honor has suffered enough."

That could have been a barb aimed at Geary, but he let it pass. "You are a man of honor, so your word will not be questioned. Emissary Rione has asked that you remain on this ship with her, and in light of her long and distinguished service to the Alliance, I have no trouble granting that request. You've both been separated for too long as it is." He looked at Rione, wondering what impact his words about her service to the Alliance had on her in light of the secrets she seemed to be keeping.

He had long since recalled the advice given him after other prisoners were liberated during earlier voyages, to give them something meaningful to do, and had regretted not being able to find tasks for so many high-ranking individuals. But perhaps it was time to offer something, anything. "Commander Benan, I regret that there are no positions on *Dauntless* appropriate to your rank and experience. However, the engineering department is in need of officers to inspect and test newly installed and upgraded equipment. If you are willing to undertake that assignment, Captain Desjani will assign you to that task." It hadn't been too easy to get Tanya to agree to that, but he had managed to convince her that useful employment and a sign of trust would both be a good idea.

Benan finally looked directly at Geary. "You're offering to let me work directly on ship's systems?"

"I either accept your word that you will not violate regulations again, or I don't, Commander. And I have accepted it."

A long pause, then Benan nodded. "I would be happy to contribute in any way I can to the readiness of an Alliance warship."

"I'll notify Captain Desjani. Thank you, Commander. Thank you, Madam Emissary."

They left without saying anything more, though Rione gave him a glance whose meaning was unclear.

IT took a total of six days to reach the jump point for Hina. Six days of futile searching for any sign of human or alien constructs. If wreckage from Syndic ships floated among the asteroids and smaller rocks of the star system, it was so old and slight that it had dispersed beyond long-range identification.

"If they wanted planets that were also suitable for human habitation, they'll be at Hina," Geary advised his fleet. "If there are still humans held captive by the aliens, they might well be at Hina, too. Be ready for action upon exiting jump."

STARS once more filled a living universe as the fleet arrived at Hina.

"Yes!" Desjani cried as the displays updated.

An alien ship, matching the turtle-like outlines of the ships seen at Midway, was right on top of the jump exit and immediately opened fire on the Alliance ships, particle beams and solid projectiles lashing at *Relentless*. That battleship and every other warship within range of the alien returned fire within less than a second, reducing the alien craft to a ruin. Before Geary could open his mouth to order probes sent over to the wreck, it exploded into tiny fragments.

"Core overload," one of the watch-standers reported. "Very powerful for a ship that size. Impossible to determine if it was accidental or deliberate."

An urgent tone drew Geary's attention to information popping up on one side of the display. *Relentless* hadn't taken any damage in the brief engagement, but the core overload of the alien ship had occurred while it was surrounded by Alliance warships. A light cruiser and a destroyer had suffered minor damage, and another destroyer had been badly damaged. "Captain Smythe, get repair assistance to *Sabar*. I want that destroyer patched up as fast as you can do it."

"That alien ship was very close to the jump point," Desjani said. "As if it was preparing to jump out, and this jump point only leads to Pele."

Geary considered that. "A picket ship that was supposed to be on station but was delayed?"

"Or else the aliens did have a surveillance satellite at Pele, one so low-power and carefully disguised as a natural asteroid that we couldn't spot it. One of their faster-than-light alerts to here, and that ship could have been on its way to finding out what humans were doing at Pele."

"I think you're right. There's not much else here, is there?" His display was changing, reflecting what was in this star system now instead of what the Syndics had once had here. "Three ships that seem to be freighters or some other kind of merchant ship, one other warship, and what's on the planets and moons."

"And that," Desjani added, pointing to the hypernet gate suspended on the opposite side of the star system, a good eleven light hours distant. "That's not a Syndic gate."

"It doesn't have a safe-fail system on it that we can recognize," one of her officers reported. "But there are other modifications to it that don't match the gates we or the Syndics have built."

"Nothing like arriving in a new star system and finding a great big bomb pointed at you," Desjani said.

"Yeah," Geary agreed. The alien species had been willing

to kill all of the wounded on its wrecked ships at Midway rather than let humans learn anything about them. They might not hesitate at all to destroy this star system if it meant also wiping out a human fleet. "We'll have to stay close to the jump exit while we look over this star system."

Rione and Charban had both come to the bridge, and Charban shook his head. "A pity our first contact with these beings had to involve our destruction of their ship."

"Our first contact happened some time ago," Geary pointed out. "When they attacked the Midway Star System. I assume you two will now attempt to speak with the aliens?"

"If they will speak with us," Rione replied.

A window holding Dr. Setin appeared. "This is astounding, Admiral. Have you looked at the primary planet in this star system?"

"We were just getting to that, Doctor."

"The towns the Syndics placed on the second planet are completely gone. There's no trace that the places they occupied ever had anything built there. The enigma race must have gone to great effort to erase any trace of previous human presence."

That was interesting as well as disturbing. Maybe having these experts along would turn out to be a useful thing.

"Have you examined the images of the alien towns on the visible portions of the planet?" Setin asked. "The images are very blurry, but the towns are not very large given how many years the enigma race has controlled this star system."

"Why are the images so blurry?" Geary asked the bridge watch-standers.

"It doesn't seem to be normal atmospherics," the sensor watch answered. "We're trying to get clearer images, but it's as if there's something fogging the imagery."

"We're sure the systems are clear of worms?" Desjani asked.

"Yes, Captain. This looks like something on the planet itself, maybe something positioned over those towns that lets through light but blocks details for anyone looking down at them."

Geary passed that on to Dr. Setin, who excitedly broke the contact to confer with his colleagues, then Geary called Intelligence. "Lieutenant Iger, what do the comms in this star system look like? Any good video transmissions we can exploit?"

Iger appeared baffled. "There's no video at all, Admiral. It's all text, and that's encoded."

Desjani blew out an exasperated breath. "No wonder the Syndics called these things the enigma race. They give paranoia a bad name."

"We can't judge them by our standards," Charban cautioned.

"I'm aware of that," Geary said. "But Captain Desjani has a point. These aren't countermeasures put into place after our arrival. The light from that planet is five hours old. The messages we're picking up are at least that old as well. These seem to be normal, routine behaviors for this species. Lieutenant Iger, I want you to look for anything that might indicate humans are still somewhere in this star system."

"We haven't seen anything that indicates that yet, Admiral."

Dr. Setin was back. "Very focused on privacy. Remarkable. Have you observed what can be seen of the towns? They are right on the coastline. As hard as it is to make out details, they seem to build right to the water's edge. What's that?" Setin seemed to be listening to someone. "Yes. Admiral, it looks like they may build *into* the water. What we're seeing continuing into the water might be piers, but it almost looks like the same construction simply continues from dry land right into the water, and those images going into water become even harder to make out before becoming impossible to interpret, which would be consistent with them continuing into deeper water."

"What would that mean, Doctor?"

"Well, one obvious possibility is that the enigma race is

amphibious. Clearly, they value being close to water and may need that proximity. We heard an alien ship was encountered at the jump exit, Admiral. Will we be able to examine it and meet with its crew?"

Geary shook his head. "I'm afraid that ship self-destructed."

"Oh. Did it evidence antagonistic or disputatious behaviors?"

"Excuse me?"

"Did it . . . attack . . . us?"

"Yes, Doctor. It opened fire the moment it saw us."

The system techs played with the sensors, trying to get clearer images but having no success. Geary waited with a growing sense of impatience, watching the alien spacecraft reacting to the arrival of the fleet but unable to move his own ships away from the jump point without risking total destruction from the hypernet gate. "Captain?" the combat systems watch said after four futile hours, her voice thoughtful. "I've noticed something in the actions of the aliens. I may be wrong, but—"

"If you've noticed anything, I'd like to hear it," Desjani said.

"Yes, ma'am. The thing is, if you look at the reactions of the alien ships, the probable freighters are reacting as the light of our arrival reaches them; but then this alien warship one and a half light hours distant also didn't react until they could see us. And a few minutes ago, we got light back from this second alien warship, about forty-five light minutes from the first warship, which showed it reacting only a few minutes after the first alien warship would have seen light from our arrival."

Desjani nodded, studying her own display. "That's consistent with our belief that they have a faster-than-light communications capability, but it looks like they don't have any faster-than-light sensors, doesn't it?"

"Yes, Captain. That first warship needed to see our light get to him before he knew we were here. But it tells us something else," the lieutenant added, "that their merchant ships don't have the FTL comms. It wasn't until one warship saw us that the other warship reacted."

"That's important to know. Excellent job, Lieutenant Castries."

Rione and Charban sent out messages, drafted much earlier, regretting past warfare, expressing interest in real dialogue, and offering to negotiate terms for peaceful co-existence.

Five hours after the fleet's arrival, a message arrived from the aliens, one definitely sent before the aliens heard the communications from the fleet. Geary saw the same sort of human avatars the aliens had used at Midway, false fronts that concealed the true appearance of the enigmas.

A "human" sat in the command seat of a virtual ship's bridge cobbled together digitally from Syndic transmissions. He frowned and made a gesture that was probably meant to be threatening but was subtly wrong to the real humans watching the message. "Go. Go now. Stay, and you will die. This star is ours. Not yours. Go or you will die. This star is ours. Go or die."

"Not much room for negotiation," Desjani commented.

"No," Geary agreed. "Route that message to the civilian experts for their input and make sure our emissaries see it." His eyes came to rest on the depiction of alien warships on his display. All of the enigma warships in this star system were headed toward the Alliance fleet, but the closest ones had veered off to hold positions a light hour distant. They either weren't planning a hopelessly outnumbered attack on the Alliance fleet or were waiting for every one of their own warships in this star system to join up before launching a still-futile attack.

"Admiral?"

He blinked, focusing on Desjani and realizing that he'd been lost in thought. "Sorry."

"You're all right?" Desjani asked. "You were out of comms for quite a while."

"I was just thinking," Geary assured her.

"Again?"

"Yes, Captain Desjani." He nodded toward his display. "I was thinking about the fact that the aliens have superior maneuvering capability; but their weapons—the weapons we've seen in use, that is—are no better than ours and may be a little inferior. It's an odd discrepancy."

"No, I don't think so," Desjani said. "Imagine that you're armed with a knife. Not a great knife, but it does the job. And you're invisible, so even though your knife isn't all that great, you have no trouble at all walking up to people and stabbing them before they even know you're there." She spread her hands with a questioning look. "Why worry about getting a new knife?"

"Because their real weapons were the worms, which allowed the aliens to be invisible on human sensors."

"Those and that damned hypernet gate. How do we deal with that?"

"I'm still thinking." Geary looked at his display once more. "Have we confirmed the Syndic information as to where the jump points are in this star system?"

"Just about." She pointed. "One of the other ones is pretty close."

Pretty close. But was it close enough?

THE fleet had continued to loiter near the jump point, close enough to it to jump out of this star system if they saw the hypernet gate beginning to collapse. But they couldn't do that indefinitely, especially when it gave them no means of learning more about the aliens.

The fleet conference room had an air of uncertainty filling it. Fighting the Syndics, even with a peace treaty in force, was a fairly straightforward thing. Dealing with the enigma race seemed to produce an unending supply of questions and dilemmas.

"Uncrewed probes sent toward the planets to find out more and get better imagery would be easily intercepted and destroyed by the alien warships," Badaya grumbled.

The images of the other fleet commanders at the conference table nodded in agreement.

"There doesn't seem to be any way to learn more here without being incredibly reckless and foolish," Duellos said. "That hypernet gate pins us near this jump point."

"Do we just leave?" Armus asked. "Why waste time just drifting here? Go back to Pele, find another way into alien space."

"That would be a long way around," Geary said. "And might just end up with us stuck the same way at Hua. There's another option," he continued, pointing to the display above the table, which currently showed the Hina Star System. "We've had time to confirm the Syndic data that there are four jump points in this star system. The one we're already at, and these two way over on the other side of the star system, and this one." He highlighted it.

"Close," Tulev said. "Close enough to reach?"

"The alien hypernet gate is eleven light hours from us. The closest alien warships are one light hour away. Even if the aliens can instantaneously send messages and react, that gives us twelve hours."

"That jump point is two point four light hours distant," Badaya observed. "We'll have to accelerate, but if we sprint up past point two light speed to the best velocity the auxiliaries could manage in that time, we could make it in almost twelve hours. There'd still be, hmm . . ." He ran some numbers. "Even if all ships attain optimal acceleration, there'd be a twenty-minute window in which we could be caught by the explosion of the hypernet gate."

"Twenty minutes?" Captain Parr asked. "If we got caught in that blast, we'd be destroyed for certain. It's a hell of a gamble. What are we waiting for?"

Geary smiled as the other officers signaled agreement with Parr's sentiments. The thought of what would happen if the fleet was caught by the explosion of the hypernet gate chilled him, but he hadn't expected to have much trouble getting them to agree to even a venture as dangerous as this would be. Rione, sitting silently, gave him a knowing look. She knew as well as he how this fleet thought. "Before we go," Geary added, "our group of experts on nonhuman intelligent species"—he hoped he hadn't sounded sarcastic— "has been analyzing what we've seen here so far and adding it to what was known before about the enigma race. They'd like to present a theory to us."

A sort of sigh ran around the table, as if a group of college students had just been told they would have to listen to a boring lecture. "Let's get it over with," someone mumbled.

Geary keyed in the commands that brought several of the civilian experts suddenly to the table, all of them appearing in a small group. Dr. Setin stood up, his expression eager. "We can't thank you all enough for this opportunity. It's very dangerous to speculate too much on too little information, but my colleague Dr. Shwartz has come up with an interesting perspective that we think you'll find very intriguing."

Shwartz stood up as Setin sat down. She peered around the table, brushing a wisp of her short, dark hair aside, then she unexpectedly smiled. "Forgive me. Like my coworkers in this field, I'm not used to anyone paying much attention to our theories. This is a very unusual experience."

She pointed to the representation of the star Hina, which floated over the table. "I believe that the enigma race differs from humanity in a very significant way. I don't have to explain to military officers such as yourselves that humans base much of our interactions on open displays of power and aggression. This is built into us, from the way our species evolved and the experiences of our earliest ancestors. When confronting a foe, we try to bulk up our own appearance of threat, standing taller, spreading our shoulders and arms, much like a feline arching its back and erecting its fur to create a larger silhouette. What we build also reflects this way of thinking. Our battleships look deadly. They are designed not just to be mighty machines of war but also to project an image of threat and power."

Shwartz paused. "But the enigma race seems to follow a completely opposite manner of dealing with threats. It's a method not unknown to humans but also not instinctual for us. I propose that the enigmas instinctively project menace to their foes not by blatant, open displays of size and strength but by *hiding* their presence and their power."

"How can someone be impressed, or deterred, or otherwise influenced," Badaya asked, "by something hidden from them?"

"Imagine yourself in a dark room," Dr. Shwartz replied. "Totally dark. Is there something in there with you? What is it? Is it dangerous? Is it dangerous enough to kill you? Do you want to fight it? Or flee? And if you wish to fight, how do you fight the unknown?"

The fleet officers were listening intently by then, and Desjani nodded. "Your theory matches everything we know about the aliens. They place a premium on hiding. The worms the aliens hid in human operating systems helped keep the aliens hidden from our sensors and let the aliens know where we were; but the worms in the hypernet gates also made them usable as surprise weapons."

"Yes," Shwartz said. "This method of attack is not unknown to us. Humans use ambushes, striking without warning while our foe's back is turned, but we regard them as unfair and improper. Fighting, our instincts tell us, should involve two combatants standing up to each other, in the open, a 'fair fight' as we call it."

"Snakes," Captain Vitali remarked. "Are you saying the enigmas are like snakes?"

"In some ways, perhaps."

"But do snakes fight other snakes by hiding and striking?" Badaya asked. "Do snakes fight other snakes at all? Here's my main concern with your idea, Doctor. Using the unknown to impress and disconcert a foe requires a foe who is capable of grasping that an unknown threat could exist. It wouldn't work against something that's oblivious. It *requires* an opponent who's aware."

"Why is that a problem?" Duellos asked.

"Because the suggestion is that these aliens evolved to fight that way. Who was the enemy that led them to that strategy? What kind of opponents did they face who could be successfully unnerved and countered by a phantom enemy?"

Dr. Shwartz frowned, but slowly nodded. "That is a valid question. Many predators can be spooked by the right kinds of threats. Perhaps the enemy was themselves, with vicious fighting among separate groups from the beginning."

"But there don't appear to be very many of them," another of the experts said. "After so much time in this star system, their settlements are still fairly small by human standards. That argues for a lower birthrate, a population that expands slower than a comparable human one would. And lower birthrates, smaller populations, should mean less conflict over resources, land, and everything else."

Jane Geary had been studying something, and looked up, saying a single word. "Neanderthals."

"What?" Badaya asked.

"Neanderthals. An evolutionary dead end, one of the prehuman species on Old Earth. They became extinct long before recorded human history began."

"I'm familiar with what's known of the Neanderthals," Dr. Setin said. "How do they factor into this discussion?"

"We know that as early humans moved into the same areas, the Neanderthals dwindled and eventually disappeared. Extinct," Jane Geary explained. "What if the Neanderthals had survived into recorded human history? What if they'd been more numerous, more powerful, able to keep fighting with our earliest ancestors longer?"

Dr. Setin took a quick intake of breath. "We don't know that early humans wiped out the Neanderthals. There was some interbreeding, but because all prehuman species died out long before recorded history, leaving only scattered remains, we don't know why they died out."

Tulev answered. "Humans have a stark enough history of struggles based on things such as specific religious beliefs, cultural differences, and ethnic variations. It is not hard to imagine the conflict that would have resulted from coexisting with a slightly different variant of ourselves. And as you say, all of those variants died out. *Perhaps* that was a coincidence."

Dr. Shwartz was nodding. "We have no way of knowing how the competition with variants of the human race impacted our own development as a species, but surely it had some impact. That could have been the same type of intelligent competition that the enigmas faced to develop this way of fighting."

"All of this is plausible," Dr. Setin said, "but we lack proof, or even sufficient substantiating detail. We need more information, Admiral Geary."

"If these aliens are so opposed to us," Captain Armus asked, "if there's no chance of getting along with them, then why not return to Alliance space now and prepare for an actual military campaign? We retake this star system, then start working our way inward until we break these bastards."

The civilians were staring at Armus, not so much shocked at his proposal as seeming to be unable to comprehend such a thing.

Badaya shook his head. "We need to know more about their strength before we plan such a campaign. Whether or not these enigmas agree to speak with us, we need to conduct more reconnaissance of their territory. Capturing some ships intact, or launching some raids, might net us some of their technology."

"We'll penetrate far enough to learn as much as we can, without getting so deep into their space that we might face problems getting back out," Geary said. "Once we get to the next star, one the Syndics named Alihi, we'll aim for long jumps, getting as far into alien space as we can as fast as we can before heading out again."

"They don't seem inclined to let us wander through their territory," Commander Neeson remarked.

"If we have to fight, we will. But our purpose is reconnaissance, not battle. Victory for us in this case consists of learning as much as we can and bringing it back to human space with us."

No one disputed that. The fleet's ardor for battle had ebbed a bit, it seemed, now that the war with the Syndics was over. He could see the weariness on everyone's faces, feel the unseen presence of countless dead friends and companions. Yet this was also the only life these men and women knew, the only life they had ever known. As tired as they were of war, like the ground forces soldiers at Ambaru station, they knew nothing else. Change, uncertainty, was in some ways harder to face than the familiar prospect of death. They would run the risk of destruction racing against time to reach that next jump point, but if he had suggested immediately following the first proposal, to fall back and look for another way into alien space, there would have been grumbling because that wasn't the sort of thing the fleet did when it faced a challenge. "Thank you. I'll swing the fleet gradually around so that the slower ships, especially the auxiliaries, are closest to the jump point we're aiming for when we start our sprint. As the fleet accelerates, the faster ships will pass through the slower ones, inverting the formation. I'll pass the exact maneuvering orders within the next hour."

After the fleet officers had left, Dr. Setin turned to Geary. "Admiral, I brought Dr. Shwartz to this meeting because I thought her proposals were truly based on observations and not preconceptions. However, there are two other . . . factions . . . within our group of experts. One of those, I am convinced, came along on this voyage already certain the aliens are morally superior to us and have only reacted with violence when humans have attacked."

Desjani laughed.

"I assure you that hasn't been the case with our encounters with the aliens thus far," Geary said. "You mentioned two factions, though."

"Yes. The other faction believes that the aliens must be hostile, that we will inevitably face a fight to the death with them."

"Did these two factions ever talk to each other before this?" Desjani asked.

"No," Dr. Setin said. "At least not when they could help it, which was most of the time. However, both factions have prepared their interpretations of what we have seen so far, and I feel obligated to ask that you review those."

"That's all right," Geary replied. "One of the mistakes the Syndics made was not considering alternatives from what they believed was true of the enigma race. I can at least skim these reports to see if there's anything in them that makes me think twice."

"Oh. Thank you." Dr. Setin peered at Geary. "You're open-minded for a military person."

"He can afford to be," Desjani said. "I'm closed-minded enough for both of us."

Setin eyed her, clearly unable to tell if Desjani was joking, then smiled politely before his image vanished.

"I'll leave you to your diplomatic discussions," Desjani said as she stood up, with a dismissive glance toward Charban and Rione.

After she had left, Rione looked at Geary. "Your orders call for this fleet to discover the boundaries of space controlled by the enigma race."

"Yes, they do. But as fleet commander, I have the discretion of responding to the situation if it requires modifying my instructions." Geary, feeling increasingly aggravated with Rione since she hadn't bent at all despite his forbearance with Paol Benan's actions, kept his speech formal. "I won't keep charging toward the galactic core as long as the enigma race and my fuel supplies hold out. We'll reach a point where our fuel cell supply, even as augmented by new cells built by the auxiliaries, will begin declining past ninety percent. At that point, we're heading back. I hope," he added to see what reaction it produced, "that the grand council wouldn't expect me to hazard this fleet by complying blindly with orders given many light years from here."

"Senator Navarro certainly wouldn't," she said, neither her tone nor her expression providing any clue to anything but the literal meaning of the statement.

"I know we've had some sharp words," Geary said, looking at General Charban as well now, "but I want to be certain you both understand that I consider us to be on the same side."

"Of course we are," Charban agreed.

Rione simply looked back at him.

THREE hours later, Geary gave the order for the fleet's ships to pivot around and accelerate all out toward the jump point for Alihi.

ELEVEN

ELEVEN hours to the jump for Alihi. An hour after the fleet had leaped toward that jump point, the nearest alien warships suddenly swung about and raced to match the movement of the Alliance fleet.

"Captain Smythe, you need to coax more acceleration out of your auxiliaries," Geary ordered.

"Yes, sir! Yes, sir! Three bags full!" As Smythe ended his words, he saluted in a grand manner. "Request permission to jettison twenty metric tons of raw material from *Tanuki*, *Kupua*, *Titan*, and *Domovoi*."

"Twenty metric tons?" By any measure, that was a lot.

"From each ship. Eighty tons total. It's the sort of thing we can most easily find along the way, like raw iron. We can just rope an asteroid or two in another star system if you want us to break it down into usable form without slowing. But I can't get any more acceleration out of my heaviest ships without lightening their mass."

It didn't leave him much choice. The acceleration rates for the four big auxiliaries weren't fast enough, and if they were destroyed here, then those tons of raw materials wouldn't do anyone any good. "Permission granted."

"Do you want us to throw it at anything or anyone when we jettison it?" Smythe asked. "It could make quite a splash whenever it landed."

"No. Just drop it in a safe orbit. We're supposed to be trying to establish peaceful relations with the enigmas, and dropping eighty tons of raw metal on them probably wouldn't further that goal."

As Smythe's image vanished, Desjani spoke in a low voice as if commenting on the weather. "You need to get some rest, Admiral."

"While we're facing the prospect of getting annihilated by that hypernet gate?"

"Yes. There's nothing else we can do for a while, and you can monitor the fleet's progress from your stateroom just as well as you can from here." She gave him a sidelong glance. "You look nervous."

He *was* nervous, but he got the point. Everyone else on *Dauntless* would be watching him to see if he was calm or worried.

Geary stood up, moving casually. "I'm going down to my stateroom to eat something," he told Desjani in a louder voice that carried easily across the bridge.

"What a good idea, Admiral," she said. "I wish I'd thought of that."

But he had barely made it down to his stateroom and checked the progress of Smythe's auxiliaries when a call came in.

General Carabali made an apologetic grimace. "Sorry to bother you, Admiral, but I feel I should inform you that Admiral Chelak has been confined to his quarters aboard *Haboob*."

"What did Chelak do?"

"He tried to pull rank on me and assume command of the Marine detachment aboard *Haboob*. Not too smart, really, since that's two hundred Marines he would have had to convince to disregard my authority."

Geary sighed. "Thank you for informing me."

"It's going to get worse, Admiral. They're sitting on *Haboob* and *Mistral* with very little to do, and they're the kind of people who are used to doing things and giving orders. I believe the only reason we haven't had more trouble before now is that all of the former prisoners are still under the influence of long incarcerations in the Syndic labor camp, and some of them are also under the influence of truly impressive doses of medications prescribed by the fleet physicians."

"Thank you, General. I'll try to think of something to occupy their time." After Carabali ended the call, Geary sat looking at nothing as he tried to come up with alternatives. *I can't assign them all to check out systems on* Haboob *and* Mistral. *Even if they'd accept that job, there are a bunch of them I can't trust with that kind of access to critical systems.*

Too bad they can't help us with the aliens.

That thought didn't fade, instead repeating itself. *Why can't they?*

He spent a moment checking on how the auxiliaries and the rest of the fleet were doing, watching the tons of raw material jettisoned by Smythe's ships floating away from the fleet like oddly angular asteroids.

Reassured that things were going as well as they could, Geary finally made a call to *Mistral*. During the brief and unpleasant meeting with the liberated prisoners, one of the freed admirals had quickly backed Geary and shown no support for Chelak. A check of that admiral's record had shown solid service and ability, with enough ambition to drive him to high rank but no indications of political ambitions. He was someone with whom Geary realized he should have already spoken and given some responsibilities. *Better late than never.* "Admiral Lagemann."

Lagemann gazed back at Geary. "What's the occasion?"

"I was hoping that you and your fellow former prisoners would help with a very important task."

Lagemann looked very skeptical. "I personally haven't

taken it badly that you haven't been able to devote your time to holding our hands, but I also know there's a pretty strict limit on the number of admirals and generals you need in command positions. I'd be glad of something important to do. We've been counting dust bunnies in the corners of the passageways for a while now, if you need a head count on them."

"I don't think dust bunnies are an endangered species, Admiral. You know that we're inside space controlled by an intelligent, nonhuman species, one which so far has acted in a hostile manner. We have little data and little experience with them, but further armed encounters are a possibility at any time. You and your comrades may not have recent combat experience, but you have a lot of knowledge and practice in operating against the enemy. You also have new eyes to look at this problem, without any preconceptions the rest of us have already developed. What I would like is for you to examine what records we have, the materials we've received from the Syndics and our fleet's records, and try to analyze how the aliens think and fight. What are they likely to do in a battle? Was the situation at Midway an anomaly or the way the aliens are likely to fight in the future? What other tactics might we expect from them?"

Admiral Lagemann was thinking, and nodded. "Not make-work after all? I can't promise anything, but that's not the point, is it? If we do come up with something useful, it could make a big difference in fighting these creatures. If we don't, you've lost nothing."

"Exactly. Are you willing to assist in this, Admiral?"

"Yes. And I know many of my comrades will as well." Lagemann looked to the side, breathing deeply. "This has not been an easy role for us. It will mean a great deal to have the opportunity to make a difference again. May I ask one favor in return?"

"I can't do much about the food on *Mistral*."

Lagemann grinned. "After seventeen years of Syndic rations, even fleet food tastes good. No, what I want to ask for is the opportunity to talk with you some more, specifically about tactics. I and some of the others really want the chance to learn from you more about how you fought those engagements that broke the back of the Syndics. The ways our ancestors fought."

"Of course, Admiral." Geary felt a pang of guilt that he had been forced to warehouse so many capable senior officers on the assault transports along with the troublemakers. "I'll arrange for all of the records I spoke of to be forwarded to *Mistral* for you. If anyone on *Haboob* wishes to assist as well, you're authorized to share the records with them. Would you be willing to have a talk this evening?"

"That would be welcome." Lagemann looked down at his hand, then awkwardly brought it up in a salute. "I understand this is the latest fashion in the fleet. We'll see you this evening, Admiral."

Geary returned the salute, smiling. *Maybe someone did try to create problems by saddling me with all those senior officers. But that doesn't mean I can't find some ways to turn them into assets.*

HE was back on the bridge an hour before the fleet would reach the jump point for Alihi and roughly thirty-five minutes before the fleet would face the possibility of being overtaken by a nova-scale burst of energy from a collapsing hypernet gate. Because of lower-than-optimum acceleration by not only the largest auxiliaries but also some of the battleships, the fleet had lagged behind projections, and so would have a slightly longer period of exposure to that threat.

"*Orion* didn't keep up," Geary grumbled to himself.

"Neither did *Revenge* and *Indomitable*," Desjani commented as if to herself. "You can test and tweak all you want, but sometimes equipment problems don't show up until you actually push your gear."

"I know that."

"I know you know that."

He decided not to continue that conversation.

Ten minutes until the vulnerability period began. Geary

found himself staring at the depiction of the alien hypernet gate, even though there was no possible way for it to have begun collapsing unless the aliens had ordered that before the fleet even left the first jump point.

Two more alien warships had joined the first two chasing one light hour behind the Alliance fleet, moving with that unbelievable maneuverability the aliens had demonstrated at Midway.

Five minutes. The watch-standers on the bridge were all trying to act as if they were carrying out routine work, but Geary noticed their gazes repeatedly fastening on one point before each of them, the place where their own displays would be showing the alien hypernet gate.

Another necessary action had to be taken now, one contrary to every instinct to keep heading for that jump point at maximum speed. But a ship going too fast couldn't enter jump. "All ships pivot one eight zero degrees at time five zero and brake to point one light speed." They would be slowing down now, lengthening the period of time when danger was the greatest, but nothing could be done about that.

One minute.

Desjani yawned. "It'll be nice to get somewhere we have the possibility of action. Right, Lieutenant Yuon?"

Yuon took a moment to swallow before he answered in a fairly steady voice. "Yes, Captain."

"How was your family on Kosatka?" Desjani continued.

"Fine, ma'am. They mainly wanted to talk about . . . you know."

Geary glanced back at Yuon, trying to match Desjani's own casual words. "I hope you painted me in a good light, Lieutenant."

"Uh, yes, sir."

"Entering vulnerability period," the maneuvering watch announced.

Desjani pulled out a ration bar. "Hungry?" she asked Geary.

"I had something earlier. Is that a Yanika Babiya?"

"No. It's . . ." She squinted at the label. "Spicy chicken curry."

"A chicken curry ration bar? How are they?"

Taking a small bite, Desjani chewed slowly, pretending not to be aware that everyone on the bridge was watching her instead of staring at the representation of the alien hypernet gate. "It's definitely got curry in it. Spicy, not so much. Some of the other stuff *tastes* like chicken."

"That doesn't narrow it down too much, does it?" Geary said.

"Every kind of meat in a ration bar tastes like chicken, Captain," Lieutenant Castries suggested. "Except the chicken."

"You're right, Lieutenant," Desjani said. "Real chicken in ration bars tastes like, what, mutton?"

"Ham," Yuon tossed in. "Bad ham."

"So this can't be chicken because it tastes like chicken," Desjani concluded.

"Fifteen minutes to jump," the maneuvering watch reported.

Geary checked the deceleration of his ships, seeing that all were braking at the proper rate to be down to point one light speed when they reached the jump point.

"What do you suppose the aliens taste like?" Desjani wondered.

"We can't eat them," Geary said. "They're sentient."

"Humans sometimes eat other humans in emergencies," she pointed out. "Like after a shipwreck. It's almost a naval tradition."

"I've heard that," Geary said. "Aren't you supposed to eat the most junior personnel first?"

"That's what I've heard." Desjani looked toward her watch-standers. "Just so we have things planned out in advance, which one of you has the latest date of rank?"

The lieutenants exchanged looks and grins. "Actually, Captain," Castries said, "Yuon and I were promoted on the same day."

"Well, we can't eat both of you right off the bat. I assume

you'd object to using alphabetical order to decide the problem, Lieutenant Castries?"

"Not if we used first names, Captain," Castries replied. "Mine is Xenia."

"That would be hard to beat," Desjani said. "Wouldn't it, Lieutenant Bhasan Yuon?"

Yuon shook his head. "I really think Lieutenant Castries would make a better meal, Captain. I'd be tough and lean."

"Five minutes to jump," the maneuvering watch said.

"Maybe you two could flip a coin." Desjani raised one finger, looking inspired. "No. I'll just get an ensign assigned to this watch team."

"Ensign slash emergency food supply?" Geary asked.

"We don't have to put that in the position's job description. It might discourage volunteers."

"Master Chief Gioninni?" Yuon suggested.

"Lieutenant Yuon," Desjani replied, "if Master Chief Gioninni were in the escape pod with us, he'd somehow trick the rest of us into getting eaten until he and any remaining survivors sailed grandly into some safe harbor, perhaps a world where Gioninni would convince the inhabitants to make him their ruler for life."

Geary was watching his fleet now, sparing only quick glances for the alien hypernet gate, which still showed no signs of beginning to collapse. None of the ships was lagging anymore, every one matching pace with the others. Two minutes remaining. The fleet would jump automatically when the maneuvering systems detected that it was in position, so he didn't even have to order the jump this time, which might have cost a few extra, critical seconds.

"One minute to jump," the maneuvering watch said.

"It takes the gates more than a minute to collapse," Desjani said, "and we haven't seen it start. We're clear."

"Yes," Geary agreed. "We are." He tapped his controls. "All units, the aliens may be using their faster-than-light comm capability to muster forces at Alihi. Be ready for a fight when we exit jump."

Forty seconds later, the fleet jumped for Alihi.

Desjani sighed and stood up as the gray of jump space replaced the alien threat at Hina. "I'm tired, and for some reason I'm hungry. I'm going to get something to eat." She leaned closer to Geary. "Next time *you* come up with something to distract everyone."

"I won't be able to equal you."

"No, but you can do your best, Admiral." With that parting shot, Desjani left the bridge.

JUMP space always tended to make humans uncomfortable. Humans didn't belong in jump space. Maybe nothing really belonged there. Maybe the strange lights that came and went were reflections of something happening somewhere else. At some level beneath conscious thought, humans could never be at home in jump space, growing more irritable with every consecutive day spent there.

But whatever was bothering Geary during this jump to Alihi felt different from the usual jump jitters. Something that Desjani had said kept coming back, like a shadow half-glimpsed repeatedly. *If you've got a knife . . .* Why did the idea of the aliens wielding knives trouble him so?

Normal communications were impossible in jump, but between the time he had fought his battle at Grendel a century ago and when he had been found still alive in survival sleep, humanity had figured out how to send brief, simple messages between ships. On the fourth day of the jump, barely eight hours from exit at Alihi, a message came from *Mistral* for Geary.

Geary read it over again slowly, despite its necessary brevity. *Regarding aliens—Watch your back. Lagemann.*

He had asked Desjani to come down to his stateroom to look at it and talk about it, and now she frowned in puzzlement. "We know the aliens can't be trusted. Is that all he's saying?"

"I don't think so. He and his fellows are supposed to be trying to guess how the aliens will fight."

"This sounds more like a warning against a stab in the back."

"What?" Geary whirled to stare at her.

She switched the puzzlement to his reaction. "I said it sounds more like a warning against them trying to stab us in the back."

"A knife. In the back."

"I wasn't speaking literally."

Geary made a fist and rapped it against the side of his head. "Damn! That's what it means! That's what's been bothering me!" He called up a display showing the Alihi Star System, or at least what that star system had looked like when the Syndics had outposts there. "They strike from hiding. From ambush. If your worms aren't working anymore to conceal you from enemy sensors, where can you hide in a star system?"

Desjani shrugged. "Behind the star. Behind a planet or moon."

"Behind a jump exit?"

"No!" She stabbed a finger at the display. "You're talking about an ambush force positioned behind a jump exit to catch an arriving force in the rear? It doesn't work. It *can't* work. The physics are against you."

"Why?" Geary asked.

"Because, one, you don't know if or when someone is arriving at a jump exit. It's hard to maintain a position close to one and even harder right behind one. You're going to do that for days, weeks, months? Two, whoever shows up is heading out of the exit, away from you, at up to point one light speed. You're starting from a dead stop relative to them, so you need to accelerate into a stern chase. Maybe you can catch them, but it'll take a while. While they watch you coming. That's not exactly a surprise."

Geary nodded. "Those are the same reasons why we never planned for ambushes like that a century ago. But what if you have faster-than-light communications?"

She paused. "Someone at the star you left could tell

someone at the star you were going to that you were coming."

"And they'd know pretty accurately when you'd appear because jump physics are consistent. If you enter jump at x time here en route there, the journey will take y time."

Desjani shook her head. "But even then they wouldn't know exactly where you'd be. They'd still have to be able to maneuver and accelerate much better than— Son of a bitch." She gave him a stricken look. "*They* could do it."

"Yeah." Geary slumped back, staring ahead of him. "The possibility didn't occur to us because we can't do it. But they have two big advantages that make it feasible. And because of the FTL communications, they might even know what our formation is like. We have to leave jump in the same formation we entered. There's no way to maneuver in jump space."

"They'll hit the auxiliaries, and maybe the assault transports. They're all in the rear of our main subformation, with no escorts behind them." Desjani pressed her palms against her eyes. "Can we get enough of our force reversed and able to cover those ships in time?"

"It takes time to recover from jump," Geary said bitterly. "And time to pivot ships and brake velocity so we can let the auxiliaries pass us. Even if we tell our comm systems to transmit prepared orders the instant we exit, it will still take precious moments for the other ships' crews to recover enough to respond, and I have a nasty suspicion that every second will count."

Desjani pointed to the message from *Mistral*. "Keep it simple, and we can send the messages in jump."

Simple. Something simple that could counter what he hadn't planned for at all.

"You've still got almost seven hours before we leave jump to think of something," Desjani added.

"Oh, *that* helps take the pressure off."

"Sorry."

* * *

THE aliens were waiting at Alihi.

Geary's brain hadn't begun to focus when he felt *Dauntless* swinging her bow up and around, the battle cruiser pivoting in response to maneuvering orders entered while the ship was still in jump. *Dauntless* was lighting off her main propulsion units, braking the velocity of the ship at the maximum rate her crew and structure could survive, when alarms began blaring from the combat systems. As Geary's vision began to finally clear, he felt *Dauntless* shudder slightly as specter missiles launched on orders from combat systems given freedom to immediately engage targets assessed hostile.

His message had gone to the other major warships in the main formation. Battle cruisers *Dauntless*, *Daring*, *Victorious*, and *Intemperate*, battleships *Warspite*, *Vengeance*, *Revenge*, *Guardian*, *Fearless*, *Resolution*, and *Redoubtable*. It had been as short and simple as required by the nature of jump space communications. *Immediate Execute on exit, pivot one eight zero, brake point zero five, engage enemy.* That was the fastest response he could create if the aliens were waiting to hit the back of his force.

There might be enigma warships waiting in front of the jump exit, but if so, hopefully the heavy and light cruisers and the destroyers remaining in the main formation would be able to handle them.

He finally managed to get a good look at his display as *Dauntless*'s hell lances started firing. Enigma warships were clawing their way toward the rear of the Alliance formation, the squat turtle shapes varying in size from rough equivalents to human destroyers to some massing a little more than heavy cruisers. Thirty . . . no, forty. Forty-one. The courses of the enigma warships altered slightly as *Dauntless*, *Daring*, *Victorious*, and *Intemperate* slowed enough for the auxiliaries to lumber past, the battle cruisers pivoting and decelerating faster than the battleships could.

Dauntless shuddered repeatedly as the aliens concentrated their fire on the four battle cruisers. Even though the battle cruisers were bow on to the enemy, their weaker shields were failing, and shots were penetrating to strike their lightly armored hulls. Geary had only a second to decide what to do, his hand hitting his comm controls as *Daring* staggered under a particularly bad barrage. "*Dauntless*, *Daring*, *Victorious*, and *Intemperate*, continue to brake velocity at maximum sustainable rate!"

As the battered battle cruisers continued to slow, the aliens accelerated past them, aiming once again for the eight auxiliaries. Grapeshot from the battle cruisers hit the enigmas as they tore past, and *Victorious* caught one with its null field, carving out a large chunk of the alien ship.

His display showed no other aliens around the jump exit, so Geary hastily sent another command. "All ships maneuver freely to engage the enemy. Captain Smythe, get your ships clear!"

The remaining alien warships, only twenty-five still in the fight, had begun firing on the auxiliaries when the Alliance battleships finally trudged even with the lightly armed support ships. The cruisers and destroyers to either side and in front of the auxiliaries were now pivoting as well, the heavy cruisers unleashing some of their own specters.

It was the battleships that made the difference, though, wiping out the nearest enigma ships, then decimating the second rank.

Only six alien warships managed to break away, twisting around in maneuvers no human warship could match, to tear away at an astounding rate.

Even though the battle was over, explosions still rippled through space as the wrecked alien warships near the Alliance forces self-destructed.

"All units, resume formation, brake velocity to point zero two light speed." He needed to see how badly his fleet had been hurt before proceeding farther into this star system.

"There's another hypernet gate here," Desjani snapped as she fielded damage reports. "Bastards."

He checked the damage reports flowing into the fleet net from *Dauntless* and the other three battle cruisers, wincing at the results. *Daring* had been hit the worst, her bow badly shot up, numerous systems out, and close to a hundred crew members dead or wounded. *Victorious* had sixty casualties, and had lost half her hell lances. Fifty-three of *Intemperate*'s crew were dead or injured, and she had taken bad damage to her bow's port quarter.

And *Dauntless*. "Twenty-eight dead," Desjani said, her voice betraying no feeling, no emotion, at all. "Forty-one wounded, six critically. I have four working hell-lance batteries." She took another report. "Correction. Three and a half working hell-lance batteries."

Geary felt a numbness inside himself as he hit his comm controls again. Such a short period of time, better numbered in seconds than in minutes, and so many lives lost. "Captain Smythe, I want auxiliary repair support mated to *Dauntless*, *Daring*, *Victorious*, and *Intemperate* as fast as you can get them there. *Daring*, *Victorious*, and *Intemperate*, advise as soon as possible if you need medical assistance. General Carabali, ensure the medical teams on *Mistral*, *Haboob*, *Tsunami*, and *Typhoon* are prepared for immediate response to requests for support."

He turned to look at Desjani, whose stony expression matched the flatness of her voice. "Does *Dauntless* require medical assistance?"

She made another call to sick bay, then nodded. "We can use support, Admiral, especially for the critical injuries."

"*Typhoon*, close on *Dauntless* to provide medical support as soon as possible." Geary noticed that Desjani was still waiting for him. "Attend to your ship, Captain. I'll look to the rest of the fleet."

"Thank you, Admiral."

THANKS more than anything to the limited numbers of alien attackers, the damage to the battle cruisers was by far the worst the Alliance fleet had sustained. A few minor hits on the auxiliaries could be repaired without difficulty, and the battleships had taken only superficial damage.

They had already seen several more alien warships pop in via the hypernet gate at Alihi as the Alliance fleet hastily repaired damage and its sensors studied the planets there. The star system had two planets deemed marginally habitable by the Syndics, one just over six light minutes from its star and the other about ten light minutes distant. Neither would be comfortable for humans, but they weren't hell-holes either. Farther out, a dense asteroid belt orbited at twenty light minutes from the star, and beyond that, four gas giants.

The enigmas had settled the planet six light minutes out, and from the sensor readings may have been undertaking the enormously difficult task of modifying its environment to be more hospitable. "Humans don't do that," one of the engineers explained. "It's not that we couldn't. We worked out the basic techniques a long time ago on that planet near Old Earth. What's it called? Mars. But we did that before jump technology made interstellar travel pretty easy. Since then, it's just far easier and cheaper to find a nicer planet in another star system than it is to go to the work of fixing up a marginal or hostile one."

"Any idea why the aliens would be doing it here, then?"

The engineer pondered that. "I can think of two reasons. One would be that the planetary modifications are much simpler and less expensive for them. The other is maybe they can't find enough better planets, like what happened when the Syndics ran into them and that region got blocked to further expansion by both sides."

"No signs of human presence," Lieutenant Iger reported, "but just like at Hina, our ability to analyze the inhabited world is severely constrained by their countermeasures."

Dr. Setin didn't try to hide his frustration. "We can only guess at the population here, but based purely on the number of towns, we think it is higher than at Hina. Can't we get closer to that planet? We've finally found another intelligent species, and we can't learn anything about them!"

There didn't seem to be much reason to stay at Alihi.

* * *

"THE hypernet gate here is only two light hours from this jump point," Geary said, his voice heavy. The images of the fleet's commanding officers focused on the star display over the conference table. "There's no way to reach another jump point without risking certain destruction. But this jump point accesses both Hina and another star, angling deeper into enigma territory. The Syndics named it Laka, but two survey missions they sent there over a century ago both vanished without a trace. We can assume Laka is also occupied by the enigmas. As soon as our four damaged battle cruisers are ready, we'll jump for Laka."

"I take it our formation will be modified next time," Armus said.

"Yes. We'll be ready for anything coming from any angle when we exit jump."

"Why not stay here," Captain Vitali of *Daring* suggested in a hard voice, "and bombard the hell out of everything until there's nothing but ruins, then go out and explore what's left?"

General Charban, looking uncomfortable, responded. "Our mission is to try to establish peaceful relations—"

"Those things have attacked us every time we've encountered them! They don't talk to us, they *won't* talk to us. They just want to kill us. Fine! Let's give it back to them!"

A low murmur of approval sounded around the table.

Duellos sighed loudly enough to be heard by everyone. "The problem we face is that damnable hypernet gate. Even if we destroyed everything, that wouldn't guarantee that there wasn't some dead-man mechanism on the gate designed to collapse it and catch this fleet in the resulting blast."

"Why not hit the gate, too?" Vitali demanded.

Commander Neeson shook his head. "If we start taking out gate tethers, we lose control over the collapse process. Once it started going, the aliens could easily have it set to go into a catastrophic collapse sequence."

"Enough rocks fired at the right tethers—" Vitali continued stubbornly.

"There are defenses around the gate. All they have to do is divert one rock slightly to throw off any collapse sequence we planned on."

"Perhaps," Charban suggested, "if we launched a limited bombardment at a few places, a demonstration of what we *could* do—"

"That didn't work with the Syndics," Badaya interrupted. "I never thought I'd be saying this, but the Syndics seem to be downright reasonable compared to these enigmas. Anything that didn't convince the Syndics won't convince the aliens."

"I have to agree," Duellos said.

"That doesn't prevent us from striking back," Desjani said. "Bombard some of those towns. They've given us more than adequate grounds to retaliate. We can show them that when they attack us, they can't just run away and avoid any more hurt."

Charban hesitated. "They'd see a bombardment launched from here early enough to easily allow evacuation of their populace. It will demonstrate our capabilities in a way impossible for them to ignore but shouldn't create any motives for vengeance based on civilian deaths."

Dr. Shwartz and Dr. Setin had been invited to listen in, and now Shwartz spoke reluctantly. "We don't even know whether they understand the distinction between military and civilian. The enigmas may be as blind to such a concept as the average human male is to the difference between taupe and beige."

"According to the Syndic records," Duellos said, "they lost quite a few ships in this region before even realizing that the enigmas existed. Many of those ships were lightly armed or unarmed. If the aliens do recognize the distinction between military and civilian, they seem more than capable of disregarding it."

Everyone looked at Geary, who bent his head in thought for a moment before nodding. "Yes. We'll send them another message saying that we want peaceful coexistence, but that if they persist in seeking war, they'll have to deal with war. I don't see any other option."

The moment of silence that followed was broken by the captain of *Victorious*. "Do we bury our dead here? Send them toward this star?"

"No," Vitali insisted immediately.

Geary nodded once more. "I agree with Captain Vitali. There's too great a chance that the journey of our honored dead to the star would be halted by the aliens. There are compartments on the assault transports for storage of casualties. We'll transfer our dead there and hold them until we reach a star system where their burials can be conducted safely. Captain Smythe, how long until all four damaged battle cruisers are back in battle-ready condition?"

Smythe scratched his neck meditatively. "None of them will be in mint condition, but give me three more days, and all of their weapons will be working again, holes in their hulls patched, and shields back up to strength."

Desjani was running some calculations. "A bombardment launched from here will take sixty-one hours to reach the planet where the enigma towns are."

"All right," Geary said. "We'll launch the bombardment within the hour, along with our message that this is just a taste of what pissed-off humanity can do. That will give the aliens plenty of time to respond with something other than more attacks, if they so choose, and give us time to see the bombardment hit and evaluate the results before repairs are far enough along, and we jump for Laka."

Most of the officers left quickly when the conference ended, but Smythe lingered long enough to shake his head at Desjani. "I go to all that trouble to get your ship's systems upgraded, and you go and get a good lot of the equipment blown apart before the work's completely done."

"I'm just trying to keep your engineers gainfully employed," Desjani replied, managing the first trace of a smile she had shown since losing her crew members.

"I appreciate your efforts, but I wanted the admiral to know that one of the hell-lance batteries on *Victorious* wasn't knocked out by enemy action. Not directly, anyway. One of the power junctions feeding it failed."

"Age?" Geary asked.

"Age and stress," Smythe confirmed. "I can't teach our equipment meditation, so I'll keep working at making it younger."

Charban sat staring down at the table after Smythe had vanished. "If they'd only talk to us. This is senseless. War always seems senseless, but we don't even know why they're hostile. Don't think I don't appreciate exactly how your Captain Vitali feels. I lost a lot of troops in my time."

He stood up and walked out, something in his movements and his bearing making Charban seem older.

Desjani glanced at Rione, who was still seated, and stood up herself. "I'll get a bombardment plan set up. Admiral."

"Thanks. Target about half the towns on the planet."

"Half?" She smiled again, this time in a feral way. "I thought you'd limit me to a quarter."

After Desjani left, Geary sat waiting for Rione to say something. Finally, she looked directly at him. "I realize that the words 'it could have been worse' are cold comfort at such times," Rione said. "But they are also true. You could have been mourning the loss of several ships, and thousands of dead."

"I know." Geary leaned back, trying to dull the pain inside as he thought of their losses. "If we hadn't reacted as quickly as we did, we could easily have had most of the auxiliaries crippled or destroyed, which could have left this fleet in a very bad position. Was that the idea, Madam Emissary?"

"I don't know what you mean."

"I think you do. I wish I had some idea of why you would have agreed to play a role in it."

"You know that I have always been willing to sacrifice myself for the right reasons." On that, she also stood and left.

* * *

FOUR hours later, Geary stood at attention in his best uniform. Beside him stood Captain Desjani, similarly attired, also at attention. Next to them were two ranks of sailors and Marines from *Dauntless*'s crew, forming two lines just outside a hatch. From the hatch, giving access to the exterior, a pressurized accommodation tube led to *Typhoon*. Everyone wore armbands showing a wide bar of gold, another of black, then a final gold bar, symbolizing the night that was only an interval between the light.

Geary brought his arm up in a salute that he held as the first of twenty-nine sealed body tubes was carried past by more crew members, moving at a somber pace, each step coming with slow deliberation. More followed, carrying the rest of the tubes. Moving down the corridor formed by the two ranks of sailors and Marines, the crew members carried the remains of their comrades through the hatch and toward *Typhoon*, where they would be kept in compartments designed for that sad burden.

Normally, cargo was simply floated through the open space between ships. But the fleet didn't treat its dead that way.

After the last tube passed by on its way to *Typhoon* and had vanished from view, Geary finally lowered his arm. Desjani did the same, turning to the honor guard. "Thank you. Dismissed."

Everyone left to change back into a regular uniform, to return to the work whose demands never ceased, but sometimes paused when tradition demanded it.

DAYS of repairing battle damage passed quickly enough. Geary noticed that now when members of the crew spoke of the aliens, they were angry, and that watch-standers viewing alien activity had the aspect of someone aiming weapons at a target they wished killed. Did the enigmas understand how their actions were impacting human feelings about them? Kalixa had been horrible, but the deaths here had been personal ones, men and women who had been friends and comrades, and increasingly the human crews appeared ready to reply to enigma intransigence with firepower rather than futile attempts to communicate.

"We received another message from the enigma race," Rione told him. "Do you wish to view it?"

"Anything new in it?" Geary asked.

"No. Same avatar, same false bridge, and same dialogue. If we took the words 'die' and 'go' away from the enigmas, most of their ability to converse would vanish."

Charban grimaced. "They're not acknowledging what we said, and they're not acknowledging events here. It's like talking to a wall."

Unable to help a grim smile, Geary pointed to his display, where the tracks from the bombardment projectiles fired days ago were finally curving down into the planet's atmosphere. "We're about to knock on that wall. I don't know if it'll do any good, but I think it'll make us all feel better. Maybe, *maybe*, the enigmas will realize how much damage their actions are doing to them."

"If they are anything like humans, that may be a vain hope. Do you think they evacuated the targeted sites?" Rione asked.

"We have no idea. That blurring is blocking too much detail."

"Are you certain this isn't due to more enigma worms?" Charban asked.

Desjani shook her head. "If it is, the worms are using a totally different principle. We have people examining every possibility, especially the ones that seem impossible, but our code monkeys haven't found anything. Our technicians all believe that this is some form of real interference near the things we're trying to observe."

Charban nodded, his eyes downcast. "I'd be surprised if it was worms this time, since the enigmas couldn't hide their own ships when they attacked us here." He stood to go.

"Don't you want to watch the bombardment hit?" Desjani asked.

General Charban shook his head, not looking at her. "I've already seen too many towns die, Captain Desjani."

She closed her eyes as Charban left, then opened them and shook her head at Geary. "We're back to bombarding towns."

"They had plenty of time to evacuate," Geary said.

"I know. This time they had plenty of time. What about next time?"

"I won't let them drive us to that."

"May our ancestors forgive us all if we sink to that level again, no matter what these things do to provoke us," Desjani replied in a low voice.

The mood on the bridge was somber rather than celebratory as they watched the time-late images. When the bombardment arrived there, the alien-controlled planet had been five and a half light hours from where the Alliance fleet hovered near the jump point. The light from that event had taken five and a half hours to arrive, and they were finally seeing what had happened as the kinetic projectiles dove into atmosphere, plummeting from the heavens to tear apart the . . . what? Homes? Businesses? Factories? Did the enigmas have such things as humans understood them?

Lieutenant Iger reported in, his own tones subdued. "Whatever they use to blur sight of their towns survived the bombardment. We can tell we tore up the targets, but that's about all."

"Fine." Geary made a final check of the status of repairs. Even badly damaged *Daring* had patched up the last systems and was ready to go. "Let's get the hell out of here."

TWELVE

LAKA Star System was empty, almost literally so. White dwarf stars didn't tend to have much in the way of planets, and Laka had only a tiny, tormented rock in a looping, close-in orbit that made it likely the minor planet had sailed in from space and been captured by the star sometime within the last million years or so. No alien presence could be detected, but after Pele, no one was sure if that meant there was actually nothing here. "Not a lot to hide among," Desjani commented.

Geary took the fleet quickly across the star system to a jump point offering a long jump deeper into alien space. The star they were aiming for this time hadn't ever officially been given a name by the Syndics, a fact that marked this as the true limits of human expansion in this part of the galaxy. "This is likely to be one of the enigmas' long-settled star systems," Geary cautioned the fleet. "They may expect us there. All ships should set weapons to fire upon any threats automatically upon our arrival." It was a dangerous policy, because even ships' combat systems could sometimes be rattled by jump exit and mistakenly identify a friendly ship as an enemy, but hopefully the radically different designs of the alien craft would minimize any chances of that.

He sat in his stateroom after the fleet had entered jump space again, feeling moody at how poorly things had gone. Despite everything that had happened with the aliens, despite everything the aliens had done, Geary realized he had still had a hope that the enigmas would come around and be willing to at least coexist with humans even if they couldn't bring themselves to be friendly.

His hatch alert chimed, then Desjani entered. "How do you feel, Admiral?"

"Lousy. How do you feel, Captain Desjani?"

"Mad." She sat down, looking at him. "Not depressed. Just mad. Unlike some others, I never expected the aliens to be reasonable. Maybe that's because of my experience with humans. What are you going to name the star?"

The sudden question threw him off. "What?"

"The star we're heading for needs a name. We can't just use its astronomical designation. Normally, there's probably a whole bureaucracy that decides the name of a star, but if you name one out here, that name will probably stick. So what are you going to name it?"

Geary shrugged. "I have no idea."

"You could name it after someone."

"Tanya."

"What?"

"I can name it Tanya."

"No," she said, "you can't. I don't want everyone looking at a star named Tanya and saying, 'Oh, isn't it sweet how much he loves her.' Gag. Name it after someone who deserves to be memorialized that way."

"All right," Geary said. "I'll name it Cresida."

"A star system controlled by aliens who are hostile to humanity? You want to name *that* after Jaylen?"

"Fine. I'll call it Falco."

"That man does not deserve to have a star named after him!"

"Tanya," Geary said, "why don't you pick a name?"

"Because you have the right to choose the name you want," she replied.

"So, what name is it that I want?"

"Something appropriate! Maybe not a person. Something unknown and dangerous." Desjani snapped her fingers. "Limbo. Call it Limbo."

"There's no star already named Limbo?" Geary asked.

"Let me make sure." Desjani's hand flew over her data unit. "No. There have been some planets, but those were all fictional, in old books. *Really* old books. Did you know people were writing about interstellar travel long before there was any?"

"It must have seemed like a pretty amazing thing to look forward to. All right. I think I'll call the star Limbo."

"I think that's a good choice," Desjani said. "Why are you smiling if you feel lousy?"

"Something struck me as funny." He leaned his head slightly to one side to look at her. "What would become of me without you?"

"You'd get by." Desjani stood up. "Four days in jump space before we reach Limbo. If we're meant to succeed in this, we will. You know that."

"Thanks, Tanya."

THIS time, when *Dauntless* dropped out of jump, no weapons fired. Geary's head cleared enough for him to assure himself that no enemies were nearby, then his eyes went to the display showing the entire star system, where fleet sensors were rapidly evaluating and adding data.

"Jackpot," Desjani breathed.

Limbo held two planets with substantial alien populations, based on the number of towns and cities visible beneath the blurring effects. Many installations orbited those worlds, and scores of freighters crossed between planets. Only a dozen enigma warships orbited the star. If this were a human-occupied star system, they would evaluate it as well-populated and fairly wealthy.

And there was no hypernet gate.

Geary kept staring at his display, wondering why that felt so wrong. There were plenty of human star systems without hypernet gates.

Captain Duellos called in, his expression bemused. "This doesn't make any sense, Admiral. It's a good thing, from our perspective, but why would the aliens have hypernet gates in such marginal star systems as Hina and Alihi, but not have one here?"

"That's a very good question," Desjani agreed. "Does it mean there's another sort of trap lurking somewhere in this star system?"

Geary braked the fleet's velocity, holding it near the jump exit, while the fleet's sensors scoured the star system repeatedly, fixing the locations of other jump points and trying to spot anything that could pose a potential danger. "Nothing, Lieutenant Iger?"

"No, sir. Just those warships that we can see. If there had been a gate here, and it had collapsed, we should be able to detect the remnants of the tethers. It doesn't look like there has ever been a gate here."

He called his senior fleet officers, asking them for opinions on what the lack of a gate here meant. None of them had good explanations.

Rione and Charban had no idea, either.

Admiral Lagemann and his fellow former prisoners couldn't offer any good suggestions except for reiterating that the aliens liked to spring traps, which did nothing for Geary's peace of mind.

Finally, in desperation, he called the civilian experts.

"Maybe the answer eludes us," Dr. Shwartz suggested, "because we're looking at the situation from a human perspective."

"What do you mean?" Geary asked.

"We're making assumptions. Examine what you're taking for granted. What are hypernet gates *for*?"

"Very-high-speed interstellar transportation." That was what he had first been told, and that was how humanity used them.

"What *else* can they be used for? Think of other potential uses that the aliens might consider primary uses."

"I can't think of anything else the gates are designed to do. As far as other capabilities, we know if they're collapsed they—" He looked over at Desjani. "They're weapons. The gates are weapons. Doomsday defenses for any star system."

"Defenses?" Desjani asked, incredulous. "Like, a minefield?"

"The biggest damn minefield imaginable." Geary pulled up a star display. "The enigmas were the ones who discovered how to build hypernets. They knew before they built any how dangerous hypernet gates could be. They never built them in their most valuable star systems. They built them on their borders."

Charban shook his head. "A willingness to deliberately employ such things as defensive weapons? A great wall of hypernet gates? It's a scorched-earth defense magnified beyond comprehension."

"They've proven willing to destroy their damaged ships," Rione pointed out, "and the crews of those ships. To us, it seems unimaginably ruthless. But to them, it seems such a defense is conceivable."

"We got past it," Geary said. "Maybe because we never intended to attack those star systems. We just wanted to get through them. Maybe that surprised the enigmas."

Dr. Shwartz had been listening. "There's also the possibility that the enigmas themselves shrank from employing such weapons. As different as they may be from us, self-preservation must play a role in their thinking even if it is species based rather than individually focused. There have been cases in human history where weapons were constructed and prepared, but not employed because their destructive power frightened those who had created them. The gates may be intended to deter attacks since their presence would make an assault on that star system impossible. The point may be *not* to use them."

"They wouldn't work as a deterrent unless potential attackers believed that the enigmas were willing to use them to wipe out their own star systems as well as the attackers," Charban insisted.

"I believe it," Desjani said.

Geary had his eyes locked on the display. Maybe there was still some hidden trap out there. The decision on whether to leave the area of the jump point and head into the inner star system was up to him. The uncertainties still surrounding what enigma technologies could do, and the enigma fondness for striking by surprise, made the decision far from easy. But in order to learn more about this race, he would have to send ships closer to some of those planets.

Split the force? Send out a strong formation, able to handle those dozen enigma warships and anything that might be expected to pop up while the rest of the fleet stayed near the jump point? "How much would be enough?" Geary wondered out loud.

Desjani frowned, then understood. "That would depend upon the threat."

"And we don't know the threat, which is why I'm considering splitting the force. Is the right response to an unknown danger to divide my own forces?"

"Not if you put it that way." She waved toward her display. "If there were a gate here, sending everyone in-system would just ensure the destruction of the entire fleet. But there isn't a gate."

He could spend a long time wondering about what to do, hoping some new information would come in. But the enigmas were pursuing this fleet, and they had faster-than-light communications. The longer he waited, the more alien warships were likely to show up. "We'll go as a fleet. My gut feeling is that any threat that appears in the next few days would be a serious challenge to part of this fleet, but together we should be able to handle whatever shows up."

She grinned. "Where to, Admiral? The closest inhabited planet?"

"No." He highlighted a decent-size installation on a large moon of a gas giant orbiting two light hours from the star. "We head for that. Isolated and not very large, so it won't have the kind of defenses we might run into on one of the planets. If the enigmas' anti-surveillance methods can even block our search efforts when we're close, then we can send uncrewed probes in."

"They might be able to destroy the probes."

"Then we'll hammer their defenses before we send the Marines to knock down doors and get some information the hard way."

Desjani approved, of course, and when Geary looked back to check on his observers, he saw Rione as impassive as usual these days, while Charban simply appeared resigned to the necessity of using force.

He put the fleet onto a vector aimed at intercepting the gas giant in its orbit around the star newly christened Limbo but kept the fleet's velocity at point one light speed.

The moon they were aiming for had been six light hours distant, making the transit there about two and a half days long. For the first day, nothing happened except that the alien warships came tearing up to a position a light hour away from the Alliance fleet, then maintained their distance, too few to threaten the fleet but a constant source of aggravation. But with the fleet only a day and a half out from the alien installation, the aliens finally reacted directly to the human movements.

"A ship has left the installation," the maneuvering watch reported. "Not one of their warships, but one of the blocky ones we think are freighters."

"Evacuating personnel," Desjani said.

Geary looked at the data. "He's accelerating slowly. Their freighters seem to reflect the same economic realities that human ones do."

"Yeah. You can't make a profit if you spend too much on

propulsion and fuel cells." Her fingers danced over her display. "Lieutenant Casque, run some intercepts on that alien freighter to double-check my work."

Casque worked almost as rapidly as Desjani, then nodded. "I come up with the same results, Captain. We can catch it."

"Send the results to the Admiral's display."

Geary watched the long curves of the projected intercepts appear. The Alliance fleet was curving into the star system at an angle. The alien freighter was heading toward the star, aiming for one of the populated worlds. Behind the Alliance fleet, the dozen alien warships trailed like a patient pack of wolves. "Our force would have to move fast to get to that freighter before those alien warships. If every enigma left that installation, we'll be left without any aliens to talk to unless we run down that ship. I'll split off a fast-moving task force to do the job and keep the rest of the fleet on course so we can still examine the installation."

"*Dauntless* is ready—"

"Tanya, she's the flagship. She has to stay with the fleet this time." He scanned the fleet's formation quickly, then paused as he was about to send a transmission. *Damn. I want Tulev running this, but I need to send the other three battle cruiser divisions, which means Badaya on* Illustrious. *And Badaya is senior to Tulev.*

All right. Badaya should be able to do it. If he might end up commanding this fleet if something happens to me, I need to see more of how he handles an independent force. "Captain Badaya, you are to assume command of Task Force Alpha and proceed to intercept and capture the alien craft that just left their installation. We want that ship intact and those on it alive." Now to call the ships that would make up that task force. It would have to be large enough to handle those dozen enigma warships if necessary, and any more that showed up suddenly, and should use ships already positioned not far from one another. "First Battle Cruiser Division. Second Battle Cruiser Division, Sixth Battle Cruiser Division, Second, Fifth, Eighth, and Ninth Light Cruiser

Squadrons, and Third, Fourth, Seventh, Tenth, and Fourteenth Destroyer Squadrons, detach from main formation and form Task Force Alpha under command of Captain Badaya effective immediately."

Desjani had slumped slightly, glaring at her display. "Every other battle cruiser division gets to go."

"The task force needs to be strong enough to handle those alien warships if they fight for the freighter. I'm keeping *Adroit* with us."

"Ha-ha. You owe me one, Admiral."

"I'll add it to the list."

Badaya didn't waste any time. *Inspire, Formidable, Brilliant, Implacable, Leviathan, Dragon, Steadfast, Valiant, Illustrious, Incredible*, and *Invincible* tore out of the formation, with the light cruisers and destroyers leaping to surround them.

In a very rare move these days, Rione came to lean close to Geary. "Badaya?" she murmured skeptically.

"He knows what he's doing," Geary murmured back. "And he has Tulev and Duellos along with him."

"You're the admiral. I'd recommend that someone else do any communicating with the aliens, though." Rione returned to the back of the bridge.

He turned to look at her and Charban. "Excellent idea. The enigmas shouldn't have any trouble figuring out that our task force is aiming to intercept that freighter, and they already know that we're heading for the installation. I'd appreciate it if you two broadcast a message to the enigmas telling them that despite their own hostile actions and provocations, we do not intend to harm anyone on the freighter unless we are forced to defend ourselves."

"Defend ourselves *again*," Desjani muttered, then frowned at her display. "That's odd."

"What's odd?" Geary asked.

"The acceleration on that alien freighter. Something didn't seem right, and now I know what. We know their warships seem to have power core efficiencies an order of magnitude higher than our own. And there's no reason to think a freighter would have military-grade propulsion. But that freighter's acceleration rate pretty closely matches that of one of our freighters. If they can build military propulsion an order of magnitude better than on our warships, why can't they build freighter propulsion an order of magnitude better than on our freighters?"

He fixed his own gaze on the projected vector of the alien freighter. "That's a good question. It's not even significantly better. Maybe we'll get an answer when we capture it."

She snorted derisively. "Don't count your freighters before you've captured them."

Charban had finished helping Rione broadcast the message to the aliens and came to stand beside Geary's seat for a moment. "I'm wondering something, Admiral."

"You, too?"

"The alien warships could have launched a bombardment aimed at that installation once they knew we were headed that way. They haven't. Why not? They're obsessed with privacy, but they're apparently going to let us examine a large installation without hindrance."

Desjani gave Charban the first look of respect she had offered the emissary. "There's a trap?"

"I would be very, very cautious about sending in a landing force, Admiral," Charban said, then nodded to Desjani before he left.

There wasn't much to do after that but watch the task force sweeping down on the freighter and wait to see how the dozen alien warships reacted. Several hours passed, with the fleet swinging in toward the installation on the gas giant's moon, the freighter moving slowly but steadily toward the inner star system, the battle cruiser task force diverging quickly from the rest of the fleet as it kept accelerating toward the freighter, and the alien warships hanging a light hour behind the human fleet. "They're not doing anything?" Geary finally demanded. He couldn't help but make a question of it, because it seemed so contrary to alien actions to date.

"It must be obvious to them that the task force is heading

for the freighter," Desjani confirmed. "And we'd have seen their reaction to that long before now. But they're just holding the same position relative to us."

"Waiting for orders?"

"Damned if I know. Sir. But with faster-than-light comms, they should have already received orders by now even if their command authority is on one of those inner planets."

The task force would intercept the alien freighter in another twenty hours. It would be five hours after that before the fleet reached the alien installation. Geary punched his comm controls. "All ships ensure that your crews get chances to rest and to eat." It could be enormously hard to stand down at times like this, even though any action wouldn't occur for close to a full day, and even if the alien warships accelerated to attack, it would take them hours to reach attack range. One of the biggest and easiest mistakes to make was sitting, tense and ready, getting worn-out and hungry as you watched ships slowly move closer to one another, even while the vast distances in space ensured that nothing could happen.

"I'm going to get something to eat and get some rest," he told Desjani.

She nodded. "I'm rotating my crews through normal watch sections. I'll take a break in a little while, too."

Despite his words, Geary once again roamed the passageways for a while to tire himself out a little more, taking the time to talk to crew members he encountered. They seemed happier now that there was a prospect of closing with the enemy, though all of them were disappointed that *Dauntless* wasn't leading the task force to intercept the freighter.

He ate a meal in one of the mess compartments, talking to more of the crew about their homes. Most were from Kosatka, reflecting common fleet policy these days of crewing ships with a majority of men and women from one planet, and Geary found that they now spoke of home as if he shared that world with them. He found himself oddly grateful for that. He had grown up on Glenlyon, but the thought of the hero worship that would surround him there more than anywhere else made that world now feel almost as alien as Limbo to him.

He also took time for a visit to the worship spaces, praying that somehow they could avoid more senseless loss of life. After that, to his own surprise he got a decent amount of sleep and quite a bit of work done before returning to the bridge.

Desjani was just settling into her own seat. "Checking on repair work," she told him. "We've almost fixed all of the things that were already fixed before the damned enigmas broke them."

"Half an hour to intercept of the freighter by the task force, Captain," Lieutenant Casque said.

"Very w—" Desjani broke off, staring at her display.

Geary did the same, barely suppressing a curse.

"They blew it up," Casque reported as if he couldn't believe what he was saying.

On Geary's display, the neat symbol representing the enigma freighter had been replaced by a spreading cloud of dustlike debris. It had happened two hours ago, but the force of the event still felt immediate. "How the hell did a freighter blow up with that intensity?"

"Run an analysis," Desjani ordered her bridge team. "Ancestors preserve us," she added to Geary. "They self-destructed their ship full of their own people fleeing that installation. Is there anything they won't do to keep us from learning anything about them?"

"I'm starting to wonder." Somehow, he wasn't surprised when new alerts sounded on the display. Fixed defenses closest to the installation had launched kinetic projectiles, whose trajectories were clearly aimed not at any Alliance ships but at the installation itself, itself still more than thirty light minutes distant or six hours' travel time at point one light speed. That volley had barely been detected when the image of the installation itself smeared and burst outward.

"They self-destructed the installation, and they launched a bombardment to pulverize whatever is left from that."

"Charban was right, though it looks like the aliens didn't want to risk waiting to blow the place until we had people down there and might have already learned something. What do we do now?" Desjani asked. "Head for one of the inhabited planets?"

"Please do not," Rione suddenly said. She and Charban had come back onto the bridge unnoticed until then. "I am very much afraid of what they would do if we tried to approach one of those worlds."

"They wouldn't—" Desjani began, then closed her eyes. "Maybe they would."

"What do you think, General Charban?" Geary asked.

"I agree with my fellow emissary, Admiral."

"It's technically not our fault if they kill themselves," Desjani grumbled. "And, no, I'm not prepared to argue that point with the living stars when I face them. But what else do we do? They have us checkmated. Either they'll blow us and themselves to hell with hypernet gates, or they'll blow themselves to hell if they can't stop us from learning anything. I prefer the second option if we have a choice, but either way, we learn nothing."

Geary exhaled slowly, thinking. "All right. We stay on course for the installation. Maybe something survived the self-destruct and will survive the impact of that bombardment."

Some time later, a short message came in from the task force, Captain Badaya looking dissatisfied. "We'll continue on course to examine the debris field in case there's anything worthwhile left, then move to rejoin the fleet, Admiral."

THE remnants of the installation were too badly torn up to reveal anything beyond the basic composition of what it had been constructed of. Carabali had advised against sending personnel down to the surface of the moon, arguing that more traps might be undetonated and waiting for human presence to further destroy the already-mangled ruins. But uncrewed probes found nothing, even the size and shapes of rooms in the installation hard to determine because of the level of destruction.

Captain Smythe called in with an engineer's perspective. "They must build things with an eye to being able to totally self-destruct. You can't just annihilate a structure this badly by setting off a few charges. You need to have a lot of explosives or other destructive materials, and they need to be placed right. I wouldn't be surprised to learn that the structures contain built-in charges."

"Isn't that extremely hazardous?" Geary asked.

"Says the man who's riding a ship loaded with weaponry, dangerous circuitry, unstable fuel cells, and a power core that can blow it into tiny pieces? And who's doing this through space, an environment totally hostile to human life? It's what we're used to, Admiral. They may be used to living inside walls packed with explosives." Smythe brightened. "They might have some extremely stable compounds that require just the right means of detonation. I'd love to have a look at that sort of thing."

"If we find any, I'll let you know. Do you think their cities might be built like that?"

"It's possible. Though placing enough nukes at the proper intervals would accomplish the same purpose."

The task force had reached the expanding cloud of debris that had been an alien freighter and slowed down to conduct a careful examination of it. When his message finally reached Geary, Badaya seemed to be in inexplicably high spirits considering the failure of the task force's mission to capture the freighter, but his first words explained his happiness. "Admiral, for once the aliens failed to totally destroy everything. *Dragon* found a partial body. At least we finally know what they look like. I have to give Commander Bradamont full credit for realizing that the aliens might well garb themselves in clothing that we'd consider stealth material. She took *Dragon* around the edges of the debris field from the freighter, looking for cool patches among the debris, and found what seems to be about a one-half-intact body that was somehow partially shielded from the blast that destroyed the freighter."

An image appeared next to Badaya. Geary flinched, not in revulsion at the alien itself but at the state of the body. Explosive decompression on top of the damage done by the destruction of the freighter had left gory remnants. Still, he could make out what seemed to be a tough skin, with patches of thin scales in a few places. The crushed skull still had a small snout visible. In life, the enigma must have been lean and long, so skinny that it looked to human eyes as if it had been stretched out by someone pulling on both ends. "Make sure medical staff and our civilian experts see this," he told the communications watch, then called the fleet's chief medical officer.

"I assume you want to look at this in person," Geary began. "Where should I have *Dragon*'s shuttle deliver it?"

"*Tsunami*, please, Admiral. They have a particularly good surgeon on there who has some autopsy experience. That's also the ship carrying the, um, experts on intelligent nonhumans. How long until we see it?"

"They're forwarding scans to us, but it will take close to a day for the task force to rejoin us so you can physically examine the remains, Doctor." Another call, this to the much more distant *Illustrious*. "Captain Badaya, my compliments to you and Commander Bradamont on a job well-done. As soon as your task force rejoins the formation I want *Dragon* to shuttle those remains to *Tsunami*."

Finally, they had found something. Perhaps his prayers had been at least partially answered.

GEARY was in his stateroom when Badaya called again as his task force rejoined the rest of the fleet, the ships returning to their places in the larger formation. "Sorry I couldn't get that freighter for you, Admiral, but at least we got that partial body. Ugly, aren't they?"

"It's hard to tell with all the damage to it," Geary said.

"That's a point. No major problems to report, but I'd appreciate it if you'd have a stern talk with *Invincible*'s commanding officer."

"Now what?"

"Captain Vente isn't taking it well that this is my division. He keeps making digs about me being junior to him, so he should be in charge. During this operation, he kept balking at orders to show his unhappiness that I was in command of the task force instead of him."

That wasn't a surprise to hear. "He hasn't done anything justifying a formal reprimand?" Which might also justify relieving him of command if it was a serious enough infraction.

"Unfortunately, no," Badaya said, twisting his mouth in disgust. "Vente's got admiral's insignia in his eyes, and he's politically smart enough to avoid going over the line while he's getting his major command ticket punched before he returns to headquarters and his hoped-for promotion."

"Somebody should have told him that promotions have hit a brick wall."

"Ha! At least as far as he's concerned, right, Admiral? But I've dealt with plenty of Vente's type in my time. They always think their connections will help them get what others can't."

Bracing himself for an unpleasant but necessary task, Geary called Vente. Nearly twenty minutes later, long enough to annoy Geary but not long enough to justify chewing him out for that as well, Vente's image and frown appeared standing in Geary's stateroom. "Captain Vente, I need to emphasize for you that I do not disrupt command relationships or positions based purely on seniority. Captain Badaya has successfully and competently led his division for some time, and he will continue doing so."

Vente's expression soured even more. "That is contrary to regulations."

"No, it is not, or you'd be citing the relevant regulations to me right now. Let me be clear that I respect the service and honor of all my officers, and I will not allow any of my officers to be treated in any manner that reflects disrespect for them."

"Admiral Chelak—"

"Is not in command of this fleet. Have I made my expectations clear, Captain Vente?"

"Yes . . . Admiral."

After Vente left, Geary ordered the fleet's support systems to provide him with more frequent and detailed updates on *Invincible*'s status. *Give me a reason to relieve this man of command. Anything that I can justify. And let's hope it happens soon.*

THE medical representatives were looking around the fleet conference room with ill-concealed curiosity. Attendance at the conferences had been increasingly restricted in recent decades, as the conferences degenerated into freewheeling political contests to decide fleet commanders and vote on courses of action. By the time Geary was awakened from survival sleep, it was rare for anyone but the commanding officers of the fleet's ships to attend such meetings. But Geary had imposed much more discipline, and the conferences no longer featured the same fireworks, which probably explained the disappointment the doctors were showing.

The surgeon who had been in charge of the alien autopsy was giving a presentation, accompanied by virtual images that would have been stomach-turning for nonphysicians even if the images hadn't been three-dimensional and as real-looking as if actual body parts were floating over the conference table. "We can't be certain why this specimen survived as well as it did, but an analysis run using injury re-creation software rates as a high probability that the individual represented here was not physically aboard the freighter when it was destroyed. A reanalysis of records from the last moments of the freighter's existence identified a stealthy object being ejected from the freighter several seconds before it exploded."

"An escape pod?" Duellos asked in surprise.

"Very likely. The distance and the structure of the pod itself would have shielded the occupant a bit." The surgeon indicated various organs. "Enough of the neck survived to identify a dual breathing system. We believe this skin flap would close, diverting breathing intake from this multi-chambered lung to these organs. They were very delicate, and not much has survived, but we think it likely that they worked the same way gills do."

"Amphibious in every sense of the word!" Dr. Setin exclaimed, pleased that his experts had called that one.

"Most likely," the surgeon responded. "There's not enough left of the eyes to be certain what wavelengths they were optimized for. It may have had six appendages, though how many of those are arms and how many legs is impossible to say from the state of this sample. We can identify the probable functions of most of the organs we found, but there's not much of those. It's clearly a carbon-based life-form, similar to our own basic makeup, and oxygen-breathing. The brain was very badly damaged. We can approximate the size, but identifying functional areas will be extremely difficult. One thing that does seem apparent is that the brain lacks bilateral symmetry. In more primitive alien life-forms that we've seen on human-colonized worlds, this translates into a lack of right- or left-handedness."

"Can you tell what it eats?" someone asked.

"No. The digestive system is completely gone except for a few scraps. It could be a carnivore, a vegetarian, or an omnivore."

"Did enough of the fingers remain to see if it had finger-nails or claws?" Dr. Shwartz asked.

"One of the fingers was intact enough to see a hard structure on the end, sort of like a conical fingernail covering the tip."

"That could be used to kill prey, or to dig up vegetables," Shwartz commented.

Commander Lomand, *Titan*'s commanding officer, had been listening intently and gestured for attention. "Sir, you spoke of gills. You're certain that this creature had water-breathing capability?"

The surgeon nodded. "Yes."

"We've seen some of where they live," Dr. Setin interjected. "Towns and cities that straddle the coastline rather than sitting on one side or the other. Water is an amazing substance, you know. Incredibly useful. Oxygen is a powerful source of fuel, so there's no surprise in seeing another highly evolved species using it. And carbon is immensely flexible. They're all tailor-made for supporting complex life. Most of the advanced life-forms we've found are carbon-based and oxygen-breathing."

Commander Lomand's fingers had been tapping out some rapid calculations, and he gave a cry of satisfaction. "I've run some initial calculations, Admiral, and checked them with some engineers on *Titan* who have some ship design expertise. We've observed the ability of the alien warships to accelerate and maneuver faster than our own ships can. If the alien warships are filled with water, instead of atmosphere, it would cushion the crew against the forces of acceleration, adding considerably to the effectiveness of inertial dampers."

"Enough to explain the ability to maneuver that we've seen?" Commander Neeson demanded.

"If the warships also had significantly larger power cores for their size than comparable human warships."

"We haven't picked up indications of that," Badaya said.

"Yes, we have," Lomand said. "The force of the power core overloads that have destroyed the alien warships that we've encountered. Those could be explained by higher efficiency levels, or by larger cores using the same basic principles as ours."

Smythe spoke carefully, trying not to publicly embarrass one of his officers. "We haven't seen emission levels from the alien warships consistent with larger power cores, have we?"

"No, sir. But if the hulls are filled with water, that would act as an additional insulator against anything emitted by the power cores. The water would not only help protect the crews from the emissions but also prevent us from remotely detecting how large the power cores were."

Captain Smythe had been talking to someone on *Tanuki*, and nodded. "I can confirm Commander Lomand's calculations. The force of the core overloads we've seen could be explained by cores of a size larger than those we use but still within parameters able to fit within the alien hulls."

"Water masses much more than atmosphere," Tulev objected. "Would this not have a negative effect on their maneuverability?"

"If the hulls were big enough. The amount of water increases dramatically as the internal volume of the hull balloons in response to larger external dimensions."

"No battleships," Desjani commented. "That's why they don't have anything much bigger than a cruiser."

Neeson was frowning as he studied something. "Even with the water insulation, having power cores that size in hulls that small wouldn't be good for the crews over the long run."

"Maybe they're not as vulnerable to the emissions," Smythe suggested, looking to the surgeon, who just shook his head to indicate an inability to answer that.

"More likely, they don't care that much about the welfare of their crews," Captain Vitali said.

Dr. Setin spoke with exaggerated diplomacy. "Clearly, the enigma race has a high level of willingness to sacrifice individuals for the good of the race as a whole. Admiral Geary asked my group to assess what we believe would happen if this fleet attempted to get close to some other installation, or a planet, to learn more about the enigma race. We have concluded that there is a high probability of mass destruction initiated by the enigma race to avoid leaving anything that will allow us to learn more."

"What if they knew we already had this body?" Duellos asked. "Would that make them conclude there was no sense in committing mass suicide to prevent us learning more?"

"I don't know. It depends on the nature of what drives

their obsession with remaining hidden. If it is deeply engraven in their very nature, then knowing that we have learned what we have might cause them to react with even higher levels of violence. I'm basing that on what we know of human and animal psychology, but that's all we have to go with."

"They're crazy," Badaya said, drawing nods of agreement.

"They're *different*," Dr. Shwartz replied. "This obsession with remaining hidden could be very deeply ingrained in them, something they don't question and can't deviate from because it was written in their distant ancestry as they evolved. Try to imagine how humans would look to aliens, with our constant, overriding obsession with sex."

General Carabali snorted derisively. "Humans are occasionally capable of going a short time without thinking about sex or letting it drive their actions. I'm speaking for the female of the species, of course."

"I once went several seconds without thinking about sex," Duellos retorted. "Though it did cause me to question my own masculinity. The fact is, though, that whatever drives the enigmas' obsession with privacy, it's something so powerful they are quite literally willing to die for it. And to kill to preserve it. No matter how much we may speculate on other aspects of the enigmas, there is now no doubt that much is true of them."

"Speaking of motivations," Jane Geary said, "does anyone have any idea why that particular alien tried to escape from the freighter?"

A long pause ensued, then Shwartz nodded toward Setin. "Perhaps this particular alien *was* crazy, by the standards of the enigma race, that is. He, she, it . . . didn't want to die for the purpose of keeping us in the dark about their race."

"A coward?" Badaya laughed. "Mind you, I'd say that particular alien had more common sense than the others, not wanting to die for that reason, but they'd call it a coward, wouldn't they?"

"Doubtless," Setin agreed.

Geary looked down the length of the table, seeing everyone looking back at him for his decision. "I see no purpose to be served in trying to examine more closely the remaining enigma presence in this star system. They might have trouble totally wiping out their own towns and cities, but they might also have the means to do just as much damage as they did to their installation. We're here to learn what we can, and it seems we aren't likely to learn much more detail. If what we're speculating about their technology is true, the main thing we'd still want to get our hands on is their faster-than-light communications system, but the odds of getting that seem too small to measure even on a quantum scale. Therefore, I'm going to order the fleet on a series of jumps, seeing how many more enigma-controlled star systems we can look over before heading back for Alliance space. Our single goal now is to gain more understanding of the strength and size of the enigma-controlled region, though our emissaries will continue to broadcast what I suspect are futile offers to establish meaningful contact."

He waited for comments or questions, but none came. "Thank you. I'll issue maneuvering orders soon."

After most of the officers had vanished, Dr. Setin lingered while Dr. Shwartz whispered furiously at him. "Admiral, there is something I wish to discuss," Setin said. "Perhaps, a single human, left behind when the fleet leaves, could learn more about—"

"No."

"I would be volunteering. The opportunity—"

"I can't allow that, Doctor. I'm sorry. From what the Syndics told us, the enigmas have already captured any number of humans. They would have no reason at all to keep you alive."

Setin still stood there, irresolute, until Dr. Shwartz said something else to him. "Yes, that's so," Setin conceded. "Perhaps we'll find another intelligent species on one of these jumps you're planning."

"That would be nice, Doctor." Especially if it was an alien race that wasn't insane by human standards.

* * *

THE fleet took a long jump toward a star newly christened as Tartarus, Captain Desjani having been disappointed to discover that there was already a star in Syndic space named Purgatory. Although, as she pointed out, Syndic space was exactly where anyone would expect to find a star with the name Purgatory.

Tartarus resembled Limbo in its population of enigmas, though Geary was bothered that the number of warships following the Alliance fleet was steadily growing and now numbered thirty-five. But there was no hypernet gate there, and after Dr. Setin begged, Geary agreed to linger in the star system long enough to send out surveillance probes and try one last time to establish meaningful communications with the aliens.

Neither method having discovered anything over the course of several days, he was preparing to order the fleet to depart when an urgent call came for him.

"Sir?" Lieutenant Iger seemed to be breathless for a moment. "Admiral, we've found some humans."

THIRTEEN

A single image appeared beside Iger, showing some blurred figures. "We only discovered it by chance," Iger explained. "One of the surveillance probes we launched cut across a data feed coming from this asteroid." Another image popped up, showing an asteroid about forty kilometers across, which was rotating at a decent rate of speed. "The intercept only lasted a fraction of a second, but we caught an encrypted video stream and were able to break out enough detail to see this."

Geary squinted at the ill-defined shapes. Definitely not the enigmas, and apparently human despite the lack of clear detail. "They're on that asteroid?"

"*In* that asteroid, Admiral," Iger said. "We're certain that's been hollowed out. We checked the rotation, and it's enough to provide roughly three-quarters of a standard gravity to someone standing on the inside surface of the asteroid." Symbols glowed on the asteroid's outer surface. "We've been able to spot some anomalies that probably represent enigma communications and sensor antennas. It's not unusual to find artifacts like that on asteroids in human-occupied star systems, items left behind by miners, but these are well concealed, and the enigmas don't usually seem to leave anything lying around."

Inside an asteroid. No way to escape, and no way to see out where the enigmas were. "The perfect prison from the aliens' perspective."

"Yes, sir." Instead of being proud or pleased by the discovery, Lieutenant Iger grimaced. "I . . . don't know of any way to get them out of there."

Tartarus. Apparently the name for this star system was a fitting one.

THE hundreds of officers around the table in the fleet conference room listened with growing enthusiasm as Iger laid out his information, but as the intelligence officer stopped, Tulev shook his head slowly. "If we move one kilometer toward that asteroid, they will destroy it. They are willing to kill their own. They will not hesitate to kill those humans, too."

"How close can we get before they do that?" Badaya asked.

Lieutenant Iger also shook his head. "I have no idea, sir. Based on our experience at Limbo, the aliens will wait until they are certain of our objective before they destroy it. And this particular target is very well hidden. If we hadn't been keyed by the intercepted transmission, we probably wouldn't have had any reason to study the asteroid closely and wouldn't have discovered the equipment concealed on the surface of the asteroid. As long as they don't believe we know humans are there, they probably won't destroy the asteroid just because we head in that general direction."

"Probably," Armus repeated with a grimace.

"It's the best we have, sir."

Bradamont had been eyeing the depiction of the Tartarus Star System floating over the table. "It must be a restricted zone for them. If we had aliens in an asteroid, we wouldn't allow unauthorized ships to get too close. If we passed inside that restricted area, it could also serve as the trigger for when the aliens decide to destroy the asteroid."

"That's plausible," Armus conceded. "Something triggered automatically by a proximity alert, or by a faster-than-light signal from elsewhere in the star system. There's no sign of alien presence on the exterior of the asteroid?"

"No, sir," Iger said. "Just some very nicely camouflaged solar cell fields."

Duellos nodded. "I can't imagine they would live inside the asteroid with humans, even if separated by a strong barrier. But if we have no idea how large this restricted zone is, I don't know how this speculation helps us."

"They need some basis for a restricted area," Bradamont said. "Both we and the Syndics measure those in light seconds, because it's a simple standard, big enough to provide security but small enough not to be triggered by anyone blundering into the wrong area by accident."

"How many light seconds do the Syndics use?" Tulev asked.

"One." No one questioned how Bradamont would know that.

"The same as our standard space exclusion zones."

Duellos frowned in thought. "The enigmas are certain to use some other means of measurement, but our parameters are based on practical considerations, as Commander Bradamont says. The physics are the same for the enigmas. If we stay at least one light second away, and don't seem to be paying any attention to the asteroid, that may be a safe distance."

"Make it four hundred thousand kilometers, well over a light second," Tulev said. "But still too far. That leaves plenty of reaction time for defenses or self-destruct mechanisms if we turn toward the asteroid. We have to reach it, match velocity and orbit, disable alien equipment on the surface, access the interior, and evacuate the humans living inside. How long to accomplish all of that? Half an hour from the closest point we dare approach?"

"More like an hour," Desjani suggested, "even if you're just using battle cruisers."

Bradamont spoke again, more forcefully. "The auxiliaries can manufacture small stealth craft carrying small landing parties. If we can—" She stopped as she saw Captain Smythe shaking his head.

"I'm sorry, Commander," Smythe said. "In the time we have, with what we have, I can't promise being able to build anything large enough to carry a few people yet stealthy enough to have a decent probability of staying undetected."

"Who would you send on a mission like that?" Badaya asked, the question apparently rhetorical yet also clearly aimed at Bradamont.

She flushed, but her voice stayed steady. "I volunteer to lead that mission."

Geary broke the silence that followed Bradamont's statement. "Unless we have a reasonable chance of success, there won't be any mission. There's no sense in killing our volunteers and the humans inside that asteroid by attempting a rescue with only a small chance of succeeding."

"We can't leave them," Bradamont insisted.

"I agree," Badaya said, "but—"

"Excuse me." General Carabali had been speaking with someone outside the software, and now her voice easily carried across those of the others. "The Marines can do it."

Badaya raised his eyebrows. "Four hundred thousand kilometers is a long jump, General. I don't think Marines could manage that even if you told them there was beer on the asteroid."

"They might if it was free beer, but we won't have to motivate them in that manner." A diagram popped up before Carabali. "Because of the nature of this mission to investigate the alien race, our equipment load-out includes a larger than usual amount of maximum-stealth configured armor, enough to equip thirty of my Marine scouts. I had some of my subordinates run the numbers, and we can do this. If the fleet launches those scouts toward the asteroid while passing by at four hundred thousand kilometers out, we should have a high probability of avoiding detection during launch and during the transit to the asteroid. Once on the surface of the asteroid, the scouts can plant scramblers and jammers, as well as disabling charges on any visible alien equipment. By blinding alien systems and jamming incoming and outgoing transmissions, we should be able to give the fleet time to reach the asteroid and launch shuttles to dock and pull people out of there as well as recover the scouts."

Tulev leaned in. "What velocity will the scouts be traveling?"

"We need it to be slow enough to not stand out too clearly against background space, and slow enough for the suit systems to manage a braked landing on the asteroid that will neither kill the scouts nor have a high chance of their being spotted." Carabali pointed to the diagram. "Average velocity would be four thousand kilometers per hour, though we'd want to be launched faster than that and be braking gradually during the last portion."

Commander Neeson gave the general a startled look. "You can brake down from four thousand klicks an hour to a safe landing velocity and remain stealthy?"

"That's right," Carabali said. "My scouts say they can do it, and they'd be the ones placing their lives on the line."

"Averaging four thousand kilometers per hour will still require four days' travel time," Geary objected. "Can your scout suits keep someone alive that long, plus the time needed to go over the asteroid and plant those charges and jammers?"

Carabali nodded. "We can hang on some extended-duty life-support packs, and use meds to slow down the metabolism of the scouts during the trip to the asteroid. That will both reduce the demands on their life support and the amount of heat and power usage that the stealth equipment has to conceal."

"Can the jammers work against anything the aliens have?" Badaya questioned. "We don't even know how their faster-than-light comms work."

"The jammers have been upgraded using some ideas gleaned from the Syndic device for preventing gate collapses," Carabali explained. "Just like our system security can eliminate the quantum probability–based alien worms without knowing how they work, we have a high degree of confidence that the jammers can halt the alien comms."

A long silence this time, as everyone studied Carabali's work, finally broken by Duellos as he pointed to part of the depiction of the star system. "There's an enigma installation on the second largest moon orbiting that planet. If we head toward it at the right time, we'll have that as an apparent goal, evidently repeating our attempt to examine a single isolated installation as at Limbo, but we can pass part of the fleet within four hundred thousand kilometers of the asteroid's orbit while seeming to head for that moon."

"It's doable," Badaya declared, and a hundred voices joined him in agreement.

"If you use the battle cruisers," Desjani added, giving Geary a hard look. "*All* of the battle cruisers. We're going to have to move as fast as possible."

Geary kept his eyes on the display for a moment longer, thinking of the lives riding on this decision. He didn't want to make this decision. But Carabali had proven her competence, and his fleet officers felt they could do their part, and those humans needed to be rescued if it could possibly be done. Ironically, one of the things making the operation feasible was the lessons learned from the Syndic device he had bargained with Iceni for. "All right. We'll do it."

This time, everyone cheered.

IT had the same strange feeling as when walking past a police officer even when you had done nothing. Look calm, look innocent, look non-threatening. That was quite a bit harder to do when you were a fleet carrying enough firepower to devastate entire planets, and you were trespassing in a star system where you were definitely not wanted, and the police officers were in fact aliens with a demonstrated

eagerness to kill you and a willingness to suicide in defense
of their privacy, and when you were in fact plotting to do
something of which the local "police" would not approve
at all.

Geary waited until the right moment to swing the fleet
onto a course to intercept the moon that was to be their apparent target. There wasn't anything unusual about shuttles
winging between warships, carrying parts, supplies, and
skilled personnel, but over the last several hours many of
those routine shuttle flights had in fact transferred Marine
scouts and their equipment to the battleships making up the
Fourth Battleship Division. *Warspite*, *Vengeance*, *Revenge*,
and *Guardian* would be the closest major warships to the
asteroid's orbit when the human fleet went past, and that
was when each would spit out seven or eight Marines aimed
at where the asteroid would be four days later, the launches
further obscured by some repositioning of the cruisers and
destroyers near the battleships as well as some shuttle
activity.

"This is Admiral Geary. At time one five, all units come
port zero four one degrees, up zero six degrees, maintain
velocity at point one light speed." It felt a little strange using
the human conventions for maneuvering in a star system
when this star system had probably never seen a human
spacecraft. But the old conventions had been developed
to ensure that every ship understood what other ships were
doing and what was meant, no matter how they might be
pointed or aligned relative to one another. Port meant
turning away from the star, starboard turning toward the
star, while up and down were designated as either side of
the plane of the star system. It was totally arbitrary, but had
worked well enough to remain unchanged for centuries.

He wondered how the aliens handled that problem. Was
it a problem to them at all? *Why the hell won't they talk to
us? Imagine the things we could learn just from understanding how another intelligent species sees the universe. What
a waste.*

"Getting moody again, Admiral?" Desjani asked as she

signed off on some administrative task. "Have you heard from Jane Geary yet?"

"Yes. How did you know?"

"She volunteered her battleship division to launch the Marines, right?"

"Correct again. I told her the decision was based entirely on which battleships could be closest to the asteroid's orbit with the least maneuvering within the formation. We want to do as little as possible to tip off the aliens." Geary gave Desjani a curious look. "Have you figured out what's motivating Jane?"

"No. I don't think it's what was bothering Kattnig"—she paused to make a religious gesture invoking mercy—"but it might be related."

"Proving herself?"

"She *is* a Geary, Admiral. You know what they're like."

"I wish I did." Geary sat back, watching on the display as his fleet swung smoothly around and settled out on the course toward the alien moon. "The hardest part is going to be waiting for a few days after the launch, then turning this fleet around to go past the asteroid's orbit again, all the while not knowing if the Marine scouts made it and are accomplishing their mission. They can't send any status reports, no updates, nothing. They'll activate the jammers and disabling charges at a set time, and we need to already be charging for that asteroid when that happens. *And* those thirty-five alien warships will surely charge us at that point."

Desjani grinned. "Finally, we get to have some fun."

"WARSPITE reports one crew member injured in an arcing mishap," the comm watch announced.

"Very well." Geary glanced at Desjani, who gave him a thumbs-up. With the quantum-probability worms scrubbed from systems on the human warships, the aliens shouldn't have any means of accessing the fleet data net or comm systems. But "shouldn't" didn't mean "couldn't," so that message had been agreed upon as a signal that all the launches had gone down without any problems.

A very long two days later, with the alien moon still more than a light hour distant, Geary brought the fleet back around as if heading back to the jump point. A freighter had already left the alien installation, repeating the pattern at Limbo. "When they see this, they should decide that we're giving up this time rather than waste more effort chasing things that are going to be blown into tiny pieces."

Desjani nodded absentmindedly, her eyes on her own display. "You know, Admiral, even if the jamming works, and even if all the alien sensors and comm gear on the surface of that asteroid are taken out, we're still going to have the alien warships coming at that asteroid as soon as they realize we're heading that way. We have no idea how many people we'll need to get off that asteroid, or how hard it will be to get inside it without triggering any booby traps. It's going to be tight."

"I know," Geary said. "That's why you're going to be calling the maneuvers when the battle cruisers brake to match orbit with the asteroid." She gave him a startled look that transitioned to a grin as Geary continued. "I'm pretty good at that kind of thing, but you're better when it comes to maneuvering battle cruisers. You're better than anyone else in the fleet."

"Yes," Desjani agreed. "Yes, I am."

"As well as being unusually modest for a battle cruiser captain."

"That, too." Desjani switched her gaze back to her display, where she was working simulations of the charge to the asteroid. "Oh, this is going to be good."

THE Marine scouts should have landed over eight hours ago. They had orders to activate the jammers, scramblers, and disabling charges at exactly zero four forty, when the fleet would be passing nearest to the asteroid's orbit on the fleet's return toward the jump point.

Aside from the asteroid itself, the nearest alien presence or surveillance devices they had been able to spot were the warships, which had stayed lurking a light hour behind and to the starboard side of the Alliance fleet, matching every human maneuver an hour after it was made. But in the last day, as the human fleet's path approached the orbit of the asteroid and this time drew closer to the asteroid itself, those alien warships had slowly closed the distance until they were only half a light hour away from the fleet.

Now it was zero four thirty eight. The asteroid was forty-five light seconds away, a mere thirteen million, five hundred thousand kilometers. At point one light speed, the human ships could cover that distance in about seven and a half minutes. But it wouldn't do much good to reach the asteroid traveling that fast since the human ships would then shoot past, unable to match speed with the asteroid. The "charge" would actually involve slowing down at a rate that would take the least time and yet leave the battle cruisers exactly matching the asteroid's velocity when they reached it. Only the battle cruisers had enough propulsion capability to brake their velocity that quickly, and they had to start immediately, or even they might overshoot their target, but they also had to avoid braking too fast and taking longer than necessary to reach the asteroid when every second counted.

Which was where Tanya Desjani came in.

Geary took a deep breath, then sent the orders. "Task Force Lima, detach and maneuver per orders from Captain Desjani on *Dauntless*. All other units, come starboard zero four five degrees, down zero two degrees, and begin braking to point zero two light speed at time four zero."

Desjani was sending her own commands the moment Geary finished. "All units in Task Force Lima, immediate execute come starboard four six degrees, down zero two degrees, begin braking velocity at maximum."

Usually, she waited silently while he concentrated on the right feel, the right moments for when to execute changes in vectors, but this time it was Desjani who was issuing

those orders for the task force while Geary watched the
battle cruisers veer away from the rest of the fleet and de-
celerate at a rate that pushed him painfully back against his
seat and caused the structure of *Dauntless* to groan in protest. Despite the temptation to watch Desjani's work, to
make sure she was doing it as well as possible, he had to let
her do the job he had given her while he kept an eye on the
rest of the fleet, slowing much more gradually and curving
on a slightly wider course, which would intercept the asteroid farther along its orbit and close to an hour after the battle
cruisers reached their objective. Geary also watched the
aliens, though it would be half an hour before their warships
saw the light from the fleet's maneuvers and realized what
the fleet was doing.

Wincing at the effort of moving under the forces leaking
past the inertial dampers, he called General Carabali. "I
want to know the moment you hear or see anything from
the scouts."

"Should be coming in any second now, Admiral." Carabali paused. "Status report. Linking to you, sir."

A secondary display popped into existence to one side
of Geary. On it, the asteroid rotated with cumbersome dig-
nity, its surface now pocked with many more symbols representing not just the positions of the Marine scouts but also
all of the alien relays, antennas, sensors, and other devices
the Marines had been able to locate. Some of the symbols
marking the alien equipment flashed red, indicating that
disabling charges planted by the Marines had destroyed
them, while other symbols pulsed yellow to indicate the
equipment was being jammed.

Also visible was a large and cunningly concealed airlock
detected by the scouts, which led inside the asteroid. "Request permission to proceed with entry," Carabali said.

"Permission granted. Why do I count only twenty-nine
Marines?"

"I've just been informed that the scout unit leader believes one suit failed to brake velocity enough and overshot
the asteroid," Carabali said tonelessly.

Ancestors preserve us. Geary activated another circuit. "Eleventh Light Cruiser Squadron, Twenty-third and Thirty-second Destroyer Squadrons, detach from fleet formation immediately, proceed to attempt intercept and pickup with one Marine scout who is believed to have overshot the asteroid."

Carabali let out a breath. "Thank you, Admiral. My scouts will be blowing the airlock any moment now."

Geary took a moment to take a long, calming breath himself, thinking of that lone Marine plummeting through space, life support slowly being expended. "Whether we can manage an intercept is going to depend on how much that Marine's velocity was slowed, General. If that scout kept going at four thousand kilometers an hour, we may not be able to get there in time."

"If the enigma warships go after the ships you sent—"

"I doubt that will happen, General, once the aliens realize that we're cracking open their human cage."

Desjani sent another order. "Immediate execute, all units in Task Force Lima reduce braking velocity to point nine maximum."

The strain on Geary eased a bit, and he could have sworn he heard the structure of *Dauntless* also sigh with relief. He spared a glance at the display, where the path of the battle cruisers arced toward the asteroid, the time to intercept constantly backing off as the ships slowed their velocity.

"Marines are inside," Carabali reported. "Possible booby-trap triggers identified. They'll have to neutralize before proceeding."

Damn. "We don't have much room for delay, General."

"Understood, Admiral."

"Immediate execute, all units in Task Force Lima reduce braking velocity to point eight maximum," Desjani ordered.

Sixteen minutes after Desjani gave her first order, and after several more adjustments to their braking, the battle cruisers slid to a halt relative to the asteroid, surrounding it. "All shuttles launch," Desjani commanded.

From every battle cruiser, shuttles rocketed out, heading for the asteroid. Each carried a few Marine engineers loaded with breaching equipment and other gear, some medical personnel, a fleet engineer to identify any alien equipment that could be looted in the time available, and empty seats for the human prisoners who would hopefully be found within the asteroid. "Five minutes to first shuttle docking at that airlock," Desjani told Geary.

"General Carabali," Geary began.

"They're past the traps," Carabali announced. "Passing empty compartments. Equipment. Another airlock. Traps visible on this side. Estimated time to disarm two minutes."

Desjani had her eyes on the alien warships. "We slowed down, they didn't. They'll see the light from our maneuvers in another ten minutes."

Geary nodded. "I guess that's when we find out if there's still a way for the aliens to blow up this asteroid." He eyed the main body of the fleet, still braking, the distance between it and the task force growing by the second. He didn't need to run maneuvering calculations to know that he couldn't turn those ships around and get them back here in time to make any difference. "It looks like it'll be sixteen battle cruisers versus thirty-five alien warships."

"Piece of cake," Desjani remarked.

The main body's formation was stretching oddly, though. Geary highlighted that area and saw that *Dreadnaught* was braking harder than ordered, *Dependable* and *Conqueror* matching her attempt to slow down. "Captain Geary, you're overstressing your main propulsion units. Ease off and remain with the fleet."

Desjani had noticed and shook her head. "She's trying to keep those battleships close enough to support us. They *can't* brake that fast."

"And she should know that."

He took another look at the light cruisers and destroyers still accelerating toward the area where the Marine might be. "General, if you can order that scout to light off a beacon, it would help."

"Already done, Admiral. The scout should have already received that order, but we've seen no response, so he might still be in a slowed metabolism state. We just sent a remote activation command to the beacon."

"Distress beacon picked up," Lieutenant Castries reported.

Geary did a quick mental check of the position of the beacon and its movement relative to the cruisers and destroyers. "That Marine did slow a lot before his suit's braking equipment failed. I think they can manage a recovery."

"Someone owes a few thanks to their ancestors," Desjani remarked.

"We're past the airlock," Carabali reported. "Another airlock, sealed, no traps. Blowing it now."

"They're moving," Desjani announced.

"Alien warships accelerating on to intercept with our current position," Lieutenant Yuon cried.

"We can hear you, Lieutenant," Desjani said sharply. "All units in Task Force Lima, recover returning shuttles nearest to you without regard for home base." She shrugged. "That should save a few minutes on the recovery," she said to Geary.

He nodded absently, most of his attention shifting rapidly from the main body of the fleet to the progress of the Marines to the shuttles to the alien warships and back again and again. "We have roughly an hour before those warships get here."

"Past final barrier," Carabali reported. "Entering large open area, multiple structures arrayed along sides of the asteroid. It's a town, all right. Humans sighted. Some are running toward our people, and some are running away."

"First shuttle docking, dropping off passengers."

"Initial estimates of human prisoners exceeds one hundred."

"Power inside asteroid has failed. Cause unknown. Deploying portable lighting."

"Enigma warships are fifty minutes from intercept."

"Light cruiser *Kusari* reports estimated time to recovery of Marine scout is one hour, forty minutes."

"Liberated prisoners being assembled, report that many of their number are *hiding* and barricading themselves inside their dwellings."

Geary resisted the urge to slap his forehead in exasperation. The reaction by these isolated, imprisoned people was understandable even if stupid. "Permission granted to break down barricades, doors, walls, or any other private structure as necessary to recover humans without delay."

Carabali seemed more annoyed than angry. "Request permission to use incapacitating agents if necessary to disable resisting humans."

"Granted. We're running out of time fast, General."

"Admiral," Captain Smythe said, "my engineers report that scans reveal the alien equipment on the asteroid is riddled with explosive devices. Trying to pull out any of it might well trigger self-destruct mechanisms unless we take the time to deactivate all possible means of activation."

"How much time?" Geary demanded.

Smythe paused for only a moment. "At least an hour."

"We don't have an hour. Have your engineers do the best scans they can of the inside and outside of that equipment, then get them back on the shuttles. They've got twenty minutes."

"First shuttle lifting from asteroid with thirty prisoners aboard," Castries called.

"They must be packing them in tight," Desjani muttered.

"Admiral!" It was the chief medical officer. "I've been evaluating what we can tell about the prisoners. They need to be medically isolated *immediately* and held there until they're scanned for any biological or artificial threat."

"Notify the ship's doctors on each battle cruiser," Geary snapped. "Have them inform their captains and ensure that's done."

"Twenty-five minutes until enigma warships achieve intercept of asteroid."

"Sir, one of the alien warships has peeled off and seems to be aiming for the Marine scout awaiting recovery."

He would have to leave that to the light cruisers and

destroyers. They didn't need to be told that they needed to get that Marine before the alien warship did.

"Ration bar?" Desjani asked.

"No, thanks. Not hungry."

"We've got half the shuttles recovered," she added. "The other half are waiting on the let's-hide-from-our-rescuers idiots that the Marines are prying out of their holes."

"Twenty minutes to alien intercept."

"Admiral, we've got equipment starting to blow inside that asteroid," Carabali reported. "Cause unknown. Maybe dead-man circuits that activate after a certain period out of communication."

"How long until you have the last humans out of there?" Geary shot back.

"Unknown. Still searching, Admiral."

"You've got fifteen minutes, General."

"Yes, sir."

Desjani was sending orders. "Captain Duellos, your shuttle docks are full. Accelerate your battle cruisers toward the enemy and engage to buy us time and even the odds."

"On our way," Duellos responded. On the display, *Inspire*, *Formidable*, *Brilliant*, and *Implacable* began moving away from the asteroid, angling toward the alien warships.

"Good call," Geary said. "There's no sense in those battle cruisers waiting here if they can't take on any more shuttles. I should have thought of that."

"You're busy," Desjani said, "and you gave me the responsibility for this part. But I would appreciate it if you would goose the Marines, so we can get the rest of those shuttles aboard before the aliens get here."

"Pulling out," Carabali reported. "We can't be certain we got everyone, but the asteroid is coming apart inside, and the interior is depressurizing, so anyone we don't have is going to be dead before we could find them. There must be dead-man circuits everywhere."

"Understood," Geary said. "Get your people out of there. How many prisoners have we recovered?"

"Three hundred thirty-three."

"What?"

"Three hundred thirty-three," Carabali repeated. "Yes, sir. It's weird. Maybe it means something." She focused elsewhere. "Now! I want every Marine out of there now! If those fleet engineers drag their feet, knock them out and haul them along!"

Small detonations rocked the surface of the asteroid, throwing out fragments that soared into space out of the weak gravitational pull, atmosphere venting in many places into the vacuum of space. Geary checked the main display. Six minutes until the alien warships reached them. "It's going to be very tight."

Desjani nodded. "Captain Tulev, get your division under way and engage the enemy."

"Understood," Tulev replied. *Leviathan*, *Dragon*, *Steadfast*, and *Valiant* began accelerating toward the oncoming enemy.

"Captain, our dock is full. Sealing it now."

"Very well. *Invincible*, why is a shuttle hanging outside your dock?"

Vente sounded as stiff as usual. "I am following proper procedure for loading sequences—"

"Get that shuttle docked *now*, or I'll have you shot! All units, we have three minutes! I do not intend engaging these bastards while we're engaged in shuttle recovery and at rest relative to this rock!"

Duellos's battle cruisers had reached the enemy, hurling out specters that the enemy twisted to try to dodge, then the two forces lashed each other as they tore past.

"Everyone is clear," Carabali reported. "All personnel accounted for. The final shuttle is en route *Incredible*."

Geary stared for a moment at the display centered on the asteroid, seeing large portions of its outer surface collapsing inward or bulging outward in response to the spasms inside it.

"All shuttles recovered, Captain. *Incredible* is sealing her dock."

"All units in Task Force Lima, maneuver independently and engage the enemy!"

Twenty-nine enigma warships were still coming, but they had to get past Tulev's battle cruisers first. Though they hadn't had a long time to accelerate, the battle cruisers were still deadly, and the enigma warships had to go through them if they wanted to reach the asteroid.

Specters volleyed out, followed within moments by hell-lance fire and grapeshot as the two forces clashed.

"They hit *Valiant* hard," Geary heard someone saying, then realized he had been the one who spoke. But only sixteen alien warships were still coming, and led by *Dauntless*, the eight remaining Alliance battle cruisers were accelerating furiously toward them.

Desjani's hand danced over her firing controls, and *Dauntless* shuddered slightly as specter missiles launched, then the battle cruiser's hell lances speared out as well, aimed and fired automatically by combat systems reacting far faster than any human could. Volleys of grapeshot followed in the instant before the far-faster-moving alien warships slashed through the human ships in the blink of an eye.

Geary kept his eyes on the display as it updated rapidly in response to sensor reports from every ship in the fleet. Only three alien warships were still moving, and they were still heading straight for the asteroid, making no attempt to turn or slow down. "What the hell?"

An instant later, the three surviving enigma warships smashed into the asteroid while moving at sixty thousand kilometers per second.

No one spoke for a long moment as the displays updated to show nothing but a rapidly expanding cloud of dust where the asteroid and three enigma warships had once been. Geary finally tore his eyes from that, only to see that, once again, every other nearby enigma warship, whether badly damaged or completely knocked out, had self-destructed.

It was close to half an hour later when they saw the sole remaining enigma warship in the star system veering off when the Alliance light cruisers and half the destroyers came right for it as the rest of the destroyers braked to pick up the Marine. "Why do they sometimes kill themselves for what seem to be totally unnecessary reasons, and other times they show reasonable discretion in the face of the odds against them?" Geary wondered. His eyes went back to the assessments of the damage to the battle cruisers, focusing on *Valiant* and her seventeen dead.

"I don't know," Desjani replied, "and I don't care anymore. If any of the aliens come within range of my weapons, I'll remove any options from their futures."

The destroyers intercepting the Marine slowed further, until *Carbine* could snag the suit and haul the scout aboard. "Goal!" The triumphant message arrived from the rescue force several minutes later, the entire group of light cruisers and destroyers by then accelerating back to the main body of the fleet.

"The destroyers are asking for ransom," Carabali reported to Geary, looking considerably more relaxed than she had during the operation at the asteroid.

"Anything the Marines aren't prepared to pay?"

"We'll buy rounds for their crews at any bar wherever the fleet has liberty next, Admiral. Thank you."

"I wasn't going to leave that scout, General."

"You didn't have to make that decision, Admiral."

Desjani glanced at Geary as he ended that call. "You should get some rest."

"So should you."

"I told you first."

"Damn good job back there."

"Why, thank you, Admiral. Can I still shoot Vente?"

"No." Geary closed his eyes for a moment, a great wave of weariness washing over him now that the days of tension had ended in success. "That threat did seem to motivate him, though. Another couple of minutes, and we'd still have been too close to that asteroid when those alien ships turned it into high-velocity junk."

Her voice sounded a little distant. "We had to succeed

this time because we can't do it again. Next time we come within a light hour of any place they're holding humans, they'll blow it apart."

He knew she was right. This had been a victory, but it had ensured no similar victories could be won.

GEARY took the time to gather the fleet and organize it back into a single formation despite the appearance of almost twenty more enigma warships at other jump points. The days required for that and the journey to the jump point they planned to use next also provided time to learn something about the humans they had rescued.

"They've never seen any of the aliens," Lieutenant Iger reported to Geary. "Even the ones who were captured as opposed to being born in there." He activated another window showing a man who looked well past middle age. "This man was a crew member on a Syndic HuK. He doesn't know how long ago that was because the humans inside the asteroid had no means of telling time, but by comparing his account to the records the Syndics provided, it was probably forty years ago when a HuK transiting through the border star system of Ina disappeared."

The old man began speaking. "I don't know what happened. I was at my watch station, and suddenly we started taking hits out of nowhere. I remember that. Everyone yelling, 'Where's it coming from?' Then we got orders to evacuate, and I made it to an escape pod with two others from the crew, and we punched clear, and that's the last I remembered until I woke up in that place. An asteroid. I always thought it must be an asteroid. I don't know what happened to the other two who were in the pod with me. I was the only one from our mobile force unit who showed up there. No. No one saw me arrive. I was just there. The lights would go out sometimes, then we'd all fall asleep, and when we woke up, there might be a new person lying next to the lock, or maybe some crates of food, or somebody who had died would be gone. When someone died, we knew that either a new prisoner would show up eventually, or one of the women would become pregnant and have a child. Always the same number of us. Yes. Three hundred thirty-three. Don't know why."

The freed prisoner had stopped speaking, blinking away tears. "I know you're Alliance, but . . . can I go home, sir? It's been a long time, and I thought I'd die in that place. I want to go home, sir."

Geary looked away, trying to control his emotions, trying not to let pity for that man and hate for his captors sway his decisions. *How would we have treated aliens that we captured? Maybe not the Alliance. But the Syndics, they could have built something like that asteroid prison.* "He can't tell us anything, Lieutenant Iger?"

"No, sir. None of them can."

The fleet's chief medical officer had an only slightly more encouraging report. "We didn't find any biological agents in them, or evidence that any such had been tested. But they did have nanodevices inside them, which outside the asteroid would have triggered fatal reactions if we hadn't neutralized them as quickly as we did."

Another form of dead-man switch. "How's their health now?"

The doctor shrugged. "Not bad, considering. They had a closed community. Human-origin equipment and devices for survival, medical care, and the like. Two of the prisoners had enough medical training to use the equipment and take care of all but the most serious afflictions. They grew crops, and occasionally, quantities of foodstuffs that had clearly been manufactured by humans appeared near the airlock. From the state of their health, they've had adequate nutrition, though of course the diet lacked variety most of the time."

"What about mentally? How are they?"

The doctor looked down before answering. "Fragile. They had constructed a society inside that asteroid, something stable enough to pass on knowledge and maintain order. There's a council of sorts that made decisions. But they've been so isolated, subject to the whims of totally unseen and unknown captors. Now . . . some of them are excited at the thought of seeing the sky. Others are terrified of the same thing. Their world, their source of stability, has been destroyed, and not just in the literal sense of the asteroid being shattered."

Geary sighed. "Surely we did the right thing by rescuing them."

"Of course. A cage is a cage is a cage. But freedom will be hard for them to adjust to. What are you going to do with them?" the doctor asked.

"Take them home." Geary paused, realizing that wasn't as simple a thing as it sounded. "They should all have surviving relatives somewhere in Syndic territory."

"Where central authority no longer governs many star systems," the doctor pointed out. "For some of these people, reunions won't be that difficult. They were first-generation prisoners. But others are the offspring of those captured more than a century ago. The only home they have ever known was the interior of an asteroid, the only family they know are the people who also lived there."

Hesitating, the doctor finally spoke more slowly. "I fear for them, Admiral. They are . . . valuable and unique research subjects. There. I said it. There are plenty of people who would be willing to treat them as lab rats, just as the aliens did, and few who could speak on their behalf, especially in the Syndicate Worlds. They need protecting from those who would exploit them and use them."

"There are limits to my ability to protect them, Doctor."

"But you can take them home to the Alliance if they wish," the doctor insisted. "Where others would stand up for their rights. And if Black Jack Geary publicly expresses a wish that they be treated as humans who have already suffered too much, it *will* influence their treatment. Perhaps even within Syndicate Worlds' territory."

It seemed a small thing to ask of him, but Geary saw the greatest roadblock to doing it. "I can and will make such public statements. But what if they don't want to go to the Alliance?"

"Admiral, what will Syndic CEOs do with those people? You know the answer. I realize it will be a while before we return to human space, but I'd like you to think about it before then."

The freed humans had all been gathered on *Typhoon*, which had required shifting some Marines, but the fleet's doctors had insisted the freed prisoners should be kept together for their own peace of mind, such as it was. Conference software was modified so that Geary could address the entire group, his image appearing simultaneously in each of their berthing areas while to him the former captives all seemed to be in one large room listening to him.

He had seen prisoners liberated from Syndic labor camps, but this was different. The humans clustered together, almost clutching one another. Some wore new clothing provided from fleet stocks, but others still had on a strange mix of clothing, styles and fashions from different periods and professions, most of the clothes threadbare and heavily patched. "We'll take you wherever you want to go," Geary said. "Some of you wish to return to homes in the Syndicate Worlds. I know that you've been told that things have changed, that life in the Syndicate Worlds is much more uncertain than you may recall, but if that's where you wish to go, we will try to ensure that you reach your former homes. All of you are welcome to come with us back to Alliance territory, where I give you my word of honor you will be welcomed and treated well."

They all exchanged glances, some looking fearful and others hopeful, a few children clinging to mothers. "How long do we have to think about it?"

"A few months. That's how long it will take us to get back to Syndic space because our mission here hasn't ended."

They didn't want to say much more than that, huddled in among themselves, so after a short while, Geary broke the connection and sat down, his thoughts jumbled. *And to think I felt sorry for myself when I came out of survival sleep to find a century gone. I was lucky in more ways than one. Forgive me, but I want to hurt those enigmas. Make them pay. But they have been hurt. A lot of them have died, and we've destroyed quite a few of their ships. Is it accomplishing anything? At least we got those people freed.*

He called up the latest status reports for the fleet. Almost thirty destroyers had suffered sudden equipment failures requiring Captain Smythe's auxiliaries to focus on those repairs as well as fixing up the latest battle damage. That had caused the planned replacement work to slide, pushing it closer to the looming rise of the failure curve waiting several months ahead.

His hatch alert chimed. He looked up, hoping for Tanya, and found himself looking at Victoria Rione. "What's the occasion?" It came out more harshly than he intended.

Her expression hardened slightly. "I wanted to inform you that Commander Benan has received a feeler about propagandizing for your replacement."

"Am I going somewhere?"

She came inside his stateroom. "Accidents happen."

"Is that a warning or a philosophical musing?"

Rione just shook her head. "I don't know of any threats to you from within the fleet."

His mind seized on part of that. "From within the fleet?"

"I said what I said. Who will assume command of this fleet if something does happen to you?"

Geary played with the idea of refusing to answer, giving back her own hidden agendas, but decided to try playing to his own strength of being honest. "Captain Badaya, who has promised to listen to the advice of Tulev and Duellos. Do you want to sit down?"

She took a seat, eyeing him. "No command role for your captain?"

"It's a safe assumption that if something happens to me, it will also happen to her. She also lacks the necessary seniority, and diplomacy isn't Tanya's greatest strength."

"Oh, you've noticed that? But, in the unfortunate event it happened, wouldn't she benefit from being the widow of Black Jack?" Rione asked.

"Tanya would never use that."

"If necessary, she should." Rione hesitated, looking for a tiny moment as if she had said more than she ought to have. "What about all of the admirals waiting on the transports?"

"They've all been officially placed on medical holds, awaiting full evaluation before being certified as capable of enduring the strains of active duty."

Rione laughed. "The great Black Jack is stooping to political games?"

"The great Black Jack knows how badly post-traumatic stress can impact someone. It's a miracle that I was able to get the fleet away from the Syndics when I was thrown into command. And none of those liberated admirals understand tactics." He leaned back. "I'm looking out for the fleet."

"By putting Badaya in command?"

"Badaya isn't stupid, and he knows that Tulev has enough seniority to challenge him if he veers off course. Badaya also knows that without me, he couldn't hope to control the Alliance. Did you come by to talk politics?"

She locked eyes with him. "Are you turning the fleet around now?"

"No. A few more star systems, then we turn."

A careful nod. "I am required to remind you that you were ordered to find the boundaries of enigma space."

"And you have so reminded me. Victoria, why did they send you as one of the emissaries?"

For a moment, her carefully shielded emotions showed. "I volunteered, after receiving an offer I could not refuse. I might have refused anyway, but I didn't know who would be sent in my place."

"Did you know your husband was at Dunai?"

"No. I knew it was a VIP labor camp, but Paol was only a commander."

"A commander married to the Co-President of the Callas Republic."

She shrugged, the defenses falling back into place. "I really should have thought of that. These people we rescued. What will happen to them?"

"We'll do our best to look out for them, but they're all free human beings, so in the end the decisions will be theirs."

"What deal did you make with CEO Iceni to get that Syndic device for preventing gate collapses?"

The question surprised him because he had thought Rione would already have discovered the answer. "Allowing the implication that I will not act against her. She is planning on breaking free from the Syndicate Worlds. It's lucky the Syndics came up with that device, isn't it? It would have been a long trip home without the Syndic hypernet," he continued, deliberately making the dig to see how she would respond.

"Yes. It would have been a very long trip." Another nod, then she stood up. "A few more star systems, Admiral? It might be tempting to keep going even after that."

Her entire attitude conveyed that she thought that would be a mistake, though something was keeping her from saying it right out. "I understand. We've plotted out a track for seven more star systems, and the seventh is as far as we're going."

FOURTEEN

FROM Tartarus, the fleet jumped to Hades, only to find another hypernet gate there. Wondering if they were already nearing the other side of enigma-controlled space, they jumped to Perdition. There was little enigma presence there, but another hypernet gate. A jump from the same jump point almost sideways to the newly named star Gehenna found no gate in what seemed a fairly well-off star system. "Did we loop back deeper into enigma territory somehow?" Desjani wondered. But another jump to Inferno found a similarly long-settled star system, also lacking a gate.

And, at each jump, more and more alien warships could be seen trailing the fleet. As the fleet jumped away from Inferno, the alien armada had grown to more than sixty.

Two more stars, both with hypernet gates. The fleet made another risky dash to the next jump point and found itself at a star once again with a gate.

"Why should we keep going farther?" Armus asked.

Geary gestured to the star display. "We're close to the turnaround. For every star we've been to, we've passed by three or four on average. It's giving us an idea of the strength of the enigmas, but they're still not talking to us, and we can't learn anything more about them without triggering probable mass deaths among them."

"You say that like it's a bad thing," Captain Vitali grumbled. Just about everybody else nodded in agreement. Anger at deaths in combat had been magnified as word got around about the state of the humans once held captive by the enigma race.

"Our mission isn't to kill them. Though we've taken out plenty of them up to now." Geary singled out a star. "This is our next objective. It's a long jump. We'll see what's there, then start jumping back, not retracing our steps, but angling along a different route to avoid running into that pack of warships that keeps following us. Maybe once we've left enigma space entirely, having demonstrated our ability to operate within their space but without trying to annihilate them or pushing any more to violate their fanatical sense of privacy, they'll be willing to consider talking to us and accepting a fixed border."

Dr. Shwartz gasped in frustration. "The border. Why doesn't our willingness to discuss respecting a single border matter to them? During the conversations you had with the enigmas at Midway, they kept emphasizing that they owned Midway and other stars, and therefore we had no right to be there. Why isn't that same thinking motivating them to negotiate with us for a mutually agreed-upon border that would guarantee their ownership of the star systems they now control?"

"It is a discrepancy," Duellos agreed. "But only one of many."

Charban, though, gazed at Shwartz as if something had just come to him, seemed about to speak, then subsided with the aspect of someone sunk into thought.

"If I could know one more thing about them," Badaya said, "I'd want to know what sort of rhyme or reason they use to decide where they put hypernet gates. The idea that the gates are last-ditch, supermines aimed at deterring conquest seems like the best explanation for the first gates we encountered, but then why all these gates inside their territory? And why do we usually see them in consecutive star systems, followed by gaps?"

Commander Neeson spoke up. "I have an idea, a possible explanation, that is." He pointed to the display. "Seen this way, in three dimensions with our path wending through them, Captain Badaya's statement is accurate. There doesn't seem to be any consistency to the placement of the gates. But it's not just the gates. Defenses inside star systems with gates are also much more robust. I tried running an analysis viewing the data in a different way." The three-dimensional star field blinked out, replaced by a simple two-dimensional graph.

"The bottom axis here is distance inside alien space, the vertical axis is the level of defenses we've seen. The initial alien star systems we entered had substantial defenses, as we'd expect. That's their border with humanity." Neeson indicated peaks in the graph near its beginning. "Then defenses tapered off, again as we'd expect. The aliens can't afford to fortify every star system any more than we can, so they place their defenses on the border."

Pointing farther along on the graph, Neeson centered the display on another peak. "But here we saw two more star systems with substantial defenses, and those star systems were neighbors in jump terms. Then some more stars without gates, before encountering more gates, again in two star systems that were next to each other for anyone using jump drives."

Tulev was the first to comment. "Layers of defense? But if so, they're not spaced in any uniform fashion, and I cannot see the sense in putting extra defenses so far from their borders."

"Far from their borders with *us*," Neeson said. "We've been looking at this as the enigma race. One entity. But if this were human space, and we saw these kind of defenses set up internally, *facing* each other, how would we interpret that? How would the border between the Alliance and the Syndicate Worlds look to an alien scouting force?"

Geary wanted to slap his forehead. "They're not unified."

"Internal borders," Tulev agreed. "Internal defenses against other members of their own species. The aliens are not unified any more than humanity is. If we judge from the frequency of the defensive lines, they are more divided than we are."

"Why did we assume they were unified?" General Carabali asked. "Because I realize that I did, too."

"Probably because we knew so little," Neeson said. "We had to fill in blanks, and they were very big blanks. That meant a lot of assumptions. Assuming the enigmas were unified simplified everything else mentally, so maybe that's what drove that idea."

General Charban nodded. "It simplified it emotionally, too, didn't it? *The* enemy. *The* alien race. I believe your officer has hit upon a very important discovery, Admiral, one that wasn't apparent on a three-dimensional display but seems obvious when viewed properly. Perhaps we can use these internal divisions among the aliens."

Duellos sighed. "General, I would be happy if that were so, but we have seen the alien forces in pursuit of us grow with each star system we pass. We did not find it remarkable that they picked up reinforcements in each star system along the way, which would have been consistent with a unified race, but a divided race should have resulted in contingents falling away as we left their particular part of enigma space. That hasn't happened. Those warships keep growing in numbers each time we see them. That argues that, whatever their internal divisions, they are more than willing to unite against *us*."

"Which also shouldn't be a surprise," Bradamont commented. "The Alliance fleet defended a Syndicate Worlds' star system against the aliens. We stood together with other humans, even humans we would not otherwise cooperate with. The aliens may dislike each other, may war with each other, but they dislike us a great deal more."

His frown growing as Duellos and Bradamont spoke,

Charban shook his head. "But when you encountered the aliens at Midway, they seemed unable to understand why you would defend a Syndic star system. They don't seem to grasp the idea of former enemies cooperating."

"And yet they seem to be cooperating against us," Geary pointed out. "It can't be that . . . alien a concept to them."

"They also thought we and the Syndics would use the hypernet gates to wipe each other out because we were enemies," Carabali said. "But we've found no star systems in enigma space where gates were used as weapons against other members of their species."

"They expected the worst of humanity," Commander Shen said in a thoughtful tone not matching his usual dissatisfied expression. "Is that some bias, the result of considering us less than them? Or was the aliens' assessment based on their interactions with the Syndicate Worlds' leaders?"

Neeson brought back the star display. "Maybe they just assume we're fundamentally different than them in every way. We all assumed the aliens were one united entity. Why? Because we thought aliens would have some fundamental differences from us, and since humans have trouble getting along with each other—"

"The aliens would be one big, paranoid-but-happy family," Duellos finished. "Yes. It's dangerous to assume anything about them, but it's probably safe to assume that they have made assumptions about us. Observing the conduct of the war between us and the Syndics, the lack of limits on what was done and the massive losses of life, and the apparently unending nature of the conflict, could have easily led the aliens to conclude that no cooperation could ever be possible between human political factions. Unlike among their own numbers, which they might well regard as infinitely more right and proper in their thinking than those strange human creatures."

Geary had his eyes on the star display. "Maybe we did exactly the wrong thing. By entering alien space, we united them against our 'invasion.' The alien force that attacked Midway was much bigger than what we've encountered so far on this mission. That argues it may have been a coalition or alliance of enigma factions. The failure of their attack at Midway could easily have shattered that coalition. But now it may be re-forming."

"If they have cooperated against us before this," Duellos said, "then sooner or later they would have again, regardless of whether or not we sent this fleet into their territory."

Badaya laughed harshly. "How can we exploit differences among them when none of them will talk to us? There's a way they're different from humans! If an alien fleet was charging through human space, there'd be people calling them to talk. Individuals and groups. All those politicians out to protect themselves or get some short-term gain. We surrender, don't hurt us! Can we make a deal? Do you need any supplies, and do you have any money? I hate these other people, so can we ally against them? The aliens wouldn't know how to handle all the conversations they'd be getting!"

Captain Shen rarely said much in these conferences, but now he spoke again as he nodded toward the star display. "They've probably devoted a lot of effort to trying to understand humans, and their problem in that respect is the opposite of ours. We have too little information about them. But, as they scouted invisibly through human space, they must have collected huge amounts of information. How do they sort it out, filter it, and make sense of it?"

"One of our first clues to their existence," Geary commented, "was finding a safe that had been broken into at a star system abandoned by the Syndics. That must have been part of the enigma collection efforts. Maybe, because of the way they think, they thought the truth behind who we are would be kept hidden in safes rather than openly displayed."

"If they do find the truth of who we are," Shen continued, "I hope they share those conclusions with us, since I've met few humans who seem to have any agreement on that topic. I endorse the suggestion that we return to Alliance space because I see no sense in continuing to go deeper in alien territory. However, I wish to point out an implication of Commander Neeson's suggestion. If hypernet gates represent defenses, we have encountered three star systems in a row holding those defenses."

"This could be another border," Neeson said.

"Yes. One the enigma race believes requires particularly strong defenses."

An alert sounded, the display over the table changing to show this star system. "Fifty more enigma warships have arrived," Desjani noted. "With more than a hundred on hand, they may think that's enough to offer battle."

Geary nodded, taking time to form his words carefully. He couldn't announce that the Alliance forces sought to avoid battle or wanted to retreat from this star system, since both ideas were still too difficult for the current culture of the fleet to accept. "If they come at us, we'll take care of them. But I'm not going to wait around here for them to do that. If this star system does represent a border, it may be a border with another intelligent species, and if they don't get along with the enigmas, they may be natural allies with us. We'll proceed on our planned course of action, and if they want to keep tagging along behind, they're free to do so."

Desjani leaned back, eyeing him, then shifted her gaze to Duellos and, as he returned her look, swung one hand to the side in a subtle gesture that wouldn't be noticed by anyone not focused on her.

Duellos frowned back at Desjani, then nodded in understanding. "Admiral, if I may suggest, perhaps the fleet should execute a preplanned evasive maneuver as we exit jump. We do have reason to think there may be something new at that star."

"Good point. We'll do that."

Admiral Lagemann had attended the conference as well, as a representative of the officers liberated from Dunai and in a goodwill gesture by Geary to those who weren't making sporadic efforts to complicate his command of the fleet. After almost everyone else had left, Lagemann lingered for a moment. "I won't deny that I'll be happy to turn toward home. A lot of us from Dunai can't wait for that."

Duellos hadn't yet left and turned a questioning look on

him. "Why just a lot of you, Admiral Lagemann? Why not all of you?"

"Because we've learned enough about things at home to expect that, with the war over and the military shrinking, we'll all be retired as soon as we get there." Lagemann smiled ruefully. "That's not quite the imagined future we hung on to in that Syndic labor camp. We'd somehow get home or escape, then lead the fleet or the ground forces in great victories, like Black Jack returning from the dead." He grinned at Geary. "Sorry. Old saying."

"I keep running into them," Geary replied.

"But," Lagemann continued, "I think the majority of us will be content with how things have changed. There are plenty who will not be happy, who will want to challenge the state of affairs and how the government is doing things. I have to admit, I don't understand why the government made it a priority to liberate us. We're going to create a lot of problems when we get home, but at least by taking us along on this mission, you delayed that happening by several months."

Something struck Geary then, a realization that he hoped didn't show. *Why did we have to pick them up before we went on to alien territory? Why did the government want them with us on a mission facing unknown hazards and the real possibility of lost ships? If something went wrong, if we were delayed getting home, if ships were lost, if disaster happened, I wouldn't be the only inconveniently alive hero the government would no longer have to worry about.*

Navarro wouldn't have set that up. I don't think Sakai would have. Who hoped for it, though? Who in the government and who in fleet headquarters, who surely don't want to deal with lots of resurrected senior officers any more than the government does?

Rione knew that was part of it. That's why she looked that way when she realized her own husband had been caught in it. But as far as I know, she's done nothing to further it happening. She isn't helping much, but she's not sabotaging us either.

The pieces of the puzzle were beginning to form partial pictures, and he didn't like the image at all.

THIS jump required tweaking the jump drives a bit to get some extra range out of them. The fleet jumped while the two groups of enigma warships were still joining up a light hour distant.

"May I speak with you, Admiral?" General Charban sat down in the offered seat in Geary's stateroom, looking around with a wry smile before speaking. "Not much, but it's home, eh? Strange how we can attach ourselves to even a utilitarian stateroom or headquarters complex, isn't it? Humans find home wherever they are. I have an idea, Admiral Geary," he added, switching the subject abruptly. "A possible means for finally getting some agreement with the enigma race on the basis of mutual self-interest."

"I can't wait to hear it," Geary replied.

"I was considering a few things, including what Dr. Shwartz said at our last fleet conference about the inconsistency between what the enigmas said at Midway and their actions since then. It may be that we made a fundamental mistake in assuming those words represented the actual motivations of the enigmas."

Geary rested his chin on one hand, regarding Charban. "Why would they have lied to us about what they wanted, about what was motivating them?"

Charban smiled slightly. "When you speak to men and women serving in the fleet, do you talk about cost-benefit ratios and the need to enhance stockholder benefits and reduce costs to the government? Or do you talk about what you believe matters to them?"

He followed where that question led. "You think the enigmas at Midway were giving us an explanation for their actions they thought we would understand or accept."

"Yes. Any exterior agent watching the war would have focused on our struggles for control of star systems. For control of territory. And property does matter to us even though it is not the most important thing for most humans. What I think the enigmas were doing at Midway, and have done since, was giving us the justifications they thought we would find plausible. Instead of giving their real reasons, they gave us reasons they expected us to expect."

Charban hunched forward, speaking more intensely. "Consider how private they are, how they give away *nothing* about themselves. Why would they offer their true reasons at Midway? Why would they tell us what they really wanted?"

"Good question."

"I was led to this while thinking about the humans held prisoner by the enigma race," Charban continued. "From a human perspective, there wasn't anything surprising about the aliens wishing to know more about us. But was that really the alien motivation? Were they researching how humans acted because they were curious, or simply because they saw us as a threat?"

Geary nodded as he thought about that. "For humans, it would be both. Even if they weren't a threat, we'd want to know more about another intelligent species."

"Because we're curious!" Charban leaned forward a little farther. "There was discussion some time ago about the human obsession with sex, and that is indeed a major aspect of us. And, of course, we fight wars over property as well as other causes. But there's another characteristic that defines us, perhaps even more so. We are curious. We want to know things. What's at the next star? How does this thing work? Why does the universe act the way it does? No matter what we learn, there's always more we want to know. We confront anything from the perspective of wanting to know more about it. Now, what is the primary characteristic of the enigma race as far as we have been able to determine?"

"An obsession with staying private, hidden." Geary took a sudden deep breath. "We want to know more, and they don't want anyone knowing anything. Matter and antimatter. We're the neighbors from hell as far as they're concerned. Is that why they attacked us?"

"It may be. I've reviewed the records the Syndics provided us," Charban continued. "As far as I can tell, the Syndics never approached the enigma race on the basis of 'We'll leave you alone.' They did the natural thing for humans, sending out exploration missions into enigma space, though the Syndics didn't then know it was enigma territory. And they planted bases and colonies, pushing farther into enigma space. Once the Syndics discovered the aliens, they tried to learn more about them, talk to them, and probably tested their defenses. And we've done pretty much the same kind of thing. We tell them we want to talk, to get to know each other, and that is exactly what they most fear and dislike about us. Look what we've done here. A mission of exploration, to learn things about them. That's a normal desire for us, but to the enigma race it must look like the ultimate act of aggression."

"We promise to leave them alone?" Geary asked. "Ignore them completely, never try to penetrate their territory again, never try to learn any more, never try any contact?"

"It's worth a try. But there are two other things. First, we need to imply that our curiosity will *never* be satisfied if we think they are still holding any human prisoners. We will keep looking. If they want us to start pretending that the universe ends where their territory begins, the enigmas will have to cough up any other humans they still hold."

"Excellent idea," Geary approved.

"Thank you, though my fellow emissary helped me come up with that." Charban paused, looking as if he were tasting something unpleasant. "The other thing. The enigmas have chosen to use military options against us. I think it possible that they will continue to attempt military solutions until we've demonstrated they can't win that way."

"That doesn't always work with humans. Beat them up, and they just come back for more."

"Yes. That's one of our particularly irrational forms of dealing with reality. But these are the enigmas. Their overriding goal doesn't seem to be survival or victory. It's keeping their secrets. Demonstrate that military force cannot succeed in that, and it may make a difference."

Geary looked at the display over the table in his stateroom, bringing up an image of the previous star system as they had last seen it, with one hundred and ten enigma warships pursuing the Alliance force. "We may have to fight again and destroy as many of those enigma warships as possible."

"Yes." Charban nodded to Geary. "You see that as a sad necessity, as do I. Victoria said you would."

"Has Victoria Rione said anything else?"

Charban frowned. "No. She just told me to talk to you. Admiral, I'm fully aware that I am far from the most qualified person to have been given this assignment. I have sometimes wondered why I was given it, whether—"

"We were being set up to fail?"

"I haven't gone that far in my suspicions, Admiral. Some of the people I have worked with would *not* have done such a thing."

"But others might?" He thought of Rione's vague warning. Many minds trying to direct a single, clumsy hand.

"Do you trust my fellow emissary, Admiral?" Charban asked.

"Yes." *But I've made mistakes before. Hopefully not this time.* "I'm glad that you told me about this idea, General. We can't consult with the civilian experts until we leave jump, but please talk with them once we arrive at the next star system and work up a way of presenting that proposal to the enigmas."

Maybe there was yet hope.

THE last thing that anyone wanted to hear when a ship exited from jump space was the frantic blare of alarms as combat and maneuvering systems screamed warnings before humans could focus their senses. Geary braced himself as *Dauntless* rolled upward and to the side in the preplanned evasive movement, trying to overcome the stresses of the motion and the confusion that came with the exit from the jump space.

"Son of a bitch!" Desjani gasped, having centered her attention a fraction of a second earlier than Geary had managed.

He still took another moment to grasp what he was seeing. "What the hell is that?"

Across the path the fleet would have taken straight out the jump point and only one light minute distant, a massive object orbited. The fleet's combat systems had already covered what seemed like every square meter of the object's surface with threat symbols, which continued to multiply as new threats were identified. Geary blinked, rereading the assessment of shield strength on the orbiting leviathan in disbelief.

One of the watch-standers answered Geary's question, her own voice filled with incredulity. "It's the size and mass of a minor planet, Admiral, and its orbit is slaved to the jump point. Either they completely turned a minor planet into a fortress and moved it here, or they built something that huge."

Desjani shook her head. "If we hadn't executed that preplanned evasion, the fleet would have gotten far too close to that thing before we could turn it. Good thing—"

She stopped speaking as more alarms shrieked from the combat systems.

Geary stared as part of the surface of the planet-fort seemed to leap into space, then saw that it was actually a dense swarm of small ships so numerous they momentarily blocked a clean view of the fortress. "How many of those things are there?"

No answer came, and Desjani spun in her seat to glare at her combat systems watch-stander. Lieutenant Castries shook her head helplessly. "System is still evaluating. Estimate greater than two hundred. Greater than four hundred. Greater than eight hundred." Castries took a sudden breath.

"Working estimate stabilizing at nine hundred, plus or minus ten percent."

Desjani also inhaled slowly, then looked at Geary. "Nine hundred," she repeated in a matter-of-fact voice.

"Plus or minus ten percent," he added, wondering that he could make a joke of such a thing. "Any idea what they are?"

"If they're missiles, they're very big missiles." Desjani tapped her display. "They have very good acceleration. I wonder if they're crewed or automated."

"They're about twice as large in mass and dimensions than standard human fast attack craft," the combat systems watch reported. "That's plenty big enough for crews."

"Or really big warheads." Desjani pointed at her display again. "They could be mostly warhead and propulsion. If they maintain that acceleration—"

"We won't be able to outrun them," Geary agreed, running another estimate on the maneuvering systems. The same answer came up, though. "Not when they're this close and coming on that fast."

The rest of the fleet had cleared the jump point by then, and all of the ships were bending onto the new course upward and to the side. "All units, this is Admiral Geary. At time four one, come port zero eight zero degrees and accelerate at maximum." That would at least line up the fleet's subformations in a column leading away from the alien force and give him as much time as possible to think of a solution to this mess that didn't involve massive losses to his fleet. His eyes came to rest on a detailed image of one of the alien craft that the fleet's sensors had compiled and his display had helpfully parked to one side. Unlike the tortoise-shaped ships they had encountered so far, these alien craft were simply cylinders with rounded bows, some kind of propulsion unit making up the entire back end, and a few low, small spines that must hold sensors sticking out from the sides. And that orbiting fort . . . "This is ugly," he said to Desjani. "But none of this looks anything like the enigmas."

"No, it doesn't. At least there's no hypernet gate here."

"One small blessing." They could race away from the jump exit without worrying about the threat of a gate. But if these weren't the enigmas . . . "Could we have found a star system colonized by humans? Some group who found themselves in enigma space and had to keep running until they found a star system on the other side of the enigmas?"

Desjani glanced back to her engineering watch. "What do you think, Master Chief?"

Gioninni shook his head. "No, Captain. None of the stuff we've seen resembles human designs. And the industrial base needed to build and maintain something like that fortress would be huge. Not something that could be thrown up overnight or in a few decades. They would have had to have been isolated out here for several centuries at least. How could they have gotten this far out that long ago? Maybe these aren't those enigmas, but I'm not seeing anything that makes me think human."

"Have we heard anything from these aliens or humans or whatever?" Geary asked. "There's been time for at least a challenge to reach us from that fortress."

The comm watch answered him. "No, Admiral. Not a word that we can tell was directed at us. And nothing that gives any clue to who they are. We're picking up lots of their comms, but it's all heavily encrypted."

"Everything?" Desjani demanded.

"Yes, Captain. There's no civilian comm traffic that we can find. It's all military-grade encryption. At least, that's what we'd call it if they were human."

"Humans with that kind of discipline? No one taking shortcuts or ignoring comm requirements?"

"That doesn't seem too likely, does it?" Geary agreed. "We don't have time to consult the experts, and as long as whoever is directing those small craft keeps charging at us, we also don't have any option but to defend ourselves." He turned to look back and saw Rione in the observer's seat, sitting silently, her eyes watching her own display. "Try to establish communications with them. Tell them we'll be happy to leave and didn't intend staying anyway and have no hostile intent. We don't have much time to get those messages across," he added, not sure if Rione understood just how bad the situation was.

Rione sounded resigned as she replied. "They have made no attempts to communicate, not even demands that we leave or surrender. I don't think they wish to talk, Admiral Geary. They appear to have enough hostile intent for both of us, and they don't seem to care about our own intentions."

"Do your best, Madam Emissary." He eyed his display again. "If we can't get them to break off their attack," Geary commented to Desjani, "we're going to have one hell of a fight on our hands."

"Target-rich environment," Desjani remarked in a cheerful voice that carried across the bridge. Her watch-standers, tense gazes alternating between their superiors and the huge number of attackers, relaxed slightly at that display of their captain's confidence.

Geary had trouble showing the same enthusiasm for the situation, though. "That's one way of looking at it. There are so damn many of them." He ran yet another maneuvering check despite knowing that he would get the same awful answer. After an awesome surge of acceleration at launch, the alien craft seemed to have steadied out at a still-impressive rate of increasing velocity. His own warships had come around to point almost directly away from the oncoming aliens and were all pushing their propulsion systems to the limit, but the maneuvering systems confirmed that the best that most of Geary's combatants could manage wouldn't be good enough to avoid interception, though the battle cruisers should be able to just pull out of contact. The cruisers and destroyers could almost match the battle cruisers, but that "almost" meant the aliens would almost certainly manage to catch many of the escorts. The four assault transports would be doomed, along with the Marines and liberated prisoners on them, and the battleships and auxiliaries also had no chance at all. Even dumping all of the mass the auxiliaries held in their raw materials bunkers wouldn't allow the auxiliaries to accelerate fast enough to give them any chance, and while the battleships could gather speed more quickly than the auxiliaries, with this little time to accelerate, the massive warships weren't all that much more agile.

Geary focused intently, trying to close out normal fear, trying to find some room to maneuver against these opponents. But there didn't seem to be any, not when the opponent had nine hundred ships too close and coming on too fast, and he usually had a lot more time to think things through, to evaluate the situation before making plans. In this situation, he knew too little and had too little time. "Advantages," he muttered.

"We've got a lot more firepower," Desjani pointed out. "And with our ships moving away at maximum acceleration, and the aliens caught in a stern chase, that reduces the closing rate. That means we'll be within firing range of those things for minutes instead of milliseconds, giving us a lot more time to pound them. On the other hand, one shot from a hell lance probably isn't going to take out one of those. We'll likely need multiple hits, and there are so many of those things that we'd have to fire repeatedly as fast as possible. The weapon systems aren't designed for that."

"I know all that!" Why was she telling him things he already knew when what he needed was answers? All right, maybe he hadn't thought all of that through yet, but he would have. His reply came out sharp and abrupt, fed by an awful sense of futility, and he saw her answering frown.

Glowering at her display, Desjani sat back, pointedly ignoring him as she prepared her ship for action.

Damn. I don't need this kind of personal distraction. Why the hell does she have to be so sensitive now, of all times? She's the best damned ship driver I've got, and if anyone could maneuver us through this, it would be her, though she'd *probably prefer just charging at those*—

Geary's mind froze, trying to retrack and find the idea

that had almost been lost as it had raced past at the speed of thought multiplied by irritation and dismay. *Charging.* "Tanya."

"What? Sir."

"We don't know how maneuverable they are. But we can judge how fast they can move since they must be coming at us at their maximum sustained capability. We have a very narrow chance to control when we come into contact with these attackers, but we'll have to time our own maneuvers just right."

Her glower didn't subside, but Desjani's expression took on a calculating measure. "They could be holding their velocity down to ensure their own targeting systems are effective and preserve their fuel reserves for what might be a long chase, but more likely we're seeing the best they can do." Desjani's eyes were narrowed as she looked at her display, as if she were aiming a weapon. Raising her voice, she addressed her watch-standers without taking her eyes from the display. "I want human eyes on the fleet sensor readings. The sensors are telling me they haven't identified any weapons on the alien craft yet. Tell me what *you* see."

There was a pause as the officers and senior enlisted personnel called up and focused intently on the depictions of the alien craft created by the sensors, then a lieutenant spoke slowly. "Captain, maybe they do things really differently from us, but I can't see anything that looks like firing ports or hard points. No external weapons are visible, and there's nothing that could blow out or open to allow internal missiles to fire. They're just tubes."

"Bullets," Lieutenant Castries said. "Really big bullets."

Desjani swung her head to look at the others, and all of them nodded; then she finally looked at Geary again. "We have to assume that those things don't carry weapons, they *are* weapons. Since those craft don't have stand-off weapons, we do have some chance to decide when we engage. That's the bright side of it. I'm not still boring you with things you already know, am I?"

"I'm sorry. I'm under a bit of pressure right now—"

"If *Dauntless* is destroyed, Admiral, then you and I *both* die. What's your idea?"

Geary kept his reply short. "Concentrate the fleet by reducing acceleration sequentially by unit type."

"Produce an easier target for the aliens that they'll catch sooner? That's counterintuitive, at least. Concentrating the force . . . sequentially?" She paused, thinking, then Desjani's hands were moving, tracing maneuvers on her display. "I see what you're thinking. It won't be pretty, but it might work, and it beats any option I've come up with."

"Link me to your display so we can do this fast." The next few minutes passed in a blur as Geary worked on his maneuvering display, planning out hundreds of ship movements in conjunction with Desjani as the maneuvering systems automatically generated orders for the necessary turns, accelerations, and decelerations for each individual ship while also figuring out how to avoid collisions as all of those ships darted through the same region of space. It was the sort of problem that would have taken humans weeks to work out, but the fleet systems produced answers instantly in response to the commands that Geary and Desjani were entering.

Of course, every system, no matter how good, still generated a few flaws, a few errors. Ideally, people would have time to discover those using the intuitive ability of the human mind to scan over a big picture and spot tiny inconsistencies. But there was no time for that now. He could only hope that those inevitable errors wouldn't be critical ones. Two ships crossing the same point at the same moment in time would produce one cloud of debris and zero survivors.

"You'll need to let individual ships maneuver independently when the attackers get close enough," Desjani cautioned. "That will seriously stress the ability of the maneuvering systems to predict movements of other warships and avoid collisions."

"I don't have any alternative, do I?"

"Nope. But you already knew that, didn't you?" she added.

Even with nine hundred alien attackers closing on the fleet, Geary couldn't help wincing at Desjani's jab. "Yes. But please keep telling me things I already know."

"I'll consider it. This plan looks as good as we can possibly manage in the time available."

He nonetheless paused to look over it, dismayed by the hundreds of separate projected tracks for individual ships weaving in and out of one another in a pattern so dense it almost resembled an impossibly huge tangle of string. The time counter in one corner was scrolling down, indicating that he had only two minutes left to order these maneuvers, or else there would be too little time for the individual ships to execute them, and a whole new plan would have to be crafted. Murmuring a prayer to his ancestors to ask the living stars to keep his ships safe, Geary hit the approve command, and the plan flashed out to every warship, transport, and auxiliary in the fleet.

"This is Admiral Geary to all units. Individual ship movement orders are en route to you. Our attempts to communicate with the inhabitants of this star system have yielded no results, and the force closing on us appears intent on a fight. We will engage these alien craft and destroy every one that threatens our ships. After doing as much damage to the attackers as we can using the orders being transmitted, be prepared for follow-on orders for every warship to maneuver independently as required by the actions of the enemy." He had a momentary impulse to add something stupid like *Try not to collide with other ships*, but managed to block the words before actually saying them. "We will re-form following the engagement." *Assuming there are enough of us left to re-form. But I do need to say something else. We're going into a tough fight. I have to tell everyone that I expect victory despite how bad things look.* "Let's show whoever lives in this star system that they made a serious mistake when they chose to attack the Alliance fleet. To the honor of our ancestors, Geary, out."

Desjani glanced at him. "You didn't tell them not to hit each other—"

"I managed to stop myself."

"—but they already know that, don't they?"

Geary paused before saying anything else, facing the reality that after very tense minutes of working and thinking as fast as possible, he would now be forced to watch events unfold, unable to intervene for a while without throwing the plan into confusion and ruining what seemed to be the fleet's best chance to defeat this threat. "How long am I going to have to pay for that remark?" he finally asked.

"I haven't decided yet," Desjani replied. "It's a good plan, Admiral, better than anything I could have come up with in the time we had. Let it run and watch the big picture so you know when to call out orders again." She raised her voice to speak to everyone on the bridge, keying a command that also broadcast her words through the entire ship. "We are heading into battle *now*, and *Dauntless* will be leading the way. I want maximum combat readiness for all crew members and systems. Let's show the rest of the fleet how it's done."

Dauntless began pivoting in response to her maneuvering orders, her bow where armament and shields were clustered most heavily coming up and around to face the oncoming horde of alien small craft. Geary sat back, watching silently as the other battle cruisers did the same.

Viewed rationally, none of it made sense. The battle cruisers were going to charge the enemy, despite the overwhelming numbers of attackers, and even though the charge was just a matter of the battle cruisers ceasing their own acceleration so that they continued moving rapidly stern first in the same direction as the fleet but also slid toward the rear of the fleet as the battleships, cruisers, destroyers, transports, and auxiliaries continued to accelerate past them as quickly as possible. Moreover, the atmosphere on *Dauntless*'s bridge could only be described as jubilant even though slightly more than nine hundred alien ships were closing rapidly and would soon enter hell-lance range. This was what the crew believed that battle cruisers were supposed to do, leading the fleet against the enemy, and between the upbeat attitude of their commanding officer and their own confidence in Geary to get them out of any mess, they were ready to fight even the odds they now faced. "All units, engage targets as they enter weapons envelopes," Geary ordered. Mines might not be of much use in these circumstances, but this was no time to try conserving missiles.

Dauntless trembled slightly as specter missiles leaped out, racing toward their targets. The other battle cruisers fired missiles as well in a staggered barrage caused by their differing distances to the enemy. "Here's where we see what kind of point defenses they have," Desjani commented.

Whatever those defenses were, they couldn't stop specters. Many of the alien small craft managed slight last-instant jogs in their vectors that caused the specters to detonate too far from their targets, but other alien vessels vanished under the blows of the Alliance missiles, blown into tiny pieces by the warheads, the force of the collisions as the missiles hit home, and the explosions of their own payloads. "Look at the size of those detonations," Desjani marveled. "Those things have some humongous warheads on them."

"Combat systems estimate from the destruction patterns that the alien craft have substantial armor of some kind in their bows," the combat systems watch reported.

"That's going to make it harder for the hell lances to achieve kills," Desjani complained. "They're not making this easy at all."

Geary, inwardly marveling at Tanya's ability to find humor at times like this, just nodded in reply and waited, wondering what hidden weapons the alien ships might be armed with. But no weapons fire stabbed out from the aliens as they got closer to the Alliance battle cruisers, which now formed a rough barrier between the aliens and the rest of the fleet. "Entering hell-lance range in five seconds," the combat systems watch reported.

One by one, the battle cruisers opened fire again, their hell lances hurling out spears of high-energy particles, the shots invisible to human eyes. The leading alien craft trembled as hits went home, knocking down shields and tearing holes in their bows, but they kept coming.

"Tough bastards," Desjani said.

"Yeah." He had one eye on the advancing aliens and another on status reports from the battle cruisers. As Desjani had noted earlier, combat systems were designed for very quick engagements, slashing firing runs in which a single volley or at most two could be unleashed. Hell lances could be fired repeatedly for only so long before they began over-heating, and now he watched the warning signs begin popping up on battle cruiser after battle cruiser.

"Hell-lance batteries 1A and 2B are experiencing serious overheating," *Dauntless*'s own combat systems watch-stander reported. "Estimated time to temporary shutdown ten seconds maximum."

"Very well," Desjani replied. "How long will the others keep firing?"

"One minute maximum estimated, Captain, but combat systems predict in thirty seconds we'll be down to only twenty percent of hell lances still firing. Five seconds to specter reload completion."

"Fire specters as soon as they're ready."

The missiles tore away from *Dauntless* again as the fire of the hell lances faltered. Geary studied the readouts for the other battle cruisers. *Leviathan* and *Dragon* had already temporarily lost several batteries to overheating, and the fire from the other battle cruisers was weakening fast. Increasing numbers of alien ships were coming apart under the battle cruisers' barrage, but so far the losses had barely dented their numbers, and the aliens were closing quickly.

Even though he knew it would happen, Geary was momentarily startled when *Dauntless* and the other battle cruisers pivoted again, putting their sterns to the enemy as their main propulsion units lit off once more. The fleet's combat systems had been able to approximate beforehand how long the hell-lance batteries could fire before overheating, so the maneuvering orders had been based on those calculations. Now the closing rate of the enemy ships slowed dramatically, but the battle cruisers also could no longer engage the enemy nearly as effectively with their bows pointed away.

Desjani had one hand supporting her chin as she watched the fight. "And here comes the second team."

The maneuvering commands sent earlier had kicked in for the mass of escorts in the Alliance fleet. Scores of destroyers and light cruisers and dozens of heavy cruisers swung around bows on to the aliens, and the Alliance battle cruisers began overtaking the smaller warships. As the alien craft continued to close, the destroyers and cruisers joined their fire to that of the rear batteries on the battle cruisers.

Alien missile craft staggered, some disappearing in tremendous explosions while others were torn to pieces. But for every alien ship destroyed, more came on from behind. Geary watched the hell-lance readouts on his escorts rapidly climbing to overheating while a third volley of specters was launched from the battle cruisers. By now the aliens were so close that the missiles were having trouble achieving lock-on before the battle raced past them, and most were clean misses. "All units, cease firing missiles unless you get a solid firing solution on some alien craft." Their hell lances falling silent from overheating, the cruisers and destroyers pivoted again, sterns to the enemy, accelerating once again at maximum, joining the battle cruisers in trying to keep ahead of the alien attackers as long as possible.

He turned to look at Desjani. "We're not whittling them down fast enough."

"Not yet. But now it's time for the big boys and girls to earn their keep," Desjani remarked, sounding jaunty again.

The fleet, once spread out in subformations, had slowly compressed down with a dense layer comprising the battle cruisers and escorts closest to the enemy and the battleships, transports and auxiliaries strung out slightly ahead of the rest. Now the battleships ponderously swung around to face the enemy bow on, their acceleration halting so that the massive warships were quickly overtaken by the rest of the Alliance warships. Only the transports and auxiliaries remained slightly ahead of the rest of the fleet, with all of the other warships and the alien craft rapidly overtaking them.

The battleships glided into place among the battle cruisers and escorts, then opened up with their immense armament. Geary felt his lips stretch into an involuntary grimace as space filled with so much energy that it began to glow slightly even to human eyes, the leading waves of the surviving alien small craft evaporating under the torrent of fire from the battleships.

"It's still going to be tight," Desjani commented as if discussing plans for dinner. "There are too damn many of them, and they keep closing on us. Our forward batteries have cooled down enough to get off several more volleys, but when we pivot again, those aliens will be right on top of us."

"Understood." This was as far as the preplanned maneuvers took them. It would be up to him to judge when to move to the final, chaotic stage of the fight. He sat, watching the aliens come ever closer, the fire of the battleships also beginning to slacken. *So close now. But I need what's left of that alien force a little closer so they have less time to react to our next move. How far to the farthest units in my formation? Factor in how long it will take those units to hear the order. Fortunately, the attackers keep aiming for the center of mass of our formation, so a slightly delayed response on our flanks won't hurt those warships. Almost time now.*

"Admiral?" Desjani asked. Her tone held only mild interest, but the fact that she asked the question was a rare betrayal of the tension she was otherwise so effectively masking.

"Not yet." He held up one hand, moving it slowly several times as if counting beats, then slapped his controls. "All units, effective immediately maneuver independently at maximum capability to avoid alien ships while continuing to engage the enemy with all short-range weapons."

He felt pressures jerk at his body despite the inertial nullifiers as Desjani yanked *Dauntless* into as tight a turn as the battle cruiser's velocity could manage, forming a huge arc through space as the warship also pivoted to immediately engage the enemy. "Fire grapeshot as the launchers bear on targets!" she ordered. "All hell lances fire and keep firing until the last attacker is gone!"

Collision alarms screamed warnings as hundreds of warships pivoted onto new vectors, Geary's display turning red as impact warning alerts covered it. Fortunately, the initial movements, when the Alliance ships were closest together, were somewhat predictable to the fleet's maneuvering systems as almost every ship turned to engage the nearest enemy craft. That, or perhaps the divine aid that Geary had prayed for, prevented any immediate disasters.

The alien craft were *here*, right on top of the Alliance warships, when metal grapeshot fired from well over two hundred warships slammed into the aliens at relative speeds of thousands of kilometers per second. Hundreds of surviving alien ships vanished in a wave of annihilation, then hell lances were lashing out with renewed fury as the bow armaments found targets again.

Geary couldn't be certain how many alien ships were left amid the bedlam as clouds of debris and energy discharges filled space, and the Alliance warships scattered as if their own formation had exploded into hundreds of individual pieces. Even the auxiliaries and transports were firing now, their meager defenses trying to fend off the remaining attackers, many of whom seemed momentarily confused by the fleet's dispersal. But other alien craft, probably sticking to targets they had already chosen, bored through the main body aiming for the auxiliaries that were the fleet's Achilles' heel and the transports, which were clearly vulnerable targets.

Dauntless, rolling as her course curved slightly downward, rocked as an alien ship twisting on an intercept with the battle cruiser caught several hell-lance hits from multiple angles and exploded nearby. Two Alliance destroyers and a light cruiser tore past, heading straight up as *Dauntless* dove beneath them, then a battleship spun by overhead so close that even Desjani looked stunned for an instant. Recovering just as quickly, Desjani cursed and prioritized two more targets, punching the firing commands to take out one alien craft homing past toward *Titan* and another near enough to *Dauntless* that the force of its explosion rattled the warship.

But *Dauntless* was committed by momentum to her current track, unable to reverse course fast enough to engage alien attackers that had made it past her. Geary could only watch with a sick feeling as more alien craft swung onto final runs aimed at *Titan* and *Tanuki*, but then, astoundingly, *Orion* was there, the battleship climbing from below, knocking out one alien ship short of *Titan*, then blowing apart the second at point-blank range astern of *Tanuki*. The resulting explosion knocked even the mass of the battleship a bit to one side.

Another alien was homing in on the transport *Mistral*, but the heavy cruisers *Diamond*, *Gauntlet*, and *Buckler* had managed to claw close enough to fire a volley of hell lances into the rear of the missile craft and shatter it short of its target.

No other alien craft had survived long enough to get close to the transports and auxiliaries. Bringing his eyes back to the wider battle, Geary tried to sort out alien ship markers from the mass of debris and the confused swirl of Alliance warships not only seeking targets but also trying to dodge one another and the bigger pieces of debris.

Nothing. The only red showing on the display were the scores of collision warnings still proliferating, then vanishing just as quickly as fleet maneuvering systems shook hands among ships and made the millisecond-fast decisions and coordinated vector changes needed to avoid crashes. The last of the alien craft had been destroyed, and now he had to figure out how much damage they had done. All he could tell at the moment was that the damage hadn't been the massacre it might have been. "All units, resume Formation Delta when safe to maneuver to station. Formation speed is point zero five light speed." Get everyone slowed down, while continuing to open the distance to that orbiting fortress, and into a simple box, as simple as any formation could be, while he tried to sort out things.

"Wow," Desjani commented, smiling, her face a little flushed. "It worked. Cool plan, Admiral."

"You're crazy," he replied, his heart still pounding.

"I thought you liked that in a woman. Did you see what *Orion* did?"

"Yeah," Geary agreed, slightly giddy with relief even while dreading what damage might have been done to the fleet. "You were right about Captain Shen."

"I'm *always* right, Admiral. Lieutenant Yuon, who was that battleship that got way too far inside our personal space?"

"The systems identify her as *Dreadnaught*, Captain. Closest point of approach was—" Yuon's voice choked to a halt, then came out at a higher pitch. "That can't be right."

Desjani checked the distance herself, then fell silent for a few seconds. "Admiral, you need to have another talk with *Dreadnaught*'s commanding officer. Captain Jane Geary owes me a drink," she added. "And I owe my ancestors some thanks."

"We all do." Both Jane Geary and his ancestors would have to wait for the moment, though. Geary pulled out the scale on his display again, finally having the luxury of viewing the entire star system in search of more distant threats. The huge orbiting fortress at the jump point wasn't launching any more ships or missiles or whatever those alien craft had been, but it wasn't the only such monster fortification here. "I have a nasty suspicion that it's not going to be hard to figure out where the other jump points are in this star system."

Desjani raised an eyebrow, then checked her own display. "Ancestors preserve us. They've got the same kinds of fortresses in two other orbits, both far enough from the star to be guarding jump points as well."

Fortresses that doubtless also carried hundreds of long-range missiles. Elsewhere in the star system, still light hours distant, numerous warships were still being identified by the fleet sensors. Geary let out a low whistle as he viewed some of that data. "Several of the alien warships are assessed by our sensors as massing three times larger than a *Guardian*-class battleship."

"They build big, don't they?" Desjani asked. "Fortunately, the nearest of those things are three light hours distant, and with that much mass, they can't be very nimble. Even I'd rather not tangle with them, though."

"We still have received no communications to us from the inhabitants of this star system," Rione reported tonelessly. "They have not yet responded to any of our messages."

Geary slumped back in his seat. "If they were human, they should have answered us by now." There weren't any imminent threats left, nothing that wouldn't take hours or days to get close enough to worry about, but that left plenty to do right away. *Evaluate damage and losses to the fleet. Get repairs going. Make sure survivors from any destroyed or badly damaged ships are recovered. Try to talk to whatever this alien species is or at least learn something more about them. Get the fleet on a course to avoid any attempts by them to intercept us again with all of the other warships they've got available.* His eyes went to the massive fortresses guarding this star system's jump points. The one they had passed at the nearest jump point might have exhausted its supply of missiles, but something that huge could have many hundreds of reloads ready to fire if the fleet approached again, not to mention other weapons. Getting to a jump point would require passing close to those forts and would be a lot more dangerous than tearing past one during an exit had been.

"Congratulations on discovering another intelligent alien species, Admiral," Rione said.

"Thanks. I'm glad the government is pleased." He didn't bother trying to keep the sarcasm out of his voice.

"Not everyone in the government is pleased," Rione murmured almost too low to hear, her eyes fixed on her display with the look of someone who had finally encountered a long-anticipated fate.

Desjani leaned closer to him. "How are we getting out of this star system, Admiral?"

"Beats the hell out of me." Actually, knowing how to get out wasn't too hard with those fortresses pointing the way to jump points. Getting out without having the fleet cut to ribbons was the problem.

But now he had time to think, and he had Tanya beside him, and a lot of good people who were depending upon him but also working with him, and while stung, the fleet was mostly intact. Perhaps even Rione would now offer real assistance again instead of that odd passivity.

Geary settled back in his seat, relaxing tense muscles by force of will so that he seemed imperturbable. "We'll think of something," he assured Desjani in a calm voice loud enough to be heard clearly throughout the bridge.

Read on for an exciting excerpt from Jack Campbell's
bold new military science fiction saga, telling of the
aftermath of the Alliance/Syndic war—
from the enemy's point of view.

The Lost Stars: Tarnished Knight

by Jack Campbell
Now available from Ace Books

TREASON could be as simple as walking through a doorway.

At least that was true anywhere ruled by the Syndicate Worlds, and when the doorway in question had stenciled on it in large, red letters the words *Unauthorized Access Forbidden OBSTLT.* CEO Artur Drakon, commander of Syndicate World ground forces in the Midway Star System, had spent his life following rules like that and only partly because everyone knew that *OBSTLT* stood for *Or Be Subject to Life Termination.* "Death" was the sort of blunt term that the Syndicate Worlds' bureaucracy liked to avoid no matter how freely it meted out that punishment.

No, he had obeyed because there hadn't been much choice while the endless war with the Alliance continued, when disobedience could leave a path open for the enemy to destroy homes and cities and sometimes entire worlds. And if the enemy didn't destroy your home as a result of your rebellious behavior, and if you somehow escaped the long and powerful reach of internal security, then the mobile forces of the Syndicate Worlds themselves would rain down death on your world from orbit in the name of law, discipline, and stability.

But now the war had ended in exhaustion and defeat. No one trusted the Alliance, but they had stopped attacking. And the mobile forces of the Syndicate Worlds, the once-unassailable fist of the central government, had been almost wiped out in a flurry of destruction wrought by an Alliance leader who should have been dead a century ago.

That left the ISS, the Internal Security Service, to worry about. The "snakes" of the ISS were a very big worry indeed, but nothing that he couldn't handle now.

Drakon walked through the doorway. He could do that because multiple locks and codes had already been overridden, multiple alarm systems had been disabled or bypassed, a few deadly automated traps disarmed, and four human sentries in critical positions had been turned and now answered to him rather than to CEO Hardrad, head of internal security. All of this had been done on Drakon's orders. But until Drakon entered the room beyond he could claim to have been testing internal defenses. Now he had unquestionably committed treason against the Syndicate Worlds.

Drakon had expected to feel increased tension as he entered that room; instead, a sense of calm filled him. Retreat and alternate paths were no longer possible; there was no more room for uncertainty or questioning his decision. Within the next several hours, he would either win or die.

Inside, his two most trusted assistants were already busy at separate consoles. Bran Malin's fingers were flying as he rerouted and diverted surveillance data from all over the planet that should be streaming into the Internal Security Service headquarters complex. On the other side of the room, Roh Morgan used one hand to flick a strand of hair from her eyes as she rapidly entered false surveillance feed loops designed to fool the automated systems at ISS into thinking that everything still worked properly. Drakon was dressed in the dark blue executive ensemble every CEO was expected to wear, an outfit he personally detested, but both Malin and Morgan were clad in the tight, dull black skin suits designed to be worn under mechanized combat armor. The skin suits also served well on their own for breaking and entering, though.

Malin sat back, rubbing his neck with his right hand, then smiled at Drakon. "ISS is blind, sir, and they don't even know it."

Drakon nodded as he studied the display. "Malin, you're a wizard."

Morgan stretched like a cat, lithe and deadly, then stood up, leaning against the nearest wall with her arms crossed. "I'm the one who got us in here and entered the deception loops. What does that make me?"

"A witch?" Malin asked, his expression and voice deadpan.

For a moment, Morgan tensed, then one corner of her mouth curled upward as she gazed at Malin. "Did I tell you that I'd calculated the lowest possible cost to fire a single shot from a hand weapon, Malin?"

"No. Why should I care?"

"Because it came out to thirteen centas. That's why you're still alive. I realized killing you wasn't worth the expense."

Malin bared his teeth at her as he drew his combat knife and balanced it on one palm. "This wouldn't cost a centa to use. Go ahead and give it a try."

"Nah." Morgan stood away from the wall, flexing her hands. "I'd still have to put some effort into it, and like I said, you're not worth whatever energy it would take to kill you. CEO Drakon, we should eliminate those four sentries. They could still betray us."

Drakon shook his head. "They were promised that if they played along they, and their families, wouldn't be killed."

"So? If they were stupid enough to believe the promise of a CEO—"

"It was *my* promise," Drakon interrupted. "I made a commitment. If I violate that, I won't be able to count on anyone else's believing I'll do what I say."

Morgan shook her head with a long-suffering look.

"That's the attitude that got you stuck out here in the back end of nowhere. As long as they're afraid of you, it doesn't matter whether or not they believe you."

Malin pretended to applaud, his palms clapping together silently. "You know the first workplace rule for Syndicate Worlds' CEOs. Very good. Now think about the fact that we *lost the war.*"

"I operate the way that works for me," Drakon told Morgan, who was pretending not to have heard Malin.

She shrugged. "It's your rebellion. I'll check on the assault preparations and get the troops moving as planned."

"Let me know if any problems develop," Drakon replied. "I appreciate your support in this."

"That was always a given." Morgan started to leave, now ignoring Malin's presence completely.

"And, Morgan . . ."

She paused in the doorway.

"The sentries will *not* be killed." He said it flatly and with force.

"I heard you the first time," Morgan replied, then continued on out.

After the door closed, Malin looked at Drakon. "Sir, if she notifies the snakes of what we're planning, she'll end up in command and you'll be dead."

Drakon shook his head. "Morgan won't do that."

"You can't trust her. You must know that."

"I know that she is loyal to me," Drakon said, keeping his voice even.

"Morgan doesn't understand loyalty. She's using you for her own purposes, which remain hidden. The moment you're no longer useful, she might put a shot in your back. Or a knife," Malin finished, raising his own knife meaningfully before resheathing it with a single thrust.

Morgan has told me the same thing about you, Drakon thought as he considered a reply to Malin. "Morgan realizes that she couldn't count on the snakes rewarding her for turning us in. They'd be just as likely to shoot her, too, no matter what agreement they had reached with her. Morgan knows that just as well as I do. But I am keeping an eye on her. I keep an eye on everyone."

"That's why you're still alive." Malin shook his head. "I'm not suggesting that you get rid of her. As long as she's alive, you need to have her where you can watch her."

Drakon paused, eyeing Malin. "Are you advising that I take care of the 'as long as she's alive' part?"

"No, sir," Malin answered.

"Then you'd better not be planning to take care of that yourself. I know it's common practice with some CEOs' subordinates, but I don't tolerate those kinds of games on my staff. It's bad for discipline, and it plays hell with the working environment."

Malin grinned. "I will not kill Morgan." His smile faded, and Malin gave a worried glance upward. "We can take down the Internal Security Service on the surface, we *will* take them down, but if the mobile forces in this star system aren't also neutralized, we'll be sitting ducks. From what I know of the mobile forces commander, CEO Kolani, she will support the Syndicate government and the snakes."

"As long as we eliminate the ISS snakes on the surface, CEO Iceni will handle CEO Kolani and the mobile forces." *I hope.*

"Sir," Malin said with exaggerated care, "if I may, I understand that you and CEO Iceni have agreed to run things here jointly. You are justified in believing that it is in her self-interest to stick to that agreement. But how will you run things, sir? I know how unhappy you are with the Syndicate government—"

"Sick to death of the Syndicate government," Drakon interrupted. "Sick of watching my every step and every word." It felt strange to be able to say that, now that the snake surveillance gear was neutralized. "Sick of bureaucrats a hundred light years away making life-and-death decisions about me."

Malin nodded in agreement. "There are many who feel the same way even though few have dared to say it, even in private. But I am unclear as to what system will replace that of the Syndicate."

"Are you?" Drakon smiled wryly. "Me, too. Iceni and I couldn't talk about it before this, before we had these surveillance systems short-circuited. Too great a chance of being caught by the ISS. We both agree that we want to get out from under the merciless thumb of the Syndicate. We both agree that the Syndicate government proved its incompetence, and that we can't depend on that government to defend this star system or to keep us safe. That's always been the argument, that we have to accept tight controls on everything we do in exchange for security. You and I and everyone else knows how false that proved to be. And now we know that the Syndicate government is moving to try to maintain control by replacing CEOs wholesale and executing anyone whose loyalty is doubted in any way. It's revolt or die. Beyond that . . . Iceni and I will talk when the snakes are dead."

"The Syndicate system failed, sir," Malin agreed. "The control has always been there, but it didn't provide the promised security. I strongly advise that you consider another way of governing."

Drakon eyed Malin, knowing why he hadn't brought that up in front of Morgan, who would surely have reacted with derision at the idea of anything less than an ironfisted dictatorship. "Your advice is noted. Our priority for the moment is survival. If we achieve that, we'll think about how to run things without repeating the mistakes of the Syndicate. I don't want anyone like the snakes working for me to keep the citizens in line, but I also know we need order and that means some control. Now I need to talk to Iceni so she knows this surveillance node is blinded, and so we both know the other is getting ready to move."

"Do it in person, sir. Even though we should've blinded ISS, they might have some security taps we're not aware of yet."

"Let's hope not." Drakon nodded farewell to Malin, then made his way out through the multiple layers of security that had protected the main surveillance node. The sensors watched him but saw nothing, feeding routine images of empty hallways and sealed doors to their masters at ISS, the men and women responsible for the very broad range of actions categorized as internal security on Syndicate Worlds' planets. He passed by the armored room where two of the turned sentries were pretending to see nothing. Then a little farther along before he reached the new, concealed access that had been painstakingly dug into this building from a neighboring structure, a task that itself had been a very delicate operation, requiring diverting and spoofing various alarms and sensors as well as the cooperation of those co-opted sentries. Walking down a roughly hewn passage, Drakon entered the basement area of a shopping center, ignoring surveillance cameras there that had also been blinded, then went up a set of stairs and through an EMPLOY-EES ONLY door whose lock combination had long since been compromised.

The ISS snakes are going to be in for a real shock in a few hours, Drakon thought. *For over two hundred years, the snakes have been staging surprise arrests and security sweeps. Now we'll see how* they *like surprises.*

It would have been nice to be able just to hit the snakes right now, but Drakon knew the process was like a long line of dominoes that had to fall in turn, each knocking down the next as the plan progressed, as sensors and spies and surveillance gear all over the planet were spoofed or silenced, as military forces loyal to Drakon began to move under cover of those actions, as rebellion gathered without the knowledge of those who could still inflict terrible damage to this world if not taken by surprise. So he kept to the plan, which had been unfolding slowly for months now and would soon begin moving very quickly indeed.

That was why Drakon wore his executive suit despite his dislike for the garment mandated for all CEOs. No average citizen seeing him could tell by his outfit whether he was assigned to overseeing manufacturing or sales or administration or any other aspect of the integrated economic, military, and political system of the Syndicate Worlds. Having spent almost his entire adult life in the ground forces, risking death and leading troops, Drakon didn't care for the thought of being outwardly indistinguishable from someone who had spent the same amount of time in advertising. He had once even suffered the indignity of being mistaken for a lawyer.

But he knew that he had to appear to conform to routine right now in order to avoid tipping off the ISS. Drakon walked briskly but without any sign of concern by storefronts and out of the mall, then turned to walk past the outside of the nondescript building that secretly housed the ISS surveillance relay facility. It took practice to look truly casual when you were guilty and strolling past those charged with enforcing laws, but no one reached the rank of CEO without plenty of experience at doing so.

The citizens he encountered on the streets automatically moved aside when they saw the CEO-level executive suit, some eagerly seeking eye contact on the chance that a CEO might take notice of them, but just as many striving to avoid attracting his attention. Citizens of the Syndicate Worlds learned their own lessons, and one of those was that the attention of a CEO was a double-edged sword that might bring benefits or calamity.

Watching the citizens react with mingled fear and fawning submission, the first real and the second probably faked, Drakon thought about Malin's recent words. What would come next? He had been consumed with figuring out how to kill the snakes without having half of this planet blown apart, and what he had said about not being able to discuss the matter with Iceni was true. They had barely been able to risk the few occasional and brief meetings in which coded phrases and words sketched out the agreement to cooperate in taking down the snakes, saving their own hides, and perhaps giving this star system a chance to survive the ongoing collapse of the Syndicate empire. Midway would either get caught in the death throes of the Syndicate Worlds or get free of that tyranny and look out for itself.

But after that? All he knew was the Syndicate way, and, as Malin said, that had failed. How else did you keep things running without everything's falling apart? The Alliance way? He had learned little about that, and what little he had heard Drakon mistrusted.

Drakon shook his head with a frown, causing nearby citizens to freeze like rabbits that had seen a wolf and now hoped to avoid notice. He couldn't afford to think about them at the moment, or about the details of what would replace Syndicate rule here. He had to keep his mind centered on getting through the rest of this day alive.

More than a few of the citizens warily watching him walk onward probably wondered why a CEO was in public without bodyguards fencing him off, but it wasn't unheard of for some CEOs to travel occasionally without guards. Drakon had made a habit of that over the last few months, casually mentioning in ways that were certain to get back to internal security that he could take care of himself. The snakes wouldn't question a CEO's being arrogant and self-assured, though in Drakon's case his ground forces training and the equipment hidden in his executive suit gave him strong grounds for feeling able to handle most threats as long as he kept varying his routine to make assassination plots difficult.

It took fifteen minutes to reach the office of CEO Gwen Iceni, the senior Syndicate Worlds' official in the Midway Star System. But Malin had been right. Any message could be intercepted, and any code could be compromised or broken. If ISS learned of their plans at this point, with Drakon too far committed to pull back, it would trigger a disaster.

Human bodyguards and automated security systems providing layers of protection for Iceni all passed Drakon without hindrance despite the hidden weapons on him. If Iceni was planning to betray him, it would probably be after his forces had dealt with the snakes that both he and Iceni needed to have cleaned out. And she had surely reached the same conclusion about him, that he would not strike her yet because he needed her to handle those mobile forces still in this star system.

But all of the screening still took time that he didn't have to spare, so that Drakon had trouble not showing any irritation or anger as he walked into Iceni's office.

That office had the grandeur expected of a star system CEO's workplace but on a level consistent with Midway's modest wealth. There was an art to such things in the Syndicate Worlds' hierarchy. Too much ostentation would have attracted too much attention from her superiors, wondering how much extra Iceni might be skimming off tax revenue and what her ambitions might be, while too little pretension in the size and furnishings would have signaled weakness to both superiors and subordinates. Now Iceni, appearing calm, waved Drakon to a seat, then checked her desk display. "Security in here is tight," she said. "We can talk freely. You didn't bring any bodyguards. You trust me that much?"

"Not really." Drakon gestured in the general direction of the ISS headquarters complex. "There's a small but real chance that one of my bodyguards might be partly turned and providing information to the snakes on my movements. Right now, those bodyguards are watching the entrance to my command center, thinking that I'm inside it. Do you trust your bodyguards completely?"

"I don't have to," Iceni replied, not really answering his question. "By the time I do something that might alarm the snakes, you'll be doing your part. Are your people ready?"

"We'll hit the four primary ISS sites on this planet at fifteen hundred, just as planned. I'm personally leading the assault on the main ISS complex in this city, and three trusted subordinate commanders of mine are leading attacks on the secondary complexes in other cities. ISS substations everywhere will be hit by squad-level forces at the same time."

Iceni nodded, then glanced upward. "What about the orbiting stations and other facilities off-planet?"

"I've got people ready everywhere the snakes are, except on the mobile forces units, of course."

"Those are my problem. You have a lot of soldiers moving around. You're sure the snakes won't be alarmed?"

He hadn't sat down despite Iceni's offer, being too keyed up to carry that off well. But he couldn't show any weakness in front of another CEO, any nerves, or Iceni would surely focus on it like a wolf seeing a stag stumble. Instead, Drakon shrugged in a show of indifference. "I can't be certain. It's a very big operation, so it's possible the snakes will see something. But it shouldn't be enough to alarm them. We had to rush things over the last few days because of the order from Prime, but everything had already been planned out."

Iceni twisted her mouth slightly. "Fortunately for us. I had been warned that the central government was sending out orders to have star system CEOs hauled in by the ISS for loyalty checks, and that quite a few of those CEOs were not being seen again after disappearing into ISS custody; but I didn't expect the government to send that order here as quickly as it did. Even before you and I launched this plot we wouldn't have survived such an interrogation session."

"You think I have the wrong kinds of skeletons in my closet?" Drakon asked.

"I know that you do. I did my homework before I made any offers to you, just as I'm sure you did your homework on me before you responded. But we didn't start planning rebellion any too soon. That order to the ISS is still held up in the comm systems, but it could pop free at any time; and then we can both expect invitations we can't ignore from CEO Hardrad."

"And he'll also have questions about how that order got held up in the message system," Drakon noted dryly. "But you did keep it from being delivered for a few days, giving us time to act on our plans. As long as Hardrad doesn't see that order for a few more hours we'll be all right. The ISS surveillance systems are disabled while still appearing to be functioning, so we can finally talk freely. The snakes should assume everything is quiet until we launch the attacks. Are you still guaranteeing to handle the mobile forces in this star system?"

"I'll take care of the warships."

"Warships? We're going to start using Alliance terminology now?"

"They did win the war," Iceni replied, her voice tinged with sarcasm. "But it's not just an Alliance term. We used to call them warships, too, before the bureaucracy 'redefined' and 'relabeled' them. We're going back to our own older terminology. Changing what we call things will be a clear signal to the citizens and our forces that we are no longer subject to the Syndicate Worlds."

"After we win, you mean."

"Naturally. I've got a shuttle lifting me to C-448 in ten minutes. I'll use that heavy cruiser to rally the other warships here to us."

"What's CEO Kolani's status?" Drakon asked. "Any change?"

"Not yet. She's still in command of the flotilla and still committed to the government on Prime."

Drakon frowned upward, as if he could see through the building and up through intervening space to where the small flotilla orbited. "You'll take her out?"

"That option fell through," Iceni replied in as casual a tone as if she were referring to a minor business deal. "Both agents of mine who were within reach of her have already been neutralized by Kolani's security, so assassination isn't one of our choices."

He felt a chill run down his back at the thought of what that flotilla could do to this planet. "You promised me that you'd handle the mobile forces." Morgan's words came back to mock him. *If they were stupid enough to believe the promise of a CEO . . .*

From the *New York Times* Bestselling Author

JACK CAMPBELL

THE LOST FLEET: BEYOND THE FRONTIER: INVINCIBLE

Admiral John "Black Jack" Geary suspects that the Alliance he serves is deliberately putting his fleet in harm's way. An encounter with the alien enigmas confirms Geary's fears. Attacked without warning, he orders the fleet to jump star systems—only to enter the crosshairs of another hostile alien armada.

Now, with a group of his officers determined to eliminate this new threat at any cost, Geary must figure out how to breach the enemy's defenses so the fleet can reach the jump point without massive casualties—even though the enigmas could be waiting on the other side . . .

Praise for The Lost Fleet series

"A rousing adventure with a page-turning plot, lots of space action, and the kind of hero Hornblower fans will love."
—William C. Dietz, national bestselling author of *A Fighting Chance*

"Military science fiction at its best."
—Catherine Asaro, Nebula Award–winning author of *Carnelians*

facebook.com/AceRocBooks
penguin.com

M1026T1211

From New York Times *bestselling author*

JACK CAMPBELL

THE LOST FLEET
VICTORIOUS

As war continues to rage between the Alliance and the
Syndicate Worlds, Captain John "Black Jack" Geary
is promoted to fleet admiral—even though the ruling
council fears he may stage a military coup. His new rank
gives him the authority to negotiate with the Syndics,
who have suffered tremendous losses and may finally be
willing to end the war. But an even greater alien threat
lurks on the far side of Syndic-occupied space . . .

M635T0811

Don't miss the *New York Times* bestseller from

JACK CAMPBELL

THE LOST FLEET
RELENTLESS

After successfully freeing Alliance POWs, Captain John "Black Jack" Geary discovers that the Syndics plan to ambush the fleet with their powerful reserve flotilla in an attempt to annihilate it once and for all. And as Geary has the fleet jump from one star system to the next, hoping to avoid the inevitable confrontation, saboteurs contribute to the chaos.

M623T1209

THE ULTIMATE WRITERS OF *SCIENCE FICTION*

John Barnes	Jack McDevitt
William C. Dietz	Alastair Reynolds
Simon R. Green	Allen Steele
Joe Haldeman	S. M. Stirling
Robert Heinlein	Charles Stross
Frank Herbert	Harry Turtledove
E. E. Knight	John Varley

penguin.com/scififantasy